To Die but Once

ALSO BY JACQUELINE WINSPEAR

Maisie Dobbs

Birds of a Feather

Pardonable Lies

Messenger of Truth

An Incomplete Revenge

Among the Mad

The Mapping of Love and Death

A Lesson in Secrets

Elegy for Eddie

Leaving Everything Most Loved

The Care and Management of Lies

A Dangerous Place

Journey to Munich

In This Grave Hour

To Die but Once

A Maisie Dobbs Novel

Jacqueline Winspear

HARPER LUXE

An Imprint of HarperCollinsPublishers

HarperCollins books may be purchased for educational, business, or sales promotional use. For information please e-mail the Special Markets Department at SPsales@harpercollins.com.

FIRST HARPERLUXE EDITION

ISBN: 978-0-06-279204-4

HarperLuxe™ is a trademark of HarperCollins Publishers.

Library of Congress Cataloging-in-Publication Data is available upon request.

18 19 20 21 22 LSC 10 9 8 7 6 5 4 3 2 1

Again, for my dad
Albert Winspear
1926–2012

A city boy who loved the land.
His story inspired this novel.

Cowards die many times before their deaths;
The valiant never taste of death but once.
Of all the wonders that I yet have heard,
It seems to me most strange that men should fear,
Seeing that death, a necessary end,
Will come when it will come.

—WILLIAM SHAKESPEARE,
Julius Caesar, Act 2, Scene 2

Prologue

Hampshire, England, May 1940

The boy had not had a day without a headache in weeks. How many weeks was it now? And how many aspirin powders had he taken, every night when he arrived back at his digs—a shared room in another lodging house in another town? Another town with airfields close by, and buildings to be painted with that viscous gray emulsion. He wondered about the aspirin and the emulsion as he walked home from the pub, and deep down inside himself, he knew that one had something to do with the other, though his mates on the job hadn't complained. Not that he'd dare say anything—no, he had to keep his mouth shut, because he was lucky to have a job at all, so there was nothing to whine about. And if truth be told, he should not have been at the pub drinking—but the landlord didn't mind, probably didn't even know. After all, the boy had come in with the older lads, and it's not as if he looked like an apprentice.

He missed his mum. He'd never have mentioned it, not to any of the lads—they teased him enough about being the boy—though he might have said to Freddie Mayes, "Freddie, you would love my mum's spotted dick pudding." And he'd describe the way she kneaded the suet dough, how she added handfuls of sultanas, currants and raisins. Then she'd take a large square of clean white cloth, place the round ball of dough in the middle and tie the ends nice and tight. Then it would go into the saucepan of boiling water to steam for hours. Hours, it would be, and the sweet smell would envelop the kitchen. And if the pudding had been put on the heat later in the day, it would be long after supper time that she'd take it out of the saucepan, unknotting the hot wet cloth with her fingertips, then she'd spoon the pudding into bowls and pour a big dollop of Tate & Lyle Golden Syrup onto every helping. If it was a Sunday, she'd make custard. She'd said in a letter that they were having to cut back on sugar, what with the war. But he couldn't complain, not really—after all, this job was on account of the war, though for the life of him he'd never come across paint like it. He sighed. At first he'd had trouble getting used to the silence in the country. In London, back in the Smoke, you never heard a footstep behind you, because there were footsteps everywhere. There were always people out on the street, and there was more life. Human life, that is. Mind you, if there was a smog, that made the footsteps sound different, as if someone was messing about with the echo, twisting it, like a plumber shaping a length of pipe to get it around a bend in the house. But now he loved being close to the land, and all that green. It was quiet. Peaceful. Well, it was peaceful once he'd done his work for the day, and when he could get over to the farm.

Not long now. Not far to his tiny room in that strange house with the loopy woman, and all them WAAFs on the floor below.

According to Freddie, they were moving on to the next job in a couple of days, though this stop had been a good one—lot of work to do, so the crew had stayed longer, had a chance to settle in a bit, get to know a few locals. And there was the overtime. More money to send home. He stopped. *Blimey my noddle hurts.* He pressed his fingers to his temples, massaging the bluish thin flesh. It wasn't only the emulsion that was giving him the pain, though he was sure it was doing a fair job of killing off a few brain cells. There had been nothing but trouble since he'd come here. Not being in the country trouble, and not work trouble—no, it was people trouble. He wanted to stay, but because of the other business, he wanted to get going. If he had to stick with this job, like his dad said he should, then he wanted to get on with it. He wanted to move on soon, and soon couldn't come fast enough, because his heart would break anyway, leaving the old boy. If only he hadn't . . . but what was it his dad always said? "You can't look back, son, not in this life. No, you can only look forward and step out in its direction." And when he'd said, "What direction?" his dad had said, "The future, son. The future—always look to your future." Well, the future wasn't turning out to be the one he wanted. Instead the future was the next place, another airfield and this painting job. The past was two days ago and two blokes he would rather not see again, though he knew he would, but for now he wanted to forget it. Forget them. *Christ, this head!*

The boy walked on along the path by the stream, then across the rickety wooden bridge, down an alley, a shortcut to his landlady's house. Freddie would wake him later when he came staggering back, in his cups, making more noise because he was trying to be quiet. But the boy knew he'd at least get a bit of shut-eye before he had to pretend to be interested in Freddie bragging about a girl he'd been eyeing up, how they didn't all go for a man in uniform, so he was in with a chance. Which was just as well, because Freddie wasn't giving up this job in a hurry—reserved occupations, it was, and he'd said he had no blimmin' intention of joining the army and going the way of his father, and look what happened to him the last time the country went to war.

What was that? The boy turned and looked back, stood for a second, perhaps two. *Nothing. Just country sounds. Probably someone's cat on the prowl.* And then the pain again. But this time it was different, this time it was sudden, a deep terrible searing crack across his skull. Nighttime turned to light, turned to lots of light, and he could hear his father telling him to look to the future, but the shock felled him, brought him to his knees, and then another wave of pain across his head again, taking him down, grinding his cheek into the path's loose gravel. He reached up with his fingers—shaking fingers, fingers he could not seem to steer—and he touched his head and brought back his hand wet. Wet with his own blood. He felt tears begin to stream from his eyes. Oh he missed his mum. He missed his dad and in that moment he even missed London. Then there was nothing more to think, no other thoughts crossed the boy's mind and time felt so slow, so very slow, though he could hear voices. Long, drawn-out voices. One seemed familiar and he struggled to find the word, the right word to call out to that person, but the word that was the person's name just would not come and he did not know if it was a man or a woman. And as he felt his body being lifted, the streetlight ahead grew faint, and at once he knew his breath was shallow, and then more shallow, and his heartbeat was slowing down, as if an engine inside him had been deprived of fuel.

It was as if someone had reached out and snuffed out a candle. Just like that, finger and thumb around the flame as he made one last attempt to form the words that would not come. Darkness enveloped him, pressed against his chest, filled his mouth, suffocated him, and the future his dad had told him to step out toward ceased to exist.

Chapter 1

Maisie Dobbs pulled off Tottenham Court Road, maneuvering her Alvis drophead coupe motor car into Warren Street. She waved to Jack Barker, who she knew should have retired by now—he had been selling newspapers on his patch outside the Tube station for years, and in that time she had seen him become more and more stooped, taking precious seconds to fold the newspapers ready to hand to busy office workers and shop assistants as they rushed to and from work. There was a time when his grandson had helped out before and after school, but now young Peter was not so young anymore, and was in the army.

Maisie wound down the window and slowed the motor car. She held out a coin for the man to take. "No need for change, Mr. Barker," said Maisie as she placed the newspaper on the passenger seat. "I bet you miss your helper."

"I do at that, Miss Dobbs. I had another one of 'em lined up to give me a hand, only he was evacuated to Wales. But I reckon he'll be home soon. His mum keeps saying that what with this Bore War, there's nothing happening. But I've told her—there's war happening all right—it's just not reached us. I reckon your Mr. Beale must be worried sick—knowing what he went through in the last war, and now his eldest is over there with the expeditionary force. He must be losing sleep over it. According to the *Express*, the Germans have marched right across the Ardennes, through Holland and now they're into France—too blimmin' close to us, for my liking."

Maisie nodded. Her assistant, Billy Beale, was indeed losing sleep worrying about his son, who was serving with the army in France, but he was also concerned for his wife, Doreen. Years before they had already lost a little girl, Lizzie, who had died after contracting diphtheria—Doreen had suffered a breakdown following the tragedy. Billy had therefore decided it was best for her to take their youngest child, Margaret Rose, to stay with an aunt in Hampshire, leaving him at home with his second son, Bobby, an apprentice mechanic.

"Did you see they've put more sandbags around the station?" said Barker. "Before long there won't be room for me out here on the pavement."

"Oh, they'll make room for you, Mr. Barker—what would we all do without you!" replied Maisie, turning her head to check for traffic as she moved away from the curb.

Barker laughed and waved, but Maisie's smile faded as she rolled up the window. While the newspapers kept up a stream of positive rhetoric, she had heard from Douglas Partridge, who now worked for the wartime Ministry of Information, that the expeditionary force in France was considered to be in a precarious position.

She drove along the street, passing the Prince of Wales pub, where the landlord, Phil Coombes, had just emerged and was ambling along to a caff just a short way down Tottenham Court Road. Maisie thought she could set a clock by Phil Coombes, for he left the premises at the same time each morning to walk to a nearby caff, where he would order a bacon sandwich and a cup of tea. It was his one break in the day, otherwise he never left the pub because he was either behind the bar or, when the doors were locked for the night, in the flat above. Coombes and his wife had raised two sons and a daughter in the flat, but now only Vivian, the middle child, remained at home.

Even before Maisie raised her hand to wave, and to receive from the landlord a desultory lifting of the hand in response, Maisie knew that all was not well. The way Coombes carried himself—with shoulders drooping and his head forward, as if trying to set a pace for his lagging feet—indicated a troubled man. As she turned left onto Fitzroy Street to park the Alvis, Maisie wondered if she should approach Coombes, ask him what was wrong and perhaps offer help of some sort. But had she not learned her lesson time and again, that not everyone in straitened circumstances wants to be helped? Yet when she looked back at Phil Coombes, she felt an ache of concern in her chest, as if the man's emotions had traced a direct line to her heart.

She was just about to set off in the direction of the caff on Tottenham Court Road, hoping to catch up with Coombes, when Billy Beale walked around the corner, his gas mask in its box hanging over one shoulder by the strap, and bouncing up and down on his hip.

"Mornin', miss." With a deft pinch to the lighted end, he extinguished the cigarette he was smoking, and put the stub in his pocket.

"Did you come up from Hampshire this morning?" asked Maisie.

Billy nodded. "Makes all the difference, not having to come into work until late on a Monday, or even a Tuesday morning. I miss my girls, so it's been handy, you giving me the extra time so I can get down there once a week. And you should see little Margaret Rose—all apple cheeks and growing like ivy. She'll be almost as tall as the boys, make no mistake."

"I thought as much when she was a toddler—she was like a mannequin even then." They fell into step toward the office on Fitzroy Square. "Have you heard from young Billy?"

Billy shook his head. "Boys of his age are not exactly known for writing, are they? Doreen sends a letter or card once a week—keeping it short because she knows he won't read anything too long—but even when he was over here in barracks, it was as much as he could do to pick up a pencil and write a quick note home. I know—I was like it myself at that age. It was only when I came back from over there that it occurred to me that it wouldn't have hurt to write a bit more—but then there's the censor peering at everything, so half the letter would have been blacked out anyway."

They reached the front door of the gray, smoke-stained mansion that housed the first-floor offices of Maisie Dobbs, Psychologist and Investigator.

"I don't like him being in France though," Billy continued. "And I reckon it was a shock to him. He only joined up because he wanted to drive a tank. Well, he's driving something, but I don't know how far they'll get with it—I heard talk in the Prince that they could be in the thick of it, if Hitler's boys get any farther into France." He shook his head. "My worst fear since the day he was born—and his brother—was that they would be in uniform. By the way, miss, where's your gas mask?"

"As usual I've either left it at home or it's still hanging on the hook behind the office door—I keep forgetting it, which means I'm in good company with almost half the people in London," said Maisie.

As they made their way up the stairs, and Maisie unlocked the door to the two-room office, Billy went on talking about his sons—not only Billy, who was named for his father, but sixteen-year-old Bobby, now an apprentice mechanic who was proving to be very good at his job. And it seemed Billy always had a story to tell about his role with the local Air Raid Precautions station—as an ARP man, he patrolled his neighborhood after dark to ensure that people had blackout curtains closed, and that everything was as it should be in case of an attack by Hitler's Luftwaffe.

"Talking about the Prince—Billy, have you spoken to Phil Coombes lately?" said Maisie. "I saw him this morning, and he seemed troubled. I—I've been think-ing about him all the time you've been talking about Billy and Bobby. Do you know anything about his sons? Perhaps he's worried about them."

"Don't know what he has to worry about. The youngest is an apprentice painter and decorator who managed to cop himself some jammy job where he won't have to enlist when his time comes, and the older boy is in some other reserved occupation, so he can sit out the war too, for as long as it lasts. I'd feel a lot better if my Billy were home on British soil."

"I know you would," said Maisie as she pulled a sheaf of papers from her bag and placed them on the desk used by her part-time secretary, Sandra. "But I can't get Mr. Coombes out of my mind. I might . . . well, we'll see."

Billy looked up from leafing through the post he had picked up on the hall table at the foot of the stairs. "Don't mind me saying so, miss, but when you have one of your thoughts like that, there's usually something to it. Do you want me to have a word with him? I can go in for a swift half o'shandy come twelve o'clock."

Maisie nodded. "Would you? That's a good idea. Just to put my mind at rest, and—"

She was interrupted by the bell above the office door—a short blast, then a second's silence before two longer blasts, as if the caller had at first been reticent, but had then drawn upon a strength of resolve.

"Bit early for a visitor. Were we expecting anyone?" asked Billy.

Maisie shook her head. "Go and let him in, Billy."

"Him?"

"Yes. I'm sure it's Phil Coombes."

Billy reached for the door handle. "I won't bet against it."

Maisie shrugged and bit the inside of her lip. "It's one of those serendipitous things, isn't it? You talk about someone or they enter your thoughts, and then there they are. And he seemed so troubled. He knows what we do here—to a point—so let's hope we can help him."

Billy returned with the caller, who was indeed Phil Coombes. Maisie held out her hand to a chair pulled up by the gas fire. "It might be spring, Mr. Coombes, but I find mornings are still a bit chilly, especially in this old building."

Coombes nodded, and looked around at Billy.

"Cup of tea for you, mate?"

Coombes shook his head. "Nah, thanks all the same, Bill—just had a cup around the corner."

"With your usual?" asked Billy.

"I didn't have the stomach for it, and I look forward to that bacon sandwich, as a rule. I just had a bit of toast and didn't really fancy that." He looked at Maisie, who tapped the back of the chair, though she realized Coombes was waiting for her to be seated first.

"Come and sit down, Mr. Coombes. You too, Billy—we can have a cuppa later." She nodded in the direction of Billy's desk, reminding him to pick up his notebook and a pencil. Bringing her attention back to Coombes, she leaned forward. "You're troubled about something, Mr. Coombes—you're not your usual cheery self, and you haven't been for a while. How can we help you?"

"I didn't want to bother you, Miss Dobbs, really I didn't, but I thought that, what with your line of work, you could help out."

Billy glanced at Maisie, and raised an eyebrow.

"We're here to listen, so please go on," encouraged Maisie.

"I—I don't have anything to pay you, and I know, Miss Dobbs, that you work for Scotland Yard now and again, and you've had all them big cases—missing persons, unexplained deaths and what have you. I don't miss much. And I'm sure you can charge a pretty penny, but we've nothing put by for this sort of thing."

"Please don't worry about money, Mr. Coombes. Really—what's important now is to talk about what's on your mind. Should Billy nip round to bring Mrs. Coombes to the office? Would you feel better if she were here?"

The man looked up at Maisie and shook his head, his eyes wide, fearful. "Oh no. No, I don't want her to know how much it's bothering me. It's best if she thinks there's nothing to worry about."

"So what is bothering you, mate?" said Billy. "Come on, Phil, get it off your chest. You'll be all the better for it."

Coombes nodded. "I know this sounds like it's nothing, but I can't ignore this terrible ache I've got here every time I think about our boy, Joe. He's the youngest one. We haven't heard from him for a few days, and it's unlike him not to get on the blower once on a Wednesday night, and again of a Sunday morning—well, I say it's not like him, but for the past couple of weeks it's as if he hasn't wanted to give us a ring, hasn't wanted to say much."

"I didn't know you had a telephone in there, Phil," said Billy.

Coombes sighed, as if answering even the most simple question would exhaust him. "The brewery had it put in a year ago now, and it's come in handy for us, not only for the business, but since the war, with the boys not at home anymore. When Joe picks up the telephone wherever he is, it's not that he can talk for long—he's never got enough pennies on him for a start, you know what lads are like—but at least we hear from him, and he knows we like to have a word, even if it's a quick one, but as I say, something feels off to me." He looked at Billy as if for affirmation. Billy nodded. *Keep going.* "Viv's a different kettle of fish," continued Coombes. "She started work at the telephone exchange when she left school, as a trainee, so she always gives us a bell when she's on her way home from a shift, and then we don't worry. What with soldiers coming in from all over—Australia, Canada, just like it was in the last war—you want to know your daughter's safe. She's turned nineteen now, doing well at her job—they've promoted her to working on the government exchanges—and she's a nice-looking girl, which is a father's worry."

Billy leaned forward. "Isn't Joe the same age as my Bobby—about sixteen?"

"Another six months. Archie, the eldest, is going on twenty-one now. Not that we see much of him—different kettle of fish to his sister and brother. Couldn't wait to get off on his own, though he sometimes comes along to see us after closing time of a Sunday afternoon, for a spot of dinner before we open again. Then he's off. It's all I can do to get him to stay and help me change a barrel—I reckon he had enough of pubs when he was a youngster."

"Tell us about Joe, Mr. Coombes," said Maisie.

Phil Coombes wiped the back of his hand across one eye and then the other. "I know it's only a short stretch since we heard from him—last Wednesday, it was—but like I said, something seems off to me. . . ." His voice tapered off, and he looked down at the carpet, as if tracing its paisley patterns with his eyes.

"Go on," said Maisie. "First tell us what he's doing and why he's not living at home—he's only fifteen."

"He apprenticed to Yates and Sons, the painters and decorators." Coombes paused and shook his head, as if not quite believing the turn of events. "One of the regulars got him the job when he was coming up to leaving school, couple of year ago, come October. Seemed a good position, learning a trade, and old Bill Yates was always very good at pushing for the big jobs, and his son, Mike, is even better at it. He gets jobs over in those mansions. Belgravia, Mayfair and the like. So Joe was learning from the ground up—and it's a job with prospects." Maisie was about to ask another question when Coombes smiled as he thought about his son. "Very easygoing boy, my Joe. Very solid young bloke—see his hands—" Coombes held out his hands. "Calm. Very precise with his hands, he was—even Yates himself said Joe's laying out of the wallpaper ready for hanging was perfect, exact, just as it should be. He said he'd known blokes on the job for years who couldn't lay out paper like that—pasted and folded, ready to hold up and brush out to keep the pattern running right."

"But does that work take him away from London?" asked Maisie.

Coombes shook his head. "Just before war was declared, it all changed. Yates had a visit from the RAF brass. They wanted him for special war work—it was a big contract, all tied up and a sizeable down payment, according to one of the other lads who works for him, name of Freddie Mayes. Yates has got a big enough business, and what with the war, both Bill and Mike Yates realized that people would probably start pulling in their horns and wouldn't be having so much painting and decorating done on their big houses, and the council contracts would probably dry up too, so they jumped at the chance. And like I said, they're being paid a pretty penny—laying out government money for the painters to be in lodgings, the lot."

"What sort of contract was it, Phil?" asked Billy.

"Joe said he couldn't talk much about it—that he had to sign some papers to say he wouldn't let on about his job. But he told me when I promised him I didn't have any spies in the pub walls, and that it was a father's right to know his son's work." Coombes looked up at Maisie and Billy. "So this is secret, right? Anything I say in this room to you two? I don't want this getting out, because if it's supposed to be on the QT, I don't want my son's name in the dirt."

"Every conversation that takes place in my office is held in strict confidence, Mr. Coombes—Phil." Maisie laid her hand upon her chest.

Coombes pressed his lips together, then continued. "Turns out the job was to take the crew to every single airfield or RAF station in the whole of the British Isles, with the most important being the ones within striking distance of the coast—they were to be the priority. Here's how Joe explained it to me—the lads on the crew go in a Yates' van down to a place—as far as I know, they've just been in Hampshire, not far from Southampton and Portsmouth, as the crow flies—and when they get there they're put up in lodgings, and they report to the airfield. Paint is brought in on a special lorry—a Yates' lorry, not RAF, but special all the same—then they have to set about painting all the buildings with this emulsion, but only the outside for most of them."

"Was it for camouflage? Did he say?" asked Maisie.

Coombes shook his head. "He said it was a sort of

gray in color, so I suppose there was that camouflage business, but that's not what it was for. It was a sort of—what do they call it?" He frowned. "For fire. To stop a building catching on fire—that's it, it's called a fire *retardant*."

"Sounds like a jammy job to me—paint buildings for the government and take their money. And wasn't it a reserved profession?" said Billy.

Coombes looked at Billy Beale. "Yes, it was a protected job—he could spend the rest of the war for however long it lasts, just painting airfield buildings for the RAF. But he said the paint wasn't like anything he'd ever come across. Sort of thick, very viscous, he said—his word, 'viscous.' And he reckoned it gave him headaches, terrible headaches, what with the vapor coming off it. It sounded like strong stuff."

"What do you mean?" asked Maisie, pressing a hand to her right temple. As Coombes described his son's work, a headache had started behind her eyes, moving to her crown. She felt unsettled, and her vision was blurred, just for a second. "Did he describe what was strong about the paint? Just the smell?"

"Joe told me that after they'd finished putting a few coats onto each wall, they had to line up a row of blowtorches against the wall, right close to where they'd just painted it, and they had to leave them there burning for a good few hours while they moved on to the next wall, or the next building."

"It's a wonder the wall didn't come down," said Billy.

"No, it didn't come down—that's the thing. Joe said there wasn't a mark on it, not even a small smoke stain. They'd run those blowtorches, and after they took them away hours later, the wall looked like they'd just finished painting."

"And what was this emulsion called?" asked Maisie.

"Oh, it didn't have a name. Just a number." Phil Coombes shook his head. "Blessed if I can remember the number—I don't know if he even told me. If I find it, I'll let you know, because I'm sure I wrote something down."

"And you think Joe has been affected by this paint, that he might be ill," said Billy, making a note in his book.

"I don't know, mate. I just know we haven't heard, and that he hasn't been himself lately. You know your own, and I know something's wrong."

Maisie allowed a few seconds of silence as Coombes' story of his son's work lingered in the air. "First of all, have you spoken to Mr. Yates? Or to a foreman at their works? Where's their depot?"

"I've been on the blower a couple of times. A young lady in the office told me Mr. Yates would return my call, but he hasn't. I had my other boy go round there to the works—it's just across the river, in Kennington—and he said there was no one there to talk to. He said the typist said she'd only been in a couple of hours, and that since she arrived, everyone was out on a job, and that she didn't have any notes regarding the whereabouts of an individual employee."

Maisie nodded. "I would imagine all the workers are out during the day, on job sites. Do you know how Joe got on with his work mates? He was an apprentice—were there others, or was he the youngest of the crew? Do you know if the men working with him were beyond apprenticeship?"

"I reckon he was the only apprentice on the crew, and the youngest of them. The other painters were always sent all around London, working for Yates—the business lost a number to the services, so apparently it sort of balanced out when a few contracts were canceled, after war was declared. Mind you, I would imagine they'll get it back if this government work goes well. But according to Joe, Mike Yates can manage the work still going on in London, plus this contract. The older painters and decorators are too long in the tooth for the army, so they can teach the apprentices, who are too young. They've got a few younger men in the crew with Joe, probably ones that don't want to get dirty fighting. Before he . . . before he sort of changed, Joe said that they were all looking out for him, being the apprentice on the job, and that he was eating well and getting his sleep. No late nights with the boys—he was brought up in a pub, so he knows how to take care of himself."

"What do you mean by 'sort of changed'?" asked Maisie. "Can you be more specific? I know it's hard, because when it's someone we're close to, it's often something we feel and it's not anything easy to describe."

Coombes rubbed his chin. "Oh, I don't know. It's been four weeks since he was last home for a Saturday and Sunday. He was quiet then. Me and the missus put it down to him being a bit tired, what with knocking around the country, sleeping in different places. She thought he could do with a tonic, and even went around to Boots, to see what she could get for him. You know, it probably seemed like a big adventure at first, this job, but them lads are working at a clip, and then there were the headaches, like I said."

Maisie allowed another moment of silence to pass before asking her next question. "Is there anything else you can add?"

Coombes shook his head. "I know he was all right

before that last visit. One of Archie's mates was stationed in the area, so he looked in on Joe at his digs in Whitchurch and said he was on top form. Those were his words. *Top form.* But I don't think he's on any top form now, or he would have picked up the blower and made a call to me and his mum. And all we know is that he's near this place called Whitchurch."

"Hampshire. I can—" Billy began to speak, but Maisie shook her head, aware Phil Coombes was watching her, waiting.

"As Billy was about to say, he's making regular visits to Hampshire to see his wife and daughter. I believe he's not too far from Whitchurch." She paused again. "Phil—Mr. Coombes—I think I should speak to your wife. She should know you came to talk to us. I understand you don't want her to be worried, but the thing is, I bet she is worried sick too, and it might help if she's given the opportunity to air her feelings without thinking she's adding to your worries. Something she says might throw more light on Joe's situation." Maisie smiled at Coombes. "I promise I will take care of her. And in the meantime, Billy here will go along to Yates' yard, and have a word with them—you know Billy, he's a terrier. He won't be put off by anyone and will find out if something's amiss about Joe's working conditions. They're probably not used to dealing with families, because their workers have always been in London, so they go home at night. Your questions might easily be settled."

"I never thought of it that way."

"But all the same, I am taking your concerns seriously, and we will do all we can to help." Maisie came to her feet. "And you're not to worry about the money."

She caught Billy's eye.

"I'll see you out, mate," offered Billy.

Coombes nodded and held out his hand to Maisie. "Thank you, Miss Dobbs. I feel better, having got that off my chest. I'll tell Sally to come round after closing time this afternoon—that all right?"

"Perfect. I'll be here. And she'll have a chance to see Sandra's baby—she comes in one or two afternoons a week with him, to catch up with the paperwork. It's a treat for all of us, seeing young Martin. Anna, our evacuee, loves it when he comes to the country."

"How's the little lady getting on?"

"Very well, Mr. Coombes—thank you for asking. We'll see Sally at about three o'clock then."

"Three o'clock it is."

Billy was holding the office door open for Phil Coombes, when Maisie called out.

"Oh, just one more small thing—do you have

the name of the lad who was in touch with Joe—his brother's friend?"

"Teddy Wickham. Nice lad—known the family for years."

Maisie thanked Coombes, and nodded to indicate that it was her final question.

Maisie was waiting, still sitting by the gas fire, staring into the flame, when Billy returned to the office and took his seat again.

"What do you think, miss?"

"I think he has cause for concern. I know it's easy to say boys will be boys, that they don't keep up with their parents when they're away like Joe's away, but he's a lad who always struck me as someone who is respectful of his family. They're a tight little unit—look at how he grew up, over the pub. In some respects, he probably was looking forward to getting away, setting out on a big adventure—but that aside, Phil's description of the past weeks is a bit unsettling. Joe might not be well and his fellow workmates have failed to notice, so he's soldiering on. Or he might have been ill and told his mates not to say anything to Yates—he might be fearful about losing his apprenticeship."

"I can see that."

"So can I—to a point. But there's something that worries me far more."

"Miss?"

"Think back to when Mr. Coombes first started telling us about his son, about his worries—not a few minutes into the conversation. He made a slip."

"What sort of slip."

"'Very precise with his hands, he was. . . .' He used the past tense, Billy. When he looked down at his own hands, and talked about his son, about his steady hands. Past tense."

"You don't think he's got something to do with his son going quiet?"

"At this point . . . no, I don't think so. But I believe Mr. Coombes has a greater sensitivity with regard to his children than he might give himself credit for. We must get to work without delay, Billy—I fear for Joe's safety."

"But if you look at it another way, he's been working for the government."

"We're at war, Billy. There are thousands of sons— and daughters—working for the government. Army, air force, navy, and in jobs like Joe's that no one knows about. They're all government jobs. No one is guaranteeing their safety."

"And don't I know it."

Chapter 2

It's so lovely how people stop to ask about Martin when I take him out in the pram—as if seeing a baby makes the sun shine a little brighter. But have you noticed, since just before Christmas there's been more children around now who've been brought back from evacuation to London by their parents? After all, it's not as if something really terrible has happened to us since war was declared. Though I think it will, what with what's gone on in the Netherlands, and, well . . ." Sandra Pickering's voice tapered off, giving the impression that she could not countenance the direction of her thoughts. She took the baby from his carrycot and handed him to Maisie. "He slept all the way here in the motor car."

"The movement of the motor can soothe a baby."

Sandra laughed. "Not when it's me slamming on the brakes every two minutes!" She smiled as Maisie gently rocked the child in her arms. "I reckon we'll all be stopping driving soon—not enough coupons for the petrol, and it's not as if you can carry them over from month to month if you don't go anywhere much. Anyway, I'll get on with these letters—and you say you have someone coming in?"

"Yes, Mrs. Coombes—Sally, Phil Coombes' wife from the Prince, around the corner." Maisie glanced at the clock on the mantelpiece. "She should be here any minute—if she keeps to the arrangement I made with Phil this morning. Would it be all right if we hand Martin to her? I think having the babe in her arms will soothe her spirit. It's about their son, Joe, you see. They haven't heard from him for a few days, and to add to their concern, they say he hasn't been himself of late. He's on a special job for the government—he works for Yates and Sons, the painters and decorators, and they've a contract to paint all airfield buildings across the county with a type of fire retardant. It sounds as if the emulsion they're using is causing Joe to have terrible headaches, and they're worried he's unwell and not telling anyone."

"I bet young Joe jumped at the chance of a job away from home."

"Have you noticed something I've missed?" asked Maisie.

"I've only been into the Prince on a couple of occasions—once with Billy after we'd left the office one evening, before I met Lawrence, and then another time when Lawrence met me from work and we went in for a drink before going home. But the first time, I remember the way Phil was talking and I thought he and Sally kept Archie, Vivian, and Joe on a very tight rein. He said, 'You see it all, working in a pub.' And then he went on to say that they'd brought up their three to know what's right and what's wrong and that there's a good sort and a bad sort and they wouldn't tolerate if one of them became a bad sort." Sandra paused, watching as Maisie settled the baby, who had whimpered as he slept in her arms. "The second time, Vivian arrived back at the pub later than expected— she was about fourteen at the time and had only just started work. But on that evening—it must have been a Friday—instead of getting on the bus and coming straight home, she'd gone out to a caff with some of the girls she worked with. I suppose it was half past seven or eight o'clock when she walked in, but Phil tore her off a strip in front of everyone in the pub. Sally was working behind the bar as well, and after Phil had had a go, she said, 'Upstairs right now, my girl—I've got some words for you too.'" Sandra shook her head. "I have no doubt they were worried, but I can see why Archie left home as soon as he could. Vivian is stuck there until she's twenty-one—she'll probably get married just to get away. It's a shame—they love their children, but they've let what they've seen while working for the brewery get the better of them." Sandra looked at her child in Maisie's arms. "I hope I'm a good mother—I hope I don't smother Martin with my worries."

The doorbell sounded. Maisie held out Martin to his mother. "Sandra, that will be Sally Coombes. I'd like you to be present for this little meeting—take some notes for me. We'll stay in here—and let's get the chairs over by the window. It's warmed up a bit now, and the sun is shining."

Maisie ran downstairs to welcome her visitor. "Mrs. Coombes—I'm so glad you could come." She opened the door wide. "The day's brighter now, isn't it? I don't know if I like the mornings so chilly."

Sally Coombes was in her late forties and looked as if she had dressed for an important appointment. Her mousy brown hair was tightly curled, and she wore a navy blue hat with a broader brim than was the fashion. Her fawn wool coat was of good quality and well cared for, and she wore shoes that seemed freshly polished—

there was not a scuff on them, and her leather hand-bag appeared hardly used, almost brand-new. Maisie thought it might have been a special gift, only occasionally taken from a box lined with tissue paper. Sally Coombes, she knew, didn't really go anywhere. Her home was her first responsibility, and it was situated above her second—assisting her husband in the pub.

"I don't like this spring cold either—I even put on a heavy coat today. I mean, it's sunny, but I can't seem to get warm these past couple of weeks." Sally Coombes held on to her bag with both hands, as if it might be wrest from her grip at any moment.

Maisie placed her hand on Coombes' upper arm. "I understand, Mrs. Coombes—you must be very worried about Joe."

The woman's eyes filled with tears as she pressed her lips together.

Maisie smiled. "Come on—I'll put on the gas fire so you can warm up. And Sandra's here with the baby." She led the way to the first-floor office. "He's such a lovely little lad—just a couple of months old now. She's lucky he's so calm."

"My first one wasn't. Or the second, come to that. But Joe was a dream of a baby—hardly a grizzle out of him. And always smiling."

As they entered the office, Sandra walked toward them. "It's lovely to see you, Mrs. Coombes. You haven't seen my baby yet, have you?"

Maisie smiled and began to move three chairs back toward the fireplace, where she turned on the gas flame. The room was not cold now, but it was clear from her blue fingertips that Sally Coombes was indeed feeling a chill.

Coombes looked down at the child swaddled in a knitted white shawl. "Look at those rosy cheeks!"

"Would you like to hold him?" asked Sandra.

The woman set down her bag on Billy's desk and took the baby.

"Let's all take the weight off our feet, shall we?" suggested Maisie.

As Coombes smiled down at the baby and rubbed a finger alongside his cheek, Maisie put her first question to the woman.

"Can you tell us what is making you so unsettled about Joe, Mrs. Coombes? Mr. Coombes has already given us his account, but I would like to know what you're feeling about the situation—as a mother."

Coombes seemed loath to shift her attention from Martin to Maisie. With a gentle touch she ran her finger alongside the baby's cheek again, and sighed. She looked up at Sandra, then Maisie. "My Joe was just like this—not a peep from him for hours, so content." She took a deep breath. "He's just not been himself. I am sure Phil said the same thing—and it's not something you can describe, though I'll do my best. Joe's been on this job for a few months now—and you know, it's hard work, outside for the most part, and through the winter too. He's a strong lad, doesn't complain, and we've brought them up to know the value of a hard day's work—so it's not as if he was moaning about the job. Well, not until a couple of weeks ago. But I think I noticed the change before Phil. Joe would telephone us—not to talk for long, but just to say hello so we could hear his voice. But his voice changed—he became sort of, well, distant, like he didn't really want to talk. It was as if he was just getting through the five minutes on the telephone, and I felt like I wasn't so much having a conversation as interrogating him, or whatever the right word is. 'How are you, Joe?' 'All right, Mum.' 'What's the job like?' 'All right, Mum.' 'Do you like your new lodgings?' 'They're all right.' It was like trying to have a word with a brick."

"I take it he was more . . . more forthcoming, before this lack of enthusiasm started," offered Maisie.

"Oh yes, Miss Dobbs—he would always have a story," said Coombes. "Perhaps something about the landlady, or a laugh he'd had with the lads. He couldn't

wait to tell us about the first time he saw a heron, landing on a lake—he'd gone for a walk after work, to get
some fresh air, he'd said, and he saw a big heron. He
was made up with seeing it—loved seeing new things."
She became thoughtful. "To be honest, I reckon he
really loved being in the country, though I think it
was around the same time as he began taking those
long walks after his working day was done, that he
first started having those nasty headaches. Perhaps he
walked to feel better."

"What about the headaches, Mrs. Coombes?"

"He wouldn't say much, just that it was as if someone had landed him a wallop on his head, and that the
light seemed blue around the edges of whatever he was
looking at. And he felt bad in his stomach at the same
time—you know, as if he would bring up his breakfast."

"I know that sort of headache," said Sandra. "I had
them a few times when I was first carrying Martin.
Came with the sickness—you remember, Miss Dobbs.
You sent me home—in fact, you had Billy go out and
find a taxi for me."

"I remember very well," said Maisie. She leaned
toward Sally Coombes. "It's a very bad sort of headache
that can often be caused by bright light, or by a certain
smell, or by strong food—chocolate will do it, believe it

or not. They can start at any age, though often at Joe's age, coming into manhood. Had he ever experienced them before?"

Coombes shook her head. "Never. My three were always in tip-top health. None of them drink—well, as far as I know, because Archie lives in lodgings across the water, in Sydenham. Close to the engineering works where he's a foreman now. And I know this might surprise you, but not one of them has ever touched a ciggie either—unlike their father."

Maisie allowed silence to settle for some seconds before speaking again. "Mrs. Coombes—Sally—why do you think Joe failed to make his usual telephone calls this past week?"

Coombes looked up, her eyes filled with tears. She appeared to increase her hold on Martin, causing him to whimper. Sandra leaned forward, concern in her eyes. Maisie lifted her chin and gave an almost imperceptible shake of her head. Coombes brought her attention back to the child. She smiled down at him, and rocked him into sleep once more.

"I think something is very wrong, Miss Dobbs. I think something is terribly amiss. I am like Phil—I can't put my finger on it . . . and I've wondered what Joe has been doing with himself when he's not working. He can't be walking all the time. But I can tell you that in the past three weeks or so, something has been wrong with my boy. I've asked myself if the headaches have been brought on by whatever it is he's working on? Or is he worried about something?" She looked up. "You see, Joe was always happy-go-lucky—that's the best way to describe him. *Innocent.* Not like some of the lads you see about—even those in uniform. Being in khaki doesn't suddenly make saints of them, does it?" She shook her head. "I'm the boy's mother, and I know—it has been as if he was a man with all the worries of the world on his shoulders. Phil can't see it like that—but he's worried sick too. We both know Joe's changed and there's got to be a good reason for it."

Maisie could see the woman's eyes smarting with unshed tears, and was about to offer her plan regarding Joe, when Sally Coombes resumed speaking. "You know, Miss Dobbs, I have worried that we've been too hard on them. That we've sort of kept them too coddled so they would be, like I said, innocent. I wonder if we didn't give them enough—you know, enough, well *tough*—to look after themselves. Especially Joe. Mind you, our Archie knows a thing or two, and Vivian isn't a stupid girl. You expect growing up in London to give them some backbone. But I still wonder if it's not all down to us, and that Joe, more than the other two, could have done with more elbow, so he could nudge back when the world nudged him."

"I'm sure there's nothing here that's your fault, Mrs. Coombes," said Maisie. "Now, I can see you're tired, and I know you need to get back to the pub and have some rest before opening time. Let me tell you what we're going to do—because we will find out what's ailing Joe and we will do what we can to put things right with him. Billy is at Yates' yard this afternoon. He's talking to people there, to find out exactly where Joe is, and whether they've heard from the crew he's with." She paused to make sure Sally Coombes was absorbing her words. "And Billy will be in Hampshire this coming Saturday, visiting his family. I thought I might take him down there in the motor—our evacuee, Anna, is very fond of his daughter, so it might make a nice excursion for her. We can go over to Whitchurch to see if we can find Joe—unless the crew has moved on. If we locate him and he's not well, we'll make sure he sees a doctor. If he's covering up these headaches during working hours, there is no reason why any of his workmates would think to help him."

"That sounds like Joe—I'm sure he would never let on. He wants to be seen as one of the men, not just the boy apprentice."

Coombes handed the baby back to Sandra, who set aside her notebook and took her son, placing him with care in his carrycot. Coombes pulled her coat around her, and took up her handbag again.

"I feel for poor Mr. Beale, you know. What with his son being over there in France, and the way things are going."

Maisie inclined her head, and was about to inquire further.

Coombes put her hand to her mouth. "Oh dear—oh dear, I shouldn't have said anything. Oh dear, I could get our Viv put in prison for that."

"I'm not following you, Mrs. Coombes," said Maisie.

Sandra stepped closer. "Your Vivian works on the government telephone exchange, doesn't she? What has she heard, Mrs. Coombes? What has she heard that hasn't been announced?"

"Oh dear, I shouldn't have said anything. But I reckon they'll sort it out, Mr. Churchill and all those army and navy men—and especially now Mr. Churchill's prime minister and that Chamberlain has gone. That stupid man and his bits of paper signed by Adolf Hitler—so much for his peace in our time. And we believed him!" She put her hand to her forehead, then took it away to grasp her bag again. "Viv was so upset yesterday when she came home—she'd been working an early shift.

She wasn't supposed to say anything to us, on account of her signing the Official Secrets Act forms, but she couldn't keep it to herself. You see, our boys are stuck over there. The Germans have already gone into Holland and Belgium, and now they're moving in to trap our soldiers. And once they've done that, you know Hitler will come over here to get us. Our boys have got a terrible job on their hands. Vivian heard it all, on the line—orders going out to prepare for a possible evacuation of our expeditionary force from France. They're already bringing home what they call non-essential staff. Viv heard that there's more calling themselves non-essential just to get away. And there's French and Belgian boys stuck too. The government's trying to plan an evacuation of as many soldiers as they can, only they've kept it quiet for morale reasons—apparently the army are trying to fight the Germans on the one hand and move toward the coast at the same time. If it gets any worse, the government won't manage to keep it a secret for much longer." She straightened her shoulders. "I suppose you could say it won't stay secret if my girl tells anyone else, but she was fair shaken about it all. Tell you the truth, I think she's been a bit sweet on Mr. Beale's eldest, ever since he brought him in for a half-pint before he went off to join the army. Mr. Beale probably doesn't know this, but young Billy came back of his own accord a couple of times when he came home on leave, just to see our Viv before he went over there. Phil frowned on it a bit, but as he said, at least he knows Mr. Beale's lads are good boys."

An image of Billy's son came into Maisie's mind's eye, a boy of eight or nine when she first met him, with wheaten hair like his father, and a swagger to his step. Young Billy, always with a cheeky grin, taking on the job of helping his father keep the family morale high, even through the worst of times. She remembered him coming into the office before leaving for France, filled with that confidence and proud in his new uniform, talking about how long it took him to get his boots to a spit-and-polish shine. And when Maisie had said, "Take care, young Billy," and had pressed four half-crowns into his hand, he had blushed and said, "Fanks, Miss Dobbs—this'll buy me and the boys a few pints before we go." His father had walked to the door with him, and had returned to the office, his head low.

Maisie could feel Sandra's eyes upon her. They both understood what the news meant for Billy and his family. The question now was whether she should tell Billy what she knew, or leave it to Pathé News to inform him. After all, perhaps his son might not be at risk.

"You won't say anything to anyone, will you, Miss Dobbs? Mrs. Pickering? I should have kept my mouth

shut, after all, it's not as if I should know anything—
but our Viv was so upset, she just had to get it off her
chest."

"We'll both keep it to ourselves, Mrs. Coombes,"
said Maisie. "I'm sure that, if the BEF are indeed
stranded, it will be in the newspapers at some point
during the next few days. And I'd already heard something along those lines from another source."

"Our boys are fighting for their lives and ours, over
there. And if they lose, if Hitler gets closer, it'll only
be a question of time before invasion, that's what worries me. People will lose their sons, and then we'll lose
our country—and let's face it, it won't be the first time.
As Phil says, look at the Romans, and the Normans,
and the Saxons before them—and those Saxons were
German, after all. Little island like this—we're sitting
ducks. I don't know what will come of us, truly I don't.
At least mine are in reserved occupations, that's all I can
say—but no one will be protected, come the invasion."

Maisie escorted Sally Coombes downstairs to the
front door, opening it wide to a shaft of sunlight. Before
bidding her goodbye, she reassured the woman. "I will
keep in touch, Mrs. Coombes, and I daresay I will have
something to report next Monday, if not before."

"Who knows what might have happened by then,"
said Coombes as she stepped out into Fitzroy Square.

As Maisie collected the afternoon's post from the table, she heard a key in the lock, the door opened again, and Billy crossed the threshold.

"Lovely afternoon, miss. Really feels like spring has sprung—and there's Sally Coombes walking down the road bundled up for a blizzard." They began walking up the stairs together, Maisie listening while Billy talked about who he'd seen on the walk from the underground station. "Now I could do with a cuppa." He continued his chatter before Maisie could respond. "Sandra here? Lovely—can't wait to see the little fella again. I bet he's a bonny boy. I remember when my young Billy was that age—I tell you, when my first boy was born, I felt like everything was getting better. I mean, I'd married my best girl, and now I had a boy."

Sandra came to her feet to greet Billy as they entered the office. But before she could speak, Billy looked from Sandra, to Maisie.

"What? Something's off. What is it?"

Maisie was used to thinking on her feet, to making snap decisions when a life was threatened, or an investigation was reaching a crucial point. Given what she knew of Doreen's vulnerability in the face of bad news, and the threat of mental breakdown that had never quite left her, she might be able to circumvent Billy's wife suffering a serious psychological response to her son's life being at risk. If Billy knew now about the situation in France, it would give him time to reach Doreen before news left Westminster for Fleet Street, before the morrow's early newspapers were stacked onto trains; trains that would take the escalating news to every household in the country—news of Britain's vulnerable army fighting for its life, and a possible eventual evacuation of the expeditionary force from the coast of France. An army of men—of husbands, brothers, sweethearts, sons—and yes, daughters too, for she knew there were young women ambulance drivers and telephonists with the Auxilliary Territorial Service over in France.

Maisie remembered being at Chelstone, in the spring of 1918—why was she there? Was she convalescing, following her own wounding in France? Yes it must have been, because she was walking at a slow pace through the village—if she moved any faster she would lose her balance. She had watched as the messenger boy went from house to house. Soon it seemed everyone was on the street, women calling to each other, telling children to find the men working out in the fields. "Who have we lost? Who have we lost?" they cried, each holding out their own telegram, just delivered following the Spring Offensive. For everyone knew everyone else, and every boy had grown to manhood with a family of mother, father and village. A man and woman might have lost their son—but they had also lost his best friends, and the boys who had played football together in the street after school, and cricket on the green in summer. "Who have we lost?" The words echoed in her ears.

"What, miss—what is it? Is it Doreen? Our little Lizzie?"

Maisie knew then that she must tell Billy, for instead of asking for Margaret Rose, his youngest child, who had been evacuated to the country with her mother, he had uttered the name of a daughter now dead—dear little Lizzie Beale, who had succumbed to diphtheria so long ago. An ingrained fear of loss had caused him to call out the wrong name. She must give him the opportunity to reach Doreen before news reached her first—surely they had time. And surely "planned" on the part of the government meant that something might not need to be put into action. There might still be a chance of success. After all, the information she'd received could be incorrect, superseded by developing events. But this was war, not a game—and if it were true, that Churchill had given instructions for plans for evacuation of the BEF to be drawn up, it meant that the situation was grave.

"Billy—you know Vivian at the pub is a telephonist on the government exchanges, and—"

"What of it?" Billy frowned, his tone had become short.

"She's bound by the Official Secrets Act, but she told her mother and father that she had overheard a conversation between callers at . . . at a very high level, discussing orders for a possible evacuation of the expeditionary force in France. The Germans have moved into the Netherlands and Belgium, and it is feared it will only be a matter of time before France falls. Our army is in fierce combat with the Germans, and already men are making their way to the coast of northern France."

Billy ran the fingers of one hand after the other through his hair. "Blimmin' hell—they're still digging up soldiers from the last war across that Somme valley, and now there'll be even more." He rested his head in his hands. "My son. My boy . . . what will we do? What will Doreen do? We can't lose him."

Instinctively Maisie moved to his side.

Sandra checked the sleeping baby in his carrycot, and stepped across toward the door. "I'll make tea—we could all do with a cup."

Billy pointed at the carrycot. "Make sure you take that boy somewhere where they're neutral, Sandra—

make sure you and Lawrence get away and take him where no one will ever be knocking at the door and wanting him for soldiering."

"Billy, I brought the motor car with me this morning, and I'll drive you down to Hampshire without delay if you think it best to go to Doreen. I just have to place a couple of telephone calls and I'll be ready to go."

"What about the petrol, miss?"

"I've motor spirit coupons in my bag, so I'm all right—let's think ourselves lucky, as I was about to retire the Alvis to the barn at Chelstone for the duration."

Billy sat down on the chair vacated by Mrs. Coombes. He leaned forward with his arms folded and resting on his knees, his gaze toward the floor. When he spoke, his voice was low. "I know there's thousands of lads over there, and I feel for every one of them and their mums and dads, and their wives, their children. But I never wanted my Billy to go, not after what I saw the last time around. And they said it would be different. War's always the same though—politicians square off and ordinary lads do their dirty work. I'd stick all of them ministers in a field—all of them, all of these big nobs from every country what wants a fight, and I'd let them have all their blimmin' weapons and tell them to get on with it. Leave us ordinary people alone to live our lives. That's what I'd do."

Maisie knew it would be of no use to comment. His need, now, was to be with his family.

"What'll I do about Bobby?" Billy wiped his hand across his forehead. "I can't believe it—for a minute I forgot all about my other boy."

"It's all right, Billy—you're reacting as anyone might in your situation. Now then, let's plan to leave within the hour, and I'll have you down to Hampshire in next to no time."

"Won't the train be faster?" said Sandra as she returned to the room with a tray set with a teapot, milk jug, and sugar. She set it down on her desk, and moved to pick up two cups and saucers along with the china mug favored by Maisie, which were kept on top of the filing cabinet.

"Billy—what do you think?" asked Maisie.

"Um—the train might be faster, but first I've got to get on one going to Whitchurch, and then there's the bus from there to the village—well, hamlet, more like, closer to Doreen's aunt. And I've got a walk after that."

"Right—here's what we'll do. Billy—I'll take you, no arguments. Sandra, can you get a message to young

Bobby—let him know his dad has had to go down to Hampshire *for work*." She turned back to Billy. "I'm sure he can look after himself, but is there anyone you want to look in on him?"

"Mrs. Relf, the neighbor. She's a good 'un, and she's taken a shine to Bobby—said she reminds him of the boy she lost on the Somme."

"Right—Sandra, would you get a messenger to take a note to Mrs. Relf—ask her to kindly look out for Bobby when he gets home from work." She turned to Billy. "Didn't you tell me he's doing a lot of overtime at the garage, converting motor cars for war work?"

"He won't be home before seven. Like I said this morning—I don't even see him much on a Sunday, because he's so tired, he's not out of bed before noon."

"Not to worry, miss—I'll look after everything." Sandra reached for the telephone receiver. "I'll get Lawrence and we'll drive over to Billy's later, if need be. And don't you worry either, Billy—he'll be all right. Bobby's more or less a man now anyway, so he won't want too many women fussing over him."

"He might be a man, Sandra—but just like his brother, he's still my boy."

Chapter 3

Billy was leaning forward in the passenger seat of the Alvis, as if doing so would make the vehicle go faster. His eyes were focused on the road before them, and each time traffic slowed, or a bus pulled out in front of the motor car, he made his complaint known with a shaking of the fist, or a curse directed toward the driver. Errant pedestrians received a loud sigh, with the exception of a woman dawdling, who was treated to a Billy winding down the side window and telling her to get a move on. Maisie knew his impatience reflected fear for his wife's emotional vulnerability, and terror for his son.

"You know what it does, miss, don't you?" said Billy, leaning back in the passenger seat. "It brings it all back. That's the worst thing about being in a war—it's not the fighting, or the tunneling, or any of the

blimmin' terrible jobs you have to do. No, it's the waiting. For us sappers, it was waiting for the coast to be
clear—laying lines, going into tunnels, putting down
explosives. Waiting to get out, waiting to get in. Waiting to go over the top. It's the waiting that makes a
brave lad cave into himself. Once you get going, once
you're doing something, you get this sort of . . . sort
of feeling like a bottle of pop just went off inside you.
And you get on and do your job, and when it's done
you drop. But waiting's terrible. Waiting bears down
on you. They don't tell you about that when you've just
enlisted and you're square bashing in Blighty. No, you
find it out once you're over there, up to your eyes in
it. I saw a bloke go down once, all his insides outside
of him—I got to him and said, 'You're all right, mate.
Stretcher bearers are coming.' And he looked up and
said, 'Thank God—the waiting's over.' And that was
him. Gone. And now there's all them lads over there."

Billy sighed as he settled in for the journey. Houses,
shops and factories were thinning out, and they began
to pass fields, farms and woodland. Maisie understood
only too well how important it was for her to counter Billy's intensity with her own modulated breathing, with measured movements and responses. The
fire inside her assistant was burning with a fury—she
would not fan the flames. Instead she meditated upon

her driving, and being safe and secure inside a shell of protection. A temper was akin to a virus, and could so easily graft itself onto another.

"You're going to have to direct me once we get close to Alton."

"The last stretch is all winding roads out to the village. It's a terror to get to—fair wears me out, it does. Doreen says they should come home, what with nothing happening. She found out that a lot of Margaret Rose's friends who were evacuated have gone home too—and the part of the school not taken over by the army is back in use, with a couple of teachers coming in every day. We don't like being apart, though I sometimes think Bobby quite likes a bit of freedom when I'm off seeing his mum and sister." He fell silent, then added, "They're good boys, my lads. A bit of lip here and there, but they're a pair of diamonds, both of them."

"Tell me what happened at Yates' yard," said Maisie. Not only was she eager to know, but the conversation would distract Billy. "It's been a rush since you came back into the office," she added.

Billy looked at his watch. "Blimey—I can hardly believe it was only this morning. Don't take long for the world to tip, does it?"

"No, Billy. Sadly, it doesn't," said Maisie.

"Well anyway," said Billy, taking a notebook from his inside pocket. He opened and then closed it again. "I'd better not read while you're driving, makes me a bit queasy. I can remember it all."

"Open the window if you're feeling unsettled, Billy."

"I'll be all right." He paused, ran his fingers through his hair, took one swift glance at his notebook again, and looked ahead at the road. "I got to the works and asked to speak to Mike Yates, but he wasn't there on account of having to go to visit a site. I should have said—when I got there, I went in through the big gates—cast iron, they are, leading onto a cobblestone yard with drains because they used to have horses and carts to take men and the paints and what have you to the jobs, but it's all vans and lorries now, with all their tools and paints stored in the old stables. There was a lorry just getting ready to leave—couple of blokes were climbing into the cab. And it was an ordinary lorry, not RAF or army. They'd just delivered paint in big tins. Now, I'm not a painter and decorator, so I don't know if this is normal, but these tins were more like barrels, and there were blokes from Yates' in their whites already starting to pour the stuff into smaller containers, then putting them into the back of a van."

"That's interesting—were any of the men wearing masks?"

"You mean like doctors? Or crooks?" Billy grinned.

"Glad to see your sense of humor hasn't completely vanished." Maisie gave a half-laugh. "No, I meant like doctors—it occurred to me that, if this paint—emulsion, Joe called it—is sufficiently vaporous to cause headaches, I wondered if wearing some sort of mask might help, and if they wore them at the yard, when they're decanting the bigger containers."

"No, they weren't," Billy paused, thoughtful. "Well, I tell a lie. One bloke had tied an old rag around his face. Over his nose and mouth. And there's more to tell on that."

"Go on," said Maisie.

"I went up to the bloke with the paperwork—he looked like he was ticking off the number of barrels—and first of all I asked him if Mr. Yates was there, and when he said no, I said, 'Perhaps you can help me then.' So, I asked him about Joe Coombes, and he said, 'Oh, he's not here—he's on a job outside London.' I asked him if he could tell me where, and he said he couldn't, because it was—what did he say?" Billy pressed his lips together as he tried to remember the conversation. "'Classified.' That's what he said. It was classified. He said Joe was working on a special . . . a special . . ." Billy opened his notebook, glanced at the pages, and closed it again, rubbing his eyes. "'A special government works order.' Then the bloke clammed up and asked, 'And who are you?' So I told him I was there because Joe's dad was a mate of mine and couldn't get away from work to come over himself, but him and his missus were a bit worried as they hadn't heard from young Joe, and they thought he might be poorly, as he'd complained of having a bit of a head a few times. And he says, 'Oh we all get a bit of that, mate—it's paint what does it, especially this new stuff. That's why Bert over there has a towel tied around his face.' Then he told me it was all right because the lads are mainly working outside, so the fumes get dispersed."

Maisie was silent, as if the information imparted were a stone found at the beach, a pebble shot through with thin veins of strata, to be traced and considered as she turned the rock in her palm.

"What you think of that, miss?"

"Did he say anything else?" asked Maisie.

"Not much—only that the older men look out for the apprentices, but at that age, they said Joe should have been pretty much able to look after himself." Billy stared out of the window, then brought his attention back to Maisie. "Trouble is, they all think they're men, these young lads, and even though I know what he meant— the bloke at Yates' yard—fifteen and already at work for a year gives you a bit more nous than you had when you left school. But take it from me—there's still something of the boy there, and without the beard of a man."

"And Joe was so attached to his family. Yet I have a feeling that he knew he would be able to establish some independence with his work. He was breaking away from Phil and Sally to grow that beard. But this government job is beginning to sound like more and more of a risk." She paused. "Do I go right here, Billy?"

"Ooops, yes, sorry, miss—I was miles away then, thinking. . . ."

"Anyway, it sounds as if the government wanted the work done as fast as possible, and sent the painters out with the best fire retardant they had to hand. And perhaps they hadn't gone through a full testing."

"P'raps they didn't want to," said Billy.

"You could be right. Look, as soon as I've dropped you at the cottage, I'll find a room at a local guesthouse—it shouldn't be too difficult, but still pushing it a bit as it will be getting dark by then. Luckily we're making good time, but I don't want to be out after the blackout. Tomorrow I'll have a look round, find out where Joe was staying, talk to the landlady, that sort of thing. It's a big county, but at least I know roughly where he was lodging, according to the notes taken when I spoke to Mrs. Coombes. I should telephone Brenda too, find out how Anna is this week. There have been some bugs going round, but so far she's managed to remain well."

"The things they pick up at school. When I was a boy, if anything was going round—mumps, chicken pox, measles—my mum used to say, 'Go on, get in there and get it and then you'll be done with it.' Makes me laugh to think of it. There's some who take very bad though. My cousin went down with chicken pox and they put her in quarantine because they thought she had smallpox. That's another nasty one." Billy seemed to stare into the distance as if the past were on the road in front of him, then sat forward in his seat. "That turning there, miss—with the pillar box at the end of the lane."

Maisie swung the motor car onto the lane, continuing along the bumpy road until they reached a cottage on the edge of farmland.

"This is it," said Billy.

"How far is it from the station?" asked Maisie.

"Three or four mile," said Billy.

"And you walk all the way?"

"Unless I can get a lift from the farmer, if he's coming this way. Doreen's aunt's husband, God rest his soul, was one of the farm workers from the time he was a boy, and the farmer said the tied cottage is hers until she dies."

"Oh look, there's Doreen with Margaret Rose

now." Maisie slowed the motor car, bringing it to a halt alongside the cottage. She shut off the engine and stepped out of the Alvis, watching as Billy's daughter ran and launched herself into his arms while Doreen stood back, watching, smiling, yet with a questioning look in her eyes, until Billy held out a hand to bring her into his embrace. Maisie caught her breath, and for a moment she imagined laughing with James as their child ran to his arms, and then feeling his arms around them both, a family of three, beloved of each other. But James was gone now, along with all hope of motherhood, and at times Maisie thought she might lose the feeling of him, lose the image of his face, of his touch, of him reaching for her. She looked away, but heard Doreen call her name.

"Miss Dobbs—Maisie—would you like to stay for tea? You must be gasping for a cup, and something to eat."

"Come on in, miss—we've been on the road for a few hours now," added Billy.

Maisie shook her head. If she were to secure accommodation for the night, she should make haste to find her way back to a guesthouse she had noted as they drove through Whitchurch. "I should be getting along—I've to settle a room for the night."

"You can stay here on the farm, Miss Dobbs," said

Doreen's aunt as she emerged from the house wiping her hands on a tea cloth, and introduced herself as "Aunt Millicent," as if everyone referred to her as "aunt" whether related or not. "They run a bed-and-breakfast up at the house, you know. The farmer's wife, Mrs. Keep, puts up a very good spread of a morning."

Realizing she had little choice—the group's faces were wreathed in smiles of welcome and all but dictated her next move—Maisie inclined her head and accepted the referral. "I'll nip along to see Mrs. Keep now." She consulted her watch. "And then I might have just enough time to go back into Whitchurch before it gets dark." She turned to Billy. "I want to find out where Joe was staying, have a word with the landlady. I've got his last address."

"Right you are, miss." Billy nodded, acknowledging Maisie's tactful decline of tea. By the time she had seen Mrs. Keep, it was likely that Doreen would be in a state of distress, for Billy would have recounted what he knew of the battles raging on the other side of the Channel, and the fact that there were plans being made to evacuate the army. Maisie wondered if being privy to classified information in advance of the general population was as useful as it appeared at first blush. And she found herself wishing she had placed a call to Dr. Elsbeth Masters, the doctor of psychiatry to whom she had referred Doreen years before in the wake of little Lizzie Beale's death. Although Billy's wife was stronger, this news of what was happening in France might distress her to the point of relapse. But Billy was with her, so at least she had someone there to share the weight of her deepest fears—and they had come through so much together.

Mrs. Keep was as good as her name. She kept a tidy house, neat accommodation and a fair price for a room, which looked out over the kitchen garden and beyond to a field with cattle grazing, and a hill flanked by a stand of oaks in the far distance. At ease in the small room with sloping beamed ceilings, Maisie closed her eyes as she stood in front of the diamond-paned window. An image of the restful landscape before her seemed etched behind her lids, as if it were a photographic negative. But she could not linger and give way to fatigue. After paying Mrs. Keep for one night, she left the house to search for a Mrs. Digby, who apparently took in lodgers—including the young Joe Coombes.

Mrs. Digby resided in a house on the Winchester Road, not far from the River Test and the old silk mill. Billy had told her something of the town during the drive down from London, informing her that the silk mill was built in 1815, but that silk only began to be made two years later, when a silk manufacturer from London bought the property. The mill had garnered some prestigious clients, and more recently Billy had been told by a local that not only was the mill continuing to make silk for shirting and legal gowns, and for the company started by Thomas Burberry, but was also weaving silk for the insulation of electrical cables. It appeared the machine of war was in operation everywhere.

Maisie had been directed to the house by the landlord of a local pub—it seemed there was a pub on almost every corner of the small town—and according to the plaque above the door of the three-storey residence, it had been built in 1790. It appeared somewhat down at heel, and for the time being had probably been saved from complete collapse by ivy leaching into every crevice of the brickwork—though that same ivy could well be the culprit undermining the mortar. Maisie knocked at the door, and when there was no answer, knocked again. No one came. She stood back and looked up at the windows, then back at the door—and only then noticed a bell pull to the right, partially obscured by creeping vine. She took the rusty cast-iron handle and gave it a good tug. This time she did not have to wait long for a response to her summons.

"All right, all right. I'm coming. What's the rush? That's what I want to know." A woman's voice, husky, interrupted by a throaty cough, grew louder on the other side of the door. "I'm here, just a minute." The yapping of a small dog inspired a scolding, and another round of coughing before the door was opened. "Yes? What can I do for you?"

Maisie estimated Mrs. Digby to be about fifty years of age, though she appeared to be doing all she could to combat the years. Dressed in a silk kimono over a pair of silk pajamas—both had seen better days, and perhaps not much in the way of laundry soap in recent weeks, or months—Digby was heavily made up, with copious amounts of powder and rouge. Maisie wondered if the woman had been on the stage, for the texture of the cosmetics reminded her of those used by Priscilla's youngest son, Tarquin, when he had been given the role of Peter Pan in the school pantomime. Regarding Mrs. Digby, Maisie remembered Douglas Partridge looking down at his son and inquiring whether he had put on the makeup with a trowel, it was so thick. The woman's eyes were bright blue, rimmed by long, thick lashes that could only be false. She held a petite white dog under her arm and jigged it up and down, as if it were a babe on her hip to be soothed. Maisie thought the dog looked more like a powder puff with eyes, nose, tongue and teeth, than something reliably canine.

"Mrs. Digby?"

The woman seemed to assess Maisie from head to toe, then smirked and raised an eyebrow, as if to have found the subject wanting. "And who wants to know?"

Maisie reached into her pocket and brought out a calling card. She handed it to Mrs. Digby, who held out a liver-spotted hand with be-ringed fingers, her nails manicured to show bright red polish to best effect. She took the card.

"Psychologist and investigator, eh? And you want to investigate me?"

Maisie shook her head. "No, Mrs. Digby. I'm here informally on behalf of very good friends of mine—their son was lodging with you, and they haven't heard from him in a week or so, and of course they are worried."

"You must mean Freddie. Or was it Len? I've only got the ladies now—three WAAFs stationed at the RAF base. Mind you—when the lads were here, it was all above board—men on the top floor, women on the floor just above mine. I don't want any funny business going on under my roof."

"Then you didn't let a room to Joe Coombes?" asked Maisie.

The woman flapped a free hand. "Oh Joe. Little Joey. I almost forgot him—mind you, easy to do as he was a quiet one."

"Was?"

"They moved on over a week ago—probably why his people haven't heard from him."

"I thought the men were still working in the area—at the airfield."

Digby repositioned the dog on her hip. "Well, there's more than one airfield within striking distance, and not many places left to lodge, what with all the WAAFs and they say we'll have land girls coming in before too long. Not that the young ladies are easier—leaving their knickers and stockings to drip all over the floor when they've washed them out in the sink. And the noise they make when they're getting ready to go out of an evening—I can hardly think. It's like a herd of elephants above my head." She paused. "No, there were three of them, the lads, and they moved out. . . ." The woman's words seemed to fade, and she glanced at the ground, frowning.

"What is it?" said Maisie.

Digby shook her head. "Probably nothing. But that boy was having terrible headaches. I mean, the other boys had headaches too—I put it down to the fact that they liked to go down the pub of an evening. But with young Joe it was bad—he asked me for a powder once or twice, and I could see he was hurting. Then all of a sudden they were giving notice—the big lad, Freddie, came to see me, said they were moving out. And that was that."

"When was the last time you saw Joe Coombes, Mrs. Digby?"

The woman stared over Maisie's head and squinted, as if the answer might lie amid the trees on the other side of the road. "I reckon it was the day before they left. They were generally off to work before it's my time to get up of a morning—they knew how to make themselves a breakfast, and as long as I don't come down to a pile of dirty plates and cups in the sink, I let my lodgers look after themselves. Then that one came back to say they'd moved on, but he didn't give an address. He brought the van and collected their belongings. Not that they had much. A small kit bag each, and that was it—I've seen evacuees turn up in the town with more. I know the lads were all working for a London firm, painting and decorating, that sort of trade. And I knew it was to do with airfields, so I assume they were doing up the officers' mess at each place, something like that. I'd been paid up until the end of next month, so I was all right."

"And they didn't give you an address for forwarding post?" asked Maisie.

"No. Joe was the only one to get any letters in any case. Just a minute." Digby held up a finger and walked back into the house. Maisie peered through the open doorway. A staircase swept up from a narrow hall, which had been painted red with a blue border, and a paper chain of dusty Union Jack flags hung in a shallow curve from the picture rail. A mirror was situated above a hall table where post had been spread out. Still holding the white dog on her hip, Digby held each letter up to her face, revealing a need for reading glasses, and a disposition too vain to admit it. Having placed the envelopes back on the table, she looked up into the mirror and squinted to check her reflection before turning back to the door.

"I could have sworn there was post for Joe. Perhaps Freddie took it for him. Anyway, he'll be about somewhere with those other lads, at an airfield. Now, if you don't mind, I can't spend all afternoon jawing away like this."

"Thank you, Mrs. Digby." Maisie turned to leave, but held out her hand and pressed it against the door. "Oh—just one more question, if you don't mind."

"Yes?" Digby sighed the word, elongating it to signal her impatience.

"Did Joe ever have any visitors?"

"Visitors?" Digby shook her head. "I don't hold with my lodgers having visitors—I like to know who's under my roof." She patted the dog, who was fidgeting, racing his little legs as if running in midair. She leaned down to put him on the ground and began speaking again as she once more stood up to her full height, by which time the dog had run to the back of the house, as if to attempt escape from his mistress. "But it's funny you should ask, because someone came to the house asking for Joe Coombes. Tall, stringy sort of fellow—about thirty, perhaps younger. He was well turned out, I remember that—very tidy, nice tie, good shoes, well polished. I thought he might be family—not that it was any of my business. I told him that Mr. Coombes had moved on with the rest of the crew." Digby placed her hand over her mouth, and whispered through her fingers. "There I am telling you all this, and forgetting what I should have remembered when that man was stood where you are now. I was told not to say anything to anyone about the lads. It was part of the contract—not a real contract, not paper, like a solicitor would give you. It was verbal—the man who booked the lodgings said that on no account must I say anything about the lads to anyone who asked, and I was to tell them if anyone came with questions or to visit. He was official, I reckon, from the government. That painting business must be making a pretty penny, if someone up in London is going to that sort of trouble." The kimono had slipped off one shoulder, revealing more of the woman's undergarments than modesty might allow. "Oh, now look at me—just as well it's you standing there, and not Sid Watkins from the ironmongers along the street. All eyes and hands, him." And with her final comment, she nodded by way of departure and closed the door.

Maisie remained in front of the door for a moment before walking back out onto the Winchester Road to collect her motor car. She wondered how the men working for Yates fared in the countryside—Hampshire had not been their first stop, and it would not be their last. Most airfields were situated in rural areas, and the painters were, in general, city men who had grown up on the streets, not close to fields and farms. She wondered if, at the end of a long day, perhaps feeling less than well, given the circumstances of the job gleaned so far, the local pubs might have offered the only place for the young men to relax. On the one hand, that might have given Joe a sense of being at home, or it might have presented him with a dilemma—too much like home.

Pulling up alongside a telephone kiosk, Maisie took the opportunity to place a call to Brenda, who would be at the Dower House, the home bequeathed to Maisie years earlier by her mentor, Dr. Maurice Blanche. Brenda and Maisie's father stayed during the week to care for Anna, the evacuee girl who had been billeted with them. Maisie drove down from London on a Thursday or Friday, returning to her flat in Holland Park on Monday morning, though if she were not busy it had become easy to linger for one more day. Sometimes two.

"The doctor's been," said Brenda. "She came over poorly and was running a temperature and he says it's definitely measles. The poor little mite is really under the weather. Doctor Stringer says it will run its course, but he said a few of the children locally have gone down with it a lot harder than he's seen before. He reckons the little ones take on more than we think they do, so they're—what did he say? Oh yes—vulnerable. Mind you, he's young—got all these new-fangled ideas. He told me he wanted to join up in the medical corps, but couldn't on account of his limp—had polio as a boy and reckons he's a lucky one because he didn't end up in a wheelchair."

Maisie knew that when her stepmother began to talk without stopping, it was generally because she was worried.

"I'll come home as soon as I can—let's see how she is tomorrow. Is everything else all right?"

"I was getting to everything else—the doctor also says that the outbreak of measles will get worse if they start a second evacuation. There's all those children who went back to London—like those boys who were here—and what with Germany going into Holland and Belgium, and now France, they're closer to an invasion, so the boys could come back to us, you never know. The new billeting officer came around today to check on Anna, so I told her she wasn't to be bringing any more children to the house until little Anna was well over the measles."

Maisie put her hand to her forehead. "Oh, poor Anna. Do you need any extra help?"

"A child lying quiet in her bed isn't a nuisance. The Ministry of Health inspector is though."

"What do you mean?" Maisie knew the Ministry of Health had jurisdiction over orphaned children, and a certain level of influence over where they should be placed. While she had documents signed by Anna's grandmother before the elderly woman succumbed to a respiratory disease, her guardianship of the child could still be challenged. However, Maisie's solicitor had considered the guardianship documents to be solid—at least until the war was over.

"She was checking on the evacuees, and knew about Anna's situation, so she was just asking questions about any plans to place her with a family. She didn't want to see her—she only found out about the measles outbreak when she arrived at the school, so she wasn't exactly keen to get close to any children. More's the pity because I've heard a few things about those poor little tykes over at Turner's Farm. They say old Jim Turner has his evacuees out working at five in the morning, before they go to school, and as soon as they're home, they're working again. I told the billeting officer about it, but all she could say was that they were a good family and the children did not seem ill-treated. I felt like telling her to put her glasses on!"

Maisie consulted her watch, and was about to speak when Brenda began again.

"Your father and I take it all in our stride, and Anna is no trouble—even as ill as she is. Emma won't leave her side, and even Jook has been up the stairs to sit in the room, and you know how that dog is with your father. If dogs could get measles, those two hounds would be down with it too by now. Anyway, one more thing—your friend Priscilla has been on the telephone. Wants to know where you are. She says it's important."

Chapter 4

It was Maisie's understanding, having spoken to one of the farm workers before she made her way back to Whitchurch, that there were several air force stations within a few miles of the farm. When she considered the reasons for such a cluster, two factors came to mind. The first was proximity to the coast, and the ports of Southampton and Portsmouth. Second was the land itself and the flight path bombers might take in the direction of towns to the northeast and to London, though airfields in the southeast—such as Tangmere, Kenley, Hawkinge, and Biggin Hill—were situated to protect the capital.

More questions queued up to be answered. Why did Yates not know the exact whereabouts of the crew? Most likely they did, but the fact that they were working on a government contract meant that secrecy was of the utmost importance—she could not expect them to have spoken freely to Billy. He could, after all, have been a spy—and hadn't the whole country been warned about the possibility of Nazi spies lurking among the general population, camouflaged by—perhaps—a British education and friendly demeanor or being a good neighbor? But what about Joe? Was his desire to be his own man overriding an ever more serious health condition? A young lad of fifteen might not consider it urgent—perhaps the headaches were easy to brush off. And who was his visitor?

Maisie's thoughts darted from one question to the next, as if she had skimmed a stone across the realm of possibilities, and was now watching ripples of suspicion form around the contours of information she had gathered so far. She checked her watch again—a wristwatch given to her by her late husband, James Compton—and looked up at the darkening sky. One more telephone call before she made her way back to the farm. She dialed the operator, gave the number, placed the requisite number of coins in the slot, and waited until she could hear the ring, and then a voice on the line.

"Partridge residence."

Maisie pressed button "A" to release the coins and

begin the call. "Elinor—Elinor, I recognized your lovely Welsh lilt. Is Mrs. Partridge at home?"

"Oh hello, Miss Dobbs—I mean, Your Ladysh—"

Maisie cut off the boys' nanny before she completed the little-used title bestowed upon Maisie on the day of her marriage to James.

"I have to be quick, Elinor—I'm in a telephone kiosk in Hampshire, and I only have a few coins on me. Is Mrs. Partridge there?"

"You just missed her. She's taken the boys—Tim and Tarquin—out for supper."

"Is anything wrong? I received a message that she was out of sorts."

"It's Tim—giving her a bit of trouble again. As you know, he's not been quite the same since Tom joined the air force, and he can't seem to wait until he gets his turn when he comes of an age to be called up. Too keen to join the navy, that one. But it won't be long, the way things are going—and more likely, he'll have to go where they put him, which might be right into the army."

"He does seem to be causing Mrs. Partridge some grief, and he has a sharp tongue on him when he likes, I know that."

"He's too much like his mother—quick with the wit,

but it can cut like a knife when he wants it to. Between us, she doesn't like it because she knows where he gets it from."

"Oh dear. I'll be back in London soon—tomorrow afternoon, hopefully—and I can usually get Tim to wind his neck in."

"He listens to you, Miss Dobbs."

Maisie was anxious to end the call, but was curious too.

"And what are you doing back in London, Elinor? I thought you were being sent somewhere with the First Aid Nursing Yeomanry."

"Oh, a couple of days' leave, and some, you know, special training."

"Sounds interesting."

"Hmmm. Must go now, Miss Dobbs. Bye!"

"Bye Elin—" Maisie pulled the telephone receiver away from her ear and held onto it for a second before returning it to the cradle. Elinor could be a bit of a chatterbox, so it was not like her to end a telephone conversation first. Indeed, Priscilla had once observed that in the midst of a conversation with Elinor one felt rather like an insect caught on sticky flypaper. The boys no longer needed a nanny, but she was so beloved, the family couldn't imagine letting her go.

After war was declared, Elinor had enlisted for service. During her years living with the family in France, she had acquired an admirable proficiency with the French language, and now thought she might be able to use her skill in war work. Priscilla and Douglas made her promise she would come "home" whenever she was on leave—her room was kept ready for her return, and she had her own key

Maisie left the telephone kiosk and returned to her motor car. The late May sun was now low in the sky, and darkness would come quickly. As she passed the cottage occupied by Doreen's aunt, she noticed the drawn blackout curtains, so not even a sliver of light could be seen.

"Oh, thank goodness you're back, Miss Dobbs." Mrs. Keep was wiping her hands on her apron as Maisie gave a quick knock at the back door of the farmhouse before turning the door handle to enter. "That road is a bit bumpy and I was worried you'd lose your way if it got too dark."

"Not to worry, Mrs. Keep—I don't like driving without a light to guide me, so I kept my eye on the time." As she spoke, Mrs. Keep turned away from her and lifted the corner of her apron to her eyes. "Mrs. Keep—is everything all right? Aren't you feeling well?"

The woman turned to Maisie. "It's the news. They

think we don't know what they're talking about, the way they give it out. But most of us have lived through one war and we know the newspapers and the wireless people are using words that mean other things. The army is in retreat in France—they told us three days ago that the Germans had broken through allied lines, and now they're reminding us that they did the same in March 1918, and we still won the war. They're not saying, but I reckon our boys will get stuck—and they're telling us about it a bit at a time so when the truth really comes out, no one is shocked. That's what my Bill thinks, and he was in the army."

"Oh, Mrs. Keep—you must stand tall, remain strong."

"Oh I know and we are strong. But we've two boys and we think they must be in the thick of it—we don't know for definite, and it's not as if you can ask the army. Bill's just gone out to check the sheep—we're lambing now, you know. Really, he wants to get out of the house, away from the waiting."

Maisie stepped to stand at the woman's side, and put an arm around her shoulders. With her free hand she pulled back a chair from the table and seated the farmer's wife, passing a handkerchief taken from her pocket. "I'll put the kettle on."

Mrs. Keep nodded her thanks. "I don't know what

to think," she said. "You bring up your sons on the farm, out in the country. And you think they're safe, that the worst that might happen to them is something horrible with the threshing machine. I mean, I lost my brother in the last war, and you think to yourself, no, it can't happen again, not like the last time. But look at it—look at us. We're all at it again, fighting each other. It looks like Holland, Belgium, and Luxembourg are going down to the Nazis, and now France." She paused, watching as Maisie warmed the teapot before adding tea and boiling water. "Mind you, they say the air force will be going out to protect our soldiers. And the navy. It'll be all hands on deck—everyone pulling together, you watch." She sat up, her spine straight, her shoulders back, as if she were convincing herself of the best outcome. "They didn't break us the last time, and they won't this time—mark my words."

Yet Maisie felt something snap within her. Priscilla's eldest son had joined the RAF only months earlier and was now flying, although he was not considered ready for aerial combat. But would that matter in an emergency? Mrs. Keep was right—all hands on deck might be a naval term, yet it extended to those who fought in the air and on the land, as well as the sea. Billy's son, Priscilla's son, Mrs. Keep's boys—it seemed everyone had something to lose, though at that very moment, more than anything, Maisie wanted only to be at Chelstone, drawn back by a feeling that her place was by the bedside of a sick child, one not her own, but entrusted to her care.

Maisie returned to the telephone kiosk after leaving the farm early the following morning. She placed a call to Chelstone Manor and asked to speak to Lord Julian Compton. Her father-in-law had contacts at the War Office—among other sources that had proven helpful to Maisie over the years.

"Maisie, my dear—how are you?" Lord Julian's voice had changed of late, and not for the first time, Maisie heard his age in the ragged edges around each word spoken.

"Very well, Lord Julian—I'm down in Hampshire, in Whitchurch actually."

"Oh, you're in the money then!"

Maisie laughed, assuming the elderly man was joking, and perhaps thought that, because she was not in London, she must be on holiday in the country. She continued. "I wonder if you could help me—I'd like to know how many RAF stations there are in the county. Could I get my hands on a list of them?"

"Tricky one, as they're building more, especially in

that area. There's about twenty-three, twenty-four, I would imagine—or there will be once they're all operational."

"How many?" Maisie was shocked. "In one county?"

"And if you're looking at proximity, you're not far from Wiltshire, and there's more there, and of course, in Dorset, and so on. I was just talking to a War Office colleague yesterday, former RAF man— he'd come down to pay a visit to the Canadian officers billeted here at Chelstone—and he was telling me they should have hundreds more airfields operational within months. Getting ready to meet the Luftwaffe on their own terms, I would imagine—that's certainly what our boys are doing at the moment."

Maisie had never known Lord Julian to be so forthcoming. He had always been helpful, yet measured in his responses. Perhaps it was because she was family now, united in grief over the loss of their only son. Over the years, Lord Julian and his wife, Rowan, had come to love her, and she had come to love them in return.

"That explains something—I'm looking into the apparent disappearance of a young apprentice painter and decorator. The business he works for landed a government contract to paint air stations with a special emulsion, a fire retardant, so they've been going from place to place spending a good amount of time in each location and painting every building, inside and out."

"There will be plenty of work for them, without doubt. And you say he's missing?"

"At the moment it might be more accurate to say 'not accounted for' by his parents. He could well just be ill and in bed at his lodgings and doesn't want them to know—he's had headaches ever since he started the work. Apparently the emulsion has a heavy vapor."

"Hmmm, yes. Fire retardant—definitely needed on those buildings. They'll be in the line of attack."

There was a second's hiatus in the conversation.

"Lord Julian—the war is close now, isn't it?"

"It was always close, my dear—close isn't simply a question of distance. The threat of war has been lingering over our heads since Adolf Hitler came to power. It was only a matter of time before we reached this point—but I don't think we could ever have foreseen having hundreds of thousands of our men at such peril almost beyond our reach. The RAF is moving farther into France to ward off the Luftwaffe—trying to give us a chance." Lord Julian cleared his throat. "Anyway—look, I can get you a list of all the RAF stations in Hampshire. Apart from the ports, it must be considered somewhat safe—after all, if it's good enough for the Bank of England. . . ." The gravely voice tapered off.

"I don't understand—" Maisie fingered a coin, ready to press into the slot should more money be required for the call.

"Their operations were moved to the county—after all, you cannot have the country's financial arm at risk in the City, not with its proximity to the Thames and the docks. And it's not a surprising choice, after all, they print the money down there, so it's considered safe enough. That's why I said you were in the money—I'm not terribly good at quips though."

"I'm afraid you've lost me, Lord Julian."

"I suppose it's a well-kept open secret. As well as the odd brewery, and of course silk, and agriculture, the place you're in is known for printing money. It's not all done in London, you know, and as much as Rowan seems to believe otherwise every time she goes to Harrods, I can tell you I do not have a press in the cellar!"

Maisie laughed along with her late husband's father, and reiterated that she would indeed find that list of airfields useful—in the meantime, she asked if he might know the nearest RAF station to Whitchurch.

"Oh, there's a few—let me think. Middle and Nether Wallop aren't far away, though Middle Wallop is for the training of new pilots—perhaps your friend's son will be sent there soon. Probably you'd want to go to Andover—again, it's mainly used for training and they have a couple of bomber squadrons there, and a maintenance division. Yes, I would imagine Andover would have been high on the list for any fire-retardant work."

As the pips sounded to indicate more coins were needed, she heard Lord Julian call out, "Must dash now, Maisie." And he was gone.

She exited the telephone kiosk and stood for some moments, thinking. How could she ever find the painting crew? They could be anywhere in the county—they could even have moved on to Dorset—so she would have to return to make a concerted effort to find Joe Coombes. Indeed, he might have already been in touch with his parents once more. She was about to step toward the Alvis when she stopped, turned around, and entered the telephone kiosk again. She had managed to obtain more change from Mrs. Keep that morning, but calls to London were not cheap. This next call, however, might cost her nothing, if it were accepted. She picked up the telephone receiver and dialed the operator.

"I'd like to place a reverse charge call please," said Maisie. "To Whitehall one-two, one-two. Tell them it's Maisie Dobbs calling urgently for Detective Chief Inspector Caldwell."

She waited, nibbling at a hangnail on her little finger. She could hear the conversation back and forth between the operator and her counterpart at Scotland Yard, and then waited until she heard a familiar voice. "Tell her I'll accept the bloody charges, though I'll live to regret it, knowing that one."

"Caldwell?" said Maisie.

"All right, what is it?" Caldwell was brusque, but Maisie could hear something else in his voice—as if he were smiling, enjoying a certain pleasure in the fact that she had called him, and it could only be because she needed his assistance.

"Hello Detective Chief Inspector. I wonder if you could give me a hand with something."

"I've already helped you out with the price of this call. Now what?"

"I'm much obliged to you for your generosity, Inspector—but I wonder if you would be so kind as to call whoever is your main liaison person in Hampshire, in the police force. I'm investigating the case of a London boy who's been working in these parts but hasn't been in touch with his parents for a while, and—"

"Oh blimmin' heck—you want me to ask Spud Murphy down there in Basingstoke if he's been nannying a boy lately?"

"Not quite. I want to know if . . . well, I want to

know if the remains of a fifteen-year-old lad—mousy hair, about five feet nine inches, freckles on his nose, medium build, no other distinguishing marks that I know of—has been found and not been identified."

"What makes you think the boy could be dead."

Maisie felt a shiver of sensation as if someone had run an icicle across her neck. "I just want to rule it out as a possibility."

"And where can I get hold of you, Your Ladyship?"

She sighed. Caldwell could never resist any chance to get under her skin. "I'm returning to London today—I would hope to be there by late afternoon, all being well. But if I can, I'll stop somewhere and call in from a kiosk—plans might change, after all."

"Make sure you've got some money on you next time, won't you."

"Thank you, Inspector Caldwell."

Maisie replaced the telephone receiver and left the kiosk. She climbed into the Alvis, and after consulting the map and the number of motor spirit coupons she had with her, she set off. She hoped to find someone who not only knew where the Yates crew were going next, but also would be prepared to tell her.

There was an element of being in another part of the country that Maisie enjoyed. Driving along main roads and country lanes, she looked out at the landscape be-yond, at the way fields were laid out that was different from the Kentish farmland she knew so well. Passing through villages and hamlets, she compared houses of stone and slate with the weatherboard cottages lining the main thoroughfare through the village of Chelstone, or the brick terrace houses of the railway towns she looked out upon during her train journeys to and from London. Soon she was approaching Andover, and took little time in locating the airfield. As she expected, her first stop—perhaps her only stop—was the guardhouse, where she was asked to state her business by a military policeman, who came out to discover the purpose of her visit.

"I wonder if you might be able to help me," said Maisie. "I'm looking for someone who can tell me if the painting crew is still here at Andover, or even in the area if they've moved on. You probably saw them—from Yates and Sons in London. They're applying a fire retardant to the buildings. My friend's son is among them—he's a young apprentice—and they fear he's ill and needs to return to his home." She passed a calling card and her identity card through the open window of the Alvis. The guard flipped from one card to the next. "As you can see," added Maisie, "I'm an investigator, and as I was in the area on a personal matter, I said I would try to find out how he is."

The guard looked around at his fellow serviceman, who was now standing outside the guardhouse.

"Call the ops room—ask Captain Michaels if he can come down, would you? Unexpected visitor. Civilian."

"Oh, and if you would like additional confirmation of my identity, you can call Detective Chief Inspector Caldwell of Scotland Yard."

"Just pull over there, Miss Dobbs. You won't have to wait long."

Five minutes later a motorbike approached the other side of the gate, its rider clad in a leather jacket over a distinctive blue-gray uniform. He cut the engine, removed the leather jacket, pulled a cap from a pannier at the side of his motorbike, and approached the guard. Maisie saw the guard pass her identity and calling cards to the officer, who seemed to raise an eyebrow as he looked at Maisie and—she thought—made some sort of joke when he turned back to the men, as the two guards laughed in response. He stepped across to her motor car.

"Miss Dobbs—Captain Michaels." He touched his cap by way of greeting. "You're interested in the painting crews."

"Crews? I am only interested in one crew—as you probably know, they're working at airfields around the country, applying a type of fire retardant. It has quite a distinctive, unpleasant odor, so I am sure if they've been here, you would have smelled it in every room."

He nodded, studying her calling card and identity card again.

"I told the guard, you can place a call to Scotland Yard, if you—"

Michaels, who Maisie estimated to be a good six feet tall, leaned toward the window, resting his right hand on the roof of the Alvis. "That won't be necessary. Your possible arrival here was already noted and clearance given to allow you to enter—friends in high places, eh?" His look was one of amused disdain.

"If you have already received clearance for me, then I suppose I do have friends in the right places—though I certainly didn't request such favoritism."

"Well, there's not much to tell you, Miss Dobbs—or I'd ask you into the mess for a chat. Yes, we've had painting crews—some working on the outside, and some working on the interiors of the buildings. They've moved on now, and I think they're over at our decoy site—but of course, now I've told you that, if I find out you're an enemy agent after all, I'll have to kill you." There was a second's delay before he grinned.

"Oh, I don't think you need to go that far," said Maisie, smiling in return. "But what's a decoy site?"

"It's fake—everything about it is fake. Fake buildings, fake aircraft, fake people—no, just kidding about the people—but from the air it looks like a place of substance and will draw enemy aircraft away from Andover. We have a lot going on here. I'm sure you know that."

"And where is the decoy?"

"Hurstbourne Tarrant. Mind you, by the time you get there, the painters could have moved on again—that one would have been faster to go over, and perhaps not so crucial. After all, if the enemy bomb the place, we want it to look like they scored a good one with lots of fire and flames. Anything to keep them away from here."

"Right—I'll go over there."

The officer shrugged. "You've got the clearance."

Maisie nodded, and held out her hand. "Do you fly, Captain?"

"Oh yes—just doing a spot of desk duty today. Had a thumper of a headache this morning, so had to go to the sick bay. But I'll be back in the air later. I'm on Blenheims."

"And you're going into France?"

The young man tapped the side of his nose and smiled. "Can't say. Even you don't have clearance for that."

And at that moment, Maisie knew this officer—who

seemed far too young for such a job—would be bound for France, and with his squadron would be doing all he could to press back the German army who were fast approaching the beaches where soldiers were beginning to gather. Without thinking she placed her hand on the top of his arm.

"Safe landings, Captain. I wish you safe landings."

"Much obliged, Miss Dobbs. Now then—must be getting on." And with that he returned to his motorbike, removed his cap and pushed it down into the pannier, and pulled on his leather jacket once more, though he did not fasten it. Maisie watched as he turned the bike, and made off in the direction of the airfield buildings at speed, his jacket flapping out with the wind like a pair of wings.

"All right, miss?" said the guard.

"Yes, thank you. Could you give me directions to Hurstbourne Tarrant?"

There were two guards on duty at the decoy airfield. They checked her identity card, and informed her that they had been briefed regarding her inquiry and that a small painting crew was indeed at the airfield— someone would be across to speak to her in about five minutes. As she waited, it occurred to Maisie that a decoy airfield was like any other RAF station, except for the silence, and the lack of activity. It was as if she were looking at an empty shell discarded on the beach. Twenty minutes later an approaching white dot in the distance revealed itself to be a van from Yates' yard in London. When it screeched to a halt a few yards away from the gate, a man of about thirty years of age emerged from the vehicle, dressed in white overalls. His pale blue shirt was visible above the collar, and he wore paint-splattered hobnail boots. He reached back into the van for a cloth, and was wiping his hands as he approached Maisie.

"Miss Dobbs?"

"Yes, that's me."

"Freddie Mayes, foreman on this job here. What can I do for you? I understand you're looking for young Joey Coombes."

"Yes, that's right—have you seen him?"

The man shook his head. "Not for a few days—he was called off to work with another crew. Trouble is, I heard he'd gone home, back to London."

"Gone home? When?"

The man ran his fingers through dark hair swept back with brilliantine, and then absently wiped his fingers against his overalls. "'Bout four days ago, I reckon. Couldn't stand the job, all the traveling around, not sleeping in his own bed of a night." He inspected his paint-stained hands. "He told me he wasn't feeling right—and I told him, don't be a silly lad. Before he knows it, he'll be seventeen and up for conscription, and then he'll know what getting fed up with being away from home is really like. I said to him, 'Stay with the crew, boy—you're in a reserved occupation, working on these airfields—you'll go through this war safe as houses, and not end up looking down at where your legs used to be and wondering how that came to happen. I told him what my dad was like when he came home from France—I was going on five years of age, and I remember. Screaming all night, not being able to walk properly ever again, and then there was his lungs. Soon as this job came up, I was in. After all this war business, I'm going back to my street and with all the bits of my body where they should be."

"So, as far as you know, he went back—and should be at home," reiterated Maisie.

"Haven't heard from him since he told me he'd had enough. To be honest, I think being the youngest was a bit much for him, because he's the only apprentice on the crew."

Maisie nodded agreement. "Yes, that would do it, for a sensitive boy."

"Sensitive? Joey Coombes? Oh, let me tell you, that boy could have his moments—probably had to, some of the company he was keeping."

"What do you mean? The Joe I know is a good lad."

"Yeah, but you know what they say—it's the quiet ones you've got to watch." He gave a snorting half-laugh, dismissive in tone, and pulled a packet of Woodbines from the top pocket of his overalls. "Can't have a smoke around here you know, not when we're working." He continued as he lit up and drew on the cigarette, holding it between thumb and forefinger, then inspecting the ashen glow as he exhaled smoke away from Maisie. "Couple of lads—older than Joe, I reckon—came down to see him. Said they were looking up their old friend, and when I told them he had work to do, they got all stroppy. Joe went out and had a word, and off they went. Looked like a pair of hounds to me—old enough to be in uniform, but in civvies. I asked him who they were, and he just said 'mates.' But I had a feeling he was well in with them though, not that I can put a finger on why." The man looked away from Maisie before she could speak, and called over to the guardsman. "What's the time, mate?"

"Not your knocking off time yet, old son," came the reply.

A second's laughter ensued, and Freddie Mayes

turned back to Maisie. "Better be off now, miss. Work to do—and there's a lot of it."

"Are you doing well out of it?" asked Maisie.

"Earning more than we were getting for touching up mansions in Belgravia for snooty women who wanted us to match the paint with the curtains or their frocks. And on this job, Joe was getting a good wad of cash in his pay packet, for an apprentice. Shame he couldn't take it—he was good at his work. Very precise, had good hands on him. Worker's hands. Then off he goes, home to his mum."

Maisie thanked the man, ignoring the tone in his voice. She had no further questions, but watched as he walked to the van, throttled the engine into life and drove at speed back to the decoy airfield, toward empty buildings that reminded Maisie of a still body bereft of a beating human heart.

Chapter 5

The black motor car visible in Maisie's rearview
mirror was not close enough to be overly obvious, but it had been in her wake a little too long for her
not to have noticed. The driver had signaled when she
had, had braked when she had, and had remained well
back when she slowed her speed. Now she would test
the driver—she would not return to London. Instead
she would detour across country, through Petersfield,
and onward beyond Petworth, taking the road on to
Uckfield and then Heathfield, across to Tunbridge
Wells and—finally—Chelstone. It would be a rare coincidence if a fellow driver were to be undertaking the
long, identical journey. For her part, London could
wait—she would go to see Anna, and along the way
find out if she were being followed.

It was close to Heathfield that Maisie looked into the mirror and saw only a green Morris Eight trailing behind her—she had first spotted it pulling out of a petrol station some two miles away. She breathed a sigh of relief, feeling the tension she had held in her neck ebb away. Already somewhat lighter, she decided to stop in Tunbridge Wells to buy a gift for Anna. Not a doll—Anna was not drawn to dolls, much preferring the company of the giant Alsatian, Emma, or her white pony, Lady. She enjoyed reading, so a book might be a good choice, a story they could read together. But Maisie had to take care and not spend a lot of money— it must be a gift without obvious high value, or she would be taken to task by her father—Frankie Dobbs had never hidden his concern regarding the bond that had grown between Maisie and the evacuee child.

Maisie parked close to the picturesque area known as The Pantiles, walked to the bookshop opposite the bandstand, and chose an illustrated edition of *The Railway Children* by E. Nesbit. Leaving the shop with her brown paper-wrapped parcel, she realized she was anxious to reach Chelstone, and she thought, then, about how Joe might have felt, far from home, moving from place to place with the painting crew. Such dislocation might well have caused distress, leading to tension, and subsequently, headaches.

She unlocked the door of the Alvis, placed her shoulder bag and the small parcel on the passenger seat and, having started the engine, was about to maneuver out onto the main thoroughfare when she saw a black motor car idling across the road. The driver's face was obscured by a newspaper, but as she watched, the corner flapped down and the man behind the wheel stole a look at her vehicle. He brought up the newspaper with a sharp snap. Maisie held her breath, but moved off after another motor car had passed, and then turned right, followed by an immediate left. She pulled into a narrow lane of terrace houses to the right of a church on the corner, stopped the vehicle beyond a tree, and looked back at the road she had just left. Only a few seconds elapsed before the black motor car passed by. If she emerged from the lane now, the driver might spot her in his rearview mirror, but at the same time, she did not want to give him time to turn around and come in search of her. She slammed the gear into reverse, pulled back onto the road, and proceeded in the direction of The Pantiles. Beyond the shops was an area of rough ground surrounded by trees—she would wait there a while before making her way to Tonbridge, and then to Chelstone. And during the time spent sitting under the broad canopy of a plane tree, she had time to speculate. Who was following her? What nerve had she touched in her investigation thus far into the whereabouts of Joe Coombes? She could not imagine the landlady in Whitchurch having given her name to another person—but perhaps someone came along with a few choice banknotes and was soon in possession of Maisie's card. Given the time of day and the encroaching evening, it would have been clear she was staying locally, so the driver had only to wait until the following day to identify her motor car as she drove through Whitchurch, and then wait for her at each stop until she was on her way back to London.

Or could Billy's visit to Yates' yard have sparked interest? Perhaps he'd asked one question too many, and had set off an alarm. And now Maisie was being followed. But by whom? A government agent? A Yates employee? Someone from the military department supplying Yates with what could well be a toxic paint?

Another hour passed before Maisie felt a sufficient level of ease to drive off, through Tunbridge Wells, skirting around Tonbridge in the direction of Chelstone, where she arrived late afternoon. When Maisie entered through the kitchen door, Brenda informed her that Anna was asleep in her room, guarded by the ever-watchful Emma.

"How is she?" asked Maisie as her stepmother busied herself making a chicken broth.

"Had a bit of a temperature today, but the fever broke last night and she's full of spots, poor little mite. I put a pair of cotton gloves on her hands—stops her doing too much damage to her skin if she scratches in her sleep. She has conjunctivitis, so I go in and bathe her eyes of a morning—she smiled this morning and said she liked feeling the warm water. So now we've got to get some good bone broth down her—and she does like chicken, so cook over at the house sent a girl round this morning with one already cooked. She said it was roasted last night for the Canadians, but they preferred the beef. Well, they would, wouldn't they? Strapping great men like that, what with all them prairies or whatever it is they have over there."

"I'll go up to see her now," said Maisie. "I can only stay tonight—I have a lot of work on my plate at the moment, but I'll be back on Thursday."

Maisie removed her jacket and slipped it over the back of a kitchen chair. She took the wrapped book, and made her way upstairs.

Anna was curled up in her bed, her hands clasped under her chin. Her eyes were closed, but the way Emma—lying down alongside the bed—was looking up at her young mistress, Maisie guessed that Anna was not asleep. She stroked the dog's head, and knelt by the bed. She placed her hand on the child's forehead and, without thinking, leaned forward to kiss the place where her fingers had just measured the girl's temperature.

"Auntie Maisie." Anna's voice was little more than a whisper.

"Oh pet, you poor little mite."

"I'm all right, Miss Maisie. Emma's here, and Auntie Brenda says she'll let me have my broth from the pudding basin—Nan always gave me broth in the pudding basin if I wasn't feeling well."

"You can have your broth in whatever bowl you want, Anna." She ran her fingers across the little girl's forehead again. "I have a present for you—a new book."

Anna nodded. Maisie set the book down as Brenda came into the room bearing a tray with a small white pudding basin filled with broth, a slice of fresh bread and a glass of Lucozade. "There you are—Anna could do with the extra glucose in the Lucozade," said Brenda. "It'll give her more energy to get better."

Maisie helped Anna to sit up, and put her arm around her as Brenda set the tray on the bed. It was as Maisie dipped the spoon into the broth and held it steady for Anna to sip, that she was aware of Brenda watching her. She looked up. "What is it?"

Brenda seemed to purse her lips and shook her head. "Nothing. Not now, anyway." She left the room, and Maisie continued to guide the spoon until Anna reached for it and insisted upon eating without help.

When the child had taken all she could, and her eyes had become heavy again, Maisie made her comfortable, watched her drift into sleep, and brought the tray back down to the kitchen.

"I took her to the lavatory, so she's settled now." Maisie took the basin and cutlery from the tray and began to wash them at the sink. "I'm concerned—is something else wrong with Anna, Brenda? What's going on?"

"I reckon the child needs to know where she stands, Maisie—makes a body weaker, not knowing your place in the world."

"She's here with us, and she's safe."

"But what about when this is all over? This war? Then what? You may have her best interests at heart, and you may now have some sort of power of attorney or whatever they call it—but I bet she wonders where she'll fetch up when all the children go home."

"She'll always have a place here—you know that—until . . . until we find a family for her."

"And that's the rub, isn't it, Maisie? It's one thing

you explaining things but I reckon something should be done about it. Now. Before she gets too settled here. We all love her—how could we not? But you promised to make sure she had a good home. What do you think you can do about it?"

Maisie nodded. "I'll talk to Mr. Klein. He'll know what to do next."

"Good." Brenda picked up a cloth to dry the crockery and cutlery Maisie had just washed. "And your friend, Priscilla—she phoned to confirm that Tim is going to come down to Chelstone on Saturday. He's had another falling-out at home, and he apparently said that he wanted to see 'Tante Maisie' because she was the only one who understood him. His mother told him you would be busy until Saturday anyway, and he was not to bother you any sooner."

"Oh dear—poor Pris."

"Poor Tim, if you ask me. Mind you, he has got a mouth on him, when he likes."

"It's just his age. He'll grow out of it, Brenda. Did she say what train he was catching?"

"She said she would put him on the train from London so he can change at Tonbridge for the eleven o'clock stopping train down to Chelstone."

Maisie sighed. "He's such a good boy—good young

man, really. He just hates the fact that Tom appears to be proving himself—proving himself to be a man—and he hasn't had the chance yet."

"He probably wants to run away, but not too far—and you two do get on, don't you?"

"That's because I'm not his mother. Anyway, let's get Dad to line up some jobs for him—and it'll cheer up Anna no end to have him here. She has a little-girl crush on him."

The telephone woke Maisie at half past six in the morning. At first its ringing came as part of a dream, a sound in the distance along a tunnel where she was searching for something—she did not know what it was that was lost, but in the dream her anxiety increased until she awoke, her heart pounding.

"Hello—" In her half-sleep, Maisie could not remember the number to recite to the caller.

"Miss Dobbs—still having sweet dreams, are you?"

"Good morning, Inspector—isn't this rather early for you?"

"Early when there's work to be done, and you know what they say about the early bird."

"What is it, Inspector Caldwell?"

"Your boy—one Joseph Coombes? Fits the description of a body found yesterday at—" Maisie heard

Caldwell pause and the sound of a sheet of paper being turned. "Basingstoke railway station. Some trauma to the noddle, but according to Inspector Murphy, it could have happened when he fell. Sounds nasty though."

"But—"

"Haven't finished yet," said Caldwell. "We need an identification, and of course there's notification of the deceased's nearest and dearest. You know the boy, so you could identify the body—in the circumstances, it might be best to save the mum and dad the grief, if you know what I mean. It's not a very pretty sight, and the better part of me—you'll be pleased to know I have one—would like to save them that last memory of their son. How do you want to proceed?"

Maisie had come to her feet as Caldwell was speaking, and pulled a dressing gown around her shoulders. "How do I want to proceed? I thought you'd just told me how I was proceeding. I'll go back to Hampshire and then up to London."

"I've already sent a motor car to take you down there. Save your coupons—we've got plenty. For now, anyway. By the time you've had your toast and marmalade, the motor will be outside your door. Murphy is waiting for you in Basingstoke. All right?"

"Yes. Of course," said Maisie, rubbing the scar on her neck. "Poor Joe."

"Poor Joe? He's out of it now. It's his poor mum and dad, that's what's poor. And you and I should have a chin-wag—the Yard's involved, which means me—and we both know I don't exactly have a lot of minutes in the day to spare, not with being short on staff. Never thought I'd see the day when I missed Able—but my able assistant Able is now Able Seaman Able—left just after that business with the Belgian refugees last year. Apparently he's been posted to HMS *Keith*. Name like his, I bet he takes a lot of ribbing."

Maisie sighed, remembering the polite detective constable and the stoic manner with which he tolerated Caldwell's insistent jokes about his name—and not very funny jokes, in her estimation. "You didn't exactly give him an easy time. I would bet he wins the respect of his fellow men—you wait and see."

"And I am sure I will—wait, that is. Right—when you're finished in Basingstoke, the motor car will bring you back to London and we can go together to see the parents. No good me bothering them before that, just in case it's not him. I'll get you a travel warrant to come back to Kent, so you don't have to pay."

"Thank you, Inspector."

"Oh, and Your Ladyship—I take it your little investigation will be coming to an end now."

"I'm sorry, Inspector, there's some interference on

the line—I can't hear you very well. Hello? Hello? I'll expect the motor car in a short while then. Goodbye." She heard Caldwell offer a muffled expletive as she returned the receiver to its cradle.

The journey to Basingstoke offered an opportunity to think about Joe Coombes—and more importantly, the precious little she had uncovered thus far. She knew that in such circumstances it was all too easy to assign importance to discoveries that were insignificant. But at the same time, every stone was worthy of a turn. And if there was nothing untoward in Joe's death—if indeed she was able to make a positive identification— why had she been followed from Whitchurch to Tunbridge Wells? For there was no doubt in her mind that the black motor car had been on her tail since she left Hampshire and might well have followed her from London. But was the driver interested due to her questioning of Joe's whereabouts? Or was it in connection with Billy's visit to Yates' yard? Then another thought came back to her—might the man following her have been a spy?

The police driver said little to Maisie, apart from the occasional inquiry as to whether she might require a break, a "refreshment stop" perhaps. But there was something about the journey that reminded her of her flight from Gibraltar into Spain, when she traveled alone with the driver who ferried her to the makeshift field hospital where she became a nurse once again. She felt the weight of remembrance bear down upon her as she recalled the young men—and sometimes women— who were brought to the former convent, often under cover of darkness, to have their injuries tended. In those days she became both doctor and nurse, and she saw, again, the wounds of battle. Joe with his headaches was now a victim of a new war. And who would be the other new victims? Yet still there would be the Tims of the world—aching to get to where the action might be, desperate to prove themselves.

She remembered, then, a saying that someone had quoted to her once. Was it her father? It certainly wasn't Maurice, because she had heard it spoken by a Yorkshireman, someone from northern England, of that she was sure. *Where there's muck, there's brass.* That was it. Was it Joseph Waite, the self-made man who had hired her to find his daughter, years ago? It had been one of her first cases after Maurice retired. Yes, perhaps it was him. *Where there's muck, there's brass.* A simple line, an aphorism that seemed to suggest the selling of manure. But it had a meaning that went so much deeper, alluding to the fact that where you find filth—where you find dirt; where you find the detritus of life—you'll also discover someone making a profit. Much money can be made from the most dirty jobs. *Muck and money go together.* That was another one. And it occurred to her that in her lifetime she had seen nothing more filthy than war itself.

"Oh, you're in the money then!" Lord Julian had said during their telephone conversation. It was a quip, a joke. But two things now came to mind. One, Joe Coombes was working in close proximity to the country's source of wealth, and secondly, that Yates had accepted a lucrative contract that was potentially harmful to his workers. It wouldn't be the first time she had seen the hardest working people become enmeshed in a web not of their making.

There's a reason they call it filthy lucre, Maisie. Maurice's words, spoken in the early days of her own apprenticeship, echoed in her mind. It was almost as if he were by her side, pushing, testing, guiding her.

Detective Chief Inspector "Spud" Murphy was a jovial man, and—Maisie thought—seemed as if he would be more suited to life as a village butcher. She could imagine him wearing a white cotton coat, a blue-striped apron and a straw boater, his drooping jowls held in place by a starched white collar and blue bow tie. Yet at the same time, it was clear, once he had introduced himself, that Murphy was efficient and businesslike—and she could not envision him wielding a cleaver.

"Caldwell said you were held in high regard by his department, Miss Dobbs," said Murphy, opening a folder presented to him by the driver who had brought Maisie to Basingstoke.

"He did?" said Maisie, her brow furrowed, though she smiled—after all, she and Caldwell were not what Lady Rowan would have called "pally."

Murphy grinned in return. "Mind you, he also said not to tell you—but I thought I would. Not a nice business, this—helps to have something positive in your back pocket to fall back on if your day includes identification of the dead."

"May I see the postmortem report first?" asked Maisie.

Murphy had placed a pair of half-moon glasses on his nose to review the contents of the folder he had just opened, and now studied her over the rims. "You can because Inspector Caldwell obviously trusts you. But do you understand medical notes?"

"I was a nurse, in the last war, and I've studied legal medicine—in Edinburgh."

Murphy looked down at his notes. "Oh yes—and you were once assistant to Dr. Maurice Blanche. I remember now." He closed the folder and put it to one side, picking up another that was already on his desk. He looked up at Maisie. "Met the man a couple of times when I was at the Yard, before I came down here for a quieter life. Impressive. Very impressive." He held out the folder to Maisie, and consulted his watch. "Here, have a quick gander at that—it'll prepare you."

Maisie opened the folder and began to read. "I don't think this type of injury is sustained falling off a wall, do you?"

Murphy turned away from his desk to look out of the window. Expanding his view, thought Maisie. It had always interested her, that physically gazing out at a landscape, even if that landscape offered a cluster of town buildings, could provide a broader view of the possibilities inspired by a question. She did the same thing herself, when something troubled her.

"On the face of it—yes. He fell straight down onto a railway line—fortunately, it was not a main line, but an old shunting line, not used in donkey's years. If it had been on another line, the skull would have been smashed beyond all recognition by a loco. So you can see, where his noddle hit the cast iron, he sustained a very, very nasty wound."

"There's something you're not happy about, Inspector."

Murphy sighed, but remained silent against sunlight emerging from behind a cloud, the beam slanting through the window.

Maisie continued. "I think you might be in two minds. On the one hand, yes, it seems from this report the victim—on account of his own stupidity or a crime—fell from a high wall and straight down onto the line, however . . . however, at the same time we could speculate that he was running from someone and stumbled from the wall in a panic. Or he could have been pushed. Or—"

"Or someone could have clobbered him on the head with a very—very—heavy object, and then the body was moved from somewhere else." Murphy turned as he finished the sentence for her and moved away from the window.

"Have you had soil particles tested? Was there any residue of decomposed vegetation on his clothing?" Maisie ran her finger down the report.

"It's right there." Murphy stood beside her and pointed to a paragraph near the foot of the fourth page. "The railway line had to some extent returned to nature—there were weeds growing between the sleepers and among the rocks underneath—and apart from some gravel in the wound, there wasn't anything to prove movement of the body, such as mineral or plant matter from another location. I think that's what you're getting at, isn't it?" He consulted his watch. "I won't rule it out though, but there are those who would. Come on, better get going."

Maisie could bear the smell of a pathologist's domain far better than most. She had known grown men—policemen with broad shoulders and a constitution that allowed them to face criminals armed with deadly weapons—fall to the ground upon entering a laboratory where postmortems were conducted. Seeing a murder victim in the place where the body was found was one thing—they could steel themselves for the discovery. But there was something about the vulnerable nakedness of a corpse having endured the attentions of a man with a scalpel, a doctor who had used sharp instruments to cut into flesh, bone and sinew, that could take that same policeman down in seconds. For Maisie there was something else that kept her standing—the fact that this moment, this very personal procedure of discovery, afforded her a chance to show compassion for the dead. Maurice had taught her that in the laboratory it was all too easy to forget respect, when there was nothing but the shell of a human being before you. "Think of a dead body as if you are viewing a set of clothing, Maisie—but consider it as the attire the soul has worn for many a year. And it is clothing that has something to teach us about the man or woman under the knife."

Without doubt, she was looking at the body of Joe Coombes. Murphy stood to one side, as an assistant informed them that "Dr. Clark" would be with them shortly.

"It's Joe," said Maisie, looking down at the body.

She glanced only briefly at the incisions where the pathologist had cut the flesh, and brought her full attention to the deep open wound on the skull—so invasive, it had allowed Dr. Clark to remove tissue from the brain. She looked closer, and frowned.

"What is it?" Murphy was standing well back, halfway to the door, yet he had been watching her every move.

"She's seen what I saw—isn't that so, Miss Dobbs?"

Maisie looked up to see a woman entering via the double doors leading into the mortuary. She stopped alongside Murphy and held out her hand. "Spud—I take it you're well?"

Murphy opened his mouth to respond, but already the woman had moved to stand alongside Maisie. She extended her hand. "Clarissa Clark—pathologist around here." The two women shook hands and Clark pulled a pair of clean rubber gloves from her pocket before reaching toward a trolley set up with an array of surgical instruments. She snapped on the gloves, picked up a scalpel and leaned back toward the corpse, using the instrument to indicate a small area in Joe Coombes' brain. "That's what you're looking at, isn't it?"

"Yes," said Maisie, taking a step to the side to provide more space for Clark to move. "It looks like some sort of tumor—yet it's not, and there is no identifiable outline or margin. And the color—though admittedly we are looking at a young man deceased for some days, but still . . ." She looked at Clark. "What do you think?"

Clark sighed. "For the purposes of this investigation, I am obviously looking at immediate cause of death. Given where he was found, I would say that, yes, it's of course possible that this injury here, on the other side, was caused by falling from a height and hitting a cast iron railway line at just the right angle." Again using the scalpel, she pointed to a deep wound—a smashed orbital bone and torn flesh above the ear revealing a skull crushed into livid brain matter. "Very bad luck indeed. Could it have been made worse by being pushed, therefore increasing velocity? Yes, I would say so. But at the same time, the injury that killed Joe could well have been done by something heavy—a crowbar, for example, especially if it came down from a height." She lifted her hand above her head and simulated bringing it down, stopping the trajectory of her hand just an inch from the open skull of Joe Coombes.

"But you've obviously thought about that too." Maisie gestured toward the naked brain matter that had first attracted her attention.

"I have, and I have never seen anything like it." Clark corrected herself. "No, I tell a lie—I've seen something like it. In Serbia, in the last war. I was working at a field hospital, and I saw something similar to this discoloration in soldiers subject to attack by poison gases."

"It's caused by exposure to toxins, isn't it?"

Clark looked at Maisie. "Yes, I would say you're right—in my humble opinion."

Maisie nodded, now pointing to the wound. "Where this young man is concerned, if you had to make a choice between falling from a height and being attacked with a crowbar, which side would you come down on."

Clark sighed. "I think you probably have an opinion, Miss Dobbs—if you are half the woman that Dr. Blanche would have taken on as his assistant."

"You knew him?" Maisie turned to look at Clark.

"He was my favorite professor, when he came to lecture during my student years."

Maisie looked down at Joe Coombes, at rest, free of pain. She closed her eyes for several seconds, and then opened them again. She looked across toward Murphy, and then at Dr. Clark. "I would say he was the victim of a vicious attack, and with a heavy cast iron object. But of course I could be wrong."

As they left the mortuary together, Murphy leaned toward Maisie, as if to share a confidence. "She lied about one thing in there."

"Yes, I know," replied Maisie.

"That woman has never had a humble opinion in her life."

Maisie laughed. And for a moment she thought poor young Joe Coombes would have laughed at that one too, for she had felt his presence so keenly.

Chapter 6

Maisie and Detective Inspector Caldwell had, for the most part, a professional association that was respectful, though at times tense. During the occasions when they worked together, she felt it was as if they were two hot electrical wires running side by side—if they came too close, there would be sparks. But over the years they had reached a point where they could avoid a fire, and had come to hold a grudging respect for one another. And on this evening, as they departed the pub where they had just broken the news of Joe's death to Phil and Sally Coombes, Maisie knew that Caldwell had been glad to have her at his side, and appreciated her company.

"That—that in there—is the very worst part of this job. It's like being in a mortuary, but instead of watching someone else take the insides out of a person, you're the one doing it to the living. I feel as if I've just ripped three people apart. And there'll be one more when their other son gets home."

"You did very well, Inspector Caldwell—it's not easy, to tell people that someone they love has died, especially in these circumstances," said Maisie.

"You did most of the telling—I just filled in the police details," said Caldwell.

"But you gave them hope that you would find out what happened. I know your hands were tied, that you could not come out and admit it was murder, when there is still a question mark over the cause of death. They believe that Joe will not be forgotten, that his screams will not have fallen into a silent void—and there's a bitter comfort in that knowing."

Caldwell nodded, sighing. "Offer you a lift, Miss Dobbs?"

"I think I'll go to my office, and then get a taxicab home. I have some work to do."

Caldwell stopped alongside the dark blue motor car parked next to the pub, where the doors were still locked and a Closed sign remained in place. A police driver held the vehicle's door open, ready for his superior to step inside. The detective inspector turned to Maisie.

"I won't stop you, you know—investigating the death of Joe Coombes. Just keep in touch and I'll do the same for you. I reckon you might have more luck than me—I've a lot on my plate, and the results of the postmortem are what they call 'inconclusive,' so I daresay the coroner will report this one as 'death by misadventure' because murder can't be proven and for all the world it looks like a risky jump on the part of the deceased, who launched himself off a wall the height of a building just for the sheer thrill and high jinks of it."

"But we know that high jinks is not something someone does alone—even a boy of that age. Joe wasn't that sort of person anyway."

"And there's them who would say that any lad of fifteen or sixteen is a high jinks sort of person." Caldwell touched the brim of his hat and turned to step inside the vehicle. "I'll send a motor car around in an hour to take you home—you'll never get a cab in the blackout. Be in touch, Miss Dobbs—and watch your back. I don't like this one."

Maisie raised her hand as the motor car pulled away from the curb, and commenced walking toward her office in Fitzroy Square. It was dark now, so she switched on the light before running up the stairs, then turned it off as she placed her key in the lock—the last thing she wanted was an ARP man admonishing her for breaking the blackout. She could hear music coming from the top floor—having once been servants' quarters in the days when the mansion had been a private home, the upper floor had been divided into separate bed-sitting rooms, and were let to students from the Slade art institute. There was no noise from the flats during the day, but at night there was often a gramophone playing, or the sound of voices—and sometimes even "high jinks."

She had not intended to remain in the office long, but she was grateful to Caldwell and his offer of a vehicle to take her home. She unlocked the door and felt her way to the windows to draw the blackout curtains before stepping through to her private office, where she again drew the blackout curtains, and turned on her desk light.

Sandra had left a few messages for her on top of a leather-bound blotting paper book that held a letter to be signed between each leaf. Maisie flicked through the messages, stopping at one in particular. She drew the light down to read.

A woman named Sylvia Preston telephoned, and said she was with the WAAF in Hampshire— apparently she had telephoned the office a couple of times, but there was no answer, so I didn't speak to her until she tried again on Wednesday afternoon.

She says she had been a lodger in the same house as Joe Coombes until he left recently—though she added that she has been sent to a new billet now. She explained that she overheard your conversation with the landlady, and she thought she should telephone, as she would like to speak to you personally. The landlady had left your card on the hall table, so she was able to obtain your telephone number. She is stationed at one of the airfields, but would not say which one. It's very difficult for her to place a call to you given her hours, however, she said she could wait at the telephone kiosk in Whitchurch on Sunday evening at seven o'clock.

A number was inscribed below the message.

Maisie walked across to the window, and fingered back the curtain just enough to look down through the grainy darkness onto the yard at the back. A sliver of light from the occupant's not-quite-closed blackout curtains illuminated the fact that nature had finally yielded to the attention of a committed tenant. She could discern the outline of a series of terra-cotta pots holding geraniums, pelargoniums and hydrangeas, and since war had been declared, the tenant had begun to grow vegetables in a series of wooden boxes. It reminded Maisie that she should have done the same and started her own vegetable garden. As an island, Britain depended in part upon its merchant navy to keep the larders stocked, and that merchant navy was now at risk from U-boat attack—the people of Britain understood only too well that men were risking their lives to put food on their tables. In the newspapers and on posters, it had been made clear that if everyone took responsibility for growing some vegetables, it would help keep families fed over the long haul of war.

She admonished herself for not calling earlier to speak to Sandra. Indeed, it was likely that Sandra had telephoned Chelstone to recount the messages, but had missed her. She sighed with frustration—she could have learned something important from Sylvia Preston—why else would the WAAF have made the effort to contact her? Turning away from the window, Maisie ensured the curtains met with no room for light to escape. She knew she would feel a greater control if she worked on a case map—it would give her direction and insight.

Joe Coombes deserved an advocate, someone who would speak for him, someone who would seek out the source of his ill health, and ultimately, his death, so she set to work, taking a length of wallpaper from a basket in the corner. Billy's friend, a painter and decorator, furnished them with the ends of rolls used in his job, and they had proven perfect for the job. It was as Maisie laid out the paper—patterned side down—on the long table set perpendicular to her desk, that it occurred to her—*painter and decorator.* What was Billy's friend's name? She stepped across to her desk and reached for the telephone. No, Billy would not be at home. But he might walk into Whitchurch to place a call to his younger son, just to check up on him. She began to dial. The telephone rang and when a voice came on the line, for a moment Maisie did not know what to say, for Bobby Beale sounded just like his father.

"Oh, I thought you were your father for a moment, Bobby—it's Miss Dobbs here."

"'Allo, miss—if you're looking for Dad, he won't be back until tomorrow. I thought you knew—he's coming back and so's Mum and Maggie-ro." Bobby yawned as he finished speaking.

Maisie smiled—unlike their parents, who referred to their daughter by her full name, the boys had always called her "Maggie-ro." But she was also concerned.

"Your mum's coming back?"

"She misses me, that's what it is." Bobby laughed, and continued. "Well, probably not, but she's coming back—not to stay, because it's better for them down there, but she's coming back with Dad tomorrow. I reckon he'll give me a ring soon, just to make sure I'm behaving myself."

"And are you—behaving yourself?"

"Can't do otherwise, can I? What with Mr. and Mrs. Pickering coming around—driving from all that way across the water, and telling me they were just passing, as if I don't know that petrol coupons are like gold dust. And then there's the woman next door, popping in to check up on me. I keep saying, 'I'm sixteen—old enough to look after meself.'"

"Could you ask your dad to telephone me, as soon as he can?"

"Will do." Bobby followed his words with a deep sigh.

"What is it, Bobby—are you all right? I can come over if you like—make you a nice dinner."

"I've loads of nice dinners in that fridge. By the way, did you know my dad bought a fridge? Never had one before and don't know anyone who's got one either—he said it was a surprise, for my mum. Well, it will be, because it's full of pies. I wish Mrs. Relf would bring cake—that's what I fancy."

"I'll see what I can do for you."

"Miss—can I ask you something?"

"What is it, Bobby?"

There was silence on the line.

"Bobby?"

"It's like this, Miss Dobbs—you remember last year, at one of your Sunday dinners, I ended up talking to Tom, the one who's gone into the RAF?"

"Yes, I remember—I saw you were deep in conversation."

"He's not really what I'd call my sort, all very posh, but he was nice to me and asked about what I do, you know, being a mechanic. I was telling him how I really like working on engines, that it's sort of like playing a musical instrument for me—not that I can play any musical instrument, but it sounded right. I told him that I listen to the engines, that I listen for them to sort of sing. I can tell when I've got an engine right, by the sound. I thought he would laugh, but instead he says, 'You should do an aircraft apprenticeship.' And he told me about the college for aircraft mechanics, at RAF Halton, in Buckinghamshire. He said I'm old enough to join the RAF as an apprentice."

Maisie felt her heart palpitate. *Oh dear . . . Tom, what have you done now?*

"Anyway," Bobby continued, "he sent me a letter

with all the details, and I found out how to apply. The woman in the library down the road helped me."

"And you didn't tell your dad, did you?"

"No. I mean, what with my brother going off into the army, I didn't want to say anything, and it might've come to nothing anyway."

"They've accepted you, haven't they?" asked Maisie.

"I had to get out of my job for two days—couple of weeks ago now—to go for an interview and a medical. They got me to work on an engine too—it was really easy for me. Dad didn't even notice I wasn't there, because he was down in Hampshire. Anyway, the letter came this morning. I'll be an RAF mechanic."

"But they need your father's signature on the permission form—is that it?"

"Yes." Bobby Beale paused again. "He'll do his nut. He won't see that it's a better job with more prospects than me converting old cars for the ARP, and spending my life in that garage. I mean, I've learned a lot, but I know I'm good at engines—I really am. Once I'm trained on aeroplanes, well, that's me—set. Tom says that when this war is over, you watch, people will be going everywhere on aeroplanes, much more than they do now. I'll have a job for life, and I could go to other places. I could even go across the world. And Tom says they have engineers on some of the actual aeroplanes. They have engineers on bombers. I could work my way up."

"You want me to talk to your dad, don't you?"

"He listens to you, miss. He says you think the right things. And what with my mum—you never know what's going to happen. All I know is that if it wasn't for Maggie-ro, she would be back in the nuthouse."

"Bobby—come on, she's your mother and she's a good mother. You shouldn't talk about her like that."

"I know, but . . . it's just that sometimes I want to get away from home."

"Look, don't tell your dad as soon as he walks into the house. Give them a chance to get settled, and if I were you, I would bide my time."

"It's because of what's going on over there, isn't it? Billy's stuck there, I know he is."

"Bobby—you've been working very hard lately. Get a good night's sleep and use that fine-tuned ear of yours to listen to your father and don't talk to him about this until he's rested—all right?"

"All right."

"And I'll see what I can do about the cake."

Bobby Beale laughed. "I'll get my dad to give you a bell."

Maisie replaced the receiver and sat down, leaning

forward, her elbows on the table, her forehead resting on her hands.

"Oh, Bobby, I wish you hadn't told me," she said aloud to the room. "Poor Billy."

Maisie kept the conversation short when Billy telephoned half an hour later. In the interim, she had started the case map and had been linking names, facts, dates, times, noting thoughts that occurred to her and questions to be answered. The diagram on paper resembled wires converging into a junction box. She now had the name of Billy's friend—Peter Sands—and Billy said he would get in touch and ask him if he could pop into the office. She reiterated that she only wanted to draw upon his expertise, and would gladly remunerate him for his time. Billy did not mention Bobby—except to say he had been a good lad, and clearly had been looked after while alone in the house. Doreen was home now, and would return to Hampshire on Monday with Margaret Rose.

The telephone rang.

"So that's where you are!" said Priscilla Partridge. "Did you forget? You're supposed to be at a special ambulance driver practice this evening and you've got five minutes to get here. Mr. Roache is about to blow a gasket as two of the younger women are not here either, and he expected us 'experienced ladies' to set an example. That was a rather strange experience, I must say—I was always the one being punished as an 'example to others' when I was at school. We may be volunteers, but this is like being in the army!"

"I'm leaving now," said Maisie as she grabbed her bag. "In fact, the doorbell has just rung and I think that's my transport. Thank goodness for the police!"

"What?"

"Nothing. Tell Mr. Roache I'll be ten minutes."

Later, after she and Priscilla had managed to take an ambulance to Marble Arch and back in the dark and then negotiated a derelict building looking for "injured"—more volunteers—and then taken them to the nearest hospital, the two women were given a lift home to Holland Park in the back of an ambulance. They stood outside Priscilla's mansion, which was a short walk from Maisie's flat. The whereabouts of Priscilla's eldest son seemed to consume her thoughts, along with worries about her middle and younger sons.

"Thank goodness Tarquin is minding his p's and q's, that's all I can say. And I am so glad Tim is coming down to you—Douglas said that he needed work to get his back into. Serious man work, he said, on the farm, or with your father. Tim should stop thinking all the time of all the things he's not doing and get on with the things he can. He's so argumentative—he's turned from my delightful second son into a little war machine unto himself."

"He can come down tomorrow, if you like—I plan to catch the train before lunch. My motor is at Chelstone, and I'm trying not to use it too much now anyway—not fond of driving in the dark and I can't afford to waste my petrol coupons."

"Oh, Douglas has something lined up for Tim tomorrow—another distraction. By the way you did all right tonight, Maisie—the way you took that turn onto Oxford Street was quite amazing. I wonder if they deliberately put other vehicles right in the middle of the road to test us—after all, when we have a real emergency, there will be a lot in our way."

"It was all the wood they scattered on the narrow alley up to the house—that was a test, because there's obviously a point where we'll have to leave the ambulance and run, and then bring the wounded to the ambulance—and reverse out again."

"God willing we'll never have to run into any burning buildings, eh Maisie? But according to Roache, we two outdid ourselves. Frankly, I think he's shocked that anyone over thirty has the stamina for this job—but we showed him, didn't we?"

Maisie laughed and kissed Priscilla on the cheek.

"Tell Tim we're looking forward to seeing him. Especially Anna. Oh, by the way—he has had measles, hasn't he?"

Priscilla waved her hand. "My boys have had everything—everything you can imagine a boy can get."

Later, as Maisie sat in her walled garden with a cup of tea and a sandwich, she gazed up at the outlines of barrage balloons obscuring the night sky, a darkness punctuated only by searchlights from a nearby anti-aircraft "ack-ack" battery scouring the heavens for possible Luftwaffe interlopers. And she wondered, then, how long the quiet would last. How long before Hitler's armies would draw even closer, their aircraft overhead raining down a blitzkrieg of terror? In Madrid she had already seen what the Luftwaffe could inflict upon a people. Or would it all blow over—would Britain capitulate to the approaching enemy, coming closer and closer with every passing day?

She went into the house, washed her plate, cup, saucer and cutlery, and went to bed. Sleep did not come with ease, so instead she opened the blackout curtain and allowed herself to be lulled by the searchlights moving back and forth, cones of light against a midnight blue sky.

At nine o'clock the following morning, Maisie, Billy and Peter Sands sat at the long table in Maisie's office.

"It's very good of you to come in to see us, Mr. Sands—I really appreciate your time."

"Aw, not to worry, Miss Dobbs—and call me 'Pete.' It's a bit of a slow day, to tell you the truth. Now if it was last week, it would have been another matter, but I'm putting the finishing touches to a job over in Russell Square." He paused, sipped from the mug of tea Billy had passed to him, and looked at Maisie, then Billy. "So, my mate here said you wanted to pick my brains."

"Yes, Pete, I'm sure you can help us—we'd like to hear what you might know about Yates and Sons. They've landed a lucrative government contract for painting buildings on airfields across the country, and the emulsion—if you can call it that—is very viscous, has a strong vapor and, from what we understand already, it does the job it was designed for, which is to stop a fire from taking over if the airfield is attacked."

"I heard they'd pulled in a big one. Of course, that's not something that would come my way, being just me and one apprentice. Nice money, especially the way things are—I reckon that one job will keep them going throughout the war, and it'll mean their boys are out of it, what with government work being protected."

"Have you ever used anything like this emulsion—do you know what they put in it?" asked Maisie.

The man shook his head. "I've heard about paint like that, but not put a brush in it myself. But you know, what with the war, I reckon they're using new stuff—and probably not tested, so they won't know how long it will last, that sort of thing. Which again means that Yates' lads will have jobs for as long as the war goes on—but let's hope it's not as long as the last one."

"Let's hope, mate," said Billy.

"One thing," Maisie interjected. "And it's a tricky question, Mr. Sands—but do you think Yates is on the up and up in his business affairs? Have you ever heard anything untoward, or critical of his business practices."

The man shrugged. "Everyone's got to make a living, haven't they? Old Bill Yates only took the firm so far, but Mike Yates worked hard, put in the hours and made the connections so it became a much bigger business—for our line of work, anyway. But a growing concern like that means more mouths to feed, because no one likes laying off their workers, especially men they've apprenticed and trained up. I mean, it's not like they're packing sausages, is it? And it's not as if any bloke with a brush can just slap paint on walls—well, they can, but you can always tell the cowboys in the trade." He paused, rubbing his stubbled chin. "I wouldn't say Mike Yates has bad commercial practices—as far as I know—but he is a terrier. He finds out about new business, goes after the opportunities, and he keeps the customers over time. The minute his crew have finished the downstairs on a job over in Belgravia, than he's over there asking about the upper floors. For every customer there's a record kept of what they've had done and when—and he's in there as soon as he thinks a room might need another coat of paint. And he's a stickler for his men looking clean and tidy—all wearing spotless whites at the start of every week and every new job, and he'll check a work site to make sure they're leaving it in good order every day. But no getting away from it—if there's business out there, then Mike Yates is on it like a fly on a corpse."

Maisie and Billy exchanged glances, then Maisie turned her attention back to the man seated between them.

"How would someone find out about a contract like this—would the government have come to Mr. Yates? Or would he have his contacts?"

"Bloke like Mike Yates? It'll be a bit of both. He's big enough to be known, and on the other hand, the people he works for are your well-heeled lot, on drinking terms with nobs in high places. And you've got to remember—like I said, a job like that won't come to a one-man band like me, or even a cartload of us—it goes to a business big enough to get the job done. And knowing Mike, he would make sure the customer gets the price they want—but so does he. His boys would be putting away a pretty penny too. I would imagine someone from the government arranged all the lodgings and that sort of thing—Mike Yates wouldn't take that on."

"Do you think Mr. Yates would do or say anything if he thought the emulsion were dangerous?" asked Maisie.

"I think that unless someone dropped dead in front of him, he would ignore it, hoping that nothing happened that he had to attend to while he was counting the money." He paused, looked at his hands, shrugged, and brought his gaze back to Maisie. "And to tell you the truth, Miss Dobbs, any of us would do the same thing—if I'm to be perfectly honest with you, we all need work and we've all had hard times, especially since the last war. No one can afford to look a gift horse in the mouth."

Maisie nodded. "Yes, you're right."

"And who knows what was causing the lad to have these headaches? It might've been something to do with the company he was keeping. He could have been smoking, and not been used to it, or trying to keep up with the older lads at the pub. P'raps that's why he ended up like he did—Billy told me about the railway line."

Billy was about to speak—Maisie heard him start, "But Pete—" when Sands continued.

"They always say, though, to follow the money, don't they? Which is why you're asking me these questions about Yates. But there's more to the money than where the boy worked."

"What do you mean, mate?" asked Billy.

"Ever seen Phil Coombes when he gets a chance to go out? I mean, you think he doesn't see the sky but for his walk down the road to the caff every morning, but I've seen him go out dressed up, suit and all—not all the time, but every now and again. And they've got the telephone—never known the brewery to do that for a publican, so he must be special." He scratched his head and put his cap back on. "It's not always the big things you notice—they don't have a motor car, and Phil and Sally Coombes aren't flash—but there are a lot of little things."

"To be fair, Mr. Coombes works very hard and they're very friendly, and that brings in a lot of custom," offered Maisie.

"So do I work hard, and I'm friendly—got to be, haven't you?" replied Sands. "But my daughter doesn't have a new pair of shoes every couple of months, or my wife her hair done regular as clockwork. Sally Coombes might look a bit dowdy at times—but she can get dolled up when she wants to. Her handbags don't come cheap and they buy quality. No, Phil is doing very well, and it's coming from somewhere."

Maisie came to her feet at the same time as Sands. Billy pushed back his chair and made his way to the door.

"Thank you, Mr. Sands." She pressed five shillings into his palm with her handshake. "Your time is appreciated—I hope I didn't drag you away from your work this morning."

Sands touched the peak of his cap. "Much obliged, Miss Dobbs—and no, it's all right. Like I said, I'm only over in Russell Square. Mind you, I hope my apprentice hasn't painted the lamps by the time I get back."

"I'll see you out to the street, mate," said Billy, holding open the door.

As the door closed behind the men, their voices muffled as they made their way downstairs to the front

door, Maisie walked to the window overlooking Fitzroy Square. She watched as Billy shook hands with
Pete Sands, and the painter and decorator walked away
in the direction of Warren Street. As she was turning
away from the window, Maisie glanced back. A black
motor car parked on Conway Street. She moved to one
side, so that she might see without being seen, for it
was as if the driver, silhouetted against light filtering
into the vehicle, were looking straight at her.

Chapter 7

Maisie and Billy sat in silence in front of the case map, looking at the highways and byways of color expressing each thought and idea that had come to them while considering the case of Joe Coombes—though the exercise seemed at that point to be getting them nowhere.

"So the air force girl didn't call back, did she?"

"She might have, but I had to rush off yesterday evening—ambulance practice, and I was late because it had completely slipped my mind."

"They won't strike you off—you're a volunteer. Apparently they've had to give quite a few of the employed ones their cards, and sent them back down to the labor exchange."

"They'll get their jobs back, and it won't be long, I shouldn't wonder."

"I thought the same thing." Billy looked down at his hands, rubbing the palm of the right up and down across the knuckles of the left.

"Everyone holding up at home?" asked Maisie.

"I'm amazed, really," said Billy. "They're keeping their chins up, especially Doreen. She said it won't get our Billy back any sooner if we all sit around in a state. I don't like what I'm reading in the papers though. They say there's going to be a service at Westminster Abbey on Sunday—prayers for the safety of our boys over there. I'm not one for all that, but I reckon it won't hurt, so we'll probably come up for it and put our hands together with the rest of them. People say it will be packed."

Maisie nodded, thoughtful as she picked up a thick red crayon from the table. "Money. Money and war. There's Yates making money out of the war, and so many others who are doing well out of something terrible—though I don't begrudge people the opportunity to put more cash in their pockets."

"My mate who works over in Fleet Street reckons that crime has gone up, and everyone thought it would go down, what with us being at war. And it's not only the criminals that are doing well. Look at the landlords who are putting up those workers from Yates—they're raking it in. And then there's the fact that prices have gone up on a lot of your basic foods," added Billy. "Mind you, they went up when war was declared, then they came down when nothing much happened, and now they're going up again. No wonder that new tenant down in the basement is growing tomatoes out the back! He'll have a cow in there next, you watch—we can talk him up for a pint of milk!"

Maisie laughed, tapping the case map.

"You know, apparently there's money in Hampshire," said Maisie. "I've heard the Bank of England has moved its operations there for the duration. And it's also where the paper supplier is located."

"Do you think it's got anything to do with this?" asked Billy.

Maisie was thoughtful, drawing her attention from Billy and the case map, to the window and the blue sky beyond. "You know, when I first started working for Maurice, I would try to put my discovered information on a given case into a box—not a literal box with six sides, but I would keep notes. And I'd ask myself if the nugget I'd collected was irrelevant, or if it was a distraction. Was it something just to be aware of? Could it be described as important? Finally I put whatever I'd discovered into the categories of significant, crucial, or essential—whatever name I'd come up with. And I would go back to the information daily and ask myself if it still belonged in that particular box—it helped me to sort through what I'd gathered, because I realized I'd been treating everything as really crucial and spent a lot of time like a dog chasing its tail, and not always managing evidence very well. It helped me to grow what Maurice termed my 'intuitive response,' though I'm not sure he quite approved of my method." She smiled, remembering the errors of her early days as an investigator. "So at first, when I considered the information about how and where money was printed and the coincidental relocation of the Bank of England to the same area as Joe Coombes' lodgings, I labeled it a distraction—something that would take time we don't have for nothing much in return. Now I think it's important—not crucial or essential, but important. Something to keep up our sleeves, something that might prove to be useful." She brought her attention back to Billy. "I always thought the Bank of England's printing works was over on Luke Street."

"Yeah, but perhaps not everyone knows that—after all, I heard the works down there in Hampshire is where money is printed for all over the world, and that sounds important enough to me." Billy leaned toward the table, resting his chin on closed fists placed one on top of the other. He studied the map. "I don't know about this headache business—I mean, I reckon young Joe Coombes had them all right, the headaches, but I don't think that's what killed him. Not what made him end up dead on a railway line."

"No, neither do I." Maisie scraped back her chair, and walked to the window. She looked down at the makeshift market garden in the yard, noticing a man's cardigan draped over a wooden chair. She realized that, apart from the well-tended flowers and vegetables, this was the first sign she had seen of whoever lived in the basement flat. She turned back to Billy.

"Right, this is what we do next—and we're limited by the fact that it's a Friday, but Phil and Sally are at the pub." She looked at her watch. "I'll catch the later train now—so I'll make a quick call to Chelstone, and we'll go round to the Prince. I'm sure Vivian will not be at work, in the circumstances, and the other son, Archie, might have come home to be with his family—it's a good time to get them together."

"Or p'raps not, what with them grieving."

"They know I've tried to do the best for them, and we'll be there just as neighbors—friends—who know what they've lost."

"Do you think they're involved?"

"In the death of their son? I don't think any parent would knowingly risk the life of their child—you wouldn't, would you?" She reached for the telephone receiver. "But perhaps . . . perhaps there's something amiss in that family, and we both know that involvement in a crime can be the result of something seemingly benign." She began to dial. "Or the family may have no connection to Joe's death whatsoever. Anyway—let me talk to Brenda, and then we'll leave."

Vivian Coombes looked as if she had slept in her clothes—a dress that was crumpled, stockings twisted so the seams were askew, and a cardigan pulled around her to ward off a chill that no one else would feel on a warm day in late spring. Maisie thought her fine fair hair had not seen a brush that morning, and she wore no shoes. A ladder had started to run from her toe to her ankle, and she had stopped its progress with a dab of red nail enamel. The landlord's daughter was usually a well turned-out young woman—today, standing in the doorway at the side of the pub, she resembled a slattern.

"Oh Vivian, I am so terribly sorry," said Maisie, as she held out her arms.

Vivian Coombes all but fell into her embrace, weeping. Maisie nodded, a sign for Billy to go up to the family rooms.

"How are you bearing up, Vivian? I know you and Joe were so very close," said Maisie.

"He was my little brother—and he was so . . . so innocent. Not like some of them. Not like other boys. He was good, Miss Dobbs."

"I know, I know. Is Archie here?"

Vivian stepped back, though remained close to Maisie, as if she needed a strength not present among her family. "He's been round. He didn't stay though—said he had to get back to work." She looked at Maisie and swept the back of her hand across her forehead, her pale blue eyes veined as they filled with tears once more. "I mean, I'm supposed to be at work—and I've got important work, especially now, what with everything happening over there, in France—but my supervisor let me have the day off for compassionate reasons. I hate Archie sometimes, really I do."

"No you don't—you're just grieving, and nothing will seem right for a long time. And perhaps it was too much for him—people deal with these things in different ways, and perhaps getting back to work is his way of trying to come to terms with Joe's passing."

"It's all he ever does, work—can't come to see us,

because of work. Work, work, work and no one works that hard, not so they can't come to see their family."

"Let's go up—I wanted to see if there was anything I could do for you all," said Maisie.

Vivian led the way upstairs, where a landing opened to several rooms—to the left a kitchen, then a sitting room, followed by the bathroom. The door of one bedroom was open, and pinned on the walls were staged photographs of film stars—Alan Ladd being the most favored. Scarves were draped over the dressing table mirror, and several library books perched next to a hairbrush. Two additional doors to the right of the stairs were closed, though Maisie assumed they led to bedrooms.

In the kitchen, Phil Coombes and Billy sat at the table, while Sally Coombes stood at the stove, watching the kettle as it came to the boil.

"Nice of you to come back, Miss Dobbs," said Coombes. "Eh, isn't it, Sal?" he continued, turning to his wife.

Maisie stepped away from Vivian and moved to Sally Coombes' side. "I am so sorry, Mrs. Coombes— yesterday was very 'official' with the police here. I wanted to come back to see how you're all faring, and if there's anything I can do."

Sally Coombes turned to Maisie, her loss writ large

in a raw desolation reflected in her eyes, and in the gray skin drawn across her cheekbones. Her hands shook as she reached for the kettle.

"Let me," said Maisie.

"We've fair drunk London out of tea," said Phil Coombes. "I'm supposed to be opening up today, but I can't. Can't face people, can't face the looks, the questions—if they bother to ask. People are probably too frightened." He looked at Maisie, who had made the pot of tea and was now setting clean cups on the draining board, ready to pour. "I'm grateful to you, Miss Dobbs—we might never have known, if you hadn't been down there trying to find Joe."

"And thank you for going down—you know—to identify him. We couldn't've done it—none of us," added his wife, who had taken a seat between her daughter and husband.

"Archie could have," said Vivian. "I can see him now, saying 'Yeah, that's my brother—now that's done, I'm off down the pub.' I can hear him now," said Vivian.

"Vivian! That's not fair! Your brother is a good young man—we brought you all up the same. He just takes it all in a different way." The girl's mother held up a finger to make a point. "You would do well to remember that—and remember who looks after you!"

Vivian scraped back her chair and left the kitchen, running along the landing to her room, and slamming the door behind her.

Coombes rubbed his forehead as his wife began weeping again. "It's been like this since the news came—I mean, aren't we all supposed to pull together? I've got two at loggerheads and we can't seem to get ourselves going—and we've got a funeral to get sorted out."

Billy nodded to Maisie, and took her place to pour the tea. Maisie sat down and reached across to lay a hand on Coombes' forearm. "There is no path set for this kind of shock, and for the grief that attends such terrible news. Vivian is in so much distress over losing her brother—that horror inside has to find a way out, so she's very, very angry. We all have a different way of dealing with loss—and sometimes our ways clash." She took a breath, knowing her words would cause more pain but had to be given voice. "You don't have to rush to plan the funeral. Joe won't be released to you for burial yet—they have more work to do, trying to find out what might have been ailing him."

"Do you think he jumped?" asked Coombes. "Do you think it was all this 'boys will be boys' business? And if he was alone—why wasn't he with the other blokes?"

Maisie nodded to acknowledge Billy as he placed cups of tea in front of each of them, and then took a seat at the table—she had noticed he had remained very quiet.

"I think the police have good reason to think he was a victim of his own ebullience on the night he died, however . . ." She modulated her speech, choosing her words with care. "However, I think the question of how Joe spent the past couple of weeks should be answered."

"The police aren't going to do any of that answering though, are they?" said Sally Coombes. "That detective—what was his name—Caldwell? He said the coroner would likely say it was either accidental death or death by misadventure."

"Detective Chief Inspector Caldwell was being honest about what was discovered, and the conclusions of the pathologist at the scene. They will look very carefully at how Joe was found—please trust that they are continuing to consider each small mite of evidence they can find, to discover what lies behind Joe's death." She looked from Phil to Sally Coombes, who were both leaning toward her, as if she had the answers to every one of their questions. "And I want to assure you that I will not cease to investigate Joe's death myself. I knew Joe—saw him grow up here—and I want to find out the truth of what was behind the accident that led to you losing him."

They finished their tea in an almost whispered quiet, with Maisie steering the conversation to Joe's childhood, so that they might remember their son as he was, and not how they might imagine him to have been at the point of his death. Maisie and Billy took their leave, receiving thanks from the pub landlord and his wife, and Maisie in turn asked them to say goodbye to Vivian, and to tell her that she was being held in their thoughts.

Billy did not speak until they reached the front door leading up to the office, whereupon he turned to look around at the square.

"What is it, Billy? What do you want to say?" asked Maisie.

"All right, it's like this: the carpet is an inch thick on those stairs, and them cups and saucers—and the teapot, sugar bowl and jug—were bone china. Matching, at that. And did you see the watch on Phil's wrist? All very nice."

Maisie waited, for she knew Billy had more to get off his chest.

"I feel really, really bad for them, miss, because that Joe was a young diamond of a lad—and Viv is a good girl, even if she does have a bit of the Sarah Bernhardts about her. But I still think something's not right, and I know where to start."

"The older son?"

Billy nodded.

"Good—because I was going to ask you to make a point of going over to see him. He works in Sydenham— easy to get to on your way home, isn't it?"

"Just a bit out of my way, but consider it as good as done," said Billy.

"One thing though," added Maisie. "Remember he's grieving too—and I meant what I said—everyone's different. We've both seen it before—when Brenda received bad news about her sister, she went out and cleaned all the windows like a demon. That could be Joe's older brother—work could be balm for his aching soul. And it wouldn't surprise me if his sister's dramatic bent didn't irritate him a bit."

"Would me," said Billy.

"So, go easy on him."

"You still think something's amiss though, don't you?"

"I do," said Maisie. "But I don't want to scare anyone either. Now, I must be getting along or I'll miss my train."

"One more thing, miss—"

"Yes?"

"What shall we do about that bloke in the black motor car over there?"

Maisie reached into her handbag for her keys. "I thought I'd wait to see which one of us he follows—and if it's you, Billy, I want you to go straight home. Your family has too much worry to risk any more problems at the moment."

From the floor-to-ceiling windows at the front of the office, Maisie watched the vehicle on the other side of the square, and sighed. Yes, she was tempted to end her own speculation, walk across to Conway Street and rap on the window. But at the same time she too had much to lose. That thought reminded her of an overdue telephone call she had promised to make. She turned away from the window, and just as she was about to reach for the receiver, the telephone began to ring. She picked up the black Bakelite receiver and recited the number.

"Is that Miss Maisie Dobbs . . . um, is she there?" The voice on the line was that of a young woman, a voice lacking the tone of maturity, but with more resonance than that of a schoolgirl. Maisie would have put her at twenty-one or twenty-two years of age. "I'd like to speak to her, please."

"Yes, this is Maisie Dobbs. Who's speaking?"

"Oh at last! I've reached you—I thought it would go

on ringing for ages, and I have so little time when I can get to the telephone box. My name's Sylvia Preston. Leading Aircraftswoman Preston, WAAF. You should have received a message I'd called before."

"Yes, I did, Miss Preston, but I thought it best not to call back as I have no idea of your shift times."

"I'm glad you didn't after that first telephone call—that nosey mare of a landlady can't keep anything to herself, and she's half cut most of the time. I'm happy to have moved out, though I sometimes wonder if I haven't gone from the fat into the fire."

"Oh dear—" said Maisie.

"It's all right really, this one's harmless—to a point. But about Joey Coombes—oh heck—" Maisie heard the woman exclaim when the pips sounded, though she was soon back on the line having inserted more coins to continue the call.

"I can telephone you back," said Maisie. "Give me your number."

Sylvia Preston read out the number and hung up. Maisie dialed, and heard one ring before the WAAF answered.

"Yes, thank you." She sounded breathless.

"Are you all right?" asked Maisie. "You're not in any danger?"

"I'm in danger every day—but not the sort you

mean." The young woman gave a half-laugh, almost a snort. "I ran to get to the telephone, and now I'm trying not to breathe in for the terrible smell in here. I don't know why people have to do some of the things they do in a telephone box. Anyway, let me tell you what I think you should know."

"Go on," said Maisie.

"I heard you talking to the landlady when you came down. She didn't quite tell you everything. There were two men came to see Joe—both of them turned out very well indeed, looking like they were in the pictures. Not in uniform—but not everyone is, though they both looked like they should be. One was about my age, I would imagine—twenty-one, twenty-two, something like that. And the other was older, thirties—he re-minded me of my brother who's thirty-six . . . I know, don't ask about the age difference between us. I reckon my mum kept away from my dad for fifteen years after the terrible time she had when my brother was born!"

Maisie smiled, then prompted Preston. "But there must have been something a bit off, for you to notice them—what didn't you like?"

"I didn't like the way they spoke to him. I couldn't hear the words, but as they walked a little way down the road, I didn't like the tone—I could hear them, friendly enough first of all—they called him 'Joe,' so they knew him—well, the younger one did. The other one was more . . . more officious, I would say. Nice enough, handing out the ciggies—Joe shook his head, he was a good boy, really he was. Shouldn't have been away from home, I reckon. Then I couldn't hear anything, but I could see, and Joe just kept shaking his head, and then the younger one got him by the arm—you know, grabbed his upper arm—and turned toward him. I don't know what he said, but it looked like Joe was scared—he held his head down, as if he didn't want to look up into their faces."

"Did he go off with them?"

"No, he didn't. They had a motor car though—I saw them get into it. But here's what happened—another one of the painters, Freddie Mayes, came along in the van, and stopped alongside them. I can't be sure, but I think he knew them. Well, he knew the older one. The younger man was in the black motor car already. And Joe got into the van, as if it had been a life raft come to save him. I couldn't make out his face, but you can see these things by the way people move—he clambered in that van sharpish."

"Then?" promoted Maisie.

"Then the van drove off, and so did the motor car—the motor went out on Winchester Road, and the van in another direction—I don't know which airfield they were at that day." There was a pause on the line, before Preston continued. "That's about it, Miss Dobbs. As I said, our illustrious landlady didn't tell you quite everything."

"Thank you, Miss Preston," said Maisie. "I appreciate you getting in touch—very much indeed."

"Well, I had to—we all liked Joe, us girls. He took our teasing in good heart, but he was a good boy." She paused, and Maisie thought she heard her begin to weep.

"Are you all right, Sylvia?"

"I just think it's terrible—that's he's missing, that he's gone off somewhere. Probably to get away from those blokes, if I know anything. Do you think you'll find him?"

Maisie drew breath and closed her eyes. Giving news of a death was never straightforward, the words caught in her heart and in her throat. "I'm so sorry, Sylvia. Joe's body was found a few days ago—he's dead, I'm afraid."

There was silence on the line, after several seconds punctuated by a sniff, and a cough. "It wasn't an accident, was it?" said Preston, her words stumbling out as she sobbed. "I tell you, Joe was scared, Miss Dobbs—I don't know what he was scared of, but he had fear written all over him during that last week I saw him."

"Would you know those men again?" asked Maisie.

"The younger one, probably. But I know how easy it is to make mistakes, so I would have to be careful."

"You're to be commended for your reticence, Sylvia, and—"

Before Maisie could say more, Preston broke in. "I've just had enough of death and bodies, really I have."

"What do you mean?"

"My job—look, sorry, I'm not supposed to talk about it."

"I can be trusted—if you want to get something off your chest."

Silence again, and more sniffing. "I'm a driver, Miss Dobbs. They taught me to drive and I thought I would be driving the officers up and down to London, and out to other airfields, that sort of thing. But you know what I do? I drive an ambulance."

"An ambulance? For practice drills?"

"I suppose you could say that, but the death is real."

"You're going to have to explain that to me, Sylvia— I'm not quite following you."

"They're training the army to parachute—all these boys coming down in big lorries so they can practice parachuting, for taking on the Germans over there. I don't know when they think they're going to do that, what with everyone talking about an invasion. But the army has already started them practicing at their barracks, jumping off walls, so they know how to land. Then they bring them here to jump from aircraft. They go up over Salisbury Plain, that's one place. We wait in the ambulances as they come down. We don't pick up many injured—if you land wrong, you're dead, easy as that. If I get one with a sprained ankle or a broken leg, or a collarbone, or what have you, I feel as if I've been let off light. Most of the time I'm with another girl loading up dead lads whose legs have gone right up through their bodies, or they're completely smashed up. That's my job. One time I had to drive back across Salisbury Plain in the dark, on my own, with six dead boys in the back of my ambulance, so no one would see, no one would know. And I tell you, I don't think aeroplanes were invented for people to suddenly get up off their seat and jump out of a door. But that's me."

"I am so very sorry, Sylvia," said Maisie. "I had no idea."

"Oh, no one has any idea. And to think I was pleased to be a driver—working outside, on the move, and none of this stuck indoors doing meteorology or typing up reports for the brass. Now I drive a death wagon— that's how it feels." She paused, drawing breath before continuing. "You won't tell anyone, will you?"

"I promise, Sylvia."

"Right. I've got to go now."

"Thank you very—" Maisie was expressing gratitude to the continuous hum of the disconnected call.

When she had raised her head from her hands, with the image of young women lifting the terribly damaged bodies of equally young men still in her mind's eye, Maisie reached for the telephone receiver and dialed a number she knew by heart. A man answered, a clerk to the solicitor she was seeking.

"Hello, Anthony—is Mr. Klein there, please?"

"Yes, Your Ladyship—I will tell him you're waiting. One moment, please."

There was silence on the line, and then a series of clicks before the measured tones of her solicitor echoed down the line.

"Maisie. How lovely to hear from you—it's about time we had a chat about your affairs. I'm afraid, what with the war, I am concerned with regard to the properties in France, however—"

"I beg your pardon, Mr. Klein—it's so impolite of me to interrupt, but I would like to speak to you about Anna."

"Ah, yes. I have held back, but if you wish, I will take your instructions to find a good family for her."

"Mr. Klein—I . . . ." She felt herself falter. "Mr. Klein, I think . . . ."

"We'd better meet, Maisie. I believe I understand completely. Are you about to leave town, or can you come to my office?"

"I'm catching a later train today. I daresay Anna is resting in any case—she has measles."

"Is she recovering?"

"I'm assured she is on the mend."

"Good—can you be here within the hour?"

"I'm leaving now."

"Excellent—I will have a series of papers for you to go over, and a list of documents required. Thank goodness the law hasn't changed—it was on the books you know, but the war got in the way. Anyway, we can make a start."

"Thank you, Mr. Klein."

"I told you long ago, Maisie—you may call me Bernard."

"Indeed—but old habits die hard."

The black motor car was still parked on Conway Street, though upon closer inspection, Maisie realized it wasn't completely black, but had a dark bottle green contrasting paint along the sides. She turned from the front window and crossed the office to the back window overlooking the yard below. There was a tall but narrow gate forming a rear exit to the alley, though probably not used—terra-cotta pots had been placed in front, filled with flowering plants. She gathered her handbag and briefcase, locked the door as she departed the office, and made her way down the stairs. But instead of leaving by the front door, she turned left at the end of the staircase and stepped across to a plain door with no number or name alongside. With her knuckle she rapped on the paneled door. There was no answer. She closed her eyes, whispering, "Please come. Please come." She rapped again. And again. It was as she turned to leave that she heard the door being unlocked and a chain drawn back.

The man before her was, she thought, a few years older than herself. Of taller than average height, he wore dark trousers, a clean white collarless shirt and an unbuttoned waistcoat. He leaned on a walking stick, and when she looked into his face, she saw a scar running from his left cheekbone, down to an uneven jaw. At one glance, it was as if she knew everything about him.

"What do you want?" asked the man.

Maisie did not look away when her eyes met his. "My name is Maisie Dobbs. I work in the office above, and I wonder—would you be so kind as to allow me to leave by your back gate? I suppose it leads into the alley. Am

I right? I'll set the plants aside, and will move them back again when I return, but I would be very much obliged if you could help me."

The man looked at her for a period of time—perhaps only a second or two, though it seemed as if he would never respond to her request.

He inclined his head, stepped back and held out his hand for her to enter. "Of course. Please, come in. And I apologize for taking so long to answer your knock. I usually use the entrance at the front, so was taken aback to hear someone at this door. Follow me."

The man led the way from the narrow landing and two short flights of stairs into a sitting room which she thought was probably also the bedroom. He proceeded through to a scullery, and out into the yard. She was still surprised by the neat order of the flat when she emerged into the small yard, and realized her view from above did not do justice to the abundance of color the man had created.

"Oh, my—this is just beautiful. So small, and so perfect, Mr.—forgive me, I don't know your name."

"I never told you." He held out his hand. "Walter Miles."

"Thank you, Mr. Miles." Maisie took the outstretched hand and returned his smile.

"Come on—let's get you on your way." Miles stepped

across the flagstones and with Maisie's assistance began to move terra-cotta pots away from the gate. "The bolt is a bit rusty, but I've moved it before." He pulled on the bolt and after some effort, it gave, shooting back and releasing the gate, which he drew back and held open.

"I can't thank you enough," said Maisie.

"It was my pleasure, Miss Dobbs. The motor car has been out there for hours now, so be on your way before he realizes you've left and starts tootling down Tottenham Court Road looking for you."

Maisie was about to open her mouth, when the man shook his head. "Go now."

And as she ran down the alley and out onto Tottenham Court Road toward Goodge Street Station, Maisie could not help but wonder about Walter Miles. She had never seen him before, never noticed him coming or going—in fact, she assumed an elderly lady lived in the downstairs flat. Yet there was something familiar about him. And she knew very well the cause of his disfigurement—wherever she went in this time of war, there was always a reminder of the last, even if it was only the sight of Billy wincing as he stood up from his desk. She reflected upon her conversation with Sylvia Preston, and the terrible job assigned to her. And she wondered how another generation of men and women in years to come would have to fight a different battle every single day—a battle against a time that would not fail to mark them, inside and out, and would come back to haunt them at moments when they least expected it. But now there was one victim of the war she would do her level best to ensure would have only joyful memories to look back upon in the years to come. After leaving the underground station at Holborn, she all but ran to the offices of Bernard Klein.

Chapter 8

Maisie arrived at Chelstone later than she had hoped on Friday—her train pulled into the sidings several times to allow other trains to pass, and the journey was longer than usual, with a change at Paddock Wood instead of Tonbridge. She asked a station guard why there was a diversion, and was informed it was due to "extra trains coming up from the coast."

Maisie's father and stepmother were sitting at the kitchen table when Maisie entered the house.

"Maisie, did you walk all the way from the station? You should have said—I would have met you, walked back with you."

"Not to worry, Dad." She kissed him on the cheek, moving to her stepmother's side for the same greeting. "How's Anna? Is she feeling better?"

"I was just going to take up some warm milk for her—it's on the side there, cooling. She's had such a sore throat," said Brenda.

"I'll take it up then." Maisie slipped off her jacket and placed it over the back of a chair. She turned toward the draining board where the red china mug filled with hot milk had been left to cool. Maisie took a spoon from the drawer, skimmed the skin from the top of the milk, and placed the mug on a saucer. "Is her honey already in, Brenda?"

"Oh yes—never forget the little one's honey!"

Maisie smiled as she left the kitchen and made her way upstairs. The door to Anna's room was ajar, so before stepping in, Maisie peered around. The child was awake, lying on her side and looking deep into the eyes of Emma, the orphaned Alsatian Maisie had rescued following the untimely death of the dog's owner. Emma's chin was resting on the counterpane while Anna was running her fingers through the dog's ruff. But Anna was yawning, her eyelids growing heavy.

"I think it's time for a little girl called Anna to have her milk and go to sleep," said Maisie.

Anna turned, and held out her arms to Maisie. "Auntie Maisie, Auntie Maisie—I've still got measles!"

Emma wagged her tail and came to Maisie, who

patted her in greeting, and pointed to the rug at the side of the bed. The dog turned and lay down, nose between paws, watching her young mistress.

"Here you are." Maisie held her palm under the cup while Anna lifted it to her lips and drank the milk in just a few gulps. "Someone was thirsty," said Maisie as she took the cup with one hand, and placed the fingers of the other to the child's forehead to feel her temperature. "How are you feeling now, my love?"

Anna shrugged. "I think I'm getting better, but Auntie Brenda says I have to stay in bed for a bit longer. Emma said so too—she likes to sleep here."

"Emma said so?"

"Yes she told me this morning that we should stay in bed another two days, to catch up on our sleep and be strong for Lady, when I can ride again."

"Well, I think Emma's quite right—she's a very intelligent dog." Maisie stood up and placed the cup on a wicker side table. "Would you like me to read a story?"

Anna nodded.

"Just for five minutes, then I'll tuck you in. You've got a special visitor coming tomorrow."

"Who?" said Anna, giggling already.

Maisie was pleased to see the girl in good heart, in spite of her appearance—dark blue smudges under her eyes, flushed cheeks and scabby spots on her face and hands.

"Your favorite young man—Tim."

"Tim! Tim's coming?"

"Yes, Tim's coming tomorrow."

The child looked at her dog, then at Maisie. "Emma says we will be ready to get up tomorrow—we're both over the measles."

Maisie laughed and reached for Anna, feeling the comfort of the small body pressing into hers. "I didn't know dogs could get measles."

"Oh they can," said Anna. "Emma said she had measles when she was a puppy, but she's felt a bit bad since I got them."

Maisie looked down at the dog, who had lifted her head as if to check her young charge. "Well, let's see how you're both feeling tomorrow. Now, how about that story?"

Anna gave Maisie one more squeeze and then lay back. Maisie reached toward a small pile of books on the wicker table, selected one in particular, and began to read.

"They were not railway children to begin with. I don't suppose they had ever thought about railways . . ."

Within just a few pages, Anna's breathing had become soft. Emma stood up, stretched, turned on the rug three times and then settled down into a comfortable crescent, giving a contented low growl as she too fell asleep. Maisie replaced the book on the table, picked up the empty cup, and leaned over the child, brushed her jet-black hair from her forehead and kissed her soft skin before leaving the room.

"She go down all right?" said Brenda, standing up to go to the stove as Maisie entered the kitchen.

"She perked up a bit—especially when I told her that Tim was coming tomorrow—but I think she needs another day or two in bed. We'll see."

Brenda pulled a plate from the oven. "There's some shepherd's pie warmed up, love, and I put on a few vegetables for you while you were up there with Anna. I bet you haven't eaten all day."

"Oh, lovely. Thank you, Brenda—just what the doctor ordered," said Maisie.

She took a seat as Brenda placed the plate in front of her, but as she picked up her knife and fork, she looked across at her father, who was regarding her without speaking.

"What is it, Dad?"

"Did you see your Mr. Klein?"

Maisie nodded.

"And he's going to help find a good family for the little nipper?"

Maisie pressed her lips together as she faced her father, meeting his eyes with her own direct gaze. "Yes. Yes, he's going to help settle her."

The following morning, after Maisie had helped Anna bathe and then dabbed calamine lotion onto the rash that dotted her back, torso, arms and face, the child asked if she could lie on top of the bed in her best dress, if she had to remain upstairs, rather than wear her nightgown.

"Oh, love—you still have lots of spots, and they won't get better if you wear your ordinary clothes. But what if you put on a fresh nightie and you can wear your new blue cardigan over the top?"

Anna seemed crestfallen, but Maisie knew she was a tractable child, not given to tantrums.

"That's a good idea," said Anna. She began to smile. "Then if I'm in bed, Tim won't know I don't have my proper clothes on, will he?"

"No he won't. He'll think you're a big strong girl. Now then, let me see your tongue—open wide."

Maisie looked into the child's mouth to check the back of her throat, searching for the inflammation that accompanied measles.

"That looks a lot better. Do you want to come down for your breakfast? You'll have to go back up again—if you rest you'll get better faster."

"Can I choose my egg?"

"Not today, pet—I'll go out and find you a nice brown one. Then I must go over to the manor, to see Lord Julian."

Anna smiled. "Before I got the measles, he told me I could call him 'Uncle Julian.'"

"He did?" said Maisie, trying not to betray her surprise.

Anna nodded. "He came to watch me riding Lady, and he said I was showing great promise."

"And that is high praise indeed, young lady. Now then, let's go downstairs."

After breakfast, as Maisie predicted, Anna had become sleepy, though her color seemed to have become more natural. As soon as she was settled in her bedroom once again, Maisie placed a telephone call to Priscilla, who confirmed that Tim would arrive at Chelstone station at twenty past twelve.

"His cheek knows no bounds, Maisie. I heard him say to Tarquin—deliberately in earshot, I might add—'Keep your head down Tarq—she'll need a target if I'm not here.'"

"And what did you say?" asked Maisie, expecting Priscilla's retort to be as filled with sarcasm as her son's.

"I told him that Tarquin and I would be going to the cinema."

"Because you know how much Tim enjoys the pictures—Priscilla, you two goad each other as if you were siblings, not mother and son."

"I know—I should grow up. I suppose if I am to be honest, there's something in me that enjoys the sparring, and at least I'm keeping him on his toes."

"Or the other way around." Maisie sighed. "Anyway, I'll be at the station to collect him."

"He'll come home a lot calmer—he always does when he's been to Chelstone. Right, I'd best be getting on—and find where 'Tarq' has got to with his head down."

Simmonds, the butler—who had once worked for James and Maisie when they lived at the Ebury Place mansion—had seen Maisie walking across the lawns in the direction of the manor house, and had already opened the door to greet her.

"Good morning, Your Ladyship—how are you, and more importantly, how is dear Anna faring?"

Maisie smiled, warmed by the affection with which

the child was held. Anna had come to them as an evacuee, and was later orphaned when her grandmother—her only living relative, as far as anyone knew—died in a London hospital.

"She's on the mend, thank you, Simmonds. She's very excited because Tim's arriving today."

"Oh good—another young person about the house is always welcome. And Lord Julian enjoys his company too—the boy seems to hang on stories of Lord Julian's years in the navy, which of course His Lordship loves to tell."

"Speaking of whom—is he here, Simmonds? I'd like to see him, if possible."

"Right you are—I believe he's in the library, but if you would oblige me by waiting just a moment, I'll have a look. He hates to be caught with his eyes closed."

"Good idea. And I'll nip into the kitchen to see Cook—she promised some more leftover chicken to make broth for Anna."

Without doubt, Lord Julian had aged since the death of his son, though his upright bearing never seemed to change. Indeed, at the memorial service for James—held in the City at Temple Church—both Lord Julian and Lady Rowan seemed a head taller, with shoulders drawn back, as if to represent the very strength and standing of their son. Maisie remembered trying to concentrate on James alive, James laughing, James running along a beach with a kite, and not the desperate yearning for her husband and their unborn child she had lost on a fine day in rural Ontario. Grief had been an oppressive weight that seemed to bear down upon her—until she regained some crucial part of her character while volunteering for nursing work in Spain. It was as if she had come home to herself, and was given leave to open her arms to all that might be possible in the future.

"Maisie, lovely to see you, my dear," said Lord Julian, coming to his feet. He had been sitting in a leather chair alongside the window. A book was open on a side table, its place kept by a weighted marker laid across the pages. He held out both hands, which she took in hers, and he leaned forward to kiss her cheek. "And how is our young horsewoman?" he inquired.

"It's lovely to see you too, Julian. Anna is recovering well, and anxious to be out on Lady again. I think we might have to tie her to the bed."

"As soon as she finds her legs again, she should be out there—fresh air, the responsibility for a pony, nothing better for a child." He extended his hand toward another leather chair close to his own. "Now then, sit down and tell me how I can be of assistance to you—

I'm sure you didn't come to tell me about Anna's recovery, though I'm glad to hear it."

Maisie smoothed the back of her linen skirt and sat down, leaning toward Lord Julian as he too was seated. "I'm curious about how the Bank of England goes about its business—not here in London, but now it's located in Hampshire for the duration. Have they moved their printing?"

Lord Julian sighed. "As you are aware, I am on the boards of various banks, so much of what I know is highly confidential. In a time of war the supply and movement of money becomes even more crucial than ever. Money is a powerful tool, and wars are about powerful men and how they use the tools at their disposal. The military is involved, in a number of ways."

Maisie raised her eyebrows. "How? I never thought the generals would have communication with the bankers."

"The prime minister—and thank goodness, we now have a man who is up to the job of war—is the linchpin. He is the man in the middle, drawing to him everything he needs to secure the country to the best of the country's ability to protect itself and its people."

"And what might the generals want from the bankers, and how is the PM a conduit between the two?"

Lord Julian looked at his hands, closed his eyes for a second and then returned his attention to Maisie.

"The Bank of England has to consider many factors in a time of war, not least the fact that the risk of forgery increases dramatically—not necessarily from local sources, but the threat of the Germans flooding the country with counterfeit money and bringing chaos to the economy is not to be underestimated. Interestingly enough, at the same time, money does not circulate in the same way—rather it is like blood around a body, and if the pressure on the system is high, blood moves a lot faster. We tend to see an increase in circulation, which means that—quite literally—paper money wears out faster, so you have to have more in hand to replace notes that have reached the end of their useful life. Of course, there are people who slow down in terms of spending, and they save their money—not always in the bank either. A tin box under the bed is often thought safer—if you have to run, you can run with your money. But on the other side of the coin there can be a tendency toward profligacy—if we're all going to die, we can't take it with us when we go."

"I confess, I had never considered any of this."

"No reason why you should, my dear. For most people, money is for saving, spending or worrying about—too much, too little, never enough—money as the devil's tool." He reached for a silver letter opener, and began tapping it against his palm. "But with the threat of invasion—and it has never been more likely—the banks have quite literally been destroying money, though at the same time notes in different denominations have been deposited with clearing banks around the country."

"So that's why, as you said, the printing, supply and movement of money is even more crucial now than in peacetime."

"Yes, that's the extent of it." He put down the letter opener. "And the Bank of England has moved some staff down to a location in Hampshire, given the risk of bombing across London. I can only tell you that money transported between Hampshire and London is an operation executed under a blanket of extreme security."

"And what about the proximity of the coast, and navy in Southampton and Portsmouth—to say nothing of the air force and army in the area."

"Our forces are in position due to the threat that has come from across the Channel since before Roman times—even the Vikings came around to the south coast!"

Maisie nodded, thoughtful. "The War Office and Threadneedle Street are therefore close."

"Very." Lord Julian looked toward the door, as if he expected someone to be there, listening. He lowered his voice; Maisie had to lean forward to hear. "The Bank of England liaises with the War Office to ensure that any special notes required for military purposes are supplied in a timely fashion and—again—under conditions of absolute secrecy." He paused, and looked out of the window, raising his hand as he smiled into the distance. "There's Rowan—I must be quick. She knows you're here now, so she will be bursting into the room in a few moments." Another second's pause. "There has to be a supply for operations such as sabotage, intelligence, and for our airmen who may find themselves in enemy territory after being shot down. They must have local currency with them, and we also have to pay the troops from our colonies—in which case it behooves us to have currency issued by British Military Authority, and in some instances those words are printed onto the currency. You will find there are notes available in sterling denominations that will never be available to the British spending public."

Maisie leaned back. "I had no idea."

"Nor should you have an idea—it's a matter of the security of our sovereign land."

"I have too many questions for the moments we have left to ourselves." She bit her bottom lip. "But regarding another matter, I have the serial number here, of a type of paint used to render airfield buildings safe from fire. Could you find out more about it?" Maisie took the note from her pocket and passed it to Lord Julian. "If possible, I'd like to know whether it's passed any tests for safety. And who manufactures it—where it's from."

"I will see what I can find out, Mai—"

"There you are! Darling Maisie, where have you been?" Lady Rowan Compton had not knocked before entering, and walked with as much speed as she could muster, now that the arthritis in her hip was becoming more troublesome. She was accompanied by a spaniel and a Labrador retriever, both dogs bounding into the room in a direct line for Lord Julian.

"Rather busy this week, Rowan. You're looking well—is your hip feeling better?"

"Oh, let's not get boring and start talking about health."

Lord Julian moved to stand to allow his wife to take his seat, but Maisie came to her feet.

"No, please—Rowan, I am just about to leave, so please take this chair."

Lady Rowan sat down with a loud sigh, and rested her cane alongside the chair. "Growing old is not for the faint-hearted, Maisie. Mark my words." She rested her hand on her chest and caught her breath. "I wanted to ask you if you would come up to town with me tomorrow morning—for the service at Westminster. George can drive us up."

"Of course—Tim will be here to keep Anna amused, and while she's asleep, my father will keep him busy. And I can drive you up to town, if you like. I left the Alvis here and I will need it during the coming week— you might have to come back on the train though, if you wouldn't mind."

"Not at all. And George will pick me up at Tonbridge so I don't have to shilly-shally around waiting for the branch line train down to Chelstone. I quite enjoy the train, so it will all be perfect! I'll be ready to leave first thing tomorrow morning."

Maisie waited on the platform, stepping back as the train from Tonbridge pulled into the small branch line station. Doors began opening and a handful of people stepped out of the train, as others waited to board. She looked both ways along the platform, to no avail. Tim was not among the passengers now holding out their tickets as they walked toward the stationmaster, who greeted everyone by name. Steam punched out from the locomotive, and as the guard stepped forward with his flag, raising his arm and blowing his whistle to signal the train's departure, Maisie turned to leave the station.

"Someone missed the train?" asked the stationmaster, touching the brim of his peaked cap.

"Yes—my friend's son. He's sixteen now, and I think he's old enough to look after himself, but I still worry."

"Coming in from Charing Cross, changing at Tonbridge was he?"

Maisie nodded. "He'll probably be on the next one."

He pulled a pocket watch from his waistcoat, extended the chain to better see the dial. Maisie knew the stationmaster would have been aware of the correct time to the second but seemed to enjoy wielding his watch with a certain flourish. "The platforms are a bit packed on that line up from the coast toward—there are men coming back from France, you see, and the seats are taken until the next train comes through. Some of them are in a bit of a state—they've got the WVS out there handing tea in through the windows as the trains pull in so the lads can get something down them. I heard they'd handed out a few hundred sarnies in just a couple of hours this morning."

"Knowing Tim he probably rolled up his sleeves and got stuck in to help," said Maisie. "He can't wait until he's in uniform."

"There's many a lad who couldn't wait the last time around—and then they couldn't wait to get home again. Anyway, better get on. Like I said, he'll most likely be on the one o'clock—due in at twenty-past." He laughed. "But I reckon you know the timetable as well as I do!"

Maisie smiled. "Yes, I'm sure you're right—I'll be back in an hour." She left the station and drove the five minutes back to Chelstone Manor.

"The stationmaster said the 'up' trains coming from the coast are holding up other services," she said, explaining Tim's absence to her stepmother. "The navy has been bringing home a good number of our soldiers, apparently—I'd heard that nonessential personnel were being sent back from France. And the trains were very unpredictable yesterday," said Maisie. "Tim might well have missed the connection to Chelstone."

Tim was not on the train at twenty past one, twenty past two, or twenty past three. In fact he did not arrive at Chelstone until long after Maisie had promised herself that she would place a telephone call to his mother. At half past six, on the train that should have arrived ten minutes earlier, Maisie felt a wave of relief wash over her as the tall, lanky lad clambered down from the third-class carriage, and seemed to lope toward her. Priscilla was right when she had observed some months earlier, "He's at that ungainly age."

"Tim, where have you been?" asked Maisie, trying to keep the mixture of relief and irritation out of her voice.

Priscilla's son leaned down to kiss her on both cheeks. "I tried to telephone, Tante Maisie, but it was rather chaotic at Tonbridge." He ran his fingers through his hair. "Does my mother know I'm late? She's watching me like a hawk these days—and I'll never hear the last of it."

"Had you not been on this train, I would have telephoned her—and she would have harangued me for leaving it so late to do so. I would have deserved her ire, because I put it off time and again. But the stationmaster told me about the trains coming in from the coast causing timetable delays. And it took me a long time to get home last night for the same reason. Now then, let's get you back to the house—your bed's made up in the conservatory. You're the only person I know who can sleep with the sunshine beaming in first thing in the morning."

"I love the conservatory—makes me feel as if I'm on a boat, hearing the wind outside and then the sunrise waking me up."

It was later, over a late supper, that Priscilla's son described the scene at Tonbridge station. "It looked as if everyone in the town was out there to help. There were women making sandwiches, brewing tea—and the men were helping to wash up the cups as the soldiers handed them back out of the train windows. I don't know how they'd heard about it, and mustered all that help—I asked a guard and he said that as some of the earlier trains stopped at the station, soldiers were leaning out and asking for water, so word went round and people started coming in with whatever they had to contribute. I'm telling you, Tante Maisie, the men looked terrible— many of them were covered in mud, and a lot were bandaged up. I left my kit bag with a guard and just got stuck in to help—handing out food and water, bringing back cups. I asked one soldier—he was only about my age . . . well, a bit older, about eighteen, nineteen, more Tom's age—and he said he was lucky to get on a ship. He told me there are thousands of them, thousands of men trying to get to the coast and waiting to get off. The navy's in there, sending over ships, but the Germans are bombing them, coming in with their Stukas. The soldiers I spoke to think they'll all perish there." He was silent for a moment, and stared out of the window into the peppery darkness of late May. "Some of them were moaning that our RAF were flying right over, and then someone else pointed out that they were going deeper into France to try to slow down the German advance to give more of our men the chance to escape. Then another came back at him and said the RAF were going after the Messerschmitts over the Channel, trying to push them back. It's a devil of a fight—and there are our soldiers, completely stranded. It's terrible. They said they had no idea how the navy would be able to get them back to England—they'll be left there, like sitting ducks."

Maisie stood up, came to her godson's side and put her arm around his shoulders. "War is terrible, Tim—and you are so young to have to learn just how terrible it is."

"You know, Tante Maisie—we haven't heard from Tom for over a week. Mother is much too calm, but she's also snappy."

"I know—but she knows how she is too, which is why she was keen for you to come down to Chelstone. She understands only too well what worry can do to her, so allow her some latitude. And you can cheer up Anna—she's come down with measles, though she's on the mend."

"I remember measles—it was horrible. Poor Anna."

"Now then, Tim—time for us all to go to bed. And your mother says you have work to do for your final school exams."

"Pointless work—pointless when you know what's going on over there."

"It seems like that at the moment. But humor your mother—and your father. They have enough to worry about."

Tim pushed back his chair and began to help Maisie clear the plates. As they moved to the kitchen, he spoke again.

"Tante Maisie. You know you said I was too young to learn how terrible war is? Well, I'm sixteen—how old were you, when you went to France?"

Maisie sighed. "I was seventeen, Tim. Your mother was a bit older than me, but no more prepared for what we encountered."

The boy nodded, though Maisie thought she saw his eyes redden, and he looked down, as if to avoid her gaze. "Tom will probably telephone tomorrow. Friday is usually his day, and he missed it." He turned, picked up his kit bag from the kitchen floor where he had dropped it as they'd entered, and made his way toward the conservatory. He did not look back, but called over his shoulder, "Good night, Tante Maisie."

"Good night, Tim."

Maisie stood for a moment, and then went to the library. She still thought of it as "Maurice's library" even now she was at peace with the legacy she had inherited upon the death of her beloved mentor. It was to this room she would come when the ache of loss was most keen, and she yearned for the comfort of his wisdom. Now, with the house full, it was her makeshift bedroom. She poured herself a glass of sherry, and as she was about to take a seat alongside the fireplace—cold, and covered with a needlepoint screen for the summer—she stopped, and returned to the trolley that held the same two decanters as it had in Maurice's day. She poured a measure of aged single-malt whiskey into a glass and set it on a small table alongside his leather wing chair. She clinked her glass against the glass she'd left for a man now passed, and seated herself on the chair opposite. She took a sip of the sherry and leaned back.

"Oh, how I miss you at times, Maurice. How I miss you."

And she waited for the counsel she would not hear, but would feel in her heart.

Chapter 9

Maisie and Lady Rowan left Chelstone Manor early for the drive to London. As Lady Rowan would doubtless have been more comfortable had her chauffeur taken her to Westminster Abbey, Maisie concluded that, in accepting her offer, her mother-in-law probably wanted to discuss something, without interruption and away from her home.

"Now we're under way, I think I can relax," said Lady Rowan. "And I must say, I do like your new motor car."

"Thank you very much," said Maisie. "It's bigger than the MG, so easier to take the family out for the day, though of course when I bought it I hadn't considered the fact that we would be dealing with petrol coupons. I have to be very careful because I have an as-

signment that's taking me down to Hampshire now—
it's a bit of a journey, and I cannot depend upon buses
and trains when I get there."

"And it's not as if you can put your toe down and
push this motor car a bit is it? I suppose it uses more
petrol if you get too enthusiastic."

Maisie looked across at Lady Rowan for a second,
then brought her attention back to the road. "I know
you, Rowan—you would be tearing around the countryside if you had this motor."

Rowan laughed. "I always liked a little speed, you
know—the wind in my hair and the feeling that I could
just drive off in search of something thrilling, if only
for a short time. The hip put paid to that though—
the wonderful hazards of riding horses diminished
the years of excitement behind the wheel. And as you
know, my son inherited the devil-may-care aspect of
my character—which . . . ." She faltered. "It's something I very much regret. I wish he had been more like
his father; more measured, more a thinking man than
a doing man."

Maisie continued to look ahead but chose her words
carefully for she understood her mother-in-law was,
perhaps, making a confession of sorts.

"The James I knew—and loved deeply—had within

him the best of both you and Lord Julian. He was also his own man, and he followed his heart."

"He followed it too high that day, didn't he, Maisie?"

"Time has passed, Rowan—time has passed for us all. It's taken me a good long while to reach this point, but I don't think it serves any of us to look back. Tormenting ourselves with 'What if?' and trying to change past events—if only in the imagination—can drive a person mad."

Lady Rowan looked out of the window. "I love the way the mist comes off the fields in the morning, just as the day is warming up. It makes me feel as if the next twenty-four hours could hold the promise of something extraordinary. Something new."

Maisie nodded, aware that the older woman had turned toward her and was now watching her as she drove on toward River Hill.

"It was the me in him that caused him to make that bad decision, Maisie. It was the me in him that caused you to lose your child."

Maisie looked in her rearview mirror to check the road behind, slipped down the gears, braked and pulled over into a lay-by. She switched off the engine, turned to her mother-in-law and reached for her hand.

"What do you want to say, Rowan? We've never

really made the time to talk, just the two of us, and we've always skirted around what happened in Canada, touching upon it here and there before escaping to our respective corners. We've let fear of what might be said prevent us from saying what *has* to be said, so we can be at peace, both of us. And I know only too well how time can cast a sort of skin over an event—a membrane that gets thicker until a point where broaching the subject is all but impossible, even when you think you can face the grief and terror once more. I did the same thing—years ago, with Simon. Remember?" Maisie looked down at Lady Rowan's hand, clasped in her own—at the deep brown liver spots, and the arthritic thumb and forefinger. It was a hand that revealed a life lived to the full. "I loved James for who he was, and he loved me for who I was. His death caused me to lose myself for a while—for years, really—you know that. But I am back. I am whole. And you do not need to make your confession to me, but I will hear it all the same. Your son loved his life, Rowan. He loved the man he became, and the man he was on the day he died."

"But he was . . . . a bloody fool." The older woman pressed her lips together, and looked away. "That was bad language, but I am so very angry with my own son and I've kept it bottled up because it's so . . . so hard to say that about someone I loved so much but am so very . . . so very . . . disappointed in. I can't stand myself for the thoughts that go through my head sometimes, and when you were away for all that time, all I could think of was, 'James did that—she lost him and her child and it's all his fault.' And if it was his fault, then it was my fault too, because I'm his mother. I couldn't talk to Julian about it, because the man is crushed anyway—there have been times when it has taken every fiber of our strength together to go from one day to the next, though it's become easier. But if I had the chance to do so, I would take my son and box his ears."

Maisie shook her head. "Oh, Rowan. James drew joy from the mystery of what each day might hold—he had come back from the dreadful years immediately after the war, and those years tormented him. That's all we should remember—that he loved his life, that he died as a man who was loved, a man filled with the promise of fatherhood and of being involved in something so important to our country. It's something we should hold in our hearts, Rowan."

Lady Rowan shook her head. "I wish I could be so forgiving."

Maisie sighed. "What might Maurice say to you, if he were here?"

Lady Rowan shifted her seat, though she allowed Maisie to continue stroking her hand. "I wish I knew," she said, then changed her tone. "Though I will add that he wasn't always right, you know."

"And there you have one thing he might have said." Maisie smiled. "He would have reminded you that we don't always make the very best decisions. That is who we are—not perfect. Yet with our imperfections we are perfect human beings; that is who we are meant to be. James died doing something he loved, and we all adored him for his passion. He chose to be an aviator, and he chose to test a new fighter aircraft for the government—it was a fateful day and it changed all our lives. Yet it serves no one to go back and forth trying to apportion blame. Forgive yourself, Rowan. Forgive yourself and set yourself free of this blame, of regret."

"But you lost—"

Maisie shook her head and released Lady Rowan's hand, patting it as she did so.

"I am here today." She reached for the ignition and started the engine again. "In Spain I was reminded of all the losses people endure. Tragedy is so personal, but it doesn't mean it hasn't happened before, to someone, somewhere—it's what helps us to understand and bring solace to others, knowing something of what they feel. And look at the family I have now—you, Lord Julian, my father and Brenda, and Priscilla, Douglas and the boys."

"And Anna," said Lady Rowan.

Maisie felt the piercing blue eyes upon her, and another unspoken question hanging in the air. She slipped the motor car into gear. "Yes, and Anna."

The long snaking line of people waiting to enter Westminster Abbey almost took Maisie's breath away. Unable to park near the abbey, she pulled in as close as she could to the gates to allow Rowan to step out of the Alvis. She then drove off to look for a suitable place to leave the motor car, which she found just off Great Smith Street. She ran back to the abbey to rejoin Lady Rowan, who informed her that because she "knew people" there were already places kept for them, so they wouldn't have to stand. But as she was about to follow her mother-in-law into the abbey, she had second thoughts.

"Rowan—I'm going to join the queue. I want to stand with the crowd. You should sit down as soon as you can—keep a seat for me, and I'll find you."

Lady Rowan looked at the growing line of people—there must have been thousands of men, women and children—and nodded. "The king said it should be a National Day of Prayer, that we should come together,

as a people, to pray to be delivered from the approaching tyranny." She cast her gaze back to Maisie. "Yes,
join the throng, Maisie—if my hip were not nipping at
me, I would too. But it's one of those days when I must
give thanks for the privilege of good connections and a
reserved seat. I'll see you inside."

As she was moving to the end of the line, Maisie
heard a voice call out.

"Oi, Miss! Oi, Miss—it's us over here. Come on."
She looked into the line of people, and saw Billy, Doreen and Margaret Rose, all waving to her.

"You don't mind if the lady joins us, do you, mate?"
Billy turned to a man and his wife standing behind
them.

"All right by me." The man stepped back. "Come
on, slip in here, love."

"Thank you, sir—I am much obliged to you." She
turned to Billy and Doreen. "It's lovely to see you
here—all three of you." She put a hand on Doreen's
arm to emphasize her greeting, and smiled down at
their daughter. "Hello Margaret Rose—oh my goodness, you've grown. You'll be as tall as Bobby soon."

The child looked down at her feet, and ran her
fingers through the halo of blond curls that fell across
her forehead, a mannerism that made her appear even

more like her father. And when she raised her head, her cornflower blue eyes staring at Maisie, she said, "Mum and Dad told me we had to come, because even if you didn't believe in God, you had to give him a chance when things get very difficult. And everybody has to pull together."

"Quite right," said the man who had allowed Maisie to slide into the queue, as Margaret Rose hid her face in her mother's skirts.

"From the mouths of babes," said a woman in front of them.

There was little time for a long conversation with Billy, but there was an opportunity for a brief chat. "Is Bobby at home?" asked Maisie.

Billy sighed, and exchanged glances with his wife. "Yep, he's at home. And that's where he'll stay if I've got anything to do with it."

"Billy—he only—" said Doreen.

Billy shook his head. "Nothing like having a sixteen-year-old know-all in the house, is there? He's gone and signed up to be a mechanic for the air force. Says it's not dangerous, that he'll be working on the aeroplanes, not in them. Well, that's all very well, but they could just as well send him up, in time."

Doreen looked at Maisie and raised her eyebrows.

Maisie realized, then, that the woman who had previously suffered such debilitating mental illness was now calm, and was likely the one keeping a level head.

"What do you think, Doreen?"

The woman linked her arm through her husband's, as if to chivvy him into a better mood. "We've got young Billy over there in France, so it's easy to think Bobby should wait, just a bit, before he goes in for anything to do with the army or air force or whatever. But one thing occurred to me—because we always call them 'young Billy' or 'young Bobby' it's too easy to forget they're men. They know what they want, and I don't think we should hold Bobby back. Not if this is what he's got a knack for—we can't expect him to want to work in that garage down the road forever, can we? And it's a good opportunity for him to get a proper profession with real prospects, isn't it?"

"It's a difficult situation, especially as Bobby needs your consent," said Maisie, drawing her attention from Doreen to Billy. "I know he's named after your brother, and you thought the world of him."

"Two peas in a pod, me and our Bobby," said Billy.

Maisie watched as Doreen bit her lip and turned away, then at once swung round again, her cheeks flushed. "And you haven't forgiven the fact that he died too young fighting over there, have you? But your son—

our son—is not your brother. The way I see it, you have a choice. You can either acknowledge him and the fact that this is what he wants. It's something he has a talent for, and he landed this opportunity with no help from anyone—and that's no mean feat, Billy. No mean feat on the part of our Bobby. Or you can withhold consent, which means you can do something you were powerless to do with your brother, his namesake—and that is to stop him." She had kept her voice low, but every word carried the weight of her frustration with her husband. "The truth is you could never have stopped your brother, because he knew what he wanted, and he wanted to prove himself to be a man worthy of his country's respect. Bobby is old enough to go to this air force college, to learn a new trade and then to take up a new job. And if you're trying to save him, my love— just you remember how Sandra's Eric died. Poor girl lost her first husband when he was working on an engine in a small garage. There's no accounting for fate's timing. No accounting at all."

Billy was silent, staring at his wife. "I'd forgotten about Eric," said Billy, distracted.

Maisie stepped forward as the queue moved. She made no comment that might come between man and wife. They had almost reached the entrance to Westminster Abbey when she heard Billy break the silence with Doreen. "Anyway, I'll think about it." She looked around at the same time as Doreen leaned toward Billy for him to put his arm around her shoulders.

"Right," said Maisie. "We're almost at the door. I have to go in that direction now—Lady Rowan has saved a seat for me. I'll see you tomorrow, Billy. In fact, I can take you all down to Hampshire, because that's where I'm planning to go."

"Oh, Margaret Rose and I are staying—we're not going to the country," said Doreen.

"And that's another nice bag of worms opened up, just as we're about to go into a church!" said Billy. "Mind you, if there's an invasion, it might be better for my girls to be closer to London."

Maisie looked from one to the other. "Well, the offer's there—I can take you all, if you wish. Anyway, Billy, we must speak tomorrow morning at the office in any case. About Archie Coombes."

"Oh yes, Archie Coombes. He's a different kettle of fish, no two ways about it. I've a few things to report on that young man."

Maisie opened the French doors that led into the walled garden from the sitting room, and went into the kitchen to put away the few grocery items she had brought back from Chelstone. She placed a bottle of milk in her new refrigerator, a half loaf into an enamel bread bin on the table, and poured a quarter pound of Brooke Bond tea into the caddy. Slipping off her pale blue summer jacket, she hung it over the back of the chair, filled the kettle with water and put it on the stove. Standing by the stove, staring at the flame licking up around the kettle, Maisie began to formulate a plan for the following day. Teddy Wickham—she wanted to talk to the young man who had decreed that Joe Coombes was on "top form." And she wanted to see the place where the lad's body had been found—there had been no time to pay a visit when she had been brought to Hampshire to identify the body. She would have to speak to Detective Inspector Murphy to gain access to the area, but she had found him to be an approachable man, so did not envisage a problem with her request.

She made a pot of tea, poured a cup and set it on a small wooden tray along with a slice of bread and jam she had prepared while waiting for the kettle to boil, then went into the garden, switching on the wireless as she passed.

Maisie had become quite used to the barrage balloons bobbing in breezes high above, as if London had been prepared for a party, not a war. But the balloons were there to deflect an attack by enemy aircraft, not to entertain. Men and women in the anti-aircraft batteries would be scanning the skies, alert for radio messages signaling imminent attack. She had almost forgotten how it might be to see the underground stations without sandbagging to protect them. And as far as keeping her gas mask with her—like many of the capital's populace, she could not quite remember where she had last put it, and made a mental note to look in the dining room cabinet.

The drive from Chelstone, the service at the abbey, along with the bobbing barrage balloons, seemed to have a soporific effect. It was from a dozy afternoon slumber that Maisie was woken by the telephone. She was rising from the chair when it stopped, so she sat down again, thinking it could not have been very important. A chill in the air wrapped itself around her arms, and she was aware that an announcement had interrupted music on the wireless, which had been beset by poor reception.

"... *owners of pleasure craft, able-bodied men with an understanding of navigation and offshore boating experience are asked to report to their local police station . . . those approved will . . . from Ramsgate . . . to France.*"

The announcer added that the same message had been broadcast several times that day. She shivered and looked at her watch as the wireless crackled and music continued; it was almost six o'clock in the evening. She had just picked up the tray when the telephone began ringing again, but this time she moved quickly to pick up the call. She was about to recite the number when she heard her stepmother's voice.

"Maisie, is that you?"

"Yes—Brenda? Brenda, what is it? Is it Anna? Dad? Is everyone all right?"

"Yes, yes—your father's well and Anna's all right too. It's Tim."

"Tim? What's happened?"

"He's not come home?"

"Brenda, what do you mean, he's not come home? Where did he go?"

"It was after you left this morning—he came in from the conservatory just as you drove out of the gates, so must have been about seven. He said that he was going off to see a friend of his who lives in Rye. I think it was Rye. Or perhaps he said he was meeting him in Rye. Oh dear . . ." Brenda's voice became faint, as if she were trying to remember exact details of the conversation. "Anyway, he said they were going hiking across the Romney Marshes. I asked him how he was going to get there, and he said it was all right, he'd looked up the trains and he would get a bus part of the way, if necessary. I told him I thought he should let his mother know, but he just said, 'Oh, it's all right, Mrs. Dobbs—she knows I'm going to see Gordon.' He was in such a rush to get on his way, it was all I could do to make him wait while I packed up a sandwich box for him, and made him take a bottle of ginger beer. If he's doing all that walking, he would need something inside him, growing lad like that."

"Priscilla didn't tell me anything about Tim going to see his friend Gordon while he was with us," said Maisie. "And neither, for that matter, did Tim."

"That's as may be, but he's gone, and I told him quite clearly that he had to be back by four o'clock, or it wasn't fair to you, as you're responsible for him." She sighed—but Maisie could hear it was an angry sigh, a sigh of frustration. "I don't think he liked it—being told that, but he said he would be back on the train that gets into Tonbridge at twenty past three, so he would be back at Chelstone in good time. He left about half past seven, marching off with his knapsack. And he's not back."

Maisie laced the telephone cable around her fingers. Tim had been pushing against boundaries for a while, but he had never crossed a line with her. Yet she knew he had been shocked at seeing young men not so much older than him coming back from France. And Tim was a bright lad—he would have taken account of the steady escalation of news regarding the German advance and the precarious position of the army. A deep collective sense of emergency was being felt by the British people; the plight of "our boys" was a national tragedy in the making—the news reports were full of it. And Tim could have overheard his father discussing the situation; after all, in his position with the Ministry of Information, Douglas was privy to reports from military intelligence.

"Brenda—did Tim make any telephone calls that I don't know about? He's usually very polite and will ask permission even to place a call to his mother."

"Not as far as I know, but—"

"But what?"

"Well, it was when you were tucking in Anna last night and reading her a story—before you sat down to a late supper with Tim. You were in with her or a while, because you were putting calamine on her spots, and bathing her eyes—those poor eyes, so sticky with this measles—and Tim said he was just going out for a walk across the field. He took Jook with him. Now, you know as well as I do, that when you go over the stile at the other end of Top Field, you're at the crossroads, and there's the telephone kiosk, right next to the bus stop."

"The bus that goes to Tenterden, where you can change for Rye."

"Oh dear," said Brenda. "Where do you think he's gone?"

Maisie felt her heart beating almost to her neck. "It's what he's done as much as where he's gone."

"But where? He's only a lad," said Brenda.

"Now, you mustn't worry, Brenda. I'll get him back—I think I know where he is. You look after Anna for me—and tell her Tim will be home soon."

"Your voice, Maisie—I can hear it—you're frightened."

"It's all right, Brenda—we'll find him, one way or another. Now, I must go. I must speak to his mother."

Maisie, what joy—you're back! Of course I knew because—" Priscilla was holding a cocktail in one hand as she opened the front door. "What is it? What's wrong?"

"Let's go in, Priscilla—is Douglas at home?"

"It's Sunday evening—where else would he be but his study?"

"Call him, Priscilla, please."

Priscilla ran to the bottom of the staircase and called out, "Douglas! Douglas? Come down—now. It's important."

Maisie heard a door open close to the stairs on the first floor, and Douglas Partridge looked over the banister.

"Maisie, lovely to see you—but what's going on?"

"I must speak to you about Tim," said Maisie.

In the hall, Maisie recounted Brenda's concerns that Tim had not arrived home on time.

"Oh, that's all right, I'm sure he'll turn up soon," interrupted Douglas.

Priscilla shook her head. "Go on, Maisie—I can tell you're worried for good reason. Where do you think he is?"

"With his friend Gordon."

Priscilla was about to counter, but Douglas interjected. "I know what Maisie's thinking. Yes, they live in Rye—and yes, they have several boats—as far as I know a rowing boat, one of those slipper boats, a sailing yacht and a motor launch of some kind. Perhaps two. Not sure if they keep them all in Rye though—I mean, the man has a veritable fleet." He turned to Priscilla. "Hasn't Tim sailed out of Broadstairs with them? Gordon has older brothers, all in the services now, I believe—and the father has a lot of money to spend on his passion, which is the sea."

Priscilla looked at Maisie. "Tell me, Maisie. Where is he?"

"I don't know if you've heard the news—I only heard part of the broadcast because my wireless has such bad reception—but there was an announcement, a call for owners of pleasure craft who have boating experience. I don't know, but following the news lately, I think it's to assist in the evacuation of the expeditionary force from France. I imagine it's turned into an all-out push now." She paused, biting her lip, looking from Douglas to Priscilla. "I doubt just anyone can take a boat and go—the authorities wouldn't allow it, but . . . but putting two and two together, I think Tim and his friend might have sailed out to find a way to join the flotilla gathering in the Channel. I know very little about this, but . . . but Tim is so desperate to prove himself, he would not think twice about it. And if Gordon's brothers are all in the services, I'd bet he's of the same mind."

Priscilla turned to her husband. "Do we have the telephone number for this boy's parents? He's been down there loads of times—I am sure we've spoken to his people. In fact, I had a word with his mother ages ago, when Tim started visiting. I'll find it."

Priscilla pulled open a drawer in the hall table. She pulled out an address book with gold leaf-edged pages and a burgundy leather cover. It was well worn, and when opened, Maisie could see names and addresses crossed out and rewritten.

"Here it is. The Sandersons. The mother's name is Beatrice—that's it, Bea Sanderson." She reached for the telephone receiver and dialed, turning to look at

Douglas and Maisie as she waited for the call to be answered. She picked up her almost empty glass and held it out toward Douglas. Her husband took the glass, but did not move. She raised her eyebrows, pursed her lips and turned away. The call was answered. "Ah yes, good evening. Yes—is Mrs. Sanderson at home? This is Mrs. Priscilla Partridge—yes, with a *P*, like the bird. *P-A-R-T*—that's it, you've got it. May I speak to Mrs. Sanderson, please?" A pause. "Not at home? When might she and Mr. Sanderson return?" Another pause. "Not until tomorrow? I see. Did Gordon go with them or is he at home?" She looked at Maisie, her eyes wide, color draining from her face. "Yes. Quite. Well, if you've put two and two together, you will understand that Tim Partridge is my son, and Gordon is most certainly not a guest in my house." She turned away again, facing the mirror.

Maisie thought that, in regarding her reflection, Priscilla was keeping her spirit present, keeping her resolve rock solid, so that she would not escape into herself as wave after wave of fear enveloped her.

Priscilla continued. "You must find Mr. and Mrs. Sanderson soonest. I fear both Gordon and Timothy have told lies to be able to do something together—no, I cannot say what that something is before I speak to his parents. And you can't let me have a number for them? Right. If I do not receive a return call within the half-hour, I will not be here to speak to them." She turned to her husband, anger and terror mapped across her face, now flushed. She pointed to the empty glass while continuing to speak to the person on the other end of the line. "Please tell them that the boys have embarked upon a rather dangerous adventure. Here's my number."

Maisie turned to Douglas. "I think you ought to get her that gin and tonic, Douglas—she is about to start shouting, then she'll break down."

Priscilla slammed down the telephone receiver just as Douglas began walking toward the drawing room.

"Can't he bloody see that when I say I need a drink, I need one! My son has gone off on a boat in the middle of the bloody Channel when, for all I know, his brother is in a piece of tin over his head taking his life in his hands trying to stop the German army—"

"Pris—Priscilla! Stop!" said Maisie, standing in front of her friend. "Stop this right now—we have to think clearly, and Douglas had every right to listen to the call because Tim's his son too—not just yours."

"But what can I do? How can we stop him?" She began to cough, tears streaming down her face, her eye makeup running across her cheeks. "It's happening again. My history is repeating itself—I'll lose them like

I lost my brothers in the last war, all three of them. Dead. Where's Tarquin." She turned to call up the stairs. "Tarq! Tarquin! Come down now!"

Douglas emerged from the drawing room, a full glass of gin and tonic in his hand. Priscilla's husband had lost an arm during the last war, and walked with a pronounced limp. He struggled to manage his cane and Priscilla's drink—but his voice was strong.

"Stop! For God's sake stop and think, darling! Tarquin is not at home. If you remember, Elinor was here and has taken him out—they're not due back yet. You can leave a note for them. Now then, first we should find out if we're completely wrong and Tim has just gone for a sail, or if he's really made for the French coast. Indeed, he could still be hiking across Romney Marsh."

"Well, of course he's gone to France, Douglas—of course he has," said Priscilla.

"Maisie?" said Douglas, as he handed the fresh cocktail to his wife.

"I'm inclined to agree with Pris." She sighed. "I know very little about nautical maps, but I have an ordinary map, one that includes the coast. I've had a look at it, and I suspect that, if Tim and his friend have indeed answered the call for seagoing craft, they would not have joined the flotilla in Ramsgate—I am sure the authorities have carefully registered boats they wanted to requisition. I imagine Tim and Gordon would have made their way out into the Channel and slipped in with other vessels."

"Oh hell! I don't know where to go, or what to do! But I know I can't stay here and just worry until he walks through the door—or until there's a policeman on the doorstep telling me he has bad news," said Priscilla, her free hand on her forehead, as she lifted the glass to her lips and took several generous sips.

"There's little you can do, Pris—but if you must be on the move, perhaps you and Douglas should go down to Ramsgate, and ask questions—someone might have seen them. And if they come in, you can stop them."

Douglas cleared his throat. "Maisie—you go with Priscilla. I will hold you up if I go."

Maisie watched as Douglas looked away in an attempt to control his emotions. She turned to Priscilla, who was staring at her husband, her own eyes filled with tears.

"I think you should discuss the situation," said Maisie. "You might hear from the Sandersons soon in any case—and all the worry might be for naught. If it is, then it's my fault, for which I am incredibly sorry—but I listened to Tim when he arrived at Chelstone yesterday, and he was full of what he had seen at Tonbridge station, as early evacuees from France were traveling through. In any case, I'll go and make ready to leave."

Maisie turned away, though as she reached the threshold she looked back to see Priscilla take her husband's outstretched hand.

"Oh Tim, you young fool," she whispered as she ran down the steps.

Fifteen minutes later, Maisie had counted her petrol coupons and gave thanks that she had enough fuel in the tank to get to Ramsgate, though not enough for the return journey—and there was likely no petrol to be had on a Sunday. As she was loading a small overnight bag into the Alvis, Priscilla came running toward her along the street.

"Bea Sanderson telephoned. They've been in Reigate with friends for a Friday to Monday, but they're on their way back now. They've checked with a friend who lives close to where their boats are docked, or kept, or slipped—or whatever it is they do with boats—and yes, it transpires that Gordon and a friend who happens to fit Tim's description went out for a sail early this morning and have not come back. But here's the thing—they took the larger of Jerry Sanderson's boats, the one that Gordon is not allowed to take out. Apparently Gordon and Tim usually go out in the smaller sailing yacht, but this is the larger motor yacht. He assures me that the boys are quite capable of taking her into the open Channel, but she's forty-five feet, and worth a fortune. He seemed more worried about the yacht, though Bea is beside herself—like me."

"Priscilla—I think you and Douglas should go to Ramsgate. He shouldn't be left here to feel he's not playing a part while his son has put himself in the path of danger. You must be together."

"But Douglas doesn't drive, and if I get behind the wheel, I know I will kill us."

Maisie shook her head and took a moment, stopping Priscilla from speaking by holding up a hand. "I have another idea. Though Billy doesn't have a motor car, I know he can drive now, because he's had a friend teach him. I'll see if he'll take you—in fact, I think he'll jump at the chance because his son is with the expeditionary force and he will want to keep himself occupied, doing something useful. I'll telephone him now."

Priscilla nodded. "Right—and if he agrees, I can at least get us to his home in Eltham to pick him up without causing too much damage." She turned to walk away, but stopped and looked back at Maisie. "And at least we'll be doing something, not just sitting around waiting."

Chapter 10

O f course I can drive them to Ramsgate—I've been thinking of going down there anyway, to keep an eye out for our Billy. Fool's errand really—I don't stand a chance of seeing him. It'll be like a three-ring circus, and they say not many are getting away, not set against the number over there. But at least I'd feel I was a bit closer. Mind you, I've got to tell you, miss, I've only been behind the wheel of my mate's little Austin, and Mrs. Partridge drives one of them really big old continental motors doesn't she? Got the steering wheel on the wrong side, hasn't it? Isn't it a Bugatti, or a Lagonda, something like that? You could probably get our entire front room in the back seat of her motor."

"She has a new Bentley, and the steering wheel is on the right side. But don't worry—she collides with something every day, so I am sure there are dents all over the coachwork. This is very good of you, Billy."

"Nah, all part of the job—and a Bentley, well, I'll never get that chance again, will I? Truth is, they must be worried sick—young Tim should have a hiding for his trouble, no two ways about it. These boys are all losing their minds."

Maisie delivered the news to Priscilla, that they should depart now to meet Billy at his home, then placed another call to Billy.

"Right you are, miss," said Billy. "I'll be waiting for them, a bag packed just in case."

"Before you go, Billy—tell me about Archie Coombes."

"Blimey, nearly forgot, what with all the worry going on. And I've been dying to tell you about him."

"Go on," said Maisie, picking up a notebook and pencil.

"He's a fitter at an engineering works in Sydenham, and has lodgings over a shop in Camberwell. One bus ride and he's at his job, though I think he's got a bike. I had a talk with him while he was on a morning break, standing outside having a smoke. It's been a while since I saw him, but he's the dead spitting image of his father, so it's not as if I had to look hard. He seemed a bit shaky, but that's to be expected, and I saw a couple of blokes walk past, stop and talk, put a hand on his shoulder, then move along to light up. Having worked with you for a few year now, I reckon it was the way he was standing—it told people he didn't want company."

"Yes, I can imagine that," said Maisie.

"Anyway, I went over, introduced myself. He throws down the ciggie, holds out his hand and thanks me for looking after his mum and dad. Then he took out a packet of ciggies again, and lit up. That was my first little niggle about him."

"Go on," said Maisie.

"He threw down a half-smoked cigarette end that still had a lot of tobacco in it, and he was not smoking cheap Woodbines sold by the ones and twos either—he had a packet of twenty." Billy cleared his throat. Maisie heard a page being turned, and knew Billy was referring to his notes. "I asked him about Joe, about his work down there in Hampshire, and if he'd been down to see him. He said no, he didn't know much about the work—he hadn't actually seen Joe for a while. And he didn't know the area. I asked him about Teddy Wickham, and he said he didn't know where he was stationed, exactly, but he knew he'd looked in on Joe and he'd said his brother seemed on top form."

"And how did he know all this—did Teddy come back on leave?"

"Yes, that's it exactly. He had a forty-eight-hour pass a few weeks ago. And he gets on the blower, apparently."

"To whom? At the pub? How does Archie take the telephone call?"

"I'm almost there." The rustle of another page turning, and then flipping back echoed as if there were interference on the line. "He didn't have much to tell me, and he was getting choked up. He said he has a telephone at his digs, because he's a supervisor and can be on call at any time. I tell you, miss, I don't believe that for a start. I know men who are supervisors in factories, and they don't all get a free dog and bone! Anyway, the horn went for the men to go back inside the works, and he had to go—pinched out another hardly smoked ciggie, threw it down and went back inside."

"But you saw him again, didn't you?" said Maisie.

"Followed him back to his lodgings, nice and easy, so he couldn't see me. Saw him go in, then come out half an hour later dressed like two penn'orth of hambone done up for the butcher's window. Good suit—well, a fifty-bob Burton's special. He looked a bit flash, if you ask me—reckon he's seen too many of those American pictures. Had shoes on you could see your face in. He waited on the street, and then along comes a motor car. Black with green down the sides, you know, the doors. Newish, I would say, with a driver in the front and someone else in the back—I could see him moving forward to open the door. Then Archie got in, and off they went."

"Do you know the make of motor?"

"It looked like a Rover Ten—a coupe, I reckon, because the fellow in the back had to push the front passenger seat for Archie to get in with him. I reckon it was the same one that was parked across the street from the office—the driver must have gone straight over there to Archie's job."

"So Archie Coombes has a bit more money than we thought he might," said Maisie. "Or at least he has friends who have money. Did you manage to look at the lodgings, by any chance?"

"I went across and knocked on the door. Nicely turned out woman comes to answer, and says I'd just missed him. I did my best forlorn look, you know, the one I put on to get round someone, and I said I wanted to leave a message for him. I pulled out my notebook and began scribbling—you know, blah-blah-blah-blah—and asked if I could put it in his room. She looked suspicious, but I said it was private, and she said she would take me up there so I could just slip it on the table. The table? Lodgings only usually come with a rotten old cast iron bed with a horsehair mattress and a couple of blankets, p'rhaps a washstand if you're lucky. So she took me up there, opened the door and there before me is a very nice gaff indeed—two rooms, one a sitting room and one a bedroom as far as I could see. 'He had his own furniture put in here,' said this landlady, all proud of the room. 'He says that when he gets his house, he'll leave it here for me.'"

"When he gets his house?" said Maisie.

"That's what I thought. Doing very well, for a lad of—what?—twenty, is he?"

"Let's not jump to conclusions—he could just be very careful with his money."

"Not buying new suits, he isn't!"

"The motor car outside—what was the driver like? Did you get a look at him?"

"Older than Archie. I'd say he was in his thirties, or even forties, but you can never be sure, not from a distance, and I didn't want to stare and draw attention. I was taking enough of a risk as it was."

"Yes, you were," replied Maisie, remembering a time when Billy was beaten up by a suspect in a case, and left for dead—she had told him then, that under no circumstances must he ever put his life in danger ever again. No job was worth his life. "It's unusual, and added to your observations about the Coombes family, it seems there are some significant contradictions."

"I'll say there are," interjected Billy.

"On the one hand they are very tight," continued Maisie. "They appear a very loving family, very honorable in fact. But these little things come to the surface—flashes of expenditure on items that would otherwise seem to be out of the budget of a family in their position, and then some discord in the home."

"So where's the money coming from?"

"I think we have to be very careful about following that particular stream—at least until we have more of an idea as to where it might lead. I'll pop in to talk to Phil and Sally again, and I'll see what I can do about finding Teddy Wickham. And I think I want to see Archie myself."

"Are you going down to Hampshire?"

"Yes, but I might wait until I hear back from you or Priscilla."

A silence descended on the conversation. It was broken by Billy.

"You think going down to Ramsgate is a fool's errand, don't you, miss?"

"I confess, it was my suggestion. And I certainly think you're right about it being chaotic there. But I know Priscilla, and I know she has to feel as if she has some control over the matter, so going to Ramsgate and being there when boats come in will keep her from losing her mind completely."

"There's talk that this evacuation could go on for days. She won't see him until the end, will she? Because what a lot of these little boats are doing is going in there, picking up men who're waiting, then taking them to the bigger ships, the ones that can't get in because of what they draw—it's too shallow."

"You're sounding like a sailor, Billy," said Maisie.

"My boy's over there, so I've been reading up on it, this business of ships and where they can dock. And I've been listening to the wireless. They don't say everything, sort of let out the news bit by bit."

"That's what Douglas said. Apparently it's being orchestrated by a man named Duff Cooper. So people are informed, but not enough to cause panic—he told Douglas that it's no good trying to pull the wool over the eyes of the British people, because they know very well when the language used in newsreels is designed to manipulate them."

"That didn't work, did it—your friend is panicking for all of us."

"I know—but most people are calm, getting on with their lives."

"Miss, you think the world of Tim. You must be worried sick."

"I am, Billy—really worried. And I'm not sure Ramsgate is the place to wait. When they come back toward the coast, I have a feeling they might make their way to Rye. They'll take their usual route, because they will want to get home—and they'll want to get home because they will have seen things they might never have imagined even in their worst nightmares."

Maisie considered her plans for the following day. Phil and Sally Coombes, Mike Yates and Archie Coombes were all on the list. And Vivian. Vivian Coombes was an interesting study, thought Maisie, not least because it was fair to assume she wanted to do what both her brothers had done quite successfully—get out from under their parents' roof.

When a telephone call came later, it was Priscilla reporting to say they had reached Ramsgate and could find out nothing.

"Maisie, I never thought I would see this sort of thing again, really I—oh hell, the pips are going . . . Douglas . . . Douglas, give me some more change. Right—" There was a brief pause as Priscilla put more coins in the slot. "It—it's taken me back, Maisie—I feel as if I've been swept into France in 1916. I remember driving back toward a casualty clearing station in my ambulance—I was so new, it was only my second or third run—and I passed a line of men walking the other way, young men who'd been in the trenches, filthy and sodden with mud, a good number wounded. It's like looking at that all over again—" The line crackled, and Priscilla's voice was clear again. "Anyway . . . anyway . . . we've spoken to some officials—well, they looked official. And no one has a record of this boat they've gone out on—*Cassandra* is her name. Well, they wouldn't, would they? The boys joined unofficially, and no one was going to turn them back because everyone was so determined to get on themselves." There was a gasp on the line, followed by a crackling silence.

"Priscilla! Pris! What's wrong?"

"There's a long line of men disembarking one of the boats, and they're walking toward the station for trains to take them back into London—it's a never-ending snake of soldiers. Billy and Douglas were waiting outside for me and—I can't quite see what's happened, but Billy just ran off. I've never seen him move so fast. I can't quite see. Oh dear, he's almost fallen—it's his weak leg, he shouldn't try to run like that." Another break in the telephone line, which Maisie recognized as the pips sounding for more money. "I think I've almost run out of coins here, Maisie," continued Priscilla. "I can't say, but . . . but I think Billy has seen his son. Gosh, I hope he's not mistaken—it would be so easy. Douglas is walking down there now. Hang on, let me open the door to get a better look." There was a pause. Maisie heard voices in the background, the muffled sounds of people moving along outside the kiosk. Priscilla came back on the line. "Oh my goodness, oh my goodness—" She wept into the telephone. "It is. It's his son—he's found his son."

And as the line disconnected, Maisie replaced the receiver, brought her hands to her face, and wept as well—for Billy, for Priscilla and Douglas, and what they already knew of war. She wept too for Phil and Sally Coombes—for whatever had come to pass in the family, they had still lost a beloved son.

Mike Yates was in his office on the first floor of the old warehouse building, overlooking the brickyard where two vans were parked and men were loading tools and materials. One of the decorators loading a van directed Maisie up to the office, which was reached via a wooden exterior staircase and through a partially ajar door. A young woman was seated at a desk piled with papers and a ledger, and was typing a letter. Maisie saw the man she assumed was Mike Yates, standing at another desk in a small office that lay beyond a wood partition with pebbled glass windows. The typist did not look up until Maisie cleared her throat.

"He's through there, if you want him," said the woman.

"Oh. All right. Then I can just go in?"

"Door's open—anyone can go in. Never disturb him if that door's closed though, not if you don't want your head blown off."

"Really?" said Maisie.

"Yes, really—he's a nasty man. I'm off to join the ATS next week, and I would rather put up with that than him. Monster. Blimmin' monster. If he has a go at me this week, I'll just down tools and leave him to it. Him and his blimmin' accounts."

"Right then. I'd better brace myself and go in." Maisie stepped toward the open door, but turned to the young woman. "What's your name, if I may ask?"

"Charlotte Bright."

"Does he let you out for five minutes in the morning?"

"He does this week—can't stop me."

"If he doesn't tell me to leave straightaway, could you meet me—perhaps downstairs or along the street, a few minutes after I leave?"

Bright looked up from her typewriter. "Go on—tell me what he's done, miserable sod. I bet he's done something—did you just find out he's married? Told you lies, did he?"

"No, not quite. I'm a friend of Joe Coombes' family, and—"

The girl's eyes filled with tears. "Oh poor Joe. We all thought a lot of Joe—he was lovely. Not like some of them, when they come up to get their wages. Anyone would think I was only here for them to make fun of, and they all think they're so comical with their jokes everyone's heard before."

"I'd better go in," said Maisie.

She approached the door to Mike Yates' office and knocked on the glass. "Good morning—Mr. Yates?"

"And who's wanting him?" said Yates, looking up from a stack of papers on his desk.

"My name is Maisie Dobbs," said Maisie, deciding to give him her full affiliation. "I am a psychologist and investigator, and I am also a friend of Mr. and Mrs. Philip Coombes, the parents of Joseph Coombes, now deceased, but latterly in your employ."

Yates' nut-brown eyes met Maisie's. He took a pencil from behind his ear, as if he were about to make a note on the top sheet of paper in front of him, but thought better of it and instead tapped the pencil against the fingers of the opposite hand. "Yeah, I'd heard someone had been round to talk about Joe—bloke with a limp. Know him?"

"Yes, that's Mr. Beale. He works for me."

"Works for you? Well, well, well—man working for a woman. New one on me. Take a seat, Miss Dobbs—you can ask me all the questions you want to ask about Joe. Silly boy, skylarking around near a railway line, not able to hold his drink and standing on top of a wall like that." He shook his head. "If he'd just had a bit of brain in his noddle, he would have seen that coming."

"How did you find out how Joe died?"

"Freddie Mayes telephoned in—he'd found out from the police, then they came here."

"I see." Maisie sighed. "I wonder, Mr. Yates, what evidence do you have that Joe had been drinking?"

"Freddie told me—I had to ask him and Len, on account of the accident, and of course the police have been around. Said it was open and shut—death by misadventure and all that. But still, I'll be going to see the family—probably tomorrow. Wanted to give them a bit more chance to get over the shock before I turned up. I've got Joe's last pay packet, and a bit extra as a consideration for the family, to see them all right. Mind you, that's if Dopey out there can pull herself together to get it all ready for me." He looked past Maisie to Charlotte Bright, and then back again. "Auxiliary Territorial Service? That one? They'll chuck her out after a week of her painting her nails in the dark when she's supposed to be operating a searchlight—you mark my words."

Maisie thought it best to ignore the comment. "It's very good of you to visit Joe's people, to help them out. They'll need it for the funeral."

"Not many firms would do it, but we like to take care of our own here at Yates. Now then, what can I do for you?"

"Mr. Yates, I am curious to know if Joe was the only one of your men to experience headaches and other symptoms, likely associated with the emulsion they've been using—the fire retardant, and—"

"How do you know about all that?" asked Yates.

Maisie gave a half-smile. "I think it's fairly common knowledge that your crews who are currently in Hampshire were working with a type of paint that prevents fire when air force buildings are under attack from the enemy."

Yates shook his head. "Not one of them can keep a thing to themselves, that lot."

"Were they supposed to?"

"Were they heck? I told every one of them—if any-one asks, you're just giving the buildings a lick of paint. Making everything nice for when old Adolf waltzes right in."

Maisie sighed, wondering how she might continue the conversation and perhaps tease more information out of Yates. "You can't stop lads talking about their work or anything else when they're away from home." She held Yates' gaze. "Do you know what's in that emulsion, Mr. Yates? Do you know if it's been tested properly?"

Mike Yates walked away from his desk toward a window. He stared down at the yard below, and after a minute had passed—an uncomfortable interlude dur-ing which Maisie thought she should have perhaps not pressed her point—Yates turned back to answer the question.

"I don't know if it's been tested at all. I was asked about the job, and I got it. You don't turn down a gov-ernment contract like that, and I know my blokes would agree—they've all got to put roofs over their heads and food on the table. If they get a headache, they can take an aspirin powder for their trouble."

"So the contract just came to you, you didn't have to bid for it."

"Sometimes it works like that. Sometimes you bid against other firms, and sometimes you're just asked to give an estimate and you're in. That was how this one was done—I was in."

"You must know some important people, Mr. Yates."

Yates' eyes appeared to narrow, as if the aperture through which he viewed her had been altered. "What's it to you, Miss Dobbs?"

Maisie leaned forward, not allowing herself to be intimidated by Yates, and this time casting several more cards on the table. "Here's what it is to me, Mr. Yates. Joe Coombes was a happy-go-lucky lad—I've seen him grow from a young boy into a thoughtful young man. Still green, admittedly, but a diamond all the same. And doing this job changed him—and not simply because he'd had a taste of being one of the older lads. I know this work had a profound physical impact upon him— but I know something else, too. Joe was worried sick. He was fed up with doing what he was doing and I don't think the painting was the 'doing' that he hated. There was something else, and I am bound and determined to find out what it was. If nothing else, so his parents can be at peace—if that's possible."

Yates stared at Maisie, then looked out of the window again. Seconds later, he turned back, taking his seat once more. He leaned forward, hands clasped on top of the sheaf of papers. "There's nothing more to tell you, Miss Dobbs. What you're saying doesn't make sense to me—you might as well be talking Greek. I sent Joe Coombes off to work with a crew on a job a lot of lads his age would jump at the chance of doing, and he goes soft on me—talking his head off about what he's doing when he was supposed to keep his trap shut, and then getting himself drunk enough to kill himself. There's your truth, Miss Dobbs—and I'm sorry I can't make it easier for you to swallow."

Maisie came to her feet and held out her hand. "Thank you for your time, Mr. Yates. I am much obliged to you for your candor. I am sure Joe's parents would love to hear from you—and for you to tell them what a wonderful young apprentice he was."

Mike Yates ignored the outstretched hand and instead yelled past her. "Oi, Miss Not-So-Bright—if you could drag yourself away from your penny dreadful for a minute, would you see Miss Dobbs down to the yard."

Maisie turned and left the small office and was joined by Bright, who put down a sheaf of papers and rose from her desk to escort her to the yard below. She did not speak until they were on the stairs.

"Don't take any notice of him—crabby human being that he is. Cheek of it! I only pick up a book when he hasn't anything for me to do, and I don't read stupid stuff either. I'd argue back, but it's not worth my breath. Him and his flash friends."

"What flash friends," asked Maisie. "He doesn't look the type."

"They never look the type, according to my mum—these crooks. I reckon it was one of his dodgy friends who got him that contract."

"Does he mix with people like that?"

Bright shook her head. "He seems the type to me—if you come from where I come from, you know about that sort of thing." She sighed. "Well, I don't really know about that sort of thing personally, but my dad does."

"What does your dad do, that he knows this 'sort of thing'?" asked Maisie.

"He's a copper. Sergeant at Carter Street police station."

"That's interesting," said Maisie.

"It probably is, as long as you're not related to him. Treats me like I'm a criminal half the time. What time are you going out? What time are you coming back? Which bus are you catching? Who are you going with?

I like to go out to the dance halls with my friends—we don't get up to anything wrong, just dancing to the swing bands playing the latest numbers, having a bit of fun. The way my dad talks, the musical world begins and ends with Gracie Fields singing about Walter taking her to the altar!" She sighed. "I know I've already told you this, but I can't wait to get into the ATS, away from all of them."

Maisie laughed. "Your dad's like that because he loves you, Charlotte. In his job he's seen too much, so he's just worried about you—give him a chance, won't you?"

"I s'pose you're right, but it don't half get on my nerves sometimes, all the questions. Anyway, nice to meet you, Miss Dobbs. And tell Joe's people I was sorry to hear the news about him. I liked Joe. He was a good sort. Not like that brother of his—"

Maisie touched Charlotte Bright on the arm as she was about to turn away. "How do you know his brother?"

"Came round here once or twice, looking for Joe. Just before this job started, the big contract. I didn't like the look of him—I mean, he was nice enough, but not like Joe—seemed a bit harder around the edges. Joe was sort of innocent, as if he would still be a bit of a boy when he was eighty. Anyway, I've got to rush—

the guv'nor will be docking my pay if I'm out here any longer."

Maisie glanced up at the office window. Mike Yates was looking down at them. She turned away and left the yard, just as a black and green Rover 10 swung through the gates.

Where's Martin today?" asked Maisie, a little disappointed to see Sandra at the office without her son.

"Lawrence's aunt is staying with us, and said she would look after him today, so I've had some time to myself. I hate to say it, but it's quite lovely—but just for a little while." She laid a hand upon a pile of papers. "I've caught up with the letters, and there are three invoices for you to sign before I send them out. And the filing is done too—what does Billy do when I'm not here? There were pages everywhere." She held up her finger, as if it were a reminder. "Oh, Mrs. Partridge telephoned. No news of Tim was her first comment. I wasn't going to ask her what she was talking about, but she told me anyway. What does he think he's doing? At his age? Going off in a boat, over there to where it's terrible. We've been listening to the wireless, and—"

"What did she say?" asked Maisie.

"Just that a coastguard had told her the best thing she could do would be to go home and wait, and not get in the way. She sounded very angry, and very distraught—and who could blame her? So she said she's coming back, and Billy's driving them." Sandra's voice changed, a smile readily spreading where before there was consternation. "Isn't it a miracle, about Billy's son? Who would have imagined that could happen? Anyway, he's with his mates now, on their way to their barracks, according to Mrs. Partridge, though she says he had some sort of shoulder wound. She told me that Billy had wanted his son to come home with them, but young Billy said he couldn't. Well, obviously he had to go back to barracks—he's a soldier, after all. But at least Billy had good news for Doreen."

Maisie nodded and placed her bag on Billy's desk as she pulled up a chair to sit down opposite Sandra. There was gentle warmth in their exchange, and Maisie felt a need for that cocoon of belonging, of being with someone she had known for a long time.

"Were there any other telephone calls, Sandra?"

"Just one. From Mr. Klein. Wants you to telephone him back 'soonest,'" he said. "There's a slight snag with the Ministry of Health that needs to be addressed. That's all he said. Is it about—"

"Thank you," Maisie interrupted. "I'll telephone him now." Maisie stood up, grabbed her bag and stepped into her office. "Excuse me, Sandra—just for a minute," she added, as she closed the door separating her room from the outer office.

Maisie was put through to the solicitor with no delay.

"Slight problem, Maisie. Not a huge one, but . . . well, any snag at this point could become more serious if we don't nip it in the bud."

Chapter 11

Maisie was torn. Should she go to Hampshire again? Remain in London? Or should she follow her heart, which would be to drive down to Rye to see if Tim and his friend would return to the place where the vessel was usually moored. She looked at the clock and turned on the wireless in her office. Stepping toward the sliding doors again, she drew them back.

"I'm about to listen to the news on the wireless—come in if you want to, Sandra."

British and French troops last night held Calais and Dunkirk. The French official communiqué stated that Boulogne had been taken by the Germans after fierce street fighting. German shock troops attacking on the outskirts of Boulogne were smashed by shells from British warships firing over the town. The battle for Calais is still south of the town. British soldiers fought magnificently with the French to repulse every enemy attack yesterday . . . and across the Atlantic, President Roosevelt told the USA to prepare for the "approaching storm." Stressing the "futility, the impossibility" of the idea of isolation, he said, "Obviously a defense policy based on that is merely to invite future attack."

The two women listened to the news for a few more minutes before Maisie switched off the set.

"It never occurred to me that it would be a good idea to have a wireless in the office," said Sandra. "But since the war started and you brought it in, at least we can keep up with what's going on. And it brings us all together, considering everyone across the country's listening."

"I sometimes wonder if the news is helpful to us," said Maisie. "Or if it just makes us more anxious. If Tim and his friend are in the midst of this, it could be days before they come home. Gordon's parents have asked the coastguard to look out for the boat, but according to Priscilla, Gordon's father has joined the flotilla, and he hopes to find them along the way."

They were jolted from speculation by the telephone. Sandra answered the call.

"Billy—Billy!" She looked at Maisie, who held out her hand. "You're just leaving Mrs. Partridge's house? All right, Billy, I'm passing you over to her now."

"Billy," said Maisie, grasping the receiver. "I've heard your good news! You must be beyond relieved—and what a miracle."

"Miracle? I never believed in them, but now I do, miss—I thought I would go on my knees right there and then. Talk about a weight off my mind—it's been like carrying around a hundred-weight of coal. But let me tell you, I reckon they need all the miracles they can get, our army over there. You should see the state of them—my boy isn't my boy anymore, miss—he looks like his granddad. And he looks like the lads I was with in the war—that long stare, as if they've seen into the devil's eyes. Put years on him, this has, but at least he's on his feet—though he's got a nasty shoulder wound. The important thing is that he's back now, he's over here and not over there. Miss, they say there's thousands of our boys, waiting to be rescued—thousands of them. And according to Billy, Hitler's blimmin' Luftwaffe are strafing men while they wait and they're bombing the ships what are coming in to save them.

And down in Ramsgate—I've never seen anything like it. There's more soldiers than I imagined disembarking, then there's the people coming in to help. You know, when we heard about the evacuation of Dunkirk, I don't think I had it in my head what it looked like, and what the soldiers and the navy are going through. Tell you the truth, I still don't, not really—I can only get a picture of it from what I've been told. Our Billy said to me, 'Dad, at least I'm home . . . I'm home.' And now I keep thinking about the ones waiting to get away. All that waiting. And the hoping."

"All right, Billy, you must go straight home to see Doreen. At least Mr. and Mrs. Partridge are safely back in Holland Park?"

"Had to all but drag Mrs. P., but the authorities don't want civilians getting in the way down there unless they've got a job to do. And even she realized that she was doing more harm than good—but who can blame her? I'm glad Mr. P. was there. He's like a solid rock, isn't he? Stalwart, that's what he is, and he takes care of her and keeps her from doing a mischief to herself—and they reckon this evacuation is going to take days and days."

"Douglas knows what she's been through. This is her most dreadful nightmare coming true—she knows the whereabouts of only one of her three sons, and it's a wonder she hasn't handcuffed him to his bed so he doesn't move while she's away."

"Well, she's home now. And that's where I'm going, off to see Doreen and Margaret Rose, if that's all right, then I'll be in the office later."

"Don't worry, Billy. Come in tomorrow."

"What about Hampshire?"

"I'm not sure—but I think I'll leave soon."

"You don't sound very sure, miss."

"It's Tim, and—"

"There's nothing you can do, miss. That's what Mr. and Mrs. P. realized. Nothing you can do until he comes back in, and if his pal is anything like him, they won't come home until it's over, until they've done everything they can for our boys."

"That's what worries me," said Maisie.

There was something about driving that made Maisie feel cocooned from the world around her. Looking out onto streets where people were going about their daily round until the town gave way to countryside again, catching glimpses of farmers at work, a horse-drawn plough turning the soil, or workers marching from one field to another—it was easy to believe the war was nothing more than a nightmare that would come to an end soon, that the country would wake up and any threat of an invasion by a ruthless enemy would have evaporated. Time would march on, the seasons would pass and death would come after three score years and ten—and with good fortune, perhaps a few more years added on to enjoy a life well lived.

Mrs. Keep welcomed Maisie with a cup of tea, home-baked scones and the promise of a room always ready for her whenever she came to the farm. Once refreshed, Maisie set her bag in the room, dropped in to say hello to Doreen's aunt, and went on her way—this time in the direction of the airfield where she believed Teddy Wickham was stationed. Would she be able to see him? Would her name still be on a list that gave her preferential access? She had not wanted to trouble Lord Julian again, but was now having second thoughts and wished she had.

As before there were two guards stationed at the gatehouse when she drove up. She pulled into a lay-by opposite their station, reached into her handbag and took out her identity card. She wound down the window and held out the card.

"Good afternoon, Sergeant. I wonder if I could speak to the officer in charge, if I may? My name is Maisie Dobbs—here is my calling card." She took one of the cards from her pocket. She did not wish to appear too confident of her position, but at the same time wanted to get answers to questions as soon as she could. "I believe my name should be on a list here—perhaps it's with the officer in charge."

"Right you are, miss. Remain in your motor car, if you don't mind." The sergeant returned to the gate-house and stepped inside. Through the open door Maisie could see him winding up the telephone and placing a call. The conversation seemed to take longer than she had expected, but at last he replaced the receiver and walked back toward the Alvis.

"Sergeant Packham had to go through some papers, Miss Dobbs. He'd remembered seeing your name, but the permission to enter had been filed away. Now then, when I lift the gate you may proceed to the building situated to your right as you drive up there. Do not exceed five miles per hour, and do not stop. You will see where to park your vehicle and a guard will be waiting to escort you to an office where Sergeant Packham will see you."

Maisie nodded and thanked the guard, who proceeded to lift a barrier, waving her through as she drove on. Taking care to keep the Alvis at the specified speed—tantamount to hardly moving—she followed instructions for parking. An armed guard approached the motor car, opened the door and instructed her to "Follow me, madam."

Upon entering the long, one-storey building, she smelled fresh paint, and could see the job had been finished recently, perhaps in the last fortnight. The guard stopped outside a door, knocked and was given leave to enter. An officer and a sergeant were waiting in the room and returned the guard's salute. The room was cool and felt damp, and seemed infused with the vapor of fresh emulsion. It was oppressive, reminding her of an interrogation room at Scotland Yard.

"Miss Dobbs," said the officer. "Flight Lieutenant Cobb, and this is Sergeant Packham. Please take a seat." He extended a hand toward a chair opposite a single desk in the room. Cobb took a seat on the other side of the desk, while Packham remained standing. "Now, how might we help you, Miss Dobbs? Is this to do with the painters?"

Maisie looked from Cobb to Packham. "Yes, I'm afraid it is in connection with the death of one of the young apprentices, Joseph Coombes. I'm given to understand that a friend of his brother, named Edward—Teddy—Wickham is stationed here. He visited Mr. Coombes a few weeks before his death, and subsequently told the deceased's parents that their son had been in 'top form.' I would like to see Wickham, if I may. I would like to ask him a few questions about his meeting with Joseph Coombes."

"Is there a suspicion of foul play in the death of the young apprentice?" asked Cobb.

"The inquest has yet to take place, but in all likelihood the coroner will conclude death by misadventure."

"Young lad playing fast and loose with fate, eh?" said Cobb.

"Perhaps not," said Maisie. "Might I see Wickham?"

Cobb turned to Sergeant Packham. "Where is Corporal Wickham at the moment?"

Packham lifted an open ledger from the desk and began to run his finger down the page. "In the hangar, sir," he replied.

"Ask the guard to fetch him, and bring him to this office." He turned to Maisie. "I should like to be present during your inquisition, if that's all right," said Cobb.

Maisie took account of Cobb's stance—he had now come to his feet. It occurred to her that, perhaps, in civilian life he had not known much respect from his peers, that he had yearned for a measure of power, some sense of having an edge over others. He had possibly been all but invisible in school days, hence his need to sit while the sergeant stood—affirming his position—and then to stand as soon as the sergeant had left the room. Maisie leaned back in the chair, placing her elbows on the arms and stretching into the space allowed her.

"I'd like to talk to him in private—if that's all right," said Maisie. "It might be easier if Corporal Wickham had no cause to feel intimidated by the presence of an officer in the room. You are, after all, his superior." She left the word "superior" hanging, suspended in the air between them, a word chosen to stroke an ego as if it were a dog to be calmed.

"Yes, quite," said Cobb.

A single knock at the door signaled Packham's entrance, with Teddy Wickham close behind. The young man was of average height, about five feet ten inches, and with reddish-blond hair. His gray eyes held no sparkle, though as soon as he saw Cobb, he snapped to attention, his chest pushed out and his back ramrod straight when he saluted the officer.

"At ease, Wickham," said Cobb. "This is Miss Dobbs. She has something to discuss with you in private—which I am allowing on this occasion." He looked at Maisie, again as if to underline his position. "A guard will be waiting outside and will escort you to your

motor car directly you've finished in here, Miss Dobbs."
He turned back to Wickham. "And, corporal, you will
immediately return to your duties." He pronounced the
word "immeejetly."

"Yes, sir!" Wickham saluted again, his heels snap-
ping together.

"And please don't do that—you look like a bloody
Nazi," added Cobb as he and Packham left the room.

"You can breathe again and sit down now, Teddy—
pull up that chair so you're on this side of the desk."

"Are you sure, miss, I mean—"

"Of course. Come on, sit down."

Wickham picked up his chair and set it down so that
it was diagonally situated to Maisie—not opposite and
not alongside. She smiled. Whether deliberate or in-
stinctive, he had seated himself in a neutral place.

"What do you want to talk to me about?" asked
Wickham.

"Joe Coombes," said Maisie.

Teddy Wickham nodded and looked down at his
hands. "I heard he was dead. Probably the job what
did it."

"Tell me what you mean, Teddy?"

"Being away from home. Joe was a soft one—and all
this business, going around painting these buildings,

it wasn't doing him any good at all." He had leaned forward, his shoulders rounded, his arms now folded.

"But you said he was on 'top form'—those were your exact words, according to Phil Coombes."

"Well, he was, in a way—but it was as if he couldn't get comfortable. On one hand he was having a bit too much fun with the lads, if you ask me. I mean, he wasn't used to the late nights, that sort of thing. And on the other, he was on his own—the apprentice, not one of the boys."

"Late nights? That doesn't sound like the Joe I knew," said Maisie.

Wickham looked up. "Didn't know you knew him."

"Yes, I know Phil and Sally, and I knew Joe. Not Archie though." She sighed. "What makes you think Joe was having that many late nights? Was he drinking?"

Wickham shrugged. "Might've been. He was away from home, away from having the collar round his neck, so he was enjoying himself."

Maisie folded her arms and leaned forward, mirroring Wickham.

"What do you do here, Teddy?"

"All sorts, but mainly stores, supplies and ordering. Boring really. But it's steady, and I won't be out there fighting, or up there in the air fighting, or on a ship fighting."

"Not a bad move," said Maisie.

"Wasn't deliberate—luck of the draw. It's where I ended up."

"Do you get much leave?"

"More than some, I suppose. More than them going up and over there to fight the Germans."

"So that's how you were able to see Joe, make sure he was all right."

"Saw him a couple of times."

"How did you manage to get into the stores job? Sounds like a cushy number to me. What did you do before you joined up?" asked Maisie.

"I worked in a warehouse. Same sort of thing—they like to use what you've already got, I suppose—and like I said, it's the luck of the draw. Always is."

Maisie nodded. "Where was the warehouse—where you worked before the war?"

"Sydenham."

"Oh, then you weren't far from Archie then?"

Wickham shrugged. "No, not far, just up the road. He's got a job that keeps him in civvy street though, jammy whatsit that he is."

Maisie nodded, and when she spoke it was with a

softer voice. "You're very upset about Joe, aren't you, Teddy?"

Wickham looked away. "Well, I would be, wouldn't I. My mate's little brother, dead because no one was looking after him."

"What do you mean, Teddy? I thought the men he worked with were keeping an eye on him."

"Well, they weren't sharp enough, were they? Didn't stop him ending up dead, did they?"

"Perhaps they didn't know what he was up to," said Maisie, her tone remaining modulated.

Wickham looked up at the clock on the wall. "I've got to get back, Miss . . . Miss Dobbs. Got a shipment coming in, big one—everything from parts for vehicles, parts for aeroplanes, medical supplies, all that sort of thing, right down to tea and Bovril—and I've got to check it all through on the ledgers."

Maisie said nothing, maintaining her gaze upon him so that, when he looked up, he found himself staring straight into her eyes.

"What?" he said.

"What are you afraid to tell me, Teddy?"

The young man shook his head, stood up and moved the chair back to its place behind the desk. He stood as if to attention in front of Maisie, and saluted before opening the door. Maisie heard his stride along a corridor, then a door opening, and as she left the room to greet the guard, she glanced out of a window and saw Wickham walking at speed toward an aircraft hangar, his hands curled into fists by his side.

"This way, ma'am," said the guard, one hand steadying the rifle slung over his shoulder.

When they reached the motor car, the guard opened the door for Maisie to take her seat. He closed the door behind her and stood to watch as she maneuvered the Alvis around, and began to drive at the same low speed toward the exit. Another guard approached the barrier, lifting it for her to pass, then directed her across into a lay-by of sorts, and held up his hand for her to remain in place. He looked along the lane leading to the airfield, and beckoned a lorry forward, which—Maisie could see—was followed by three similar vehicles. The guard checked the papers handed to him by each driver, and as the lorries moved off, the engines roared and whined. Having secured the gate, the guard waved her forward and on her way.

A mile or so along the road she passed two more lorries, with boxes being loaded from one to the other. The first lorry was similar to those she had passed at the airfield, and the second bore the Yates' company livery. There were no tins or barrels or anything that might contain paint to be seen.

Making her way back along country lanes, Maisie was thinking about Teddy Wickham, when she heard the low drone of aircraft approaching. She stopped the motor car next to a five-bar gate overlooking the green fields beyond, and stepped out. Leaning on the gate she looked up at the aeroplanes as they flew overhead— two Hurricanes and three Spitfires if she were not mistaken—toward the coast, and in all likelihood bound for France. And she remembered another time, at an airfield outside Munich just two years earlier, when she watched a young aviatrix, Elaine Otterburn, take off on a mission to save the life of a man valuable to Britain's preparations for war, and her words as she had watched the aircraft disappear into the clouds: "God Speed." Maisie whispered those same words again as the aircraft became specks in the distance.

The interview with Teddy Wickham troubled Maisie, not simply because she believed—indeed, she knew— that he had lied to her, but also for one other reason. As Teddy Wickham had left her he was fighting back tears. But were they tears of the bereaved? Tears of guilt? Or perhaps an expression of fear? She stopped at a bakery to buy a cheese roll, and then at a grocer's where she bought a bottle of ginger beer, and considered her next move. She wanted to see Freddie and Len again, the two painters who were working with Joe, and who—as the senior men—were supposed to be training him in his job. In particular Freddie Mayes. Driving back into Whitchurch, she stopped at the telephone kiosk and placed a call to Yates' yard. As soon as the singsong voice answered, she knew she was in luck.

"Yates Painting and Decorating, how may I help you?" The speaker's tone seemed to begin on a low note and end on a high one.

"Hello—is this Miss Bright? Charlotte?"

There was a pause before the woman replied with a lowered voice. "That's Miss Dobbs—I recognize your voice."

"Charlotte, would you be able to give me some information please?"

"What sort of information?" Her voice was now little more than a whisper.

"Can you tell me where Freddie and Len are today? I'm in Hampshire and I'd like to see them."

"Hmmm, let me see—just a minute."

Maisie could hear the turning of pages, then Bright was back on the line. "Yes, I thought so. They moved on from that last airfield, and they're now at another place. RAF Templeton. Nearer the coast it is—have you got a map?"

"Yes, I have, and I've also a list of the RAF stations, so I have everything I need. Is everything all right, Charlotte?"

"Mike Yates gave me my cards this morning—said that seeing as I was leaving anyway, I might as well be gone sooner rather than later, especially as he had another girl coming from the labor exchange with better qualifications than me. Made a point of telling me she was 'brighter' than me. I hate that man—and I'd like to know what someone with so-called better qualifications is doing coming here."

"You'll be in uniform soon, anyway," said Maisie.

"Counting down the hours, Miss Dobbs. Counting down the hours."

Maisie laughed. "Charlotte, I've another question. As I was leaving the other day, a motor car came into the yard—it was a black and green Rover Ten. Do you know who it belongs to?"

There was a brief pause before Bright answered. "I shouldn't say, you know, what with that form I had to sign, the one about keeping quiet about what I do here—but seeing as this is my last day, I don't give tuppence ha'apenny for Yates and his secrets. That motor car belongs to a bloke called Jimmy Robertson, but that wasn't him driving it. No, that was one of his tea boys—that's what my dad calls them, the blokes down the ladder from the top. Robertson has a finger in a lot of pies, and he comes here because one of the pies he has a finger in is the painting business. He supplies that special paint and helped get Mike Yates that contract. I'm not supposed to know that, but I do—oh, hang on." There was a pause, then Bright came back on the line. "No, madam, I'm afraid it wasn't Yates Painting and Decorating—I've looked up the records. However, Yates would be more than happy to give you an estimate—shall I get Mr. Yates to telephone you? No? All right. Thank you, madam."

"Charlotte—could you give me your address quickly, just in case I have any more questions for you."

The young woman recited her address in a low voice, adding a hurried good-bye.

Maisie left the telephone kiosk and sat in her motor car, staring straight ahead, deep in thought, paying no attention to her surroundings. She sighed, shook her head and spoke aloud, as if someone else were in the Alvis, and she had asked for their opinion. "Jimmy Robertson. That's all I need—Jimmy Robertson."

Maisie had never met Jimmy Robertson, though she had heard of him. Had not everyone in south London heard of the Robertson family? In the office, where she kept the card file started by Maurice, a resource used throughout her apprenticeship and which she continued to refer to, there was a clutch of cards, each one bearing a Christian name followed by the surname "Robertson." The family's tentacles reached into almost every business south of the river, and—she had heard—possibly even into Westminster. No wonder Sergeant Bright worried about his daughter—it beggared belief that he had ever allowed her to work for Mike Yates, if that was the company he kept. Jimmy Robertson was known to be ruthless with those who crossed him. She remembered hearing about one of Robertson's "tea boys"—a man who had, on the orders of Jimmy Robertson, been dismembered before his body was set in concrete and thrown into the Thames. It was Caldwell who had told her. "The word on the street is that Barney Coleman's now holding up Rotherhithe Docks. And they say Jimmy Robertson started cutting him before he was dead!" Robertson was not someone to be underestimated—Barney Coleman was his cousin.

She had intended to place a call to Chelstone to ask after Anna's health, but looked at the single penny left in her purse—she would have to do it later. Instead she started the engine and slipped the motor car into gear, her thoughts on the conversation with Charlotte Bright. An unexpected thread was now running through the web. It happened—though not often. But this time perhaps that single thread might be the one to pull. As she made her way to RAF Templeton, checking the map at every junction, she wondered what counsel Maurice might offer. She remembered a story he had told about a sojourn in Morocco as a young man. He explained that in times past, for the early morning and evening Muslim call to prayer, the muezzin had no means of telling the correct time—the exact moments of dawn and dusk—so from their balcony high up on the minaret, they would hold two threads in the palm of one hand: a black thread and a white thread. When they could see no distinction between white and black at night, that was the time to begin their call. And in the morning, as soon as they could distinguish the white thread, so they would summon the faithful to prayer. Maurice had taken a pencil and paper and drawn a minaret, so that she might know what this tower, part of the mosque, looked like. She knew, then, as she turned off onto another lane, that for all her work on a case map and despite the colors used to follow each thread of evidence collected, she was still at the dawn of her investigation, for she could not distinguish black from white. Indeed, as she followed directions to the airfield, she was reminded of the difficulty of the task—all road signs had been removed. It seemed to be a reflection of her investigation into the death of Joe Coombes.

Once again Maisie had to go through the procedure of identifying herself to a guard, for someone at an office in a low building on the airfield to approve her presence, and only then would she be authorized to wait for the person she wanted to see. As she stood alongside the Alvis, she saw a van coming toward the guardhouse, a cloud of dust rising up behind the back wheels.

"I'm going to give that lad a bit of a talking to about his driving," said the guard. "He looks as if he's in a race to get over here. Pity he's in civvy street and not one of ours—I'd have him on latrine duty for that."

The van screeched to a halt on the other side of the barrier, and Freddie Mayes stepped out, slamming the door behind him.

"Before you leave your old jam-jar in the way, mate, you'd better put it over to one side—there's people driving up and they want to get in and out," the guard admonished the painter, who—thought Maisie—if looks could kill, had just committed murder.

The van was moved and Freddie came to the barrier, ducked underneath and approached Maisie.

"Miss Dobbs. You're back again. Mr. Yates said none of us were to talk to you. Sorry about that."

"Nice to see you again too, Freddie." Maisie followed the sarcastic quip with a question. "When did
you speak to him last—he was very cordial to me when
I visited."

"It's this business about Joe," said Freddie. "Got
him worried, I suppose."

"In case you're all getting ill, is that it?"

Mayes shrugged. "Not as bad as Joe, but it makes
us feel a bit queasy at times. Nothing that a pint won't
cure of an evening. Anyway, I'm going back up to the
Smoke soon. Not for long, just for a couple of days off,
then back down here. Like being in the army it is, stuck
where you don't want to be."

"Just as well you're not in the army, don't you
think?" Maisie regarded the painter, who took a packet
of cigarettes from his pocket. It was a full packet of
twenty expensive cigarettes, not the Woodbines he had
smoked before. "I'd like to ask a couple more questions,
about Joe."

"All right then—fire away," said Freddie.

"Can you tell me honestly—did Joe drink at all?
Was he ever the worse for wear after you'd been down
to the pub in one of these villages where you've been
staying?"

Freddie shook his head. "Joe wasn't what you'd call

a drinker. Mind you, I suppose it's my fault that once or twice he was a bit tipsy. He was all wound up, you see. Like a spring. I put it down to missing his mum or something like that—p'raps he's got a girl back at home. So when he asked for a shandy a couple of times, instead of his usual Vimto, I got the landlord to make it more ale than lemonade—which is the opposite of what Joe liked. The way he ordered it, it was a glass of lemonade and a spoonful of ale on the top! Who would have believed his old man was a publican?" Freddie took a long draw on his cigarette, pinched out the lighted end and threw it into the bushes. He was staring at the ground as he spoke. "So, I suppose a couple of times he was a little bit not-quite-there, but at least he wasn't so nervy. Just before it happened—just before he died—he was in a bit of a state. Every time someone came into the pub, he almost jumped out of his skin. I reckon it was the paint—it was doing something to his mind." He looked up at Maisie. "But do I think it was doing enough to his mind to make him jump onto a railway line? I really don't know. None of us was with him, and he wasn't one for skylarking around. And I've thought about it a lot—I reckon Joe was like he was because he wanted to be different from some of the sorts he saw in his dad's business. But he told me his dad warned him about it too—that the pub should be a lesson to him. It put dinner on the table and clothes on their backs, but there were better ways to earn a living."

Maisie said nothing for some seconds, allowing the silence to distill her thoughts, and the picture Freddie Mayes had painted of Joe Coombes away from home. "Did he get any visitors—either at the lodgings or while working?"

The painter and decorator shook his head. "Not as far as I know—although he mentioned his brother's mate coming over to see him. Ted—Teddy—something like that. But he went out for walks. He said it was to clear his head, though it might have been to see someone. We were in Whitchurch for a good while and he started talking to one of the farmers in the pub one night. Bloke had a sheepdog with him, and Joe was telling him how it fascinated him, the way the dogs worked on the farm. The old boy said he should come over to watch, perhaps have a go—and I know Joe walked over there of an evening sometimes—he liked the old boy's company."

"No one has mentioned this before," said Maisie.

Mayes shrugged. "Didn't seem important, I suppose—going off to look at a sheepdog messing around with some sheep." He held out his hands, palm up, and shrugged again. "Look, Miss Dobbs, I'm a London boy, born and bred—the only thing I know about these animals is when I put a few pennies on a greyhound at Catford dogs."

"What was the farmer's name?"

"Hutchins. Phineas was his name. Funny old name for a funny old bloke. They called him Finny. Looks like he came out of a book. I think it's Moorwood Farm—ask a publican in Whitchurch, any one of them would know how to get there. Not that old Finny could tell you much. Oh, and he has a bit of a smell about him—being a farmer, I suppose."

Maisie regarded Freddie Mayes. "Do you know where the paint comes from?"

Mayes took another cigarette from the packet and lit up. Maisie wondered how long this one would last, and again how he could afford to be so cavalier about his expenditure. Recalling how Billy always kept the unsmoked portion of a cigarette, perhaps the only reason for such waste was a good supply, and at little or no cost.

"It comes in big tins in a big lorry, that's all I know."

"I meant its place of origin—where it begins its journey?"

"Not my business, is it? Probably from a government depot, something like that. All I know is we get the paint, put it in our buckets, and we brush it on the walls."

"And the only friends outside of you and the lads that Joe had while you've been away is this old farmer and his dog."

"Far as I know."

"All right, Freddie—I've kept you from your work for long enough. You'd better get back. Thank you for your time."

The young man drew on the cigarette a couple of times, blowing the smoke to one side. "Got to do our best by Joe, haven't we?" He turned to leave.

Maisie watched as he took two steps, and then called to him. "Freddie—just one more thing. Sorry, but I have to ask this—you all seem to have a good supply of smokes. Where do you get them—you're out of the way down here?"

"Mr. Yates sends them. They come with the supplies." He gave a half-laugh. "In fact, they're probably from the same place as that paint—" He stopped abruptly, raised a hand as a final gesture of departure, and turned back to his van.

As Maisie stepped toward the Alvis, she heard the guard shout across. "And watch your bleedin' speed, sonny—you're on government property and you'd better follow the rules. This ain't your cushy civvy street."

"Oh wind your neck in, getting upset because you're stuck out here and not one of them fly boys up there," came the retort from Freddie Mayes.

She started the engine, and as she slipped the motor car into gear, she wound down the window to thank the guard, who shook his head.

"That bloke and his mates on the painting job— untouchable, that's what they are. They're all right, I suppose, but sometimes that one can get mouthy. His mate said it was on account of the paint they're using. Well, all I can say is, he should be over there with our lads in France. Then let's see where mouthy gets you. You'd be wishing all you had to do all day was paint so the buildings don't burn."

Maisie bid good-bye to the guard and drove away from the airfield, and at a very low speed.

Chapter 12

Consulting her watch, Maisie realized there was no time to locate Phineas Hutchins, though she dropped into a local pub to get change for the telephone kiosk, and directions to the farm visited by Joe Coombes. The publican gave her plenty of coins for her telephone calls, and she discovered that the farm neighbored the Keeps' land, and was leased from the same owner. She would visit tomorrow, before making her way back to London. But there was more she must do before she returned to her room at the farm for the night.

Brenda picked up the telephone after the first ring. "Anna's been asking for you—and for young Tim. She's in a bit of a state about it, poor little love."

Since the evacuee came to live at the Dower House, Maisie was aware that the child had a sensitivity shared with her grandmother.

"What is she saying? What has she been told about Tim?"

"Nothing—but she already knew he wasn't here without us even telling her. She said she watched him hiking out over the fields on the morning he left. She said she knew he was going to leave, because she could see it in his head. I tell you, that child makes me wonder at times, Maisie. Your father says it's nothing to worry about, that children on their own see all sorts—little friends who aren't there, and other strange things. He said your mother always told him they had to just accept anything you said that was like that without comment, when you were a child."

"Yes, Dad's right. And she is still not completely well, is she?" Maisie knew her stepmother meant well but worried she might say something that would make Anna feel different from other children. "Did Anna say anything specific—about Tim?"

"She said she had a big dream, that he had a bad arm and that he was on a boat."

"She knows he likes to sail—he's told her enough stories about his trips to see his friend Gordon."

"And what do you say to the bad arm?"

Maisie was quick to answer. "Oh, you know—she's seen his father many times now and understands that Douglas lost an arm, so in her dreams it all becomes mixed up. That's how dreams are."

"Well, when the woman from the Ministry of Health came, I had to whisper to Anna not to say anything about her dreams and what she imagines. Last thing we want is for the woman to write something critical about it in the report."

"She came today? I thought she wasn't coming until I was present. Oh my goodness."

"Don't you worry, Maisie. Your father and I made a good account of ourselves, and so did Anna—we'd brought her downstairs to lie on the bed you'd made up for Tim in the conservatory, so she could look out over the fields. She wanted to watch Lady in the paddock, and Emma when your father took the dogs for a walk. And she keeps saying she wants to see Tim when he comes home."

"So, what happened? Tell me—this is so important, and the woman will have thought the wrong thing because I wasn't there."

"I told you, it's all right—don't worry. Your father explained that you were involved in war work, that you could not discuss it. He told her that you had to go to

London a couple of times a week, but that Anna was in our good hands when you went—just like any other woman might leave her child with relatives."

"Oh dear—"

"She asked questions and wrote on a form that I couldn't see. She said 'Right you are' a lot, and asked about your marital status—again. They asked that the last time. I reminded her that you were widowed, and I pointed out that your in-laws are over at the manor. Then she checked her notes and said, 'Oh yes, your daughter is Margaret, Lady Compton, isn't she?' So I reckon it will be all right. What does Mr. Klein say?"

Maisie sighed. "That there is an issue because I'm a widow—husbandless is what they mean."

"There's a lot of women going to be husbandless in this war, and children going to be fatherless. And at least this will be one they don't have to worry about."

"Mr. Klein said they asked about her father. All her grandmother knew was that his name was Marco, and that he was a merchant seaman from Malta."

"You could make a verse out of that." Brenda laughed.

The pips sounded, and Maisie pressed more coins into the slot and pushed button "A" on the telephone box.

"I wish I could laugh too, Brenda. Mr. Klein has

pointed out to them that, what with the situation in Malta and the paltry amount of information we have on the father—and it might not even be correct—there is almost no chance of locating him. I'm used to looking for people, and I doubt I could find Marco from Malta. And Anna is five years old, for goodness' sake!"

"I can hear you getting worried again, Maisie. Try not to—you've had references from some very good people—Lord Julian, Lady Rowan, that Mr. Huntley, and Mr. MacFarlane."

"I think Robbie MacFarlane might not have been the best choice."

"It'll be all right, Maisie. He might be a bit brusque, but he'll do you proud, just you see—and after all, he is a policeman. And for now little Anna is here, and she is safe—and she knows she's safe. I just wish she would stop fretting about Tim. She says he will be home in a few days. What with that little determined face of hers, I wouldn't bet against it."

Maisie bit her lip, imagining Anna, her black hair braided in two long plaits tied with ribbon at the ends. She would be kneeling on her bed looking out across the fields, her brow knitted, waiting for Tim to come home.

"I must go now, Brenda—I'll be back in London tomorrow and will telephone again. Perhaps I can speak to Anna then."

"All right, Maisie, love. You look after yourself. I'm glad you finally told us about your plans. And Maisie—remember, that little girl loves you. She told me so yesterday. She asked when you were coming home."

Maisie felt words catch in her throat, and could bid only a faint good-bye to her stepmother.

Composing herself, Maisie picked up the receiver again and placed a call to a number seared into her memory. Whitehall-one-two-one-two. Scotland Yard. She was put through to Detective Chief Inspector Caldwell without delay.

"I was just about to go home, get an early one, and there you are. If I could have put money on anyone messing up my plans, it would have been you, Miss Dobbs. Now then, what the you-know-what can I do for you?"

"Two things. Perhaps three. First—would you pave the way for me to see Inspector Murphy again tomorrow? Late morning would be best, if you can. And the other thing is this—do you know what the Robertsons have been up to lately?"

There was a pause on the line, followed by a loud sigh.

"For a minute there, I thought you asked me about the Robertsons. In fact, I could have sworn you asked me about London's most notorious family of criminals who—for reasons best known to the gods—keep slithering through the fingers of the law. Yes, I thought you asked about them, just for a minute."

"Inspector Caldwell—please—"

"That means I should be getting you in here to have a chat with me and my esteemed colleague from the Flying Squad, because we both know there is no smoke without a fire." Caldwell cleared his throat. "Now then, what do you know, that you're asking me what I know?"

"Just a guess."

"What is it?"

"I think Jimmy Robertson is involved in the death of Joe Coombes."

"Pull the other one. Jimmy Robertson would not be messing about with a wet-behind-the-ears apprentice. You're wasting my time, Miss Dobbs. Right now we don't have anything concerning Jimmy Robertson on our department's books, though I like to know what him and his kin are up to. Harry Bream in the Squad has a few robberies he's looking into, and what with the war on, you can bet the Robertsons are making hay at everyone else's expense. They say crime will go down, what with all the bad blokes joining the army, but I haven't seen a lot of evidence of it, not yet. In fact, it's the opposite. But as I said, I can't see your lad being mixed up in all this."

Maisie felt a sudden lack of patience. "Have it your way, Inspector Caldwell. I'll pull the other one somewhere else!" She slammed down the receiver.

But instead of picturing Caldwell looking at his own receiver and laughing at her expense, Maisie could only see in her mind's eye a little girl kneeling on her bed, her elbows resting on the windowsill, her chin on her hands, looking across fields, waiting for those she loved to come home. Maisie had come to love Anna too, and now, in the telephone kiosk, she leaned against the doorframe and began to weep with fear, that—despite documents signed by the child's grandmother and all the other required elements that had been gathered by her solicitor—her dearest, most heartfelt wish might come to nothing.

Maisie's eyes were still raw, smarting as she sat in her car along the road and watched a van—she suspected an armored van with a guard alongside the driver— leave the works where paper money was printed for the Bank of England. She had not sought nor did she wish to gain access to the establishment, for she could acquire all the information she needed from Lord Julian. No need to cause a problem where none were necessary. She had learned that security was tight around the establishment, due not only to the amount of currency being taken to and from London, but because of the special notes produced for airmen. She pushed away thoughts of Tom—he was young to be so vulnerable away from home. Yet so were all the airmen taking to the skies. Eighteen, nineteen, perhaps just into their twenties—so much rested on the shoulders of youth.

She had waited outside the gates, having observed that the van would leave at different times of day. She had also learned from Lord Julian that a variety of steps were taken to ensure the safe arrival of money in London or wherever stocks were bound. Alternate routes were chosen, selected just before the van left, and a certain understated police presence along the way meant additional security. How tempting it must be for someone like Jimmy Robertson—though would even a family such as the Robertsons risk so much? She knew only too well that the darkest inhabitants of London's underworld were not stupid—though they were informed enough to slip through the law's dragnet.

Maurice had taught her early in her apprenticeship that she had to be something of a chameleon. On one hand, she was an advocate for the dead. In viewing the deceased she had to endeavor to understand every inch of their being—and not only from the perspective of the pathologist's craft. He cautioned her to accrue knowledge of the "forensic science of the whole person." Hence she was accustomed to being alone with the deceased, to absorbing an aura others might not feel. But Maurice also imbued in her the need to understand the mind of a criminal—and the criminal in question might have the equivalent of a doctorate following long study of his or her subject. Or he might be a neophyte, a mere novice who sees only the fortune waiting at the end of crime's rainbow rather than the nuances of color in the job to be done. And now, having satisfied herself that she understood what was required in the transportation of considerable amounts of money, she decided that Jimmy Robertson would not have ventured beyond a red outer ring of that rainbow—at least not if there were easier pickings closer to home. But what were those easier pickings? And how did Yates and Sons fit into the picture? What was the pot of gold the man in the black and green Rover 10 was looking for—or perhaps protecting? Before driving away she decided she had chosen the correct category for the presence of large amounts of new money in the same place as Joe Coombes had been lodging. It was not a distraction, neither was it crucial, but this particular shoe fit somewhere. For now she would still consider it important, something she would perhaps come back to.

The following morning, Maisie declined a fried breakfast in favor of a soft-boiled egg and two thick slices of Mrs. Keep's homemade bread, toasted, with butter and honey from the farm's hives. She packed up her overnight bag, and left, waving to Mrs. Keep as she drove away. The Keeps—still anxious for news of their sons—had assured her that Phineas Hutchins was a "good sort" who kept to himself but knew the land and his livestock better than anyone.

Grateful for such a solid motor car, Maisie drove at low speed along the pitted track down to the farmhouse where "Finny" Hutchins resided. It was a timber-framed home with a thatched roof and well-tended vegetable garden in the front. Maisie came to a halt alongside the farmhouse, stepped out of the motor car and walked to the front door. She knocked twice, but was not surprised at the lack of an answer—a farmer would be expected to be out on his land long before breakfast. Maisie never embarked upon a trip to the country without her stout walking shoes—which she appreciated as she entered the muddy cobblestone courtyard beyond the house, leading to a series of low buildings. Two border collies—one young, one more mature—saw Maisie first, and came running toward her. The older one seemed more measured, the younger one was yapping. The experienced dog maintained a low trot around her, as if she were a sheep to be kept in place. Hutchins looked up from his work, mending a fence. He was not a tall man—Maisie had an inch or two on his height—but he had a solid bearing, a strength to his body. She thought he might be in his sixties. His gray hair was clipped in a tidy fashion, and he was clean-shaven. And though his attire—corduroy trousers, a gray shirt, woolen weskit—showed age, it would appear they were clean. She wondered what Freddie Mayes might have meant by his comment about the aroma that followed the farmer to the pub.

"Lads! Lads! Get back 'ere!" Hutchins commanded. The dogs ran to heel as the man wiped his hands on a handkerchief pulled from his pocket. He took his tweed jacket from where it had been hung on a fence post and collected his shepherd's crook, which was leaning in the same place. He walked toward Maisie.

"Hello—Mr. Hutchins? Good morning—my name is Maisie Dobbs. I wonder if you could spare me a little of your time." Maisie held out her hand.

"Depends upon what you'll be wanting with that precious time of mine. We've got to get up to the big field presently—so the lads and I shall be tapping our feet to be off before you know it. Eh, lads?" He passed the crook into his left hand, with which he also held the jacket, and accepted Maisie's hand. "My, that's a strong shake you've got there, young lady. Can't abide a wet fish in my fingers, no I can't—can I, boys?" He looked down at the dogs, then back to Maisie. "And I like to see a person come to a farm with good solid footwear. Not like some of them land girls I've heard are turning up without even a pair of good boots. Now then, Miss whatever-your-name-was—state your business, because I've got to get about mine."

Maisie smiled. "Mr. Hutchins, I want to talk to you about Joe Coombes—I'm a friend of his parents, and I am also an investigator, so I'm trying to help get some questions answered for them, about his passing. Can you help me?"

The man's ready smile evaporated. He looked down at his feet. The older of the two dogs whimpered. "You'd best come in then," said Hutchins, pointing to the farmhouse with his shepherd's crook.

Maisie declined the offer of tea, and Hutchins joined her at the kitchen table, where he had drawn back a chair for her when they entered. The kitchen was neat, as if everything was in its designated place. The pine table was scrubbed and clean. The red-tiled floor smelled of disinfectant.

"You keep a comfortable farmhouse, Mr. Hutchins," said Maisie. "I live in the midst of several farms, and I know a good farmer when I see one."

"Farm has to run like a ship—otherwise you never know what might end up overboard in a storm." He rapped the knuckles of his right hand on the table. "Right then, miss—let's get down to it. What do you want to know about Joe?"

"I'd heard that you'd befriended him, and that he had visited you here at the farm."

"That's true," said Hutchins. "Took to my young pup there, and started asking me about him, and about how I train them for sheep. I don't only have my own two, but that one's mother, and I sell the pups when she has them. I breed a good sheepdog, and there's farmers who know it. The bitch whelped again just afore Joe died. I let him have first pick."

"Really? Joe?" said Maisie.

"Don't look so surprised! He might have been a London boy, but he soon had the country in him. Loved it here, he did. And he came over to the farm many an evening, and would sit here talking to me, asking me questions. Came out with me to watch the dogs working. He asked me for one and I told him—put one of them dogs in London and you'll have a lunatic on your hands. Fifty mile a day that dog can do—easy. Been bred for a job, not to sit in front of a fire. Mind you, mine always like the fire of a winter's evening, I must say. My late wife said I was a soft touch with the dogs. But they work for it, and they're good 'uns. Joe said he wouldn't want a dog in London, that he wanted to work for me here on the farm. Said he'd had enough of it all, London, the painting, and going round the country to these airfields."

Maisie leaned forward, resting her elbows on the table, and drawing closer to Hutchins. "I am not shocked, Mr. Hutchins, but perhaps a little taken aback. I'd heard that Joe missed home, and that he wanted to finish with the job."

"Right enough he did. He'd had enough of all of them. But he didn't want to go home, and that's a fact."

Maisie looked down at her hands. She was in no hurry to continue, and felt that Hutchins was waiting for her to say something. And she suspected he was waiting for her to ask the right question—a question that he could answer without feeling as if he had revealed a confidence.

"Was Joe troubled, would you say?" Maisie looked up into the farmer's eyes.

"He was."

"And what was he troubled about?"

"I don't know, though I tried to find out."

"And how did you do that—how did you try to find out?"

"We'd go out to the fields, check the sheep of an evening after he'd finished at one of them airfields, and then we'd come down to the house for a cup of tea and perhaps a bite to eat. Sometimes he'd stay and sometimes he had to get back to the other lads, or to have the dinner his landlady had put out for him. He'd sit there, right where you are now, and we'd talk, and as time went on, it was always as if he wanted to tell me something, but just couldn't get the words out."

"Do you think he was in trouble?" asked Maisie.

Hutchins shook his head. "I know what a lad looks like when he's in trouble, when he's been up to something, and that wasn't the look he had. No, it wasn't that kind of trouble. But it was close—it was as if he was trying not to get into trouble."

"Do you think someone was making him do something he didn't want to do?"

"Well, his father was for a start."

Maisie frowned, and was about to speak when Hutchins continued.

"Far as I can make out, Joe wanted to ask for his cards from this Yates business and get another job—he wanted to come to work on the farm. But he said his father had put his foot down, that he said that if he gave up working for Yates, then he might as well never come home again. He told Joe you don't give up a chance of a craftsman job, an apprenticeship that could lead to something. I remember him sitting there, and saying, 'I don't want to go where this job is leading though. I want to stay on your farm.' He was only a boy." He sighed. "I can see his father's point, but Joe told me his father had just brushed it off when he told him about the headaches. Not sure I would have done that—but I don't know. Not my place to comment upon how another man raises his son. But I know this—they're soon gone, especially if there's a war on."

Maisie nodded. "Do you think Joe was scared of anything?"

Hutchins met her eyes once again. "I do, Miss Dobbs. Yes, I do. Only I don't know what it was. He wouldn't tell me. I said to him, one evening, out there with the dogs, I said, 'Come on, lad, a problem shared is a problem halved. Tell me what's bothering you, and it might not seem so bad—like putting on the light in a dark room.'"

Maisie smiled. "A very dear friend of mine once said the same thing—about putting on the light in a dark room. He told me that when we keep secrets they grow inside us, and we can't see the truth of them anymore."

"That's about the measure of it," said Hutchins.

"What Joe couldn't tell me could have been a small thing, or it might have been something much bigger than he could manage. But he was scared—and he seemed fearful of what might befall me if I knew what it was."

"Did he say as much?" asked Maisie.

"Just that it was best if I didn't know. That's words of a fair size for a young man."

"Yes, you're right."

Phineas Hutchins broke the silence that followed.

"Now, Miss Dobbs, you can answer a question for me. You've been looking a bit surprised ever since we met. First out there in the courtyard, and now in here. You keep looking around my kitchen, as if there's something you find curious about me and my house."

"Forgive me, Mr. Hutchins—but I was told to expect a quite different person."

Hutchins laughed. "Bet it was that Freddie, the one who was supposed to keep an eye on Joe. I surmised he was the foreman, and in that position, he should mind the apprentices. It's part of the job—just like Odin here looks after his apprentice, Loki." The dogs pricked up their ears as their names were spoken. "First time Freddie saw me, I'd been out there in the courtyard loading up two pigs being taken to market. I'd had a miserable time of it. As a rule I'd have a good old wash and brush up before I went to the local, but this time I had a thirst on me and I didn't care what anyone thought—and me and the landlord grew up together, so he knew I was usually better turned out. Anyway, that was when Joe came over to talk about the dogs, and we became friends." The man looked down at his hands, and in that moment it was as if every line on his forehead, every fold of skin on his face, became more apparent. "He was a good boy, Joe. He was my friend and I do miss him. Nice to have a lad around again, here in the house."

Maisie nodded, and took one of Hutchins' hands in her own. Some seconds passed before she spoke again. "I should be going, Mr. Hutchins." She slipped her hand away and took a card from her pocket. "This is my card. If you can think of anything else that might help me, please get in touch."

"'Fore you go, miss—come out to the barn. Want to show you something."

Hutchins led the way, first to the courtyard, then to another small outbuilding. He drew Maisie inside and pointed to a large boxed-in area filled with straw.

"Oh, my goodness. May I?"

"The mum's name is Freya. She's not as protective as she was—she's already started nipping at them, telling them who's boss. Take a pup away from the mother too soon, and you take away the first lessons in life, so I leave them with her a bit longer than some might. She's letting them all know they can't be top dog. She'll let you pet them."

Maisie knelt down to stroke the pups, who nipped and tumbled trying to get to her outstretched hand.

Hutchins pointed to one of the pups. "That one there—with the one blue eye, one black—he's the one I earmarked for Joe. They're all spoken for," said the farmer. "Even with the war. Work has to go on and a farmer needs good dogs." He knelt down beside Maisie and picked up the one he had chosen for Joe, holding it to his chest as he stroked the pup. "This one stays though. Not getting rid of Joe's boy. Going to call him by the name he chose for his dog. He went to the library and looked up names so it fit with my little gods here—and of course, my goddess." He smiled as he reached across to ruffle the bitch's ears, setting the pup in front of its mother. "Joe wanted to call him Magni. That's the god of strength. Seems only right he'll have that name, even though Joe's not here."

Later, as Maisie bid good-bye to Phineas Hutchins, she wished she had known about him sooner, for the perspective he offered regarding the final weeks of Joe's life was not quite what she was expecting, though she was not surprised. Despite taking more time than she had hoped, it seemed the mystery surrounding the

death of Joe Coombes was beginning to give up its secrets. "Everything yields to pressure, Maisie," Maurice
had taught her. "The slow drip of water on stone will,
in time, wear away a ridge. Even the strongest metal, if
enough weight is applied, will start to bend. Some cases
will begin to give quickly. But do not despair of the as-
signment when it seems to defy every effort. Just give
it time. Continue with your work, with your questions
and your observations. Wait for the yielding."

There was one more task to be completed before
setting off on her journey back to London. She slowed
down alongside All Hallows Church, parked the motor
car and entered the place of worship. The church was
cool and damp, and to the left as she entered was the
town's war memorial plaque. One by one she read
down the long accounting of young men from the town
who had perished in the years 1914 to 1918. And there
he was. Joseph Hutchins. Age nineteen.

She returned to the Alvis, took the driver's seat once
again, started the engine, slipped the motor car into
gear and drove off toward the Winchester Road. At
last, slowly but surely, the yielding had begun.

Chapter 13

Detective Inspector Murphy met Maisie at the entrance to Basingstoke Police Station.

"Caldwell was on the blower, telling me you were coming in and to accord you any assistance you required," said Murphy.

"He did?" said Maisie, taken aback.

"He holds you in high regard, but he is one of those people who seems to enjoy being contrary, doesn't he?"

"That's one way of putting it—though we get on a lot better than we used to."

Murphy laughed. "I bet it only took one case where you proved your point, eh?" He opened the door to the street and indicated a waiting black motor car, the engine idling, a driver at the wheel. "I'm not so against private inquiry agents myself, as long as everyone plays fair and isn't like a dog in a manger with the details. And especially now—I've lost a few lads to the services, and that makes surveillance of criminal activity very tricky, with men thin on the ground."

The driver stepped out of the motor car as Murphy and Maisie approached, and opened the rear passenger door. They took their seats and were soon under way.

"You'll see that where we're going is more or less around the back of the station. There's a high wall, the one we believe Joe leapt from, and the railway line below. That part of the line was laid down when the railway was built, and is used to shunt a loco into for a while—perhaps while it's awaiting maintenance or cleaning. It's not been used much in recent years, and you'll see the buffers end at another part of the wall—it takes a dogleg turn there."

"Right, I understand."

"Up above and behind the wall is a road usually used as a shortcut down to the station—busy enough during the day, but not at night. Never at night—too quiet and what with the blackout, no light at all. The railway line at that point is not exactly looked after. You won't see any hanging baskets of flowers, and there's weeds all over the place. Broken bottles where lads have thrown them over, and all sorts of mess. Even if that lad had lived, tetanus would have got him, the state of the place. But like I said, not used much in years."

At the station, they were met by the station master, who led them out beyond the platform. Looking both ways, he waved them across the lines to the other side, then behind a series of red brick buildings coated in smoke dust.

"It's very dirty back here, madam, so watch yourself," said the station master.

Soon they stopped at a place where brick walls rose up on two sides—one tall enough to reach the street above, and the other joining railway buildings. Maisie thought it was like being in a three-sided brick box, a cul-de-sac for trains. Turning around from the buffers toward the open side, she could follow the weed-clogged line to where it joined a main line, with the signal box in the distance. Even on a warm day it was a cold, dark place.

"I'll stand over there, Inspector, so you can go about your business. Just shout if you need me, though I know you've got my statement," said the station master.

"Much obliged to you. We shan't be here long." Murphy beckoned to Maisie as the stationmaster walked along the line a short way.

A train passed along another line, punching out steam as it slowed for the platform. The stationmaster took out his watch, checked the time and nodded to himself. He kept the watch at the ready, studying the platform from his vantage point, waiting for the whistle to blow and the train to begin the onward journey.

Murphy didn't begin speaking again until the train departed. Maisie wiped a few smuts of damp coal dust from her jacket.

"Can you imagine working in a railway station?" commented Murphy. "You'd be forever washing your clothes!" He shook his head, then turned and walked farther along the short disused stretch of line. "Just along here."

Chalk marked the spot where Joe Coombes' body had been found. Maisie knelt down and ran her fingers along the cast iron railway line.

"Was there much blood?"

"Not as much as you might have thought," said Murphy. "But we were hampered by all this muck around here—and whatever it was that Dr. Clark found in his brain matter."

"I don't think that would have affected blood flow when he fell." She looked up at Murphy. "If he fell."

"All the other indicators are there, that he fell from that wall," said Murphy, pushing back his hat and scratching his head. He continued as Maisie looked up at the wall. "In the dark it might not have looked like a long way down—he probably thought it was only a couple of feet."

"Have you searched the area around here?" asked Maisie.

"With a fine-tooth comb."

She nodded, coming to her feet. "Inspector, would you mind if I spent just a couple of minutes here alone. I'd just like to think a bit, and have another poke around."

Murphy nodded and turned to join the station master. Maisie remained in place until he was some yards away, then she knelt down again, this time placing both hands firmly on the railway line. She closed her eyes and imagined the Joe she remembered, the happy-go-lucky lad she would see walking along Warren Street toward the pub where his family lived above the business. She modulated her breathing.

"Come on, Joe. Give me a clue. What happened to you?"

The pain did not come on slowly—instead it was as if she had been struck by a piece of iron as hard as that she was now clutching to retain her balance while kneeling. She gasped and raised one hand to the back of her head, feeling as if she were in a dark, narrow thoroughfare. She could hear water running. Or could she? The sensation lasted only two or three seconds, but it had taken her breath away. She opened her eyes, and began searching the ground between the railway lines, brushing debris from the black creosoted wooden sleepers, picking through the rocks between them. She poked here and there with her fingers, sure—though she knew not why—that she would find something.

"All right, Miss Dobbs?" Murphy called to her.

"Just another minute, Inspector. I'll be ready soon."

She stood up and looked down. To one side she saw a stick, which she picked up and used to move stones and gravel. Then it caught her eye—a glint as the sun emerged from behind a cloud. She knelt again, using her fingers to pull out a small metal disc from between two pebbles. She turned it in her fingers and read the word engraved upon it. *Magni*. Magni, the Norse god of strength. It was meant for Joe's pup. She wrapped her fingers around the disc, and came to her feet. Was there any meaning in her finding the small round of silver metal? Or did Joe simply want his dog to have the name on his collar lest he be lost, and the disc had fallen out of his pocket as he fell? Or was he clutching it, for the comfort, and perhaps in the hope that he might live? She looked at the name again, and turned the disc. *Joe Coombes, Moorwood Farm.* It appeared Hutchins was right—Joe had never intended to go home.

This time she was not followed on the journey back to London. As tempted as she was to go directly to Chelstone, there were other matters to attend to. The first was Priscilla. Though it was evening by the time she arrived in Holland Park, she went to her friend's house first.

When Maisie was shown into the drawing room, she found Priscilla sipping a gin and tonic and smoking a cigarette, which was pressed into the long holder she had favored since she first began flirting with tobacco in her late teens.

"At last!" said Priscilla, coming to her feet. Still holding her cocktail and cigarette, she fanned her arms out to each side so as not to burn Maisie or spill her drink, and pressed her cheek to Maisie's.

"Sit down, Pris, before you lose your G and T," said Maisie.

"Want one?"

"Small—more tonic, less gin. Thank you." Maisie took a seat at the opposite end of the chesterfield while Priscilla poured a drink for Maisie and refreshed her own.

"We've been cast into the ambulance driver failure pit, you know. I made a point of telephoning to tell our supervisor that due to personal reasons—my son is missing, possibly on a boat going back and forth to Dunkirk, and that you are in pursuit of the truth, as always—we would not be at drill this week, and next week looks dodgy."

"What did he say."

"Let's just leave it that we're still on the roster, by the skin of our teeth. They need us, Maisie, but they need us back soon."

Maisie nodded and sipped her drink, then looked at Priscilla, who had taken her place on the chesterfield.

"It was bloody dreadful, Maisie. I know we shouldn't have been there, and it was a nightmare, but I had to go. There were men coming off those boats who looked as if they had seen into the jaws of hell. They were utterly exhausted, filthy, many emaciated and yet they were holding up the wounded." She raised her free hand to her eyes, as if to banish the images, then continued. "But to a man they were doing their best to remain of good heart—raising a smile as they said thank you for a blanket and a cup of tea. I had to go there just to find out, Maisie, and then it was clear we had to leave—there were so many people there, and most seemed to have a job and know what they were doing. We were just in the way. Douglas has been my rock, and Billy's miracle gave me hope—no one could believe it happened. It was heartbreaking, Maisie, seeing him try to run, stumbling toward his boy—and it might not even have been him. It could have been an hallucination driven by hope. To be honest, at first I thought Billy was imagining it, because they all looked the same. Tired beyond measure, relieved, streaked with oil—and so many coming off the ships with that long stare, as if there was nothing but emptiness behind the eyes. We used to see it in France, didn't we? When men came back down the line from the front. The doctors called it the ten-thousand-yard stare." She looked down at her drink, turned toward the ashtray on a side table, and extinguished the cigarette. "Bloody things. I know I must smell like a chimney at times. I should give them up."

"Priscilla," said Maisie.

"Yes?"

"I think Tim and Gordon will come back into Rye. I just feel they will set a course for home, and home means Rye—it's where they sealed their friendship while sailing, and the place they know."

"According to Gordon's father—before he left for France in his other launch—he was told that no boats were officially sent from Rye to Dunkirk. Mind you, we know of one, don't we? I can't see them out on the ocean wave this long for a pleasure sail, can you? And this could go on for days. Days! If I know my boy, he won't come back before he's done what he set out to do. Stubborn since the day he was born, that one. Tom's a gentleman, Tarquin is tractable and Tim is bloody stubborn. My mother said she had to watch my middle brother more than the others." Priscilla rested her head back on the chesterfield.

"Trust in Tim, Priscilla. Trust in him. He will be home. I know it." She took a breath and exhaled, reaching for Priscilla's hand. "And anyway, Anna said so."

"Oh, I would trust that girl of yours before I would put my faith in anyone else I've met, and that's no exaggeration." She looked at her now empty glass, then at Maisie. "I'm going to telephone the coastguard again and get on their nerves. I've sent Tarquin off to stay with a school friend to take his mind off his brother and his mother, and Douglas is up to his eyes with work at the ministry, which is good for him—if he's writing about this bloody disaster making it seem all very under control, then it gives him hope." She sighed. "When shall we go to Rye, Maisie?"

"Not yet. But I think soon. Perhaps you'd all like to come to Chelstone at the end of the week—get away from London."

"Might be a good idea," said Priscilla. "By the way,

forgive me, I should have asked—any news from the inimitable Mr. Klein?"

"A few stumbling blocks."

"Like life. One bloody stumbling block after the other," said Priscilla. "Oh hell, I'm having another drink."

The following day Maisie stood outside Faraday House in the City at a quarter to twelve, and waited. The Faraday Buildings housed not only the General Post Office headquarters, as well as international and government telephone exchanges, but was also known to be an alternative fortification for the government, should Whitehall come under attack. The outside was packed with sandbags several layers deep, and it seemed to Maisie that it was almost as if she were waiting for insects to start leaving their nest, ants running out of the mound.

She checked her watch. At noon a stream of women began emerging from the building, some in groups, others on their own. It was lunchtime, a break in a long day spent staring at a switchboard, connecting people across the country, the world, across London and—for Vivian Coombes—from one highly confidential government office to another.

Half-past twelve. No Vivian, but it seemed to Maisie that the women took staggered breaks, and there were also shift changes. Quarter to one. One o'clock. At two minutes past one, Vivian Coombes emerged from beyond the wall of sandbags, and looked up at the sky. As she walked toward her, Maisie noticed how well she was dressed—a powder blue skirt, white blouse, navy-blue jacket and matching navy-blue shoes and bag. She carried her gas mask over the same shoulder as the bag, and her hat was a pale blue with navy band. She called out to her as she came closer.

"Hello Vivian—what a coincidence! I just left a meeting and was passing when I saw you."

"Oh, Miss Dobbs—I almost didn't recognize you."

"That happens when you see someone away from the place where you usually expect to see them. Takes you aback. Are you on your lunch hour?"

"Lunch half hour if I'm lucky, you mean!" said Coombes. "There's a big cafeteria at the top of the building, but it's nice to get a bit of fresh air, so I come out for a walk sometimes—bring a sandwich from home, or just have a cup of tea somewhere."

"There's a Kardomah not far from here—may I buy you a sandwich and cup of tea?"

The young woman consulted her watch. "All right then. But I've to be back by half-past."

The entrance to the Kardomah coffee house was

packed with sandbags from top to bottom, with the word *KARDOMAH* the only indication that the narrow doorway led through to the café. It was busy, but they found two seats together. Vivian checked her watch again. Maisie ordered tea and sandwiches for two.

"What I'd really like, to tell you the truth, is a bacon sandwich—makes me wonder when it's all going to come off ration," said Coombes. She looked around the café, and raised a hand to acknowledge a couple of fellow telephonists.

Maisie knew she had not much time, so she broached the subject sooner than she might otherwise have done.

"Vivian, it's fortuitous I saw you—I'd like to ask a couple of questions about Joe."

The young woman looked at Maisie. "I hope you're not going to make me cry—I can't go back in there with big red eyes. The supervisor takes a dim view of a poor appearance."

"I don't think so, Vivian—but I'm trying to get to the truth about Joe's death, and I believe you want me to find out, don't you?"

Maisie noticed the slight delay in Coombes' reply, as if she were weighing the meaning of Maisie's words.

"Yes, we're all wanting to know, my family and me."

"Good. First of all, did you know Joe wanted to

leave his apprenticeship? He had a very specific job in mind that he wanted to take up instead."

"Dad said he had a stupid idea about becoming a shepherd, if that's what you mean. My brothers can come up with cockeyed ideas at times."

"Joe was quite serious. He had a pup ready to train—did you know that?"

Vivian Coombes rolled her eyes. "No, I didn't, but it wouldn't surprise me."

"Your other brother, Archie—he looks after the family to some extent, doesn't he?"

"What do you mean? Looks after?" Coombes straightened her shoulders. She folded her arms, and leaned back, taking herself out of the sphere of her interrogator's influence—Maisie knew this was the first move of the defensive person. She pulled her chair closer to Coombes.

"I meant that he seems to be a good lad—he works away from home, but he clearly earns a fair wage, and I understand he makes sure his family benefit from it too."

"We all look after one other. Archie and me, we were always close—Joe was our little brother."

"Then you must know Teddy Wickham."

There was a slight hesitation before Coombes responded. "Of course I do—he was always over at the pub, when we were younger. Him and Archie are good mates."

Maisie held Vivian's gaze. "They still keep in touch then—has Archie visited Teddy?"

The young woman shrugged. "I dunno." Another glance at her watch. Another sip of tea and bite of the sandwich.

"What do you know about a man named Jimmy Robertson."

Her color heightened, Joe Coombes' sister picked up her cup again, and took another sip. She lifted her wrist to look at her watch.

"I only know what's in the papers—if that's the Jimmy Robertson you mean. From the Robertson family." She set down the cup. "I've got to get back now—my supervisor will be after me if I'm late."

"I'll walk with you. I've a couple more things you can help me with."

"All right. If you want."

They emerged from the coffee shop and, almost by instinct, both looked up at the barrage balloon floating above their heads.

"I don't think them things are going to stop old Hitler, do you?" said Coombes.

"Fortunately, there's the air force, the army and the navy between him and us," said Maisie.

"Not much army and they're keeping back the air force because they'll need every man they've got up there when the invasion starts—you should have my job, you'd know what's going on."

"Yes, I suppose I would." The two women fell into step toward the Faraday Buildings. Maisie took the opportunity to ask another question. "You must hear quite a lot, and you have a weight of information on your shoulders that you have to keep secret. It can't be easy, can it?"

"You just have to forget it and connect the next call. I'm on the government exchanges, and I'm younger than others in my room, so I have to do as well or better than them. Or I'll be back connecting women crying about their husbands to their sisters."

"I'm sure you must be privy to some quite emotional revelations. Oh, and of course here you're not far from the Bank of England too—I expect those calls come through your exchange, money being so important to the country, to the government."

"We get all sorts of calls, like I said."

They had reached the entrance to the Faraday Buildings. Maisie looked up at the structure, and then at Vivian Coombes.

"You've done well to secure a good position here, Vivian."

"I had to work for it, Miss Dobbs. The civil service exams, memorizing exchanges, learning correct enunciation, all that sort of thing—and then you have to be tall. They only take you if you're over five feet six, otherwise you wouldn't be able to reach the top jacks on the board." She looked at the top of Maisie's head, as if to assess her height. "You'd be all right for this job, being as you're tall too."

Maisie smiled. "Perhaps we can talk again, Vivian—you probably know so much about Joe that would be helpful, and I know it's difficult to discuss it because the shock of his death is still very raw."

Coombes' eyes filled with tears. "I just never thought it would come to this, that's all."

"What do you mean, Vivian? That it would never come to what?"

She shrugged, composing herself. "That it would never come to it that Joe would be the first of us to go. That's all. Because he was the youngest. He shouldn't have been first. Now then—I've got to get back to work. Bye."

Maisie watched the telephonist vanish into a snake of young women making their way back through the sandbagged entrance to the Faraday Buildings. Returning to a place where they were sworn to keep all manner of secrets—between husbands and wives, between lovers, government departments, long-lost friends. And even, she thought, secrets concerning the movement of money.

It was as Maisie walked away, toward the underground station, that she realized she had forgotten to impart an important piece of information to Vivian Coombes. She would have liked to let her know that young Private Billy Beale was home safe from the shores of Dunkirk. But perhaps it was best she hadn't. For as they'd walked away from the coffee house, along streets flanked by sandbagged buildings, Maisie had taken a moment to mirror the way Vivian Coombes carried herself. So much was revealed in the way a person walked—and it was a simple technique, a means of understanding something of a person without their knowledge. But it was important to be distinct in the interpretation. By the time she made her way through the turnstiles at the underground station, Maisie was wondering how best to describe the waves of fear and regret she felt emanating from Vivian Coombes as she walked alongside her.

"Billy, look at this," said Maisie, pointing to the case map. She had been back in the office for only twenty minutes when Billy came in, his footfall heavy on the stairs before he entered.

"Aren't you even going to ask where I've been?" said Billy. "Any other employer would."

"I know where you've been, Billy—your son is at home now, probably on a few days' leave before he has to report for duty again, and you wanted to see a bit more of him."

"He says I'm the only one he can talk to, that he can't talk to his mum about it, or his brother. And he definitely can't talk to his little sister—won't even let her near him when she wants to give him a cuddle to make it all better. That's what she keeps saying. 'Let's make Billy all better, Daddy.'"

"Billy—you should be at home, really."

"Nah, he was sleeping when I left. Like the dead. Got a nasty tear along the shoulder, where a bullet just skimmed along. Could have killed him, miss—could have killed my boy."

"But it didn't kill him. Someone was watching over him."

"Our little Lizzie. That's who." Billy took out a handkerchief and blew his nose. "They patched him up at the military hospital and sent him home for a few days."

Maisie pulled out a chair for Billy, and leaned back.

"It must have brought back a lot of difficult memories for you, Billy—would you like to take the load off? And I don't mean your feet."

Billy gave a half-laugh, slumping into the chair. "I can't let it take me down again, miss—I need the backbone for our Billy." He looked at his hands, then back to Maisie. "But what he told me made me sick, miss. And he said, 'Dad, I was lucky—I got away early. It's bound to be worse now.'"

"Go on," said Maisie.

"He told me all about it—and, miss, I don't know if I can bear to think about what's going on over there. Billy says the expeditionary force is being driven right back to the coast by the Germans. And I mean, right back. There's men out there, our boys—and the French—holding the line so more can get to the coast, and when they get there, they're lining up, masses of them, hoping to get onto a boat and sail for home. Some even tried to swim for it. And the blimmin' Germans are coming down, flying above the beach and strafing the poor buggers. They're bombing the navy ships and gunning them—coming in right overhead so the navy boys can't get their big guns raised vertical enough to defend themselves. He saw one ship—a hospital ship, with a blimmin' great red cross on it that you couldn't miss from Mars—and the Luftwaffe came in for the attack and it sunk in seconds. There were doctors and nurses on board, wounded, and any other poor sods they could take. And Billy said he almost got on that one. The army's having to leave everything—tanks, guns, motor cars. I tell you, miss, a miracle got hold of my son, pushed him to the front of the queue and brought him home."

Maisie said nothing, allowing silence to wrap itself around Billy's story. A minute passed before he looked up, pinched the bridge of his nose and sighed.

"Now then, what was it you wanted me to look at, miss?"

"The case map—here." Maisie's voice was little more than a whisper, as she pointed to a long red line between two names, then linking it to a third.

"I should've seen it coming—if anyone's going to make money out of a war, it'd be that one."

"I just don't have the links in place, Billy—that's the trouble. I have to find the links."

"I'll go over and—"

Maisie shook her head. "Not this time, Billy. Doreen's coping very well, all things considered, and I don't want her given cause to slip. Life is too fragile, isn't it? In fact, considering the situation, I am wondering about the future of the business—for the duration of the war, anyway."

"You'll still be busy, mark my words."

"That's not it—though I can see that pile of inquiries Sandra has left for me on the desk."

"And this one," said Billy, tapping the case map. "Is one you're doing for nothing, no payment from anyone."

"That's why there are some in that pile we have to start working on. There's nothing big in there—I just glanced through them. But enough to keep us on our toes." She reached for the sheaf of six or seven inquiry messages and placed them on the table. "I've just been considering how we should work—if the worst happens and there's an invasion, or London is targeted by the Luftwaffe. It might be an idea to limit the time we spend here, don't you think?"

Billy shook his head. "Everyone has to go to work, miss—you can't let them win, not this easily."

"I wasn't planning to lose anything—especially not my employees."

"And I'll second what Billy said," said Sandra. Maisie had not heard her enter the office. "Lawrence says life has to go on, so we're staying."

Maisie looked at Billy and Sandra. "All right—that subject is out of bounds for now, but I may come back to it. Your safety is paramount in my book." She beckoned Sandra to a chair on the other side of the table bearing the case map. "Indeed, we'll discuss it again when this case is closed. Right now, it seems to be splitting open wider every day."

With Billy dispatched to call upon three of the prospective new clients, Maisie spent some time with Sandra going over the afternoon's work, and then made her way downstairs to the front door—she had an appointment with her solicitor. As she closed the front door behind her, she heard someone calling after her.

"Miss Dobbs—Miss Dobbs."

"Mr. Miles—how are you?" Walter Miles reached the top step of the stairs that led from the basement flat up to the street. "Oh, and I must thank you once again for getting me out of a tight spot the other day."

"I was wondering if everything was all right now— are you safe?" asked Miles.

"I'm not sure I was particularly unsafe, but I didn't want to be followed by that motor car."

"They have been back, you know," said Miles.

Maisie felt the familiar ice cold sensation across her neck, as if a finger had traced the old wartime scar that was now hardly visible.

"You've seen them?"

He nodded. "You weren't here, nor were your two friends, as I discovered. There were two men, one older, one younger. The older one waited across the road in the motor car, while the younger came toward the square, lingering over there with his newspaper and cigarette. When one of the students who lives upstairs left, the younger one sprinted across and caught the door just in time. I'd been tending my plants down there." He pointed to a lower window, where a series of flowers struggled to bloom in terra-cotta pots. "That area never catches the sun, but I try, though my ministrations are not as successful as they are in the courtyard at the back. Anyway, I'd come up a few steps to look across, that's how I knew what was going on. I was worried that Mrs. Pickering was upstairs on her own with young Martin, so I went into my flat and then up to your office via the inside staircase. I found the man outside the door, looking at the lock. It's a good one, isn't it?"

"What happened?"

"I asked him if he needed assistance, and he—very quickly—asked me if it was where Vivian lived. I told him he had the wrong address, and sent him on his way. I would say he picked the name out of thin air—it was probably his mother's name, which is why it came to mind when he was put on the spot."

Maisie nodded. "Thank you, Mr. Miles—I am much obliged to you for looking out for us." She smiled, not wanting him to know her level of concern. "And thank you for being so thoughtful regarding the safety of my staff—especially Mrs. Pickering. I—I didn't know you'd already met."

"Oh, she always says hello. Such a nice young lady, and not often you see a woman working following marriage and especially now she has a child. I suppose times are changing. But that lock stood you in good stead."

"Yes, it certainly has been worth it." Maisie paused. "Actually, before her marriage to Mr. Pickering, she was a widow—her first husband was killed in a terrible accident. But he had put in those locks for me when they were courting, and the subsequent tenant obviously kept them—I've leased the office twice, you see."

Miles nodded and began to retreat down the stairs, holding on to the railing for balance as he took each step. "I'd better get back to work, Miss Dobbs. Always much to do."

As she walked toward the Tube station, Maisie considered two elements of the conversation with Walter Miles—first, the fact that the younger man Miles had intercepted had said he was looking for "Vivian." The second was that Miles had seemed so easy to confide in.

Sandra had clearly made his acquaintance, to the extent that he was concerned for her safety. And for her part, she had told a story about Sandra's past—something that, as a rule, she wouldn't do. Now she was intrigued, though the intrigue did not extend to the man looking for Vivian. She already knew his identity.

Chapter 14

Four days had passed since the service at Westminster Abbey. Four days since Tim's disappearance. Later in the afternoon, Maisie would collect her motor car, pick up Priscilla, and the two would drive to Chelstone. Priscilla would be distracted from worrying about her son by the journey, then—hopefully—by life at Chelstone and being away until Monday, at least.

The more she thought about it, the more sound Maisie considered her plan to limit the time she, Billy and Sandra spent in the office during the week. Sandra was already working only on those days when administrative tasks had piled up, and she seemed to enjoy coming in. She and her husband were renting Maisie's old flat in Pimlico, and had made no plans to move, despite having a new baby to consider. Lawrence's small publishing firm was located in London, and employed several people, so they could not up and move. Indeed, Sandra's fears while expecting—of bringing a child into a country at war—seemed to have been put aside, which surprised Maisie. Billy lived outside the capital, and if need be could work from home on occasion, traveling as any investigation demanded. For her part, she was beginning to begrudge time spent in London when she could be in Kent, at the Dower House and closer to her family. Fortunately, as she had told Billy and Sandra, business was still coming in, and in fact seemed to have increased of late—which in turn could mean her plan might not work.

The telephone was ringing when she entered the office. She ran to the desk and picked up the receiver. The caller addressed her before she could issue a greeting.

"Is that Miss Dobbs?"

"Yes, speaking," said Maisie, recognizing the voice.

"Clarissa Clark here. Do you have a moment, Miss Dobbs?"

With one hand, Maisie removed her hat. "Of course, Dr. Clark."

"It's regarding Joseph Coombes. As you know by now, I have had to be less decisive in my report than I might have wanted to be—to be fair, it was entirely possible that the injury to the skull could well have taken place during a fall onto the railway lines. But that's not why I'm calling."

"Go on," said Maisie.

"I've been studying Joe's brain matter. By the way, I hope you don't mind me calling him 'Joe.' The police don't always like it—they want to remain detached, claiming it makes them lose focus or some such thing. But Dr. Blanche taught us that we should speak to the dead by name—it helps us to remember respect, and to keep our questions coming. I'm sure you know that. Anyway, I've always done it—I find it's led me up some very fruitful alleys of inquiry, and reminds me I'm dealing with a human being who was alive and in the world until fate stepped in to stamp the time card." She paused, and Maisie heard a leaf of paper turn. "Right, anyway, as I said, I was studying Joe's brain matter, and as you know it bothered me, this discoloration. So I spoke to a neurologist friend of mine because I know he's interested in diseases of the brain and how they affect behavior. He came down to the lab here to have a look, and we've come to the conclusion that it's likely that Joe was suffering from more than the physical sensation of headache, but also dizziness and swings in mood. He might also have been sensitive to sound."

"Traffic, and such like."

"Yes."

"That explains one thing—he didn't want to go back to London. He wanted to leave his job and stay in the country, working on a farm."

"Hmmm, psychology is more your bailiwick, but I would say the physical trauma to the brain from whatever toxins he had been exposed to would have led people to say things such as 'Joe isn't himself these days.'"

"Yes, that's why his parents came to me. But what about the injury that killed him."

"To be fair, it could just as well have happened as a result of a fall as a blunt instrument." Clark sighed, and Maisie thought she sounded exasperated. "There were tiny specks of cast iron in the hair and brain, but the railway line is iron, so that doesn't help. And the behavior I've indicated might have led him to jump—my colleague has pointed that out."

Maisie picked up a pencil and tapped it on the desk, mindful of Clarissa Clark's position. "I applaud you for keeping an open mind, Dr. Clark—but I have a feeling you believe he was killed elsewhere. Since we spoke, have you encountered any evidence to suggest his death might have happened at another location?"

"That railway siding is a dirty, filthy place. People have thrown fish and chip wrappings over the wall as they passed on the road above, cigarette stubs, and even urinated onto the railway. There's over a century of accumulated debris down there, and it was last cleaned decades ago because it's not even used much for shunting engines back and forth these days. The station master likes everything to look shipshape where people can see the platform, but this part of the station is out of the way."

"So, the rubbish on the line made it difficult to reach a final conclusion."

"Not quite," said Clark. "In fact, I was a little surprised because, having been to the location where the body was found, I would have expected to see more evidence of debris from the site in the actual bone matter and hair, and on the clothing. But I didn't. He either had a clean fall, or he was laid there after the point of death. The police are quite within their rights to have asked for a declaration of death by misadventure. What I am telling you is just speculation."

"Your word counts for something, Dr. Clark."

"Which is why I have to leave the door open for the possibility that Joe jumped from the wall above, perhaps while in an unstable frame of mind."

"I think you want to add more," said Maisie.

Clarissa Clark cleared her throat. "Miss Dobbs, you are engaged in a search for the truth, are you not?" Clark did not wait for a response from Maisie. "Then you should follow the injury sustained by Joe before the wounds that took his life. Look at what happened to his brain before his skull was cracked open. That's what killed Joe—whether he jumped, or not. In my humble opinion, of course."

"It's a web, though."

"I deal with them every day. Dr. Blanche gave us sage advice in order to untangle them. Patience, and one thread at a time."

Maisie smiled. "I've been thinking the same thing lately. Your conclusion confirms I'm going in the right direction. Thank you."

"Of course. Now then, I have to get to work. Joe's remains will be released to his family for burial soon, but I assure you I have kept copious notes, and also brought in a medical artist. It's something I do at times, if I feel it necessary."

"As evidence."

"Yes. Indeed. Now, I must go. Good day, Miss Dobbs."

"Thank you for telephoning, Dr. Clark."

Maisie replaced the receiver. Much of the pathologist's report was already known to Maisie. But she appreciated having her suspicions substantiated by Clark. She also rather liked speaking to a woman known for never having had a humble opinion in her life.

Maisie crossed the room to the window and looked down at the explosion of color now gracing Walter Miles' postage-stamp yard below. Her own walled garden in Holland Park was much larger, and laid to lawn with shrubs around the perimeter, and various vines clinging onto the bricks—wisteria, clematis, climbing roses. A gardener came in once a fortnight, and though she kept it tidy enough in the interim, she would never have considered herself proficient in the realm of horticulture—indeed, the flowering vines in Miles' yard were much further along than her own, and her garden received more direct sunlight, so it should have been equally abundant. Miles clearly had more than a green thumb—he was a gifted gardener. A book had been left on the small table, half read and upside down to keep the place. There was a cardigan over the back of one chair, and a notebook, as if he had only just left his seat. She wondered whether he worked, and if so what his profession might be. She was curious about Walter Miles.

"Morning, miss," said Billy, entering the office.

"Oh, hello Billy. Everything all right?"

"Our Billy is still spending most of the day in bed, but that's to be expected. He's received orders to be back at barracks on Monday for a medical exam, so the doctor can look at that wound and tell him whether he's well enough for service, or if he gets signed off for a bit longer. And Monday isn't many days to go, so I said to Doreen that he should try to be up and about today. Get Margaret Rose to nag him a bit to take her to the park when she comes home from school. He thinks the world of his little sister, and I know it's probably a bit odd, a man of his age having a young sister, but it would do him the power of good, I think, to go out to the park for a bit of a play."

Maisie looked over toward Billy.

"What? What did I just say?" asked Billy.

"You just referred to Billy as a man. Not a boy, and not a lad—you called him a man. And I think you're quite right—playing with a child will do him the power of good. You don't have much time to lighten the load on his shoulders."

"I'd like to see mine lightened, miss." Billy shook his head. "I signed the papers for Bobby last night. That's one thing his brother said to me, he said, 'Dad, if our Bobby is in the RAF as a mechanic, the chances are they can't send him anywhere they can send me.' And he reckoned his brother would be a lot safer on the ground, working on aircraft engines, so I signed it, and even his mother said I should. Bobby is now as happy as a sand boy, which is a mercy, as that face was getting as long as a week, and there's only so many miserable faces you can bear at the dinner table. Thank our lucky stars for Margaret Rose—she's our gem, truly she is." He exhaled, and continued relating family business. "So, you could say I've got two men now." He nodded toward the window. "And what's Farmer Miles up to out there? Put in a row of potatoes yet?"

Maisie laughed. "No, but he's certainly trying to better Kew Gardens. I'm amazed he has managed to do so much—remember how that used to look? Then the last tenant tried to make an improvement, but it took Mr. Miles to really change that yard into a very small smallholding!"

"He had some operations on his legs, but he's got his strength back, I would imagine."

"How come you and Sandra know so much about Walter Miles, and I didn't even know he lived there until a week ago? Who is he?"

"I was told by the woman at the dairy shop across the square, that she'd seen him quite a few times before he moved into the flat. He'd come in for some odds and ends—and then one day he told her he wanted to live in the square. She said he had been looking for a certain sort of rooms, with both a front and back entrance and a small yard, like the one he's got, so it all came right for him. He'd just come back from living in the south of France, apparently—he returned to see his doctor. The stairs at the front aren't too bad for him, and of course he can just let himself out the back, if he wants to. I've heard he's a lecturer at the university, over on Malet Street."

"Really? Then he's probably *Dr.* Miles. What does he teach?"

"Oh, I think you'd have to ask Sandra that one."

"I just don't know how I missed all this."

"You weren't paying attention—you rush in and rush off, and he's not exactly out there all the time waiting, is he? He keeps to himself, though he's been out the front a few times when I've come in, and he's always friendly. Interested in people who live around the square, passes the time of day and then goes on his way, or back downstairs."

Maisie shook her head. "Well I never. Anyway, I want to talk to you about the Coombes case."

"We're close, aren't we?"

Maisie nodded. "Yes, in a way, we are. I know the people, and I think I know the why—but bringing them to justice will be difficult, not least because the solid evidence is proving hard to nail down. I have lots of pieces, but making them fit is quite another thing."

"What do you think we should do next?"

"I'm leaving for Kent later today—taking Mrs. Partridge down to Chelstone, and then tomorrow we're driving along the coast from Rye to Ramsgate, stopping at every possible place where Tim and his friend might come in with the boat, which will be tricky, considering all the barbed wire laid across the beaches. But my money is still on Rye. Admittedly there's that long journey along the River Rother estuary to the Channel, but it's home for the boys, where they've always sailed from together."

"And the case?"

"I think it should stew in its own juices for a few days, but with a little help—I'm going along to see Phil and Sally Coombes in a minute, try to get them before opening time. I'm sure that somewhere, there's a connection with those Robertsons."

"There is, but not probably what you're looking for," said Billy.

"What do you mean?" said Maisie.

"I made a note of it so I'd remember to tell you before you went out today, and I only reminded myself yesterday evening."

"Go on, Billy." Maisie moved to the large table and sat down, pulling back another chair for her assistant to be seated alongside her. She unfurled the case map, and brought the tin filled with colored crayons closer.

Billy placed his notebook on the table and unfolded

a press cutting. He ran a palm across the scrap of news-paper, making it as flat as possible before pushing it toward Maisie.

She looked down at a row of faded faces, young men in uniform, smiling at the camera, as if sharing a joke at the photographer's expense.

"Are you in this?" asked Maisie.

"No, not me—never one to get my name in the paper. This was sent to me by my mum in the war, be-cause one of my cousins was in the photograph. Here, you can see, it says, 'London Boys Leave for France to Take On the Hun.' They're all lined up, waiting to get on the boat. See? That's Arthur, my cousin—Mum and her sister, my aunt, said we always favored brothers more than cousins. He was in the artillery though. I was showing Billy my war photographs last night—pictures of me and the lads I was with, over in France. I was trying to sort of get him to talk a bit, letting him know I understood how things are, when you're soldiering."

Maisie was already running her finger along the line of men. "Who am I looking for? There's someone here you want me to see, isn't there?"

"Right there, miss. You have to take account of time don't you, but I think that's Phil Coombes—look. If you can imagine Archie—he's the dead spitting image of his dad, when he was his age. That's what made me stop and look again."

"It's hardly surprising he was in the army though—there's more, isn't there?"

"You ever seen a photo of Jimmy Robertson?"

"Not recently, no," said Maisie.

"I was a bit late today because I had to go down to see my mate, the one who works for the *Express*. We went down to the newspaper storage place, and we found a picture of Robertson from a few year ago, when he was hauled up for armed robbery and the beak let him off. You see, I'd seen more recent photos in the papers, and it seemed to me that the bloke right there could be him. And it was him—there, next to Phil Coombes. In the artillery together."

"And someone like Jimmy Robertson doesn't forget anyone—because the anyone in question could be useful later." Maisie looked at the grainy cutting again, taking care not to tear the thinning folds. "Can I keep this?"

"It's all yours, miss—I never wanted it in the first place. When Mum sent this to me, she wrote in the letter, 'How come you can't get into the papers and make me famous on the street?' Which was a bit rich, if you ask me."

"I'll bring it back, Billy—this is part of your family's history, after all. You might change your mind." She placed the photograph in her bag. "Now then, I'm off to see Phil," said Maisie. "Any luck with those new inquiries?"

"Two on the go, miss. One woman thinks she's just married an officer in the navy who's married to someone else, and another who only really wanted some company, I reckon. She asked me about her missing watch and necklace, but I found them for her before twenty minutes was up—then she wanted me to stay for a cup of tea and insisted on paying me for the time—I'll put it in petty cash. She was just lonely, I reckon. Sad, eh?"

Maisie nodded and passed a crayon to Billy. "Would you do the honors and bring us up-to-date?" She tapped it onto the desk in front of him and gave a half-smile, knowing he was put out that she intended to see Phil and Sally Coombes on her own. "Look, I know you want to be helping with this case—but as soon as Jimmy Robertson's name came up, I knew we had to proceed with care." She sighed. "Billy, you almost died a few years ago, and even if you can't remember because you were in a coma, I remember the effect it had on Doreen. I can't risk that again, which is why I want you to take charge of the new cases. Just for now."

Billy shook his head. "But you could be walking

right into danger, and you've got little Anna to consider. I know she's only your evacuee, but there's more to it than that. We've all got people to take account of, but this is what we do, after all—and haven't you always said we've got to get to work when truth comes to us for help? Or something like that, anyway."

"Oh, touché, Billy—touché!" She paused and dropped the crayon. "All right, come on. Let's get over there to see Phil and Sally—but take my lead, as I don't want to show too much of my hand. Just enough. Then we'll let it simmer, like I said we would. All right?"

Billy grinned. "Ready when you are, miss."

Phil Coombes came down from the upstairs flat the third time Billy rapped on the door.

"Thought you'd all left home, mate," said Billy.

"Oh good morning, Miss Dobbs, Billy." He looked from one to the other. "Got any news for us?"

"I'm sorry, but we've a few more questions, if that's all right," said Maisie, stepping into the deserted public bar when Phil Coombes stood back to allow them to enter. The smell of stale smoke and the yeasty odor of yesterday's beer was overpowering. Dust motes danced and settled in a shaft of sunlight slanting through the window to the dark stained floor.

Coombes led the way up the narrow staircase to the flat above, and called out to his wife. "Sally—got company. Miss Dobbs and Mr. Beale. About Joe."

Sally Coombes stood in the doorway to the kitchen, drying her hands on a tea towel. "Oh, hello—come in. I've just put the kettle on."

"What time does Vivian start work in the morning?" asked Maisie, taking the seat proffered by Phil Coombes.

"Half past eight, as a rule." He sat down opposite Maisie. "Sometimes it's earlier. Usually, though, when the women finish their day, the men telephonists come on for the night shift. She's a clever girl—top marks in her civil service exams."

Maisie engaged Phil in small talk about Vivian's prospects, until Sally had placed cups of tea on the table and taken a seat. She paused, stirring her tea and taking a sip before speaking again.

"I want to go back over Joe's apprenticeship, if I may. How did he find out about the job at Yates? Wasn't it someone you knew who put in a word for him?"

Phil Coombes glanced at his wife, then at his hands as he answered. "It was through Archie, who found out from his mate, Teddy Wickham."

"And how did Teddy know about the opening?"

"Can't say as I remember now—but must've been through someone he knew who does business with Yates. Or a relative. Teddy was looking out for Joe, and thought it would be a good start for him, to learn the trade—like I said before. Being in a trade sets you up, and he did well to get in at Yates." He drummed his fingers on the table.

"Right, yes, I know you wanted him to become a skilled craftsman. Are you sure you can't recall who gave Teddy the tip-off?"

Coombes shook his head and turned to his wife. "Sal—can you remember?"

Sally Coombes shook her head. "Can't say as I do."

Maisie continued. "I remember you saying that Joe had changed—when do you think that started?"

Coombes looked at his wife again, as if her face would jog his memory. She raised her eyebrows and sighed.

"I reckon it was after he'd been put on this new job a month or so. Before the headaches, if I'm remembering rightly," said Sally.

"Nah, the headaches came before. Don't you remember me saying, 'Joe's been very quiet when he gets on the blower.'" He looked at Billy, as if the father of sons would understand. "Then when he came home one Saturday afternoon, he didn't want to go out much. Said it was being in the country—made him not like all the noise out there."

"And what about his wish to give up his job because he wanted to work on a farm?"

Coombes rolled his eyes. "Oh that business. Might've known that would come up. Joe had this idea he wanted to be a farmer. Said he'd been offered an apprenticeship by a local bloke with a farm. All on the up and up, it was supposed to be." He stared at Maisie. "Give up a good job to be planting turnips? The boy was off his rocker."

"By all accounts he loved the country," said Maisie. "You said so yourself when we first spoke."

"No, I told him he had to stay with Yates. You don't give up a good job." Phil Coombes looked at the clock, and pushed back his chair. "Getting on for opening time."

"Just another minute or two, Mr. Coombes—it's important," said Maisie. She cast her gaze from Coombes to his wife. "What would really have been the consequence of Joe leaving his job at Yates?"

"I don't know what you mean. Mind you, there's always a consequence of giving up work. Joe remembered how it was when he was younger—grown men on the streets begging for money to keep their families fed. Lining up for work, time and again—saw it myself, and we vowed that was not going to happen to our boys." Sally Coombes looked at her husband.

"And I knew the consequence of going into the army," added Coombes. "I saw enough myself in the last war. You did as well." He brought his attention to Billy, then Maisie. "There's consequences your mum and dad know about that you don't, when you're still wet behind the ears. And Sally and me, we knew it was our job to steer our children on the right path. Ours learned how to put in a day's work, and they knew they weren't going to fight any wars, not if I had anything to do with it. Joe's job was reserved, and so was Archie's. Vivian wouldn't be in uniform either."

Maisie nodded, as Coombes took account of the hour again, shifting in his chair as if to render it obvious he was checking the clock. "One minute, then we'll let you get on, Phil. Do you know how Mike Yates managed to obtain the contract for painting aerodromes? And have you any idea about the source of the paint Joe's crew were using?"

"How would I know?" said Phil Coombes.

Maisie came to her feet. Billy followed her lead. "I wondered about it, that's all." Again she turned from Phil to Sally Coombes. "You see, if my son were being killed by a certain substance, I would want to know exactly where it came from." She turned to leave.

"Now, Miss Dobbs, I know he wasn't feeling well, but—"

"The paint was toxic," said Maisie. "It was poisoning his blood and affecting his brain. Joe knew it—and he knew, if only by instinct, that he had to get away from it. And the only person who truly listened to him was a farmer, a man who had lost his son in the last war."

As they reached the door, Maisie turned back. "I'm sorry to be so blunt, but that is the way it stands. I am trying to find out who killed Joe, and I have to do all I can to turn not only stones, to see what lies underneath, but in this case I have to move boulders. The truth can hide in some very troubling places, Mr. Coombes, and you asked me to find out the truth."

"I know about war, Miss Dobbs. I fought in the war."

"Yes, I'm aware you were in Flanders. As was Billy, and I was a nurse in a casualty clearing station, so I know how it was." She paused. "In fact, Billy showed me that newspaper cutting today—you were a local somebody for a short while, after appearing in the *South London Press*. How many of you came home, from the lads in that photograph?"

"You had that photo?" said Coombes, his face registering surprise.

"Arthur Beale. Artillery. Passchendaele, 1917. He was my cousin," said Billy.

"Oh blimey," said Coombes. "I never knew."

"No need for you to have known. I've got a common name, and it's not as if we talk about it, is it?"

Coombes stared at the ground and nodded. "Not as if we do." He looked up. "Only two of us came back, of the lads in that photograph," said Coombes.

"Yes, I already know," said Maisie. "I'll be in touch—and thank you, Mr. Coombes. Mrs. Coombes."

They began walking back to the office without speaking, until Billy broke the silence. "Not like you to be so hard on someone, miss. Never heard you talk like that to people grieving. Fair surprised me, it did."

"Sorry, Billy. There's a time for everything, and this was a time when I needed to poke with a knife instead of a gentle touch with a fingertip."

"Why?"

Maisie sighed. "Let's just see what happens next. Then I'll explain." She stopped and turned to her assistant. "Trust me, Billy."

"Always have, miss. I always have. But what do you want me to do next?"

Maisie began walking again. "There is something, before you start on the next three cases that came in. I want you to find out more about Teddy Wickham."

"What about him?"

"His parents—mother's maiden name, that sort of thing. Uncles, aunts, brothers, sisters. School. Best friends—though we know his very best friend is Archie Coombes."

"Right you are, miss. Good as done."

Walter Miles emerged from the downstairs flat and greeted them as they reached the steps leading to the office. He was wearing a cream linen summer blazer with beige trousers and brown leather shoes, and wore a white open-neck shirt. He carried a brown leather document case, and used a cane to steady his walk. Passing the cane to the opposite hand, he raised his cream straw fedora. Maisie realized that, despite the scar along his jawline, Miles was a very handsome man, and somewhat reminiscent of her late husband.

"Good day to you, Miss Dobbs, Mr. Beale."

"Good morning," Maisie and Billy replied in unison.

"You're like the number thirty-six bus," continued Maisie. "We don't see much of you—and then here you are several times in a row."

"I'm on my way to the university now," said Miles, his smile broad as he regarded Maisie.

"What do you teach?" she asked.

"Botany, usually, though with a few colleagues being called up, I'm now teaching other sciences as needed—and I'm often at Bedford College as well as Malet Street. Anyway, I'd better be off, or I'll be late." He lifted his hat to signal his departure and gave another smile.

Maisie watched as Miles made his way toward Warren Street.

"Seems to be a good bloke, eh miss?"

"Yes, very nice indeed."

"He might be sweet on you," added Billy. "I haven't see him much, then—like you said—there he is a few times in a row."

"That doesn't mean anything, Billy."

"It meant something that day Mr. Stratton came to take you out to lunch. Last month, it was."

"I don't understand—what do you mean?"

"Oh, you two were off across the square, going out to have lunch somewhere, and I was leaving to see one of our new clients. Up comes Mr. Miles from his downstairs flat, and says, 'Miss Dobbs seems to have a nice gentleman.' Of course, I told him Mr. Stratton was only a friend, someone you'd worked with. And then he asked what he did, and so I told him Mr. Stratton used to be with the police, before he left to become a teacher, but has to come into London for war work now. I think Mr. Miles was a bit downcast, you know, as if you were walking out with Mr. Stratton and he was sad about it."

"Hmmm, I think you're seeing things, Billy," said Maisie.

"P'raphs he'll come up and invite you down for a cuppa."

"Oh, I don't know about that, really I don't."

Later, in the office as she packed papers she might need during her absence, Maisie walked across to the window to look down at the garden Walter Miles had created. She found it calming to stand there. Perhaps it took a botanist to have such luck in a postage-stamp yard where sunlight only seemed to flash through at certain times of day.

Chapter 15

I felt quite bad about going to Ramsgate, to tell you the truth," said Priscilla, flicking ash from her cigarette out of the open passenger side window. "I mean, there I was, jumping up and down, talking to anyone who looked official, trying to find out if they knew where my son was. And they had enough on their hands dealing with the men coming off the boats, without a lunatic mother screaming at them." She coughed and patted her chest. "I don't know whether that's the gasper I'm puffing away on, or all this fresh air. Lovely to have a motor car with a roof you can put down though—I adored driving with the wind in my hair when we lived in Biarritz." She paused. "Sometimes I wish we'd have bloody well stayed there, because now I have a son in the air force and another who thinks he's Lord Horatio bloody Nelson."

"It's best you're not in Biarritz, Pris—not with what's happened in France. And you know it." Maisie shifted gears as she slowed to drive through Chelstone.

"I absolutely adore this village, Maisie. Perhaps I should sell the family home and buy something here—it would make sense, because we hardly ever use the house now, and I've only kept it, really, for the memories. But I think Kent would be so much more convenient, after all, we would be in the country, yet there's the train or the coach to go back and forth from London." At that moment, a trio of RAF Spitfires flew overhead. "Then of course, I remember that Kent has taken the brunt of invasions for centuries, and I don't particularly want to be on the front line," she added, shielding her eyes with a hand to follow the aircraft until they disappeared into the clouds. "Wouldn't it be simply the strangest thing if one of those boys were my son, flying off to France?" She turned to Maisie, then raised a palm to blow a kiss in the direction of the aircraft.

"Nearly there," said Maisie. "Brenda will have baked a bounty of cakes, I'm sure."

"Thank heavens for your chickens and their eggs!" said Priscilla.

Maisie pulled into the lane leading to the back of the Dower House, parking the Alvis under a tree.

"Tomorrow will be the last time I can drive—it has to go into the garage until after the war now. I can't push my luck with the special allowance anymore."

"Ours has gone into storage too—going to Ramsgate was its swan song until this war is finished," said Priscilla. "And there's your greeting party," she added, pointing to the back door of the Dower House.

Frankie Dobbs stood on the threshold, holding Anna's hand. The child was in her pajamas, her feet drumming the ground, running on the spot as she waved to Maisie.

Maisie stepped from the motor car as Frankie relinquished his hold on Anna's hand. The little girl ran to Maisie, Emma ambling from behind Frankie to remain close to her mistress.

"You're home, you're home, you're home!"

"And you've forgotten your slippers, your slippers, your slippers, young lady," said Maisie, lifting the child and holding her on her hip. "My, for a little girl who's had the measles, you're getting heavy! And what time is this? It's past time for a measled girl to be in her bed!"

"Hello, Auntie Priscilla," said Anna, as Maisie let her slither to the ground.

"Hello, Anna," said Priscilla, leaning forward and tapping her own nose and cheeks. "One there, one there, and one on the other side."

Anna giggled and kissed Priscilla on both cheeks and her nose, as instructed, then reached for Maisie's hand.

"Tim's coming back tomorrow," she said, leading Maisie and Priscilla into the kitchen. The women exchanged glances.

"Hello, love," said Frankie, kissing his daughter. "She's gone on and on about Tim coming home all day." He looked at Priscilla, who had moved to kiss him in greeting. "Sorry, Mrs. Partridge—I told her to keep her dreams a secret, because I wouldn't want you to be upset. But Anna's been waiting for Maisie and you to get here—she was so excited she couldn't rest."

"What will upset me is you not calling me 'Priscilla'—how many years have I known you now, Mr. Dobbs?" She paused and pulled a face. "Oh dear, I don't practice what I preach, do I?"

At that moment, Brenda entered the kitchen. "Hello, Mrs. Partridge—I've made up the guest room for you and Mr. Partridge, and we'll put Tarquin in the conservatory when he gets here—Tim always loves sleeping there."

"That's perfect, Mrs. Dobbs—thank you so very much." Priscilla turned to Maisie. "And I suppose you're still bedding down in the library."

"It's very comfortable, and if I can't sleep, there's plenty of reading material to get on with." She reached for Anna's hand. "Now, while you all catch up with your news, I'm taking Anna upstairs. It's time she was in bed again—we don't want all the excitement to set her back."

Maisie was stretched out on top of the covers reading a story, with Anna in bed resting against the crook of her arm, when Brenda entered with a mug of warm milk.

"Looks like she's not far off sleep now," said Brenda.

"Almost in the land of nod, aren't you," said Maisie, sweeping a tendril of black hair across Anna's forehead, away from her eyes. "Come on, time for your milk."

As Anna reached for the mug and began to sip, Maisie continued to support the child, who was leaning against her.

"Heard from your Mr. Klein, Maisie?" asked Brenda, standing by the door.

"Yes, I saw him this week. It was a short meeting, not very long at all."

"And?"

Maisie shrugged, not looking at Brenda, paying attention to Anna as she finished her milk. "Just a few little things to get over."

"Oh," said Brenda. "We'll talk about it later."

"Yes," said Maisie.

Brenda left the room as Anna took a final sip and handed the mug to Maisie.

"A widow is a lady whose husband has died, isn't she?" said Anna.

"Yes, that's right." Maisie stood up and set the mug on the side table. She had answered the question as if it were the most ordinary inquiry. "Now then, snuggle down and close your eyes ready for the sandman."

"I know your husband died," whispered Anna.

"Yes, you probably heard someone mention it," said Maisie. "It's not a secret, but I don't talk about it much."

"Lady Rowan came over to read to me when I first had measles. I heard her talking to Auntie Brenda downstairs. She said it doesn't help that you're a widow."

"Probably because sometimes being a widow makes other people sad," said Maisie.

"Who's Mr. Klein?" asked Anna, resting her head on the pillow.

"He's what they call a solicitor. A man who draws up papers to do with the law."

"Did he draw up papers for you because you're a widow?"

"Yes, he helped me with all sort of things," said Maisie

"Is he drawing up papers so you can keep me?"

Maisie knelt down at the side of the bed and held Anna's hand. Emma, who had been lying close to the door, raised her nose.

"What made you say that, Anna?"

The child looked into Maisie's eyes. "Because you want me. That's what nanny said, before she went to heaven. She told me that everything would be all right, because the lady wanted me."

Upon reaching Hastings at ten o'clock the following morning, Maisie parked the motor car close to the Stade, the shingle beach that was home to the town's fishing fleet. Most had returned home with the morning's catch several hours earlier, though one of the heavy clinker-built boats had just been winched ashore.

"Wait a moment, Pris—I won't be long," said Maisie as she took one of several bottles of water she had packed in the motor car, and walked across the shingle to speak to a fisherman. He was standing to one side, his waxed overalls and jacket sodden and stained, his face and hands black with oil and sweat. She uncorked the bottle and passed it to him. He nodded his appreciation.

"You've come back from Dunkirk, haven't you?"

The man drank several mouthfuls and nodded again.

"I wonder if you could help me. My friend's son and another boy went out in a launch—a forty-five-footer. They've not come in, and I wondered if—as you were making your way back—you saw a vessel returning in this direction. She's usually moored at the harbor in Rye. So not far."

He shook his head, took one more long draw from the bottle, and wiped his mouth against his sleeve, spreading another line of oil across his cheek. "Can't say as I have, love." The man leaned back against the boat behind him, and sank down to sit on a mound of nets. "Sorry. We only just came in." He raised the bottle as if in a toast. "Much obliged to you. Much obliged."

"Thank you, sir. Thank you—for going over there."

"It was terrible. Never get the pictures out of my head. Never. Once seen, never forgotten." He closed his eyes.

Maisie moved to walk away, then heard the fisherman speak again. "Just because I never saw the boat, don't mean it weren't there." He sipped more water and nodded toward the boat that had just been winched in. "It was all I could do to get us back here, what with her taking on water. Didn't like to leave, because there's still more to bring home. Brave boys. All brave boys. And your lads might've been out there. I just never saw 'em. 'Twas all I could do to see my way home."

"Thank you, sir," she called out, raising her hand to bid him farewell again.

"Now Rye," said Maisie as she reached the motor car and opened the driver's door.

Priscilla took one final draw on her cigarette—this time without the holder—threw it down and ground it into the dirt with the toe of her shoe.

At Rye there was no sign of the *Cassandra*, but as Maisie and Priscilla left the motor car to walk across to the harbor, a member of the local constabulary approached to query Maisie's authority for running a motor car, and also asked to see her motor spirit coupons and both their identity cards. They complied with the request.

"All looks in order, madam. But I wouldn't chance another run in that motor car—and I hope you've got a full tank there because there's not much to be had at the petrol stations."

"Yes, fortunately—and my vehicle is going into

storage tomorrow. We just had to make this last journey along the coast, looking for my friend's son." She explained what had happened with Tim and his friend Gordon.

"Oh yes, know the *Cassandra*—and now I come to think of it, I've seen those boys before, taking out one of the father's boats. Got a veritable fleet, the Sandersons. Sailing family through and through."

Maisie was aware of Priscilla's mounting frustration, as her friend tapped her foot and folded her arms.

"Here's my telephone number, Constable," said Maisie, handing the man a calling card onto which she had written the Dower House number. "I know you're a very busy man, but perhaps someone could place a call to me should this particular member of the fleet return."

He nodded and placed the card in his breast pocket. "Right you are, madam. I'll keep an eye out. So, you said you're making your way along the coast."

"Yes, we are," interjected Priscilla. "It stands to reason my son and his friend will end up somewhere between here and Ramsgate, so we're on our very own personal patrol to find them."

The man smiled, as if to mollify Priscilla, then turned back to Maisie. "Drop into the constabulary at every town, madam—tell them you've already spoken to me, Constable Sheering, from Rye. We're all doing what we can for the boys coming in and the boats that bring them, so my colleagues along the way will give you a hand, and if they can, they'll let you know if he's come in." His eyes met Priscilla's once again. "Your son and young Gordon are courageous boys, madam. They're made of the best of us all."

"Yes, quite," said Priscilla, who turned and walked away.

"Her other son is in the RAF, so she's not herself," explained Maisie, as she watched Priscilla light another cigarette.

"Didn't think so," said the constable. "I wouldn't want to be in her shoes. I'll let you know if I find out anything."

Maisie nodded, thanked the man, and walked back to Priscilla.

"Sorry about that," said Priscilla. "I could just see us tearing along the barbed-wire-wrapped coast— Dymchurch, Hythe, Folkestone, Ramsgate—having these little chats with policemen and old salts along the way and getting nowhere fast. Finding out absolutely nothing while my son could be dead somewhere!"

"I just told that man a terrible lie, Pris—I told him you weren't being yourself, but really I should have said you are being exactly yourself! The first fisherman had just returned from Dunkirk, having saved heaven knows how many lives, and that constable is going to look out for Tim. We will find him, but we won't find him in an instant!"

"I should have let you do this alone, but I could not sit still. Just could not sit still a minute longer." She folded her arms.

"Then let's get on our way."

They were silent along the route, stopping in Dymchurch and then Hythe.

"Never mind water and a bottle of ginger beer each, why didn't I think of bringing a flask of something to soothe my nerves? That was a huge error on my part," said Priscilla, lighting up another cigarette, then extinguishing the lighted end with her thumb and finger, and throwing it out of the open window. "I should probably slow down with these things—luckily I've got a stash, but they'll go on ration, and—"

"Oh dear, I wonder what he wants?" Maisie looked into the rearview mirror, at the police motor car gaining on her, bell ringing. The driver had opened his window and was waving at Maisie to pull over.

"I'm not surprised—your foot turned into lead as we left Hythe," said Priscilla.

Maisie maneuvered the motor car to the side of the

road. Both women once again took out their identity cards. The police vehicle stopped in front of them, and the policeman in the passenger seat left the motor car and walked toward Maisie.

"At a rough guess, I would say you're about to go to Holloway Prison," said Priscilla.

"Oh, Pris, give it the elbow!" said Maisie. She opened the door and stepped out, ready to meet the policeman at her full height.

"Miss Dobbs?" said the policeman, as he approached. He bent down to look at Priscilla through the open window. "And Mrs. Partridge?"

"Yes?" Maisie and Priscilla responded at once.

"Not many motors on the road, and certainly not one like this. We had an urgent telephone call from our colleagues along in Sussex, and we thought we should intercept you. You're looking for a vessel named the *Cassandra*? Shortly after you left Rye, a fishing boat came in and the skipper raised the alarm that another boat had found her drifting without power and is towing her back to Rye. It's a distance and slow going from the Channel, but she should be home before dark—and of course, there's the tide to consider."

Priscilla had already leaped out of the Alvis to join Maisie. "My son. Is my son all right? Timothy Partridge. Is Timothy Partridge on the boat?"

"I understand there are two boys, and some soldiers. There are some wounded, but both are on board."

Priscilla ran back around the motor car to take her seat once again. "Come on, Maisie. Hurry up. Hurry!"

The policeman addressed Maisie. "Best if you follow me, miss. Best all-around."

"Yes, thank you, Sergeant," said Maisie. She placed a hand on his arm, and felt her eyes fill with tears. "Really—I can't thank you enough."

"All part of the job. Much prefer being the bearer of good news—and it's not me to thank, but Constable Sheering down at Rye. He's the one who put out the call. Now then, before your friend becomes a casualty, let's be on our way. You follow—I'm the one with the bell."

Two ambulances were standing by at Rye Harbor, and members of the local Women's Voluntary Service, with their distinctive green uniforms, had set up a table with sandwiches and flasks of tea. Another woman was folding a pile of blankets. As soon as Maisie had parked the motor car, Priscilla ran across the road toward Constable Sheering. He held out a hand as if to steady her. In the meantime, Maisie stopped to speak to the coastguard.

"According to Mick Tate over there—in the fishing

boat—he saw the *Cassandra* being towed back toward Rye by the *Mistress Mollie*, another of the fishing boats. They'd found her out there, making her way back from France, but she had almost run out of fuel. She had been attacked by them bloody Germans." He looked up at Priscilla. "She one of the mums?"

Maisie nodded. "Yes, her son is a very good friend of the owner's son—they sail together a lot."

"I heard. Those lads took out the *Cassandra* without anyone knowing; went off and joined the flotilla of boats going to Dunkirk to help bring our boys off the Mole there. Bloody little fools—but you've got to hand it to them, haven't you?" He paused, but before Maisie could reply, he continued. "Young Gordon's mother is in Ramsgate, and as soon as we've found her, we'll get her here—she's looking out for her husband as well as her son."

"Poor woman—to have that worry."

The coastguard nodded toward Priscilla again. She had begun walking along the embankment as if to follow the River Rother out to sea, her hand to her forehead looking toward the point where the estuary met the sea, though it was far in the distance and not visible.

"You're going to have to keep an eye on your friend. Mick said they'd had a good number of soldiers on board, but some went onto the other boat towing them.

One of the boys was down, so the other lad was working himself silly to keep her going, and he's been injured himself, quite badly."

"What do you mean—one of the boys is down?" asked Maisie.

The coastguard shook his head and half turned away. "I mean he's gone. He's dead."

Maisie brought her hands to her mouth. She had become light-headed, yet her feet felt as if they were indeed made of lead, as if it would take every ounce of her resolve to move.

"You all right, madam?" said the coastguard.

"Tim is my godson. Oh heavens—this is terrible. I must go to Priscilla, to stand with her."

"P'rhaps I shouldn't've said anything," said the coastguard.

"No—no, you did the right thing. I'm prepared now. I've got to be Priscilla's strength. And I must telephone her husband, to get him down here. I know where to contact him—I can get him here soon."

The coastguard directed her from the harbor to a telephone kiosk. Maisie ran along the road, rummaging in her pockets for change. As the door closed, the odor from every human being who had ever stood in the kiosk seemed to be leaching up from the floor and enveloping her. Struggling for breath, she opened the door, keeping it ajar with her foot as she asked the operator to connect her call.

"Chelstone Manor." The butler answered the call.

"Simmonds! Simmonds, is Lord Julian at home?"

"Yes, indeed, Your Ladyship. Just one moment please, hold the line."

One minute. Two minutes. Maisie made a small cylindrical pile with her coins on top of the telephone box, ready for use if the pips sounded. She adjusted the pile, counting the coins once more. Then a click on the line.

"Hello, Maisie—how are you?"

"Lord Julian—thank you, yes, I'm all right. Well, no, not quite. You are the only one I can trust to keep calm. Douglas Partridge should have just arrived at the Dower House with Tarquin. I would like George to collect him and bring him to Rye Harbor as soon as possible. But not with Tarquin. You must find a means of drawing Douglas away from his son to tell him the reason." She recounted the news she had been given by the coastguard.

"Right you are. It will be done exactly as you've asked. Leave it with me, Maisie. I will also let your father know what's happened—I am sure Mr. Dobbs will find an enjoyable means of distracting the boy." There was a second of silence, and the pips sounded.

With shaking hands Maisie pushed more coins in the slot, cursing when a coin dropped to the floor.

"Lord Julian, are you still there?" she asked.

"Yes, still here." She heard a catch in his voice. "I imagine George could get him there in about forty minutes, at a fair clip. And Maisie—do keep us informed."

"Yes, of course. I must go now."

She replaced the receiver, and stepped out into the fresh air. Priscilla had walked back and was standing on the harbor wall, binoculars to her eyes. Constable Sheering gently placed his hand to one side of her, not touching her clothing, but close. Maisie saw Priscilla nod, and move back to a safer point from which to keep her vigil.

"See anything yet?" said Maisie as she approached her friend.

"You can't see anything much from here, but when I walked alongside the river, I saw a little speck in the distance. But it's difficult—the marshes can give you an optical illusion, so what you think is a boat, is probably a farmer crossing his field with a horse and plough." She tapped the binoculars. "The coastguard kindly loaned these to me."

At that point the coastguard called out. "I can see them. They're coming in."

Priscilla drew the binoculars up to her eyes again. "Where? Where? I can't see them. Where are they?"

"Let me look, Pris."

Priscilla passed the binoculars to Maisie, and stepped closer to the water again. And again the policeman drew her back. "You don't want your son to see you in the drink when he brings that boat in, do you?"

Maisie trained the binoculars into the distance. At first she could see nothing, not even a farmer with his team of horses drawing the plough. Then a speck appeared, glistening mirrorlike in the mid-afternoon sunshine. Yet instead of anticipation, she felt dread—for until the boat docked, until the lines had been drawn in and the vessel tethered, the wheel of fate would continue spinning. Only when those on board were home would it stop—and for one mother the terror would not end.

The dot in the distance continued to grow in size as time passed. Two fishing boats cast off in the direction of the *Cassandra* and her savior, the *Mistress Mollie*. Soon another motor car was parked alongside the Alvis, and as Maisie looked up, she could see the effort with which Douglas Partridge wielded his cane as he limped toward his wife.

"Oh, darling! You're here!" Priscilla rushed to her

husband's side. He allowed his cane to drop and pulled her to him. "Tim's coming home. Tim's coming home and he's almost here."

"I know. I know, my love. He's almost here."

Maisie knelt to retrieve the cane.

"Thank you, Maisie," said Douglas. "And thank you for sorting everything out—for getting me here."

"You spoke to Lord Julian?" asked Maisie.

"Yes. He brought me up-to-date—I know what's happening."

"What's happening is that our son is almost home, Douglas!" She took his arm and began leading him toward the harbor wall. "I promise I will not admonish him in front of everyone for this escapade. I may have to fling my arms around him, though."

Maisie and Douglas exchanged glances.

"Don't embarrass the boy, whatever you do, Priscilla." He pointed his cane toward a cluster of people waiting alongside the women with their tea and sandwiches. "There's a newspaper reporter and photographer over there, and I am sure Tim would not want to be on the front page with his mother clinging to him. Whether you like it or not—our son is a hero."

Priscilla shook her head. "I never wanted heroes."

It was late in the afternoon when at last the *Cassandra* drew into full view, behind the fishing boat towing her in. The two vessels seemed to stop their progress, as another fishing boat joined them. People around began muttering, speculating about what might be happening. Douglas grabbed Priscilla's arm to stop her running in the direction of the boats. Then a fisherman pushed back his cap and smiled.

"Good on 'em. Good on 'em."

"What is it? What's going on?" Priscilla called out.

"I know what he's doing," said the policeman. "He's giving the *Cassandra* enough fuel to get to the harbor. He's letting her come in under her own steam."

And as the crowd became silent, the rumble and fail of an engine trying to start echoed along the river, until after a chug-chug-chug the engine fired and began running. A cheer went up and the boats began moving again toward the harbor.

Priscilla screamed out her son's name. People clustered together to watch the launch pull in to dock, the young man at the helm calling out instructions to soldiers on board, who threw out lines from the bow and stern to waiting fishermen. The soldiers' faces were stained and drawn, their exhaustion evident in the way they half-stumbled toward hands waiting to receive them. Maisie could see the skipper, his face black with oil, his shirt red with blood and bandages wrapped around his left shoulder and arm. A fisherman from one of the boats was standing behind him, as if to support the boy should he fall. The coastguard clambered on board to reach him, turning off the engine, then joining the fisherman to help the young man remain upright.

"I can't see who that is," said Priscilla. "He's hurt. I hope it's not Tim, I hope he's not been wounded."

Maisie looked at Douglas, who rested his hand on his wife's shoulder.

"You should wait here." He walked toward the *Cassandra*, just as two ambulance men made their way on board with a stretcher.

"Maisie, what is it? What's happening?" As Priscilla struggled to speak, it was as if she were learning every word anew.

Maisie held on to Priscilla's arm. "There are wounded on board, Priscilla. The man at the helm will not leave until everyone has left the boat—even if he's falling down with exhaustion, he will not leave. He may be young, but he is the captain." And in that moment, she felt a glimmer of hope.

Priscilla watched as the ambulance men began to leave the boat. And with movements that showed a deep respect and—Maisie thought—gentleness, they brought a blanket-draped body ashore. The crowd moved aside for them to continue on.

"Oh my God." Priscilla turned to Maisie. "Is that Tim. Is that my son, Maisie?"

"We mustn't think like that. Let's wait and see." She felt her voice crack, as she again drew her attention toward the *Cassandra*.

The two ambulance men approached the boat once more, this time without a stretcher. They made their way on board, then stopped and stood aside. Instead, Douglas was helped onto the boat by a fisherman. Maisie squinted, watching Douglas approach the coastguard and the young man who had brought the *Cassandra* home. And as Douglas allowed his cane to fall a second time, to pull the young man toward him, she felt Priscilla begin to give way.

"Don't fall, Priscilla. Don't fall. He's home. Tim's home."

The coastguard handed Douglas his cane, and guided him off the vessel. He turned back to watch as Tim began to walk toward the stern.

Priscilla ran toward the *Cassandra*, with Maisie following. Reaching the vessel, she opened her arms to her son, yet as she witnessed the reunion, Maisie saw the blood running down Tim's arm, his hand limp as his mother relinquished her grasp.

"Priscilla—hold on to him! He's going down!"

And as Maisie knelt alongside Tim, she pulled

back the dressing on his arm and saw the extent of his wounds.

"He was hit, miss," said one of the soldiers. "The same one that got his mate. They came out of the sky right at us, and them two couldn't get down in time because they were trying to get us home. Pair of bloody heroes, them boys. I don't know how that one got us so far, but he kept saying he had to get Gordon home, that it was his job."

Chapter 16

A s soon as Tim had been placed on a stretcher and lifted on board the ambulance, Maisie gave instructions for him to be taken to the Royal East Sussex Hospital in Hastings, then she ran to the telephone kiosk once again. George, the Comptons' chauffeur, pulled out to follow the ambulance, and as the two vehicles drew onto the main road, a cheer went up from the soldiers for the two boys who had fought to bring them home to England.

Once again Maisie piled her coins onto the telephone kiosk and began to dial a number she knew by heart.

"Andrew Dene." The greeting was short, with no reference to the number called.

"Andrew! I am so glad you're home."

"Maisie, hello! And I'm only just home—I almost

remained in London. Had soldiers with some terrible wounds being brought in. We've been operating around the clock since the evacuation began."

Maisie had once walked out with Andrew Dene, but friendship had replaced courtship, with cards exchanged at Christmas and Easter, and birthdays remembered. Andrew was now married with two children, and had risen to become not only a renowned orthopedic surgeon, but also a professor of orthopedic medicine in London.

"Andrew, I know you're exhausted, but this is terribly urgent. It's Tim—Priscilla's son." She explained what had happened, and gave Dene her assessment of Tim's wounds.

"Right. Consider me on the way. I'll telephone the hospital now and have a theater prepared and Tim made ready as soon as he's brought in. I know the best vascular man to assist, and I'll get him over there. I'll be at the hospital by the time you arrive, Maisie."

In the hospital waiting room Maisie, Priscilla and Douglas spoke little, each immersed in their own thoughts. As she sat, and stood, and paced, Maisie remembered Billy, and his prescient words. "That's the worst thing about being in a war—it's not the fighting, or the tunneling, or any of the blimmin' terrible jobs you have to do. No, it's the waiting." Soon enough, though, the door opened and Andrew Dene beckoned them into a private office. Once they were seated, he ran his hand through hair slicked back with perspiration.

"First of all, I have no idea how Tim managed to garner enough strength to bring a boat back from France—his resolve was a miracle in itself, as is the fact that he is alive."

"But how is he, Andrew? And when can we see our son?" Priscilla's hands were balled into fists.

Douglas reached out to cover one hand with his own. "Go on, Andrew—please tell us how Tim is faring."

"I will tell you now that, having examined him when I arrived, I took Tim into that theater not knowing if I would be able to bring him out alive. The operation was a long one—you know, you've been waiting—but he endured the anesthetic and the procedure." He cleared his throat. "The fact is that the humerus bone in the left arm was shattered. He had sustained vascular damage and various connective tissue was all but lost. I am afraid devastation to the limb, together with the huge risk of spreading infection, meant that the arm could not be saved—I had to amputate just here." With his finger he drew a line across his arm just below the shoulder.

Maisie heard both Priscilla and Douglas gasp.

Andrew Dene sighed. "I'm so very sorry—if I could have saved the arm, I would have. In the meantime, infection remains a great risk, but I have used something very new—a purified type of fungus known as *Penicillium,* though it's now known as penicillin."

"Fungus? You've put a fungus into my son?" said Priscilla.

"It's terribly new, as I said—well, it's new for use in the medical field—and I was fortunate to have been asked to contribute to research regarding its application in hospitals, as a tool to use against possible sepsis. It's not available to most doctors yet, but I have great faith in it—and in my work so far it seems to far exceed the results we've had with the usual sulphur-based compounds."

"When my arm was amputated, it was in France, at a casualty clearing station," said Douglas. "I remember that terrible smell of sulphur."

"But better than gangrene," said Maisie.

"And I'll never forget *that* smell," added Priscilla. "It was the odor of death in the back of my ambulance."

"If there is a saving grace, it is this," said Dene, looking at Douglas. "Tim has a strong family, and a father who knows exactly how he is going to feel. He will require all your support and guidance as he emerges from this trauma." He paused, drawing his attention to

Maisie, then to Tim's parents. "What Tim witnessed during the evacuation will remain with him forever—it's something we cannot imagine, and those memories cannot be taken away. This is all more in Maisie's line of work than mine—but he will have many mountains to climb, especially the weight of survival because his friend was killed. He will regain dexterity—as you know, Douglas, the other arm becomes stronger—but he will be forever changed." Dene stood up, his shoulders rounded with fatigue. "I am a surgeon, and when operating I have to be dispassionate, seeing the body as a machine. It is my task to give the machine every chance of working properly again, though the cogs might look a little different. But I also know the difficulties involved in true recovery—and it can take a long time. Tim has an advantage I cannot prescribe—his spirit."

"When can we see him?" asked Douglas.

"Not before tomorrow. My suggestion is that you all go home to Chelstone and get a very good night's sleep, if you can. Tim will prevail—the fact that he came home, that he kept his wits about him when the pain would have felled a lesser man, is testament to his ability to endure."

The sun was shining as George drove Priscilla and Douglas back to Hastings the following day, along with

Tarquin, who had been told about his brother's journey to Dunkirk, and what happened when he came home. Having waved them off, Maisie brought the Alvis around to the Comptons' garage, where she parked it and left the keys on George's work bench. She patted the bonnet, and closed the door behind her. It was not a great loss, the lack of a motor car to hand, though it might prove to be inconvenient. She hoped the day ahead would be a quiet one. Perhaps she would read to Anna, prepare Sunday lunch, and visit her in-laws, who were anxious for news of Tim.

Brenda was waving to her as she reached the path that led from the garage up to the Dower House.

"Telephone for you, Maisie," she called out. "It's your Mr. Beale, says it's important."

Maisie ran to the house, and picked up the telephone receiver.

"Billy—how are you?"

"All right, miss. What about Tim—did you find him?"

"Yes, we did. He's home." Maisie recounted the story of Tim's arrival back in Rye, and the news of his operation.

There was silence on the line.

"Billy?"

"Yes, miss, just thinking about Tim and his mum and dad. I know this sounds a bit off, but I half envy them?"

Maisie nodded. "I think I know what you're going to say, Billy."

"I thought you would. I mean, it's a terrible, terrible thing, but the boy has been to war now—so he'll never be blaming himself for not going. And he did something not a lot of lads his age would've done. So, he's lost his arm—but the fact of the matter is that now no one can send him anywhere to lose his life, can they? He can get on with it and make something of himself, like his father's done."

"Yes—yes, I believe you're right." Maisie paused. "But you called for another reason, Billy—what did you find out?"

"I think you had an inkling of this, or you wouldn't have been so specific with what you wanted me to look into. It's Teddy Wickham."

"Go on," said Maisie.

"His mum—maiden name was Doris Robertson. And there's more."

"Sally Coombes."

"Right first time. She's Jimmy and Doris Robertson's sister."

"And probably met her husband through Jimmy Robertson, because Phil Coombes was in the army with him."

"What's that you're always saying, that line—didn't you say Walter Scott wrote it? 'Oh what a tangled web we weave . . .'"

"'When first we practice to deceive.'"

"But why did—?"

"Not yet, Billy. Having dodgy relatives doesn't make people criminals. We've a little way to go—as I said, they can stew in their juices. I think I understand this particular web, but I need more evidence."

"All right, miss. See you tomorrow?"

"I'll be back in the office late morning. I'll tell you what I think we need to do then. We've time."

Maisie replaced the telephone receiver, and thought for a moment, her hand remaining ready to make another call. She picked up the receiver and dialed.

"Chelstone Manor?"

"Hello, Simmonds—is Lord Julian in his study?"

"I have just taken him his morning coffee. Her Ladyship has departed for a walk with the dogs across to the stables. Shall I tell him you'd like to speak to him?"

"I'm going to come over to the house now, Simmonds. Please let him know I'm on my way."

"Right you are—and may I say how glad we all were to hear that young Timothy Partridge is on home turf. It might have been better news, but at least he is home."

"Yes, he's home. That's the most important thing. I'll see you in a few minutes."

When Maisie entered the manor house library, Lord Julian was standing behind his desk looking out at the grounds. He turned as the door opened, and came toward her, his hands outstretched.

"Maisie, my dear—what a trial, seeing your dear friends go through such a terrible time, waiting for news of their son, and now this. We have come to enjoy their company. If there's anything we can do . . ."

"Thank you so much," said Maisie. "I think, though, it's going to be a time of waiting and helping Tim through the coming weeks and months of recovery. I believe he will be spending a good deal of time here at Chelstone, along with his family."

"Full house eh? We're at capacity here too, what with the Canadian officers. Good group though, we've grown to enjoy having them here—the supper conversation has been very lively." He motioned to Maisie to take the chair on the opposite side of his desk. "Coffee?"

"I'll pour," said Maisie. She topped up Lord Julian's

cup and served herself a half-cup of the thick black coffee from the silver pot bearing the Compton family crest, a coat of arms also engraved on the matching tray, milk jug and sugar bowl.

"What can I do for you, Maisie?" He took his seat.

"It's about the Bank of England. Do you think you could find out if there have been any attempts to mount a robbery—I'm thinking of the transportation bringing notes of currency from Hampshire into London."

"I can find out."

"And I know I've asked this before, but I assume every precaution is taken to reduce the risk of such an attempt."

"I have been informed that it is so." He took a sip of coffee, then replaced the cup in the saucer, returning it to the silver tray. "What do you know, Maisie?"

"I am not sure—it's pure speculation, really. But I would advise extra precautions for the next week or so. I think the risk of a criminal act has passed, but one cannot be too sure."

"Have you alerted the police?"

"The police need evidence, Lord Julian, and I don't have any at the moment. All I have is a series of observations. But the real crime I'm concerned about is not one of theft, but of fraud. And I believe it has to do with the War Office."

Lord Julian raised his eyebrows and leaned forward. "Go on."

"How does a business land a government contract in a time of war?"

"Pretty much the same procedure as when the country is not at war, though with a few degrees more secrecy. Companies are invited to tender their estimates for work or supplies, and also provide references to support their work. The government does not necessarily award a contract based upon price, but other aspects of the supplier's credentials are taken into account—delivery record being of prime importance."

"I see. And how does a business become known to a government department? Previous work? References from another source?"

"Both of those might be the case, and of course sometimes the principals in the business receive word that there is a contract to be awarded, and they request to bid along with everyone else."

"I suppose no one would admit if there were some degree of . . . of—"

"Would that American word *graft* do? Is that what you're looking for?" Lord Julian sighed. "Interesting that here the same word means hard work." He shook his head. "I can't say corruption doesn't happen, and in a time of war, especially, it could be seen as a treasonable act, given that it undermines the integrity and therefore strength of government. It diminishes us all." Lord Julian held Maisie's gaze. "You would tell me if you had knowledge of such an act."

"It's down to evidence again, Lord Julian—and making the connections between people I've met. I don't want to point a finger at the innocent."

Maisie looked out of the window behind Lord Julian. "Oh, here's Rowan now."

"Don't dare leave before seeing her. This business with Tim, you see . . . we've become very fond of the boy, and when we heard what had happened, it brought back such memories of . . . well, you know."

"Yes. I do. There's always something to remind us of James, isn't there?" As Maisie turned to leave, she noticed a uniform laid out on one of the leather armchairs. "Lord Julian—the uniform? Is it yours?"

"'Fraid so. Our newly formed Local Defense Volunteers unit. And I seem to have been volunteered in my absence to be the figurehead of the Chelstone brigade! Seriously though, with the threat of invasion, and with our proximity to airfields and being between London and the coast, it's a case of every man being called upon to bear arms to protect the country—and as the prime landowner in this area, I have a responsibility to do what I can. We've a good number of men in the village and beyond who fought in the last war, and of course some who cannot fight in this one, so it's time we all stepped forward to do our bit." He smiled, shaking his head. "Rowan thinks it's terribly funny, seeing as I was last in uniform a good few decades ago, and rarely even lift my gun to go after a pheasant now—though with this rationing business, I might sharpen my eye on bagging a few. Anyway, they've already started calling us the Home Guard, which I think sounds more like a shield you put in front of the fire to stop sparks catching the carpet."

Maisie laughed. "I am sure you're the very best leader they could hope to find anywhere—a catch indeed."

Lord Julian placed his hand on Maisie's shoulder as they walked to the door. "Let's hope we can catch the odd German parachute-landing in a field, eh? That'll show them what we're made of!" He took a deep breath, and a wave of gravity seemed to envelop him. "Maisie, I know I can tell you this in confidence, but it's important for us to consider the possibility that we may all have to move—and in a hurry. The fall of France does not augur well for us, and the prime minister is ordering authorities in Kent and Sussex to prepare for complete evacuation in the case of imminent invasion. It obviously hasn't come to that yet, though children are already being evacuated from certain coastal areas—but we must be prepared."

With Anna now almost fully recovered, Maisie relented and agreed it would be perfectly all right for Frankie to take her down to the stables to groom Lady, her pony, though she cautioned against tiring the child.

"We'll have no backsliding," added Maisie, smiling as she waved to her father as he led Anna by the hand, along the path toward the stables.

Brenda put the kettle on the stove and sat down at the kitchen table, patting the place opposite.

"You've not yet told me what Mr. Klein wanted to see you about," said Brenda.

Maisie rubbed her forehead, her mind still lingering on the conversation with Lord Julian. "Just a few minor points."

"Minor?" said Brenda.

Maisie avoided Brenda's gaze. "They prefer to approve adoptions where married couples are concerned, not widows, or spinsters, and definitely not bachelors."

"But you are already her guardian—her grandmother signed the papers."

"Guardian in a limited capacity—there was no time

for Mr. Klein to prepare the documents required for full guardianship, so my standing is as a sort of temporary guardian with a responsibility to place Anna in a good home."

"This is a good home," said Brenda. "The very best for Anna."

"Don't worry. All is far from lost, Brenda," said Maisie. "The new stricter adoption laws on the books for ratification were canceled when war broke out, so there are avenues remaining to me. And the local billeting officer has commented in her report that it might be difficult to place Anna elsewhere anyway, given her parentage—which really means her coloring. Then the problem of her father came up, Maltese Marco, who came and went out of Anna's mother's life before she was even born. So, as I said, there are avenues—I have great faith in Mr. Klein. I just have to be patient."

"So, the war that brought us Anna could be the war that helps keep her with us."

Maisie nodded. "I really do hope so, Brenda. But I'm almost scared to imagine it."

Brenda reached for Maisie's hand and held it tight. "It'll all come right, love. I believe it will all come right."

By every canon of military science the BEF has been doomed for the last four or five days. Completely out-numbered, out-gunned, out-planned, all but surrounded, it had seemed certain to be cut off from its last channel of escape. Yet for several hours this morning we saw ship after ship come into harbour and discharge thousands of British soldiers safe and sound on British soil.

Maisie had read enough, so she folded the copy of the *Manchester Guardian* and placed it where she had found it—on the seat next to her, discarded by a previous passenger. The train began to slow, signaling that the last stop—Charing Cross—was only a few minutes away. She opened the *Daily Herald*, this one left by a woman who had been sitting opposite her, until departing the carriage at Waterloo. She glanced at the front page headlines, and turned the page, where a smaller lead caught her eye.

BOY, 16, YOUNG HERO OF DUNKIRK.
Timothy Partridge, 16, of Holland Park, London, took to the high seas last week in a motor boat belonging to his best friend's father. Tragically . . .

She rolled up the newspaper and slid it into her bag. She could not bring herself to read another word, but would clip the column later, in case Tim wanted to keep it. But perhaps not yet. That morning she had left the Dower House before breakfast, agreeing with Brenda that it would be best not to disturb Priscilla and Douglas. The pressures of the past week had weighed heavily on the family—and they were all becoming more and more anxious about Tom, who had not been heard from for some days.

At the office, Maisie went straight to her desk, where she removed her coat and gloves and placed her briefcase and shoulder bag on the table. Yet again she had left her gas mask hanging on a hook behind the door when she last departed the office, and upon seeing it made a promise to take it with her today. She would also make more of an effort to keep the gas mask to hand at all times. Maisie took out her notebook and began reading through notes she had made on Sunday afternoon, devising her plan for the coming several days, when she would—she hoped—track down the evidence to support her belief that Joe Coombes' death was no accident.

A noise outside distracted her, so she stepped across to the window, where she saw Walter Miles on a step-ladder, weaving fresh clematis shoots up across new trellising. It appeared the plant had sprouted up a few inches almost overnight, and was reaching toward the gutter downspout. She watched for some moments as the man worked in the color-filled courtyard.

"And why don't my clematis bloom like that?" she whispered to herself.

"Miss—something you should know," Billy called out to her as he entered the office, throwing down his newspaper and wiping his brow with a handkerchief.

"And what's that, Billy?" she replied, frowning as she drew away from the window.

"Been talking to Phil—he was outside when I came past the pub. Smoking enough to put a chimney to shame, he was. I asked him what was troubling him, and he said it was his Archie. You should see Phil—he's got a temper on him when he likes, and right now he's like a madman."

"What did Archie do?" asked Maisie.

"He's thrown in his job at the engineering firm in Sydenham, and he came round this morning to tell his mum and dad he's enlisted and is going in the army. He's not even waiting for his call-up papers to arrive."

Maisie grabbed her bag and jacket. "Just when I need the Alvis, she's in the garage at Chelstone!" She did not stop as she ran toward the door. "Come on, Billy."

As they reached Tottenham Court Road, a taxicab screeched to a halt as soon as Maisie raised her hand, and they clambered into the back of the vehicle.

"Faraday House, please," said Maisie.

"Faraday House? What are we going there for?"

"Just a guess, but I think Archie has planned the imparting of his news down to the last minute. Vivian will leave the building for lunch in about fifteen minutes, and I would bet that Archie is waiting there for her."

"Why? I mean, I know she's his sister, but—"

"I believe she's also an informant for Jimmy Robertson. Consider this—the Coombes family are a good family, and you can tell that Phil and Sally have done their best to bring their children up to know right from wrong. But just because you know right from wrong, it doesn't mean you stay away from the wrong part. The family is still connected to the Robertsons—they've grown up in the shadow of Uncle Jimmy. I would say they've kept it quiet, but a man like Robertson keeps his hooks in."

"Blimey," said Billy.

"I can't explain now," said Maisie, as the taxicab drew up alongside Faraday House. "But what would you do if your uncle was Jimmy Robertson, and you've reason to be scared of him, perhaps because you're in deeper than you thought you would ever be?"

"Blimmin' 'eck, I'd run away."

"That's what Archie is doing, and the war is giving

him a good opportunity to make his bid for freedom from those hooks."

The taxicab began to slow down as they reached their destination. Billy leapt out as it came to a halt alongside the curb, and held the door open for Maisie. She paid the driver and looked up and down the street. "Now we wait, but not for long. If Vivian comes out to go for a sandwich and a cuppa, and Archie isn't here to say good-bye to his sister, then we've missed him. It means I've guessed wrong."

They stood for a few minutes, Maisie fixing her attention in one direction, while Billy kept his eyes on the other.

"I think that's him, miss—see? Coming toward us, along the pavement."

Maisie cast her gaze in the direction indicated by Billy. "Yes, that's him. Let's go toward him—if he meets Vivian, there will be strength of denial in numbers, and I want him on his own."

"Right you are, miss."

Maisie and Billy walked toward Archie Coombes, who seemed dressed for a cooler day, in a dark suit, a black overcoat and with a dark gray fedora on his head. He was smoking a cigarette, cupping the lighted end in his hand.

"Hello, Archie. How about that—what a coincidence, bumping into you. How are you?" Maisie smiled.

"Hello, Miss Dobbs. What're you doing here?"

"Actually, Archie, I am so glad to see you—I've been meaning to have a chat. Can you spare a moment? I know where there's a caff quite close by."

"I can't, miss—I'm meeting my sister, and she's due out of work any minute, and she don't get long for her break."

"Oh, not to worry—Mr. Beale will wait for her."

"Good as done, miss," said Billy. "Meet you at that place you told me about? Where you went with Vivian before?"

Maisie nodded. "Yes—when I've had my chat with Archie, we'll join you. Come on, Archie."

"But, Miss Dobbs—"

"Archie—I want to talk to you about Joe. And about your cousin—Teddy Wickham. You can't all enlist to get away from your uncle Jimmy—the next thing we know, Vivian will be in the ATS. Or even the Wrens—I hear all the girls enlisting want to get into the Wrens for the uniform, and your Viv is a stylish young woman." She laid her hand upon his arm. "Help me, Archie—this is about your brother, not the supplies, or the Bank of England, though I think I know why that might in-

terest you. Come on, Archie—take the brave way out.
You can't run forever."

"You don't know what he's like—he'll kill us. I told
Joe. I told him—keep your mouth shut about those
bloody headaches. I got him some aspirin powders, and
told him to just knock a couple back every day and he'd
be all right." Tears welled in Archie Coombes' eyes,
and his hands were shaking. Rivulets of perspiration
beaded his forehead, and began to stream along his
temples, down to his jawline.

"I will do everything I can to protect you—but help
me, Archie. Help me for Joe's sake. Help me for your
brother."

Archie Coombes looked from side to side, then back
to Maisie.

"I'm so scared, Miss Dobbs. I never thought I could
be so scared. I thought it can't be any worse, being in
the army, being shot at, than looking over my shoulder
at every motor car, wondering if my number's up." He
began to weep.

"Come on, Archie—let's go over the road. Let's find
a place to sit down and have a chat."

Chapter 17

Some fifteen minutes later, Maisie and Archie reached the café where Billy was waiting with Vivian Coombes.

Billy stood up as Maisie approached. They exchanged an almost imperceptible nod, and Billy smiled at Archie and his sister.

"I'm leaving you two to talk to Miss Dobbs now—lovely to see you again, Viv. And thank you for asking after my Billy. Can I get anyone another cuppa before I go?"

"I think we're all right, Billy," said Maisie, taking a seat and pulling out the chair next to her for Archie to be seated as Billy left the café.

"Vivian, Archie has been talking to me about the difficulties involved in being related to Jimmy Robertson, and I wonder if I can ask you a few questions—I just want to connect the dots, if I may."

"Uncle Jimmy's not a *difficulty*, Miss Dobbs. People thinking he is, that's the difficulty. He's been good to us." She turned to face her brother. "And you should learn to keep your mouth shut, you stupid idiot."

"But Viv—"

Maisie held up a hand. "A row between the two of you isn't going to help matters—and neither is denial, Vivian. You could be in a lot of trouble, and lose a very good job. I just want to get some things sorted out. And you probably don't know this, Vivian, but Archie was on his way to barracks and was coming here to say good-bye to you when I bumped into him—he's enlisted, so you don't have a lot of time with your brother."

"Oh that's just wonderful." Vivian glared at her brother. "You yellow-bellied twit! Off to join the army because you can't get anything right—see what good that did Teddy. You're like a child with his hands over his eyes who thinks no one can see him."

"Oh, leave off, Viv—things are bad enough as it is." Archie rested his head in his hands, elbows on the table.

"And don't loll around on that table—I know people in here. You'll have everyone looking at you and you'll show me up," added his sister.

"All right, Vivian, here's your choice," said Maisie.

"You either talk to me now, or you'll be talking to the police for hours on end. You're going to have to talk to them anyway, but you can make it easy on yourself by starting to tell the truth right now. Get into practice. You're in trouble—but it might not be as bad as you expect, if you cooperate."

"I've been cooperating since I was a child—I'm fed up with cooperating with someone. Mum and Dad, and now Uncle Jimmy. I suppose you want to know all about Teddy too, don't you?"

"Actually, no—I know about Teddy, and I know all about Archie. What I want to know about is every step that was taken so your uncle was awarded the contract to supply Mike Yates with a special paint to use as a fire retardant on airfields."

"That? You want to know about that? That was nothing much." Vivian Coombes smirked and turned away, her back to her brother, and her right shoulder to Maisie. She lifted up her handbag, which she had placed on the floor, and took out a lipstick and compact. She proceeded to apply the red lipstick, rolling her lips together before closing the compact with a snap. Maisie could see she struggled to control her shaking hands. "And how long do you think I can stay here in this café? I've got to get back to work."

Maisie looked at her watch. *Not long now.* "Just another couple of minutes, then you can go. But first—that contract, how did you find out about it?"

Vivian Coombes sighed and flapped her hand at Maisie, as if the answer were hardly worth her time.

"I'm on the government exchanges—you know that. And I heard it on the line—it's not as if they're all scrambled, after all, and not all the calls are important or top secret. Most of the time it's just one boring civil servant speaking to another boring civil servant. Anyway, it was before the war, when I'd just been promoted—I heard this bloke talking to another bloke about putting the contract out to tender, that it had to be done quickly, none of this waiting for months. Painting the airfield buildings with that special paint to stop fires was urgent, on account of the expected attacks and the chance of invasion if war were declared. I knew Uncle Jimmy was always looking for a new bit of business, and that he'd sold paint to Yates before, so I let him know. After that I didn't do anything—he's got his ways of finding out about the other bids, so he made sure he got it. I can't go about my job listening to everything."

"Just as well." Maisie sighed. "But you were rewarded for your trouble, weren't you?"

"I don't know what you mean," said Vivian.

"Come on, Viv—she knows," said Archie. "And this

is about our Joe. Uncle Jimmy wasn't on the up and up, not with that paint."

Maisie watched as Vivian Coombes looked at her brother, then at her hands, and when she met Maisie's eyes, her lips trembled.

"You're a strong young woman, Vivian, and you are loyal to your family. Your uncle has seen you all supplied with some lovely things in the past, gifts that made life a little easier. You've had brand-new clothes, good shoes, nice furniture, all sorts of little extras. And he had that telephone put in at the pub. It wasn't the brewery, was it?" She looked from Vivian to Archie. "Your family were the recipients of stolen goods, and have been for a long time. Being a 're-ceiver' of such items is a crime in itself, but the passing on of confidential information carries a different kind of punishment in a time of war."

"We weren't at war, not when I told him," said Vivian. "I just thought I would let him know."

"All in your favor, Vivian, that there was a limit to your sharing of information from a confidential government call. But the judge might see it as simply a question of semantics," said Maisie.

"Of what," asked Archie.

Vivian rolled her eyes. "She means it's down to how the judge sees it. That big bits of information are the same as small bits, when it comes to language—it's confidential whether it comes from the prime minister or the cleaner, when it's on a government line. You dopey item."

"It's the seriousness of the crime that counts, and character," said Maisie. "Fortunately, you weren't in on the most egregious part of the crime."

"What was that?" said Vivian.

Archie began to weep, his head low, his shoulders revealing his grief and fear.

"Oh you, you blimmin' watery head. I wish you'd pull yourself together," said Vivian to her brother. She took her bag and began to stand up.

Archie looked up at his sister. "You're not as hard as you try to be, Viv. Uncle Jimmy killed Joe. He might have got him that job, so he was in a reserved occupation, but he was killing him slowly because he was adding other stuff to the paint to make it go a lot further. He wasn't supplying Yates with the stuff exactly as it was shown to him by the RAF bods and the government officials. I know—I'm a slave in his blimmin' engineering works. I know what he does, and he was doing things on the cheap so he made more money—a lot more money. He was thinning it down so he could sell it to other businesses, for painting factories, shops and all sorts of other buildings, telling the landlords that it would save their properties from burning down when the invasion came and we were bombed. He couldn't use water because it would have just gone lumpy like rotten eggs, so he used chemicals. Mike Yates was in on it. And yes, Dad wanted me and Joe to have jobs where we wouldn't be called up, but what were we really protected from? Eh? No one protected Joe, did they? That stuff was killing him."

Maisie watched the siblings argue back and forth, then saw her chance to interject.

"Joe was made very ill by the paint—possibly he was more susceptible to the toxins due to his age, and the fact that he was still growing. And because he was the apprentice, he was set to work on tasks that demanded most exposure to the poisonous vapor—decanting the paint into the smaller pails, stirring it to mix the chemicals, and then the final testing, setting the blow-torches on the finished walls where he was breathing in even more danger. There are more pathology reports to come through. But ultimately Joe was not killed by the paint or an accident—he was murdered, and his life was taken because people knew about his health and that he was suffering. He had to be stopped, because the more he talked about his headaches, and the more he wanted to leave an apprenticeship that was considered an otherwise good opportunity, the more attention was drawn to him and therefore to the job he was doing and the materials he was using. If he continued complaining, it was only a matter of time before the paint was subject to renewed testing by the authorities. Your uncle Jimmy needed time—time for the contract to run its course, enabling him to make as much money as possible. And the contract could go on for a long while, given the number of new aerodromes being built and any repainting required after the job was finished."

Vivian stared at Maisie, her mouth open.

"You want to watch that, love—something might fall in if you keep it that wide." Caldwell stood over Vivian Coombes, then pulled up a chair and sat down.

Maisie shook her head and sighed. "This is Detective Chief Inspector Caldwell with the golden tongue from Scotland Yard. He would like to speak to you both on his premises, and not here in the café. A motor car is waiting outside, so my advice is to accompany him without attracting attention." She turned to Caldwell. "Thank you, Inspector."

Vivian Coombes came to her feet. "But I have to get back to work—you don't understand, I have a shift—"

"All sorted out, love—your supervisor knows you've been a witness to a serious crime and that you are providing us with invaluable information, for which you could well receive an important reward. *Your life.*" He drew his attention to Maisie. "Now then, Miss Dobbs, would you be so kind as to lead the way, and I'll bring up the rear, as the saying goes."

Outside the café, Caldwell shepherded the siblings into a police vehicle, and turned to Maisie. "They'll be at each other's throats all the way to the Yard, mark my words." He held out his hand to Maisie. "My colleagues with the Flying Squad will love this one— nailing Jimmy Robertson will be a coup."

"There's more, Inspector Caldwell—I just had to get them into safe hands. What about Teddy Wickham?"

"Steps have been taken to question him. His testimony will come in useful to snare his uncle, though he will most likely end up being reassigned to another military capacity—and that's after a good spell of cleaning latrines before being promoted to peeling spuds and chopping cabbage. And after that, he won't be in any cushy number like looking after stores." He shook his head. "The forces have lost enough men and they can't afford to lose more, so they're making allowances." He sighed. "Anyway, getting Jimmy Robertson off the streets will be a dream come true for us at the Yard. Trouble is, the nasty bugger gets others to do his dirty work, so he's hard to nail. But this time, it's his family telling us the story." He turned to get into the motor car. "I'll see you at the Yard, to make a full statement."

"And what about Joe Coombes' killer?"

"Got Murphy on it, down in Basingstoke. Should be picking him up at any minute. How did you know it was him?"

"It was a process of elimination. Freddie Mayes had a lot to lose, with Joe being so ill and him worried more people would notice and then the balloon would really go up. Mike Yates, Freddie—they're all Jimmy Robertson's men, one way or another."

"The money way," said Caldwell.

"The past ten years have been bad for a lot of people—no work to be had, and even when you get a job, you're not being paid as much, or you're on short time. I would bet that Freddie had more going on at home than we know about—and responsibility brings a need for more money. I have no idea who Jimmy Robertson's driver is, but I imagine he was the man with the cosh, and Freddie just knew the route that Joe took when he was out for a walk, trying to clear his head. He was an accomplice, not the perpetrator."

"We found the motor, and the driver—he's got previous as long as your arm, including grievous bodily harm—good old GBH. In fact on his record, there's a long line of GBH, GBH, and even more GBH. His name's Sidney Spooner—the initials suit him. He should be over there with old Hitler." Caldwell paused, then inclined his head toward the back seat of the motor car. "And what about their parents? I'm looking forward to hearing their side of the story."

"Can I talk to them first?" asked Maisie.

Caldwell nodded. "All right. This time, yes—I owe you."

Maisie watched as Caldwell moved away. His rhetoric was the same, but it was tempered, flat, as if someone had stepped hard upon an essential—and not entirely likeable—part of his character. And such was the air of melancholy that emanated from him, underlined by his willingness to follow her lead, that she reached out to touch his shoulder.

"Inspector Caldwell—wait. There's something amiss." She kept her voice low as he stepped back to face her. "What is it? What's wrong?"

Caldwell shook his head. "I don't like to admit it, but there's not much anyone can get past you, is there, Miss Dobbs?" He took a deep breath, looking up at the barrage balloons, then casting his eyes down to the sandbags and barbed wire. He exhaled as he brought his attention back to Maisie. "It's Able—you remember Able?'

"Yes, of course—of course I remember. You said he joined the navy."

Caldwell nodded. "He did—and I made a joke of that too. Able Seaman Able. That's what I said when he joined up. And the lad took it all in good heart." Caldwell looked at his feet, then at Maisie again. "HMS *Keith* went down on Saturday. She came under attack by German aircraft, taking out her steering gear first, then they dropped a bomb right down her funnel. And she'd already done one run to Dunkirk, evacuating over nine hundred soldiers—she was on her way back to get more when they attacked her. A lot of men were saved, but Able wasn't one of them."

"I am so sorry, Inspector. I'm so very sorry."

"I feel bad about it—the way I teased him, made everyone laugh at his expense."

Maisie shook her head. "Don't—don't blame yourself for anything. Able was a good sport, and even though you ribbed him, he would smile and laugh in return. You noticed him, Inspector—even though you had a joke about his name, he was never invisible, and was held with great affection by the other men because of the way he took it. I believe he knew it too—knew he was popular, and well liked."

"Thank you, Miss Dobbs. Thank you very much for that. Now then—I'd better get these two over to the Yard, before they kill each other in the back of my motor car."

Maisie watched the vehicle drive away.

"I heard that—about Able. Terrible shame," said Billy, who had been waiting outside the café for Maisie. "Miss—did you really mean it, about Able knowing he was held with affection? By Caldwell? I mean, does that man hold anyone in any sort of affection?"

Maisie raised a hand to hail a taxicab. "He was a good assistant to Caldwell, and though Caldwell could be merciless in his teasing, Able had a gentle kindness about him, and I believe he would see no advantage to saying anything that would add to Caldwell's grief and guilt."

A taxi stopped, allowing Maisie and Billy to climb aboard.

"So, why do you think someone like Able joined the police in the first place, if he was that gentle? I mean, you really need to be a bit of a tough nut to do that job, unless of course you're on the beat in a little village somewhere."

"I don't really know—and by the way, from my experience, being on the beat in a village can be fraught with danger. But I would imagine that if we delved a bit further into his motivations, it might have something to do with his father. Perhaps he was a policeman, and even in a small village—a man who aspired to Scotland Yard and pressed his son into the same profession. Perhaps when war was declared, the navy offered a way out of the family business for Able, so he jumped at the chance of enlisting into the senior service." She paused. "It's all perhaps, perhaps, perhaps. And on that note—talking about a family business—we're going to see Phil and Sally Coombes."

Maisie and Billy sat in the saloon bar and waited until afternoon closing time before the pub was empty. Phil Coombes did not even ask if they wanted to speak to him, but as he chivvied the last customer out of the pub and locked the door, he turned to them.

"Better come upstairs. Sally will have heard me bolt the door, and the kettle will be on."

"Thank you, Mr. Coombes," said Maisie.

Sally Coombes demonstrated no sense of surprise as her husband led the visitors into her kitchen. She set two more cups and saucers, a pot of tea, a jug of milk and the sugar bowl on the table.

"Take a seat," said Coombes. "You too," he added, pulling out a chair for his wife.

Maisie looked in silence from Phil to Sally Coombes, and Billy shifted in his seat.

"You know why I'm here, don't you?" said Maisie.

"It's about my brother," said Sally. She pulled a handkerchief from her pinafore pocket and pressed it against her eyes.

"We couldn't go to the police," said Coombes, putting an arm around his wife's shoulder.

"Couldn't go to the police? He was killing your son!" Billy's outburst came without warning.

"Billy—" Maisie raised her hand to settle her assistant. She drew her attention back to Phil Coombes. "Mr. Coombes—Phil—correct me if I'm wrong, but here's what I believe has happened in this family." She looked toward Sally. "Would you pour the tea, Mrs. Coombes—I know I could do with a cup." She continued while Sally Coombes poured. "Sometimes these things start in a small way, don't they? I've seen this so many times in my work—the very worst trouble that people get into doesn't begin with a big leap to the dark side. It's rather like when you run a hot water tap—it first runs cold, then slowly the water warms, until the hot water comes through and it's so uncomfortable you have to draw your hand away. You can run the cold water to moderate the heat. Or you can just get used to the increasing temperature."

Sally Coombes set a cup of tea each in front of

Maisie, Billy and her husband, then took a sip from her own cup while continuing to stare at Maisie, as if she had been anticipating every word spoken.

"Phil—you were in the army with Jimmy Robertson, and you two became tight—he's a charismatic person, after all. I've heard he's a bit of a Jack-the-Lad with a quick turn of phrase, and a very good head on his shoulders. A very bright man."

"He kept our boys out of the army," said Sally.

"Indeed." Maisie glanced at Billy, then brought her attention back to Sally. She had expected her to make at least one defense of her brother. "And he's seen you all right," she continued. "You've been well taken care of as a family. But there's a price, isn't there? And what was that price? Selling his stolen goods through the pub—perhaps the holiday clubs? People put money in the kitty every week to buy themselves a good Christmas, or Easter, and you not only keep it for them, but then you can sell the goods acquired by your brother."

"It didn't do anyone any harm," said Sally, folding her arms.

"Sal—hold on," said Coombes. "All right—yes, it was just like you said. A bit of knocked-off stuff here and there, and holding on to some money until one of his blokes came for it—he made it worth our while. Kept our three in better clothes than we could afford, and all we had to do was the odd favor. Nothing wrong with that—not really."

"But it began to get bigger, until—I suspect—you both would really rather not be doing what you were doing anymore. And that's why, when Joe didn't telephone as usual, and when he complained about the headaches, you were too scared to go to Jimmy, because really—" Maisie turned her attention to Sally Coombes. "Because really you know that Jimmy might have the veneer of taking care of his own, but anyone in his pay is dispensable, one way or another. You could not go to the police directly, because you have—whether you like it or not—committed the crime of receiving stolen goods, and you've done it for years. Probably all your life."

Maisie reached to take a sip of tea, choosing her words. "You, Phil, started the ball rolling when you came to see me. I think you hoped that I would find Joe alive, bring him home, and then all would be well. But I also think that, in the deepest place of your heart, you knew your brother-in-law would sacrifice your son to save himself. He is a ruthless man."

Phil Coombes began to weep, his shoulders shaking as the mournful keening took over his body. "I thought Jimmy was saving him, I thought he had helped us by putting in the word at Yates, and then getting him the job there. I knew that if this war went on, he'd reach conscription age, and after what I saw in the last war, I didn't want my sons to go, and Jimmy helped."

Sally's voice was cold, her words delivered in a tone that made Maisie think of shards of shaved ice. "Jimmy expects loyalty."

"I'm sure he does. I think it's something we all like—but you knew, deep down, that something was not quite right with the work, and instead of allowing Joe to leave Mike Yates' employ—and Yates is in the palm of your brother's hand—you forbade him to take up the opportunity to work on a farm."

"You're right, Miss Dobbs." As he spoke, Maisie could see that Phil Coombes wore the demeanor of a resigned man—his shoulders were rounded, his head low—and in his voice she could feel the deep chasm of grief in his heart. "I was scared, and I was scared of Jimmy—of what he could do. I knew he would have had no patience if Joe's complaints led to him losing money. Archie and Vivian know exactly what their uncle is like, and they've toed the line—they've done very well—but Joe was different. He didn't really see it. And what future is there on a farm, for a London boy?" Phil Coombes held out his hands, palms up, as he asked the question.

"There's life," said Billy. "A boy on a farm would be alive. And in one of your precious reserved occupations."

Maisie cleared her throat. "Billy, would you telephone Caldwell. Tell him Mr. and Mrs. Coombes are ready to make a statement. I think it would be a good idea if he sent a motor car."

"Right you are, miss," said Billy. He left the room to go down to the saloon bar, where he could place the call.

"I could have stopped it all, if I'd gone to the police earlier," said Phil. "But, I mean, it was only headaches, and it was probably his age."

Maisie leaned forward, her brow knitted. "Phil, you're playing a devastating game of snakes and ladders, going back and forth with the truth. One minute you're confessing and the next denying complicity to the rest of the world. You must face up to the fact that Joe suffered terrible pain due to your brother-in-law tampering with the paint he was supplying to Yates. And who knows how many others have been affected."

"But Teddy said—" began Sally.

"Teddy is only protected now because he is in uniform and the services need people working, not in prison—but he may still risk incarceration if he has to stand a court-martial. The authorities know he was under the influence of a man of whom he was fearful, so that may help him—believe it or not, the police have spoken up for him. But you knew Teddy worked in his uncle's warehouses before the war, and it was fortuitous that his experience took him right into a similar position with the RAF—looking after stores. But was it fortune, or another of his uncle's contacts? Either way, that's where Jimmy Robertson came in again—and Teddy wasn't safe in the RAF."

"What do you mean?" asked Sally.

"Teddy was falsifying deliveries. No less than a third of each shipment was going straight to his uncle's warehouse. And a good deal of each shipment was foodstuff—which is becoming harder to get already. It's very nice money for Jimmy, a quite significant black market income. There's probably food in your larder that should have gone into an RAF store. Sally, your brother has tentacles that reach everywhere—but you know that, you've lived with it all your life, because your father before him was the same. It's the family business."

"We wanted only the best for our children, Miss Dobbs," said Phil Coombes. "We might have been strict, we might have been a bit hard on them, but it's no good bringing them up soft, is it? And we provided for them the best we could."

Maisie sighed, relieved to hear the sound of a motor car pulling up outside.

It was not Caldwell who entered the kitchen moments later, but another man, along with Billy and a uniformed policeman. The man in civilian clothing addressed Maisie first.

"Harry Bream. Flying Squad. Pleased to meet you." He turned to Phil and Sally Coombes. "If you wouldn't mind accompanying me, Mr. and Mrs. Coombes. It's very quiet outside, and we just want to take you along to our gaff to ask a few questions."

Sally Coombes came to her feet, aided by her husband.

"If you don't mind, Mr. Bream—in fact, I'm sure it's Detective Inspector Bream—I'd like to change into my best costume, fetch my coat and pay a visit to the lavatory," said Sally. She smiled at her husband and reached across to squeeze his hand.

Bream stepped aside to allow her to leave, and as she did so, Maisie came to her feet and stood still, watching the first steps she took across the threshold onto the landing. As Sally Coombes' footfall receded along the passageway first to the bedroom, and then a few minutes later to the bathroom, Maisie felt as if she were watching a moving picture reduced to slow motion. And then the screen turned black.

"Oh no!" cried Maisie, rushing down the passageway. She had just pushed open the bathroom door when the shot rang out.

Chapter 18

Maisie bent her head as the flash from camera bulbs erupted, and reporters approached, notebooks in hand, asking for comments on what had happened in the private residence of the popular watering hole. Billy raised his hand to shield his employer, taking Maisie by the arm and falling into step as she walked at speed along Warren Street toward Fitzroy Square. Behind her she could hear Jack Barker, the newspaper vendor, who had hurried across the street when he saw what was happening. "Come on, gents, that's enough for today. You've got your pictures and you've got the story, now get back to your little desks down there in Fleet Street and fiddle with your pens because I've got to sell your wares tomorrow morning."

"That's all I need," said Maisie, as they reached the front door, her key at the ready.

"Nearly there, miss. Another nice cup of tea with a lot of sugar is what we need. Terrible day—miserable day all-around, and that was a blimmin' horrible thing you saw in there."

Maisie was standing by the window, staring down at Walter Miles' garden when Billy entered her office, placing a tray with two mugs of hot tea on the long table, the case map still drawn out across its full length.

"I know you prefer a mug, miss, so I didn't mess around with them china cups. Reminds me of being in the army, that there's still a fight to be had and we'd better drink it all up and get some courage in us."

Maisie took a seat at the table, clutching the mug with both hands as she sipped the piping hot, sweet tea.

"Funny, innit, miss—how it's a nice warm afternoon out there, but now we're both feeling like it's a winter's morning?"

"It's the adrenaline, Billy. The rush of adrenaline that gets you through a shock leaves you cold once it diminishes in your body. At least we can still be shocked—I would hate to have to accept the death of Sally Coombes as something perfectly normal."

"I know what you mean." He put down the mug and tapped the map. "I can see all the links now, but some still seem a bit faint." He paused. "And I've a question, miss—if you don't mind me asking."

"Go on, Billy. We should sit here and talk over everything that's happened—so we can begin to take it all in, along with the outcome. This has been a testing case."

"It's been an odd one, no two ways about it. All these threads and lines of inquiry, and you're not the one tying them all together. Well—you were when it came to Sally Coombes, but . . ." Billy reached for his mug again. "Anyway, I don't want to speak out of turn."

Maisie looked up at the man who had been at her side as her assistant for the best part of eleven years, a man she had seen struggle with lingering pain from war wounds sustained in 1917, with addiction, the loss of a beloved child, a very ill wife, and the challenges of bringing two sons to manhood as war approached. In turn he had witnessed Maisie battle her own shell shock along with the physical wounds of war, and then her blossoming when finding love again. He had known her through widowhood, through a homecoming from another war, and had returned to work for her as she reestablished her business.

"You have every right to express your opinions, Billy—and if I am not mistaken, you have been harboring feelings about the way I've managed this case."

"It's just not like you—you've almost got there, you've all your notes from the investigation. You've got this." He tapped the case map. "And you've handed the lot over to Caldwell and that bloke from the Sweeney Todd—Harry Bream. You're not going to be on the spot when they bring in Freddie whatshisname, and you never faced up to Jimmy Robertson—never even attempted to see him. That's not like you at all. Now, admittedly, being in the same room with that felon would be a bit of a chance—after all, he's not known for taking prisoners, but still . . . why? Why aren't you in at the end? Is it because you've not got the motor car anymore, and you can't exactly nip here and there on the train and the bus? Or is it to do with the money? Because as far as I can see, there ain't some fancy client falling over himself to settle an account on this one. All the costs are down to the business."

Maisie took another sip of tea before responding. "Certainly giving up the Alvis has clipped my wings— it's hard to act at speed without a motor car. And it's not the money, Billy. I daresay there will be some 'consideration' coming from Scotland Yard—after all, I've given them almost everything they need to make arrests. Or I will have by the time we make our statements. And there are funds in the business account to absorb a few losses." She sighed. "No, it's something quite different. I have to be careful for another reason."

"I reckon after all this time, miss, you could tell me what it is," said Billy.

Maisie set down her mug, pushed back her chair and walked to the window, her eyes drawn to the thriving clematis. She lifted a hand to wipe away a tear, and turned back to Billy, leaning against the windowsill as she sighed before beginning to explain herself.

"You're right—together we've put all the pieces on the table for Scotland Yard, and yet I am not the one constructing the final picture, though it's pretty obvious—it'll fall into place without any more help from me."

"But, miss—"

"Wait, Billy—just wait." She cleared her throat. "You've probably gathered—indeed, I think it's fairly obvious—that I have become very fond of our little evacuee, Anna."

"She's a treasure of a child, a real treasure," said Billy.

"She is indeed." Maisie nodded, struggling to swallow the lump in her throat. "And whilst her late grandmother—just before she passed away—signed forms naming me as Anna's guardian, my stated responsibility was not only to offer Anna a good home, but to find her a family who loved her. My role was to be temporary, a place for her to be safe until she could be settled forever. It's implied in the language."

Billy opened his mouth to speak, but Maisie raised her hand and shook her head. "Let me get to the end, Billy." She took another deep breath. "I decided to take steps to adopt Anna—to become her mother. But of course there are hurdles to leap across. I have managed to persuade the authorities that it would be nigh on impossible to find her Maltese father—at first they stipulated that I should prove that both parents had relinquished interest, either through death or a signed contract. And then without any prompting from me, they concluded that it might be difficult to place her, as she is not exactly colored like an English rose. But neither am I—and I have had very mixed feelings because on one hand I was glad they identified a problem with placing her, which gives weight to my application, yet at the same time I was filled with anger that they dared to voice such . . . such . . . prejudice." She sighed, shaking her head. "And I couldn't exactly take them to task for it—that would have definitely put someone's back up, and I need people on my side, not against me. To the good, I have been fortunate in the references I've been able to submit, but two things stand in the way."

"Just two?" said Billy.

Maisie nodded. "Oh, but they're big. One is that I am a widow, though I am a woman of independent means, and of course I have a title bestowed upon me by marriage that has smoothed the way a little." She shook her head. "But to tell you the truth, that infuriates me too. I was brought up by people who, when all is said and done, did their very best for me. No matter what privations we faced as a family, I was loved. That's all that really matters. Anyway, my references are excellent and my house passes muster with the Ministry of Health."

"So, one thing is that you're a widow—a woman with no husband."

Maisie nodded, wiping away a tear.

"And what's the other thing?"

There was a moment's silence before Maisie could speak.

"My work."

"Oh," said Billy, nodding his understanding. "Yes, I'm beginning to get the picture."

"So you see, I have to 'box clever' as the saying goes. I cannot be identified as being at the closure of a case, for example. You know how the press have reported it in the past—that I have been involved in an investigation. That's why I could only go so far with

Vivian and Archie, why I could not go to challenge Jimmy Robertson. I'm worried enough at how reports of Sally Coombes' suicide might look in tomorrow's papers."

"What don't they like about it—your job? You're doing something decent and good, not like some people—and it's to do with justice, after all, and helping put wrong things right."

"First of all, it's the danger inherent in the work— and we know it carries a risk, even though we are careful enough. And then there's the fact that I am likely to come into contact with a criminal element of society."

"But if it's dangerous, what do they think of you joining the Auxiliary Ambulance Service, as a volunteer? That's blimmin' dangerous too! Or haven't you told them?"

"I've declared my involvement in volunteer work with the ambulance service—but that's seen as me doing my bit, as a citizen, and we've all been called upon to do our voluntary service, haven't we? And they don't see that as dangerous at the present time. They don't even mind the fact that I spend several days per week in London, though that may have to change."

"These people make me ill—can't see to the ends of their noses. And what about little Anna, bless her?"

"She's very happy. She adores Dad and Brenda, and even Lady Rowan and Lord Julian have started treating her as if she were the grandchild they always wanted."

"Can't they speak up for you?"

"They provided my first references."

"And I suppose there's a pen-pusher somewhere who doesn't want to feel pushed around by the upper classes."

"Something of that order."

"Blimey." Billy finished his tea and placed his mug on the tray. "So what are you going to do?"

"I'm going to keep my nose clean, so to speak. I can continue my work, though I will have to be careful, not do anything to draw attention to myself. I have never liked it on those occasions when my name has appeared either as a special witness in published court proceedings or the newspapers—I've tried to remain as anonymous as possible. But I admit, in terms of securing new business, it's useful. Anyway, a hearing has been set for September. I'll have to go before a panel, which includes a special judge, to state my case for becoming Anna's adoptive parent. I almost dare not hope—"

"Oh, miss, it'll all come out in the wash—that's what my old mum used to say. Just you wait and see." Billy moved to Maisie's side and put an arm around her, pulling her to him as she wept. "You have a good old cry. It'll do you good, what with everything that's gone on lately, and seeing Sally Coombes top herself today. Let your tears fall, and then come out fighting. It'll be all right."

"Oh, I hope so, Billy. I do hope so. I don't want to lose her."

"I know, miss. I know."

"I love Anna, Billy. I love her as if she were my own."

"But she is—she is yours. Anyone who sees you two together knows that—she belongs with you. If your Dr. Blanche were here, I reckon he would say she's always belonged to you."

Maisie slumped down onto one of the wicker lawn chairs without even entering her garden flat in Holland Park. There were telephone calls to be made, for her day's work was not yet done, and she was anxious to find out if Tim was improving. Every time she thought of her beloved godson, she felt her breath catch. She wondered how he might be feeling, now that the enormity of his undertaking—and the loss of his best friend—was in all likelihood beginning to come into focus. She allowed herself another five minutes outside, before opening the French doors wide for the fresh evening air to blow through. She removed her jacket and hat, and placed her document case and shoulder bag on top of the desk in the corner. Once again she had left the office without her gas mask.

She was just about to sink into the armchair when the telephone began to ring. She lifted the receiver.

"Tante Maisie! Thank goodness! Where is everyone? I can't find my parents or my brothers—have they all trotted off on holiday?"

"Tom! Tom! I am so relieved to hear your voice. Your mother and father have been worried sick about you—we've had news reports of RAF fighting over the Channel, and there was no word from you."

"Sorry about that—we weren't allowed to use the telephone during the evacuation—and it's all right, I wasn't flying. Well, I was, but not on ops. Where is everyone?"

Maisie realized it would fall to her to break the news to Tom about his brother—his bravery, and how he now carried the wounds of war. She told Tom the story from beginning to end, and then answered his questions, one after the other in quick succession revealing his fear and concern.

"I'll put in for compassionate leave. I can't stay here, flying all over the place like some gnat without a purpose—I'm coming home."

"Wait until you've spoken to your parents," said

Maisie. "Tim will be at the hospital in Hastings for a few weeks, I'm sure—they have to wait to see if any infection emerges. Everyone's at Chelstone, staying with me—it's not too far a drive to Hastings from there, and there's the train too."

"Can you fit in another, if I can get away?"

"Of course I can, Tom—you'll have to bunk in with Tarquin though."

"For once I won't mind his snoring. I'll let you know when I'm coming, Tante Maisie. But I'll try for Friday."

"I hope to see you then, Tom—and do take care."

"I'm up in Northumberland—shouldn't really tell you that, should I? They put us pilots into three big groups, and we're all over the place—there's us newish boys, who have to get our practice in, and then there's the next group, which is a mix, so everyone gets experience flying with more seasoned chaps, and then there are the pilots with the hours on them—they're a year or so older than me, the old salts! I started flying an old Tiger Moth—doing the sort of aerobatics that Uncle James would have done in the last war. I kept thinking of him, actually." He paused for breath, and to put more coins in the slot. "Then they put me on this American aeroplane, called a Harvard. I thought it was a lovely kite—even had automatic wheels up. But now I'm really excited, because the very good news is that I'm transferring to RAF Hawkinge next month—they're moving me into Hurricanes. I'll have had about ten or twelve hours flying by the time I'm on ops over to France, which isn't bad as I think some of the men coming up after me will have less, what with one thing and another. And Hawkinge is in Kent, so you'll see something of me when I've a day or two off."

Maisie nodded, as if Priscilla's eldest son were in the room. "Telephone your parents at the Dower House this evening—they should be there in an hour or so. Let them know you're doing well—they will be so relieved."

"Will do, Tante Maisie. I want to know how my brother is—he'll get better when he knows I'm coming. The way this family is going, we'll make a good team of one-armed bandits—I'd better be careful!"

"Yes, you had. Now then, call your parents and I'll see you at the week's end. You can tell me then what a one-armed bandit is!"

Maisie replaced the receiver, knowing that Tom's nonstop light banter at the end of the call was his way of assimilating his brother's plight, of trying to appear as if everything was normal. All the emotions that Priscilla and Douglas had experienced since they learned that Tim was missing would have hit Tom at once, with relief coming on top of fear, and—she thought—some anger toward his sibling under the surface, in the place where deep brotherly love resided. Every member of the family was affected—that was how it was. And now Tom was being posted to RAF Hawkinge. Northumberland seemed a lot safer. *They're moving me into Hurricanes.* Maisie shook her head. It felt as if they had all been moved into a hurricane, right into the eye of the storm.

She went into the kitchen, took a bottle of white wine from her new refrigerator—she still had not become used to the intermittent running noise—and poured herself a glass. She stood for a moment, looking out of the kitchen window across the garden, to her clematis still in bud, and then to the barrage balloons in the sky. Soon she would have to think about closing the doors and drawing the blackout curtains. She thought of Tim, looking back at his homecoming, the image of him being taken from the boat on a stretcher, and the terrible wounds to his arm. And she remembered the description Sylvia Preston, the WAAF, had given her—of driving her ambulance onto Salisbury Plain and picking up the bodies of young men who had failed their first parachute jump. She pictured Tom stationed at an aerodrome in Kent, which—it now seemed— would be on the front line of the invasion, if it came.

And then Anna. *Anna.* How could she ever keep her safe? She sighed. Her heart was heavy. It was time for the next call.

She had no need to look up the number before dialing.

"MacFarlane!" The greeting was as brusque as ever.

"Robbie, when will you answer the telephone as if there's a human being on the other end of the line, and not a charging bull elephant," said Maisie.

Robert MacFarlane, formerly a senior officer with Scotland Yard's Special Branch and now working with the Secret Service as a linchpin between the two, laughed when he heard Maisie's voice.

"It's been a while, has it not, hen? And to what do I owe this intrusion into my first wee dram of the day?"

"Bit late for you, isn't it, Robbie? From my garden the sun is already over the yardarm."

"I'm a-mending of my ways," replied MacFarlane. "That sounds almost poetic, doesn't it? Now then, seeing as you didn't mention taking me out for a nice four-course luncheon tomorrow, I take it this is a business call."

"It is, yes."

"Come on then, tell me what's going on."

"I could be wrong, Robbie, but I think I know of the whereabouts of an enemy agent—and even if he's not

German, I think he's someone who's probably not on our side."

"I see. Pray tell," said Robbie, his tone now weighted with the gravity of her news.

Maisie described her fears, and her reservations. "I just didn't think it was wise to wait any longer to tell you."

"No, you're right there. I'll get on it. Don't go into your office tomorrow, and keep those two employees of yours out of the way."

"Yes. I'll telephone them both immediately." She paused, curling the telephone cord around the fingers of her left hand. "Robbie—he's a nice man. Go easy on him."

"If the creeping vines are innocent, he won't even know we've been there. I'll put my little wee white gloves on for him."

"But not your white boxing gloves."

There was silence on the line before MacFarlane spoke again.

"My nephew didn't get out of Dunkirk, Maisie."

"I'm so sorry, Robbie. Truly I am. But please remember, I could be wrong about the man."

"I know you, Maisie, so in my gut, I doubt it. Now then, stay away tomorrow—treat yourself to an outing. Go home to the country to see that little girl of yours."

Maisie was grateful for a chill in the air as she walked along the Embankment toward Scotland Yard. Having confirmed that Sandra would not be required in the office, she had arranged to meet Billy outside the police headquarters at half past nine and instructed him not to go to the office first, as she had just remembered that some essential plumbing work would be in progress.

She had slept little the previous night. Priscilla had called late in the evening to let her know that Tim was weak, but improving, and had been awake long enough to talk briefly about Gordon's death. He had become distressed and was given a sedative. Andrew Dene had paid another visit, and estimated that it would be another two weeks before Tim would be discharged. He counseled against Tim returning to London, as fresh air and the chance to begin walking each day would help with balance and well-being. Priscilla and Douglas would therefore be looking for a property to rent in Kent, and ideally as close to the village as possible. "We're family, Maisie. We all need to be near those we love—don't you think?"

At Scotland Yard, Caldwell took Maisie's statement, starting with the day Phil Coombes came to her office to talk to her about his son.

"Do you think the man knew about his brother-in-law and the paint at that point?" said Caldwell.

"He knew what sort of man Jimmy Robertson was. He knew he was a criminal—but remember, they had served together, had gone over the top into battle together. They were connected by the horrors they'd seen, and by the fact that they both came home. I believe that as time went on—and of course, Phil married Sally Robertson—Phil did his utmost to turn a blind eye to the way Jimmy Robertson operated. And Robertson looked after the family, providing many little extras that make life easier. I believe Phil at some point began to doubt Jimmy, and he had to face up to the reality that the man is very dangerous indeed. He couldn't go straight to Jimmy about Joe, because he knew, deep down, that Jimmy cared only about number one. So, he came to me. Phil Coombes came to me only to say he was worried about his son. And if I found Joe safe and well—all to the better. But if not, then there was a detachment—it wouldn't be Phil who shopped Jimmy, it would be me. If luck held, Joe would come back, everyone would keep their mouths shut and life would go on. And as far as Phil and Sally Coombes were concerned, Jimmy had done more than provide those little extras I mentioned—he made sure both Archie and Joe were in reserved occupations. Vivian did well for herself, but there was always pressure to do anything she could for Uncle Jimmy—and that was probably true of the whole family."

Caldwell nodded. Maisie thought she had never seen him look so drawn. "Detective Inspector Murphy has brought in the painting crew, and Freddie Mayes has been charged with accessory to murder, following his confession today. He was acting on the instructions of Jimmy Robertson, who—it transpires—showed his face, along with Mike Yates, at their lodgings in Whitchurch. They wanted Joe to be quiet about his headaches, and—according to Yates—they told young Joe that it would be very bad form for his parents to know he wasn't pulling his weight in the job. We're getting enough to put Robertson away, and we hope for a long, long time. He has been brought in and is cooling his heels in a cell, though his brief is coming in to see him soon—the one who has had a fair bit of luck in allowing him to slide off our shovel in the past. Anyway, he's not been charged, but we have time. I just didn't want him to go anywhere. Not that getting away to the Continent is a good idea at the moment."

"I see—and what about the Bank of England?"

"Yes, that. All very interesting, I must say." He shook his head and gave a satisfied chuckle. "Young Archie had what he thought was a bright idea when he went down to see his brother, and it came to his attention that there was money in the area, quite literally. He considered the possibilities and thought he might be able to make himself a lieutenant in his uncle's business if he had a potentially lucrative plan. He was scared of Robertson, but decided that if he could make himself more valuable, he'd be safer, and his opinions would carry more weight. He's admitted he tried to get Joe involved, but Joe didn't want to have anything to do with any cockeyed plans involving robbery. Now, Jimmy Robertson likes a good idea resulting in great sums of cash coming his way as much as the next villain, but he also knows when it becomes a nonstarter. He considered Archie's plan, looked at it from all angles, and then thought better of it."

"It distracted me for a while, I must admit—though I always felt it might turn out to be important. My mistake," said Maisie.

"Oh, it could end up being important—as another nail in Jimmy Robertson's coffin. We know he eventually dismissed the plans, but at first he couldn't ignore information about large sums of money going to and fro between London and Hampshire. Robertson and his boys were interested enough to put some quite detailed plans on paper and ask Archie to get more information before deciding the risks outweighed the benefits—

and those incriminating papers were found in Archie's gaff with Robertson's scrawl across every page, along with his signature because he loved his name so much. Bit of a narcissist, is Robertson, and those papers signify intention, which is important, because he's been up for armed robbery more than once—so you might say they're a tool. And while we're about it—I've never known a lad of Archie Coombes' age to put so much into where he dosses down. This lad had his digs decked out like he was a matinee idol."

"I think he just wanted something more out of life," said Maisie.

"Don't we all?" replied Caldwell.

They discussed the revenue Robertson and Yates had brought in from the business of painting commercial buildings with the diluted fire retardant, and the fact that most were owned by people coerced into agreeing to the work by Robertson. The racket amounted to a pretty sum for the Robertson coffers. Maisie made a further statement, recounting how she had witnessed two lorries unloading and reloading stores on a country road close to the aerodrome where Teddy Wickham was stationed. It was not firm evidence, but enough to support deeper investigation. At the point where Caldwell began to shuffle his pages of notes, with only a few more questions left for Maisie to answer, there was a knock at the door, and a uniformed policeman entered.

"Oh sorry, guv, didn't know you had a visitor," said the policeman. "I thought you'd finished taking a statement in one of the interview rooms and was back up here on your own."

"I can take a statement here, where Miss Dobbs is concerned—she's one of our special advisers."

"I'm just going round collecting for DC Able, sir. To send something to his mum and dad. They're having a memorial service at their local church, and a few of the lads are going, especially on account of his dad."

Caldwell took out his wallet at the same time Maisie reached for her purse. The sergeant thanked them for their contributions, and left the room.

"Able's dad is in the force, you know," said Caldwell. "He was on the beat, but he's now a desk sergeant, out in Essex. I was told he always wanted his son to follow in his footsteps, so of course he was really chuffed when young Able came to work at the Yard. It had been his ambition, when he was a lad, but he never quite made it out of the village. I bet he wishes his boy had stayed here."

"Yes," said Maisie. "Yes, I'm sure he does."

Epilogue

Billy was waiting, pacing back and forth along the Embankment when Maisie came out of Scotland Yard.

"All right, miss? I suppose that's that. It seems they've got Jimmy Robertson cornered, though I must say, that Flying Squad bloke looks more like a bit of a villain himself—no wonder they call them the Sweeney Todd!"

"It's getting into the criminal mind that does it," said Maisie.

"But you don't look like a criminal—well, not all the time." Billy grinned, pleased with his quip.

"Thank you very much!" said Maisie. "How's your Billy getting on?"

"I forgot to tell you—he's been given another nine

days leave by the docs. They reckon he needs extra time to get over that shoulder, and then he'll be right as rain. They don't want blokes with one shoulder up and one shoulder down on the parade ground, and to be honest with you, I think another week or two at home will do him good. Mind you, it's going to take longer than a few weeks for him to get over what he saw in France—and don't I know it."

"Then take the week off, Billy—it's time you had a holiday. There's no need to come into the office."

"But what about the work? We've got new business to consider."

"Make your calls, tell the clients that you are recommencing investigations in a week or so. There's no need to go to Fitzroy Square."

"What about you?"

"I'm taking a week to myself too—perhaps more. I've work to do to bring the case to a proper close, but I don't need to go into the office. And I've to see Robbie MacFarlane this afternoon, then I'm going down to Chelstone. Sandra knows not to come in, so that's all right. We could all do with some time away."

Billy looked at Maisie, raising his hand to shield his eyes from the morning sunshine. "What's going on, miss?"

"Nothing more than me deciding that we could all do with a little holiday."

"Right then." Billy sighed. "I'm off home." He patted the pocket where he kept his notebook. "Got everything I need here, so I'll keep them security cases ticking over, and I'll spend that time with my family. Bobby's off to his air force engineering college soon, and there won't be many more opportunities for us all to be together. Thank you, miss."

Maisie watched as Billy walked away, a spring in his step compensating for a war-wound limp. She turned to walk toward Whitehall.

She had no fixed appointment with Robbie MacFarlane, but throughout the meeting with Inspector Caldwell at Scotland Yard, she was thinking of the report she had made the previous evening, and was curious to know the outcome. MacFarlane would be back in his office by the time she arrived.

Entering the building, she was about to approach a security guard when two young women came down the long flight of stairs to her right. The sound of their footfall and voices distracted Maisie, mainly because they were conversing in French.

"Elinor?"

The woman who had been the nanny to Priscilla's

sons only just managed to disguise her shock at seeing Maisie.

"Hello, Miss Dobbs." She held out her hand, turning to her friend. "This is my former employer's neighbor, Miss Dobbs."

The friend, who was dressed in the uniform of the First Aid Nursing Yeomanry, as was Elinor, turned to Maisie and smiled. "How do you do—I'm very pleased to meet you."

"And you," said Maisie. She was about to comment on how surprised she was that their paths should cross here, when Elinor stemmed any further conversation.

"We're in rather a hurry, Miss Dobbs," said Elinor. "Do give my best to Mrs. Partridge."

Maisie watched the women leave, then brought her attention to the security guard and stated her business. The guard turned to the telephone at his station, and picked up the receiver. Half a minute later he called out to Maisie, who had begun pacing back and forth along the tiled floor.

"Mr. MacFarlane says you know the way—he's ready to see you in his office."

Maisie made her way along the labyrinthine corridors until she saw MacFarlane waiting for her in the corridor outside his office. He waved as she approached, and held open the door for her.

"Sit yourself down, lass," said MacFarlane. He was a tall, heavyset man, indeed, Maisie always thought he appeared less than comfortable seated at a desk. His bulk was more suited to movement, or a much more forgiving chair than those found in government buildings. MacFarlane cleared his throat, as if preparing his deep Scottish burr for oratory. "Following his arrest early this morning—the early bird catches the worm, as the saying goes—we've been interviewing your Mr. Walter Miles for several hours now, and look at this pile of notes I've amassed already." He tapped a thick sheaf of papers on the desk. "We might run out of paper with this case, and that's not an exaggeration. What with shipping affected by the war, even the daily newspapers are worried about supplies." He cleared his throat. "As you suspected, the blooming clematis was not a clematis after all—well, it was, but it was a very good fake. Its true purpose was as an aerial to connect wireless transmissions. Very nicely tucked away too. Frankly, we knew there was someone in the area up to funny business with a set, but we couldn't locate him. His English is perfect, but he's a German citizen, true name of Walter Maier—so he wasn't far off with his invented identity. Always best to stick to a name you know, if you're an agent. And he was also a lecturer at the university—so that bit was right. He was a botanist originally, but more recently he taught physics and had been doing so for a year. Took the place of another physicist who is now working for the government—one of those boffins we've got tucked away out in the country."

"I see," said Maisie.

"Not sure if you do quite yet—because there's more."

"Go on."

"It seems our Walter had a chip on his shoulder, and you were a way he could get rid of it."

"Me? Now you've lost me, Robbie."

"It's like this. Your upper classes—of which I could say you are one, though we both know your roots run deep the other way—but as I was saying, your upper classes, until fairly recently, were used to embarking on a very expensive round of traveling known as the Grand Tour, when they reached a certain age, of course. Off they went around the castles and estates of Europe on something of an aristocratic pub crawl. Bavaria, Rome, Florence, Paris—all very nice if you've got the wherewithal." He rubbed his forefinger and thumb together.

"What are you getting at?"

"Turns out that Walter was born out of wedlock, though his mother married eventually, but to a man without the funds his true father would have had to spoil him. I tell you, that Walter is holding nothing back now—the man is throwing his whole life story at us." MacFarlane cleared his throat. "But if his beloved mother had been a satisfactory match for his sire, then his name would have been Compton."

"No. I can't believe it. Not . . . not Lord Julian?"

"Don't be daft, lass—even I know your father-in-law is too much of a gentleman to get himself into that sort of pickle. Mind you, his brother was less than careful with regard to the family's reputation, and on this tour went about sowing his wild oats."

"His brother? His brother died over forty-five years ago or thereabouts. I don't know much about him—in fact, I can't remember anyone even mentioning him to me before I was married." Maisie was thoughtful. "But now I remember James telling me his late uncle was something of a dilettante. Lady Rowan apparently could not abide him. His name was Rupert—and he died in a hunting accident, in Bavaria."

"Ah, but Rupert the spare—the one the old lord and lady had just in case the heir, Julian, died—had impregnated a little fraulein at some point on that very excursion, as far as we can establish."

Maisie looked out of the window, then back at MacFarlane. "So Walter Miles—Walter Maier—is really my late husband's cousin."

"And with a hefty chip on his shoulder. He was targeting you, Maisie."

"He seemed a kind man, though I always thought something was a bit off. Yet you say he was focused on me?"

"He was here in England with a job of work to do for his country—for the Fatherland. And I'm under no illusions as to why he's giving us his sob story. He's giving us his poor boy background to try to soften us up before we dig deeper with the really important interrogation. And he wants to avoid the gallows. As if we haven't had enough trouble with Nazi sympathizers in our own upper classes—and even higher than that!" MacFarlane turned a page of notes. "He was targeting you as a means to gain an introduction to the Compton family, and—he hoped—to receive an invitation to the Chelstone Manor estate. I suppose he wanted to look at a life that had eluded him by a whisker of fate." Another page turned, and then MacFarlane raised his eyes from the report to look directly at Maisie. "And needless to say, you are not to inform your father-in-law that his nephew—or the man who says he is Rupert Compton's offspring—is languishing in no less a place than the Tower of London."

Maisie nodded. "Of course I won't say anything, though Julian is very well connected—I am sure he'll know in time. He might even know already." She paused. "Now, you can do something for me. I just saw two young women, both with the First Aid Nursing Yeomanry—one of them was previously my friend Priscilla's nanny. She still has a room at their house. What's she doing here?"

"You know better—"

"I do," interrupted Maisie. "But it's a fair trade of information, is it not?"

"At the moment, she's probably just doing clerical work."

"And in the future?"

MacFarlane seemed to waver. He pushed back his chair and walked across to the window, looking down at the street below, then shaking his head. He turned back to Maisie, but did not take his seat. "It's a fresh idea from our new prime minister—though you could say he's not that new, having just had a baptism by fire in the exalted position. The young lady to whom you refer is one of the women we've earmarked as having special skills." He took his seat once more, and turned to his notes, waiting for the penny to drop.

"Seeing as I doubt you're interested in her quite amazing proven ability to silence three rambunctious boys," said Maisie, "then I suppose you can only be interested in her fluency in French—especially colloquial French—and her familiarity with French culture. What's going on, Robbie?"

"Something we were going to speak to you about, in time, Maisie. This new plan from our higher-ups. Not that I hold with it completely, but I see the value in it—especially now."

"My French isn't good enough for whatever you have in mind."

"Of course it isn't—we had enough trouble with you and German. Languages are not exactly your abiding strength, are they, Maisie? And you won't leave that little evacuee girl—I know that now. September isn't it, that you've got your hearing?" He raised his eyebrows in a conspiratorial fashion. "Anyway, where was I? Yes—as I was going to say, you may not be the most fluent speaker of French, but you know character, Maisie, and for what we have in mind—someone who can judge whether a man or woman has the very long list of qualities we'll need—you're the someone we think could be very valuable in this department." He paused. "And there's always the promise of such joyous repartee whenever you and I work together, isn't there? Anyway, all in good time, all in good time. Can't say any more now. But it might be what you're looking for—in a few months, perhaps next year. A way to do your bit without your life being in danger while you're careening around in an ambulance—yes, I know all about you and your friend putting your best foot forward." He gathered up the papers in front of him. "Right, that's enough of that. I've thanked you for serving your country and bringing an enemy agent to our attention, and I have given you more information than I should have about our aforesaid spy. Now you have to get on and we'll both forget we saw each other this afternoon."

"What will happen to him, Robbie? What will happen to Walter?"

"Eventually? He'll be hanged. Very, very slowly."

Maisie shook her head. "But—"

MacFarlane held up his hand to silence her. "Timothy Partridge. Wounded. Gordon Sanderson, a boy of sixteen doing his best for his country. Dead. Francis Able, Caldwell's former assistant. Dead. And Sandy MacFarlane, eighteen years of age. My nephew. Dead," said MacFarlane. "If you'd been caught in Munich, you would have faced a firing squad. Need we say more? I'll be in touch."

Maisie spent some eleven days at Chelstone. During that time Priscilla and Douglas made the decision to move into a tied cottage that had become vacant on one of the manor's farms. The former tenant had died several months earlier, and the cottage had lain vacant, so Lord Julian suggested that the family could take up residence while Tim convalesced, though until essential work had been completed on the cottage, they would be staying with Maisie.

Tom had returned to Northumberland, having spent much of his compassionate leave at his brother's bedside, his uniform working a magic on the matron, who failed to reprimand him when he overstayed visiting hours. Now, on a day when the sun was shining, Maisie and Priscilla had thrown a blanket down on the Dower House lawn, and were lazing in mid-afternoon warmth. Only the occasional cumulus cloud passing across the blue sky cast a shadow before moving on.

"Surprisingly, I am not at all in a hurry to return home to London full-time," said Priscilla. "Yes, there is the issue of Tarquin finishing the school year, but I have found an excellent tutor locally—a former teacher at Tonbridge School—and Tarquin's studies will be directed by him until he starts again in September, when he will most likely go to Tonbridge anyway. The man only lives in Plaxtol, so my son can rumble off to see him on that old bike he found in your shed. And if Tarq doesn't like that school after he starts, then we'll find him another. My younger two have rather rebelled against the yoke of discipline."

"That's got one of you sorted out. And Douglas seems quite content working in the library, though we have to prepare for Tim coming home. Anna is very excited." Maisie looked at her watch. "She'll be back from school soon. Dad has taken out the governess cart to collect her—I'm amazed he's trained Lady to draw a carriage, and Anna thinks it's wonderful!" Maisie stood up and pointed to the estate's entrance. "I can tell they're on their way because Emma is waiting by the gates at the end of the drive. And I bet the first thing Anna does is rush to the conservatory to see if Tim's home."

"Perhaps she'll be able to bring him out of his funk when he's here. Tom did his best for a couple of days, but I fear it's going to be terribly hard, getting him to buck up." Priscilla tapped the silver cigarette resting on the arm of her wooden chair, but did not attempt to light up. "Douglas says we must let him grieve the loss, but at the same time, he must be kept occupied, and then he must also rest. Your stepmother swears by the efficacy of slowly simmered bone broth, and I have lost count of the gallons we've taken into the hospital. The staff have been very good about it."

"Brenda will make sure Tim wants for nothing—and I think it's given her another cause," said Maisie.

"Brenda likes a cause—for her Maurice was a cause, and so was I. In fact, I believe I'm still one of her causes!"

Priscilla was about to comment when Anna came running into the garden, her leather satchel bouncing against her hip. She made a beeline for Maisie's open arms.

"Oh that's a full satchel!" said Maisie as Anna slithered to the ground, giggling.

"Auntie Pris—is Tim home?"

"I'm sorry, sweetheart, but not yet. Soon though."

"Come on, let's all go inside," said Maisie. "Auntie Brenda's made some Eccles cakes and I think they're still warm."

Tim had still not been discharged from the Royal East Sussex Hospital when Maisie caught the early train up to London on the morning of June 17th. In the meantime, life at the Dower House had become more settled, despite news of the fall of Paris on June 14th. It was time for Maisie to get back to work, and more especially to embark upon her final accounting. For work to commence on a new case, it was necessary to visit the people and places that had become significant in the course of bringing an investigation to a satisfactory close. It was a wiping of the slate—to a point—because it also encouraged greater understanding of lessons learned, and errors made, so that those mistakes might not be repeated in the future.

Billy was waiting for her in the office following their extended leave. "There you are! Miss, you will never—never—guess what!"

"I'm sure I won't," said Maisie, taking off her hat and placing it on the long table in her office. The case map outlining the Joe Coombes investigation had been folded and filed away, consigned to the past after the contents were revealed to Inspector Caldwell. She looked from Billy to Sandra, who came into the office as Maisie was responding to Billy's greeting. "And good morning to you, Billy, Sandra—did you both have an enjoyable holiday away from Fitzroy Square?"

"I could have done with a holiday from Lawrence's aunt," said Sandra. "She's overstayed her welcome. She is good with Martin though—but we're relieved she's leaving at the end of the week."

"And how about your Billy?" said Maisie. Her tone was measured, knowing that Billy was bursting with news.

"I'll tell you in a minute about him—but what about Walter Miles downstairs? He's been arrested! I came in this morning and bumped into a couple of the students who live upstairs—told me everything. The police came—all on the QT, looking around in his garden, and especially at that thing he has growing up the gutter—and the next minute he was being carted off. Happened that day we went to Scotland Yard."

"Oh dear," said Maisie. "I wonder what he's done."

Billy looked at Maisie, his eyes meeting hers, then he went on. "Anyway, you asked about our Billy. He's right as rain and gone back to barracks now. He asked me if I'd seen Vivian Coombes, but I said I thought she was walking out with a fellow, and it was serious. I mean, I don't want to protect him from everything, but that Viv, well, he would need evacuating all over again if he took up with her!"

Much of the work involved in the final accounting kept Maisie in London. The pub on Warren Street had been closed, with a sign informing regulars that new tenants would be taking over soon, and it would be business as usual. Mike Yates' yard was also closed, with the tall wooden gates pulled across the cobblestone courtyard where lorries had unloaded the toxic paint that had caused Joe Coombes so much suffering.

Maisie visited Phil Coombes, who was living temporarily with his sister in Norwood. They talked for only a short while, as Maisie understood that Coombes might still face charges of receiving stolen goods. She wanted, however, to discuss Joe's final resting place.

"I thought about having him laid to rest with his mum, but I don't know," said Coombes. "I reckon he would like something different, and not be in a cemetery with that side of the family."

"His body has been released to you, Phil. May I make a suggestion?"

Phil Coombes nodded. "My other two only seem to care about themselves at the moment. I reckon Archie will get off light, considering what he has to say about his uncle, and he's a young man, so they'd like to see him in uniform. Enough were lost at Dunkirk, so they've got to make up numbers. But Viv—well, she violated the Official Secrets Act, and no matter how small the crime, they look upon that very seriously. She could be in Holloway for a long time—if she's lucky. At least she's not been charged with treason."

"I've spoken up for her, Phil," said Maisie. "I think there's a case for her to receive some leniency, though even leniency can be hard in this situation."

"I know." Coombes nodded, biting his thumbnail. "I know it's no good wishing it were all different, but I knew what Jimmy was like years ago and I should have put my foot down and taken on a brewery tenancy out of London. We should have gone somewhere else, well away from him."

"But Sally was his sister. She was loyal to her family. And I think Jimmy would have put upon you anywhere you ended up."

"Sally should have been a bit more loyal to our family, that's what. And now I've lost her too." Coombes seemed overcome, and turned away for a moment. As he regained control of his emotions, he spoke again. "What shall I do about Joe, Miss Dobbs?"

Maisie took a deep breath and exhaled. "I think that, when all is said and done, perhaps having Joe cremated might be the better course of action."

"Then what? I don't want him sitting on my sister's mantelpiece, or coming with me to prison if I'm sent down."

"No, that's not what I had in mind. Phil, Joe wanted to live in the country. From the moment he went down to Hampshire, he loved it there—and he loved the land where the farmer Phineas Hutchins had offered him a job. Mr. Hutchins thought a lot of him, Phil. I can ask him if Joe's ashes could be scattered across the land."

Phil Coombes nodded. "All right. All right. Yes, I reckon that's the best thing. Then I can go down there to the farm and imagine my Joe working there, on the land—if the old boy lets me."

"Oh, I think he will."

Maisie made the journey to Whitchurch by train, and walked around the town, stopping on a narrow bridge to look at the old Silk Mill, then wandering farther afield until she was ambling alongside the River Test, following the route Joe was believed to have taken during the last moments of his life. Later, she met Phineas Hutchins in the pub, and afterward he drove her back to the farm in his old van.

"He'll rest up there, by that stand of trees," said Hutchins. "You can tell his father that he'll be looked after. I'll watch over him, and so will these two— and his pup, when he's ready." He pointed to the two dogs—one a seasoned sheepdog, the other a youngster ready to learn the ropes. "They'll know it's hallowed ground. Dogs always know."

Maisie bent down to stroke the dogs, and when she came to her feet she pressed the small silver disc engraved with the name "Magni" into the farmer's hand.

Phineas Hutchins drove Maisie back into the town just in time to meet Sylvia Preston for tea. The young

WAAF arrived in her distinctive "air force blue" uniform, a halo of coppery brown curls bubbling from under her peaked cap.

"This is awfully good of you, Miss Dobbs. I'm starving!" Preston tucked into a scone with jam and clotted cream. "I'm always starving—the food they give us is terrible and what that landlady puts on the table isn't much better at all. My staple diet these days is toast!" She held up half a scone. "And who knows how long we'll be able to get this sort of thing."

"I'm very grateful for your help, Sylvia," said Maisie. "The information you gave me was invaluable, and has helped to put those responsible for Joe's death away for a long time."

"That detective from London was a bit sharp, wasn't he?"

Maisie laughed. "Detective Chief Inspector Caldwell? Consider his job—I think it would make anyone sharp."

"Well, he didn't keep me for long, but it raised a few eyebrows at the airfield, I must say. I think it might be part of the reason why I've been promoted—well, not exactly a promotion, but it feels like it, not to be driving that ambulance. I'm being transferred to a new job—much better."

"Oh? That sounds exciting—well done."

Preston used her handkerchief to dab her lips, and took a sip of tea. She looked around at others enjoying their afternoon tea, and turned back to Maisie. "I'm sure you don't know any German spies, so I'll tell you what it is—sort of." She looked around again, and leaned toward Maisie. "They're sending me to one of the Chain Home stations."

Maisie moved closer to Preston. "The what?"

Preston cast her glance around the tea shop again. "Chain Home stations—they're stations where they have a special early warning system and they've been set up all along the coast, so we can tell when there's an attack coming from over there. It's using radio signals and I'll be a plotter for what they call 'radio detection and ranging.' We can use this system to instantly know where the enemy aircraft are located and how many of them are coming over here, so we can get our boys up there to intercept them. We'll be able to give a decent warning if bombers are on their way." She leaned back and began spreading clotted cream on the remainder of her scone. "That's all I'd better say. They're sending me to Ventnor on the Isle of Wight, so that's me—away from the ambulances and that terrible job. And you won't tell anyone, will you?"

"I wouldn't tell a soul," said Maisie. "And I don't think you should tell anyone else—not even your family. I think this information is too important, Sylvia."

Maisie met Dr. Clarissa Clark at the hotel in London where she was staying while attending a series of meetings—one in connection with her findings during the postmortem on Joe Coombes.

"The interesting thing, Maisie, is that—having done more research—we discovered that while the various substances used by Robertson to thin out the fire retardant and to make it go further, were fairly nasty, they were not what was causing the more serious problems. The paint had been developed and then tested only to discover whether it had the required fire-retardant qualities. The testing was arbitrary, a very basic affair and not conducted by scientists at the level I would like to see—they just wanted the paint on their buildings to protect them, because they were racing against time."

"Will they discontinue use?" asked Maisie.

"I doubt it, not the way they're constructing new airfields around the country. No, it's a time of war, so a worker who has a particularly bad reaction—someone like Joe—is only so much concomitant damage along the way."

"That's terrible," said Maisie.

Clark pressed her lips together before speaking again. "It *is* terrible, Maisie—but so is a burning building. To die in a fire is a dreadful death—I've seen my fair share of burn victims and I am sure I will see many, many more before this war is done. Will there be more Joes? I don't know—though certainly there are going to be precautions now. I've asked for even the most simple masks to be provided to the workers, especially those apprentices who are still so young. And I have stipulated that they should wear gloves, though they tend to limit the dexterity of the working painter. And a list of guidelines I've drawn up will be issued to the companies who are currently taking over the Yates' contract— that's what my meetings here in London have been all about." She paused. "The thing that worries me is not what happens to these workers now, or even in a few months, or a year—it's what happens when years have passed. This very powerful fire retardant is poison, and such contamination can remain in the body for decades, affecting every part of the human system. I am sure men will suffer in the future and never know it was all due to a job they took on when they were little more than boys."

Tim Partridge came home to Chelstone toward the end of June, to a welcome from all but his brother Tom, who was already stationed at RAF Hawkinge, flying Hawker Hurricane aircraft and preparing for whatever might come next in his life. Anna had taken to grabbing Tim by his right hand and insisting he accompany her to the stables to help her groom Lady. And when he objected, maintaining that a person with an arm missing could hardly groom himself, let alone a pony, she replied, "Tim—you've got another arm, haven't you?" And to the delight of all who observed the exchange, Tim agreed to be pulled this way and that wherever Anna wanted his company. His recovery had begun.

With her routine reestablished, of weekdays in town and toward the week's end, the journey back to Chelstone, it was toward the end of the month when Maisie persuaded Priscilla to accompany her to Rye.

"I don't know if I can bear to go back there," said Priscilla. "Gordon's funeral was hard enough on everyone. Tim was so upset that he could not leave the hospital, but I think it was for the best."

"You should come," said Maisie. "You know what you always say about the dragon. Look it in the eye, and then keep it mollified."

George checked the amount of petrol in the tank, and decreed that Maisie had enough fuel in the Alvis for one more excursion. They set off mid-morning on the last Friday in June for the drive down to Rye.

Parking the motor car alongside the harbor, Maisie and Priscilla walked past fishing boats unloading their catch, and stood to remember the day Tim came home from Dunkirk.

"I still can't believe he did it, Maisie. I've been moaning for the past three years that Tim was the one causing me trouble, and that this sailing lark at least kept him out of the house for a while. Now he's the one who has surprised me the most—and of whom I am so proud."

"They're good young men, Priscilla," said Maisie. "Tim was incredibly brave."

"I can still see him struggling to bring in the boat—and that fisherman helping him do it on his own, knowing it was only right that he be given the chance." Priscilla wiped a tear from each eye. "I think this war is going to make a lot of mothers proud—but for the wrong reasons. What was it Churchill said? You know—it was on the wireless. 'The Battle of France is over. The Battle of Britain is about to begin.' It makes my heart so heavy. Young men shouldn't have to die, and their parents shouldn't have to go through the rest of their lives making everything seem right by saying, 'At least my boy was brave.' Or, 'We're proud he did his bit.'"

A now familiar low rumble of aircraft engines caused

Priscilla and Maisie to look up, hands shielding their eyes from the midday sun. Three Hurricanes flew in formation overhead, out toward the Channel.

Priscilla stood on tiptoe and waved at the departing aircraft, then turned to Maisie. "Just in case that's my Tom up there."

Maisie waved along with her until the aircraft were out of sight. And she wondered, then, how it must feel flying across the Weald of Kent, across Sussex, over ancient woodland and patchwork fields of barley and hops down below; over farms with oast houses, their white cowls like witches' hats poking through the morning mist, and above market towns and small villages, with children looking up and waving as they passed, until they left the English coast behind.

"It's time to drive back to Chelstone, Pris," said Maisie. "They'll all be wondering where we've got to."

"And Anna will be home from school by the time we get there."

Maisie linked her arm through Priscilla's, and nodded. Yes, Anna would be home.

Acknowledgments

During the years 1941–43, my late father, Albert Winspear, was the young apprentice who inspired this story. It was only during his final weeks that we talked at length about the job he'd started as a fourteen-year-old apprentice, joining a crew of house painters who were taken from one RAF base to another around the country, applying fire retardant to the buildings. He told me that it was one of his jobs to line up a series of blowtorches close to each wall to test resistance to fire after the emulsion was applied, and described his initial shock when the torches left no mark following four hours of blasting heat. When I asked him what the paint was called and he told me it didn't have a name, only a number, I knew that in time it would become a story. My father died from a serious blood disorder termed "idiopathic"—there is no known cause—though there is evidence to indicate that his particular incarnation of the illness is associated with exposure to toxic materials. We were fortunate it took so long to catch up with him. My parents left me with many stories of the Second World War, which deepened my appreciation of the ways in which individuals are affected by conflict, with their scars lasting a lifetime.

My cousin, Larry Iveson, inspired me to use the area around Whitchurch in Hampshire, England, as a backdrop for a novel. From the moment he told me about the town's connection to the Bank of England and the business of manufacturing paper money, I was hooked! My "research" involved some lovely walks together around the town where he has lived for many years. Coincidentally, my father had worked at some of the airfields in the region during his apprenticeship. In addition, the experiences of one of my late aunts inspired the character of Sylvia Preston, the young WAAF (Women's Auxiliary Air Force) in *To Die But Once*. My aunt drove ambulances across Salisbury Plain, collecting the bodies of soldiers who hadn't survived their first parachute jump. Of my uncles, two were among the thousands of soldiers who stood for days on the beaches of Dunkirk waiting to be evacuated in the spring of 1940, again rendering *To Die But Once* personal.

In our very large extended family, almost all theaters of the Second World War were experienced by at least one of my uncles or aunts, or my parents—from Dunkirk to the Battle of Britain, the war in France, Italy, Asia, the African desert, D-day, the Blitz, and in Germany, plus of course the dark side of childhood evacuation—thus the stories that were retold during my childhood, along with those of my grandparents and their lives during the First World War continue to inspire my writing.

My thanks, as always, to my literary agent and dear friend, Amy Rennert, along with my amazing editor Jennifer Barth—I am a very fortunate recipient of their wise counsel and guidance. I have great admiration for the team at HarperCollins, including marketing wizard Stephanie Cooper, who stuns me with her new ideas, and Katherine Beitner, PR and publicity maven, whose support and encouragement mean so much to me—thank you, Katherine. Deepest thanks to Josh Marwell and his team—Josh, I truly appreciate your enthusiasm and hard work on behalf of the Maisie Dobbs series. And many thanks, as always, to Jonathan Burnham, senior vice-president and publisher of

Harper Books. Creative director Archie Ferguson is one of my all-time heroes for his work on the iconic covers for the Maisie Dobbs series. And I am filled with admiration and gratitude for the imagination and skill of Andrew Davidson, artist and craftsman, who has created works of art to grace the cover of each new book—thank you for your attention to detail and for your appreciation of my work, Andrew.

My husband, John Morell, is my support on the home front, and for that he deserves a medal!

Finally, having grown up in the Kent countryside, and later living in Sussex, where my parents resided close to Rye for over thirty-five years, I have an abiding love of the area, and equally so for London, where my family's roots run deep. Thus any geographical wide turns are usually deliberate—sometimes when writing a story, you just have to get everyone from A to B.

About the Author

JACQUELINE WINSPEAR is the author of the *New York Times* best sellers *In This Grave Hour*, *Journey to Munich*, *A Dangerous Place*, *Leaving Everything Most Loved*, *Elegy for Eddie*, and *A Lesson in Secrets*, as well as seven other bestselling Maisie Dobbs novels. Her stand-alone novel, *The Care and Management of Lies*, was also a *New York Times* and national best seller, and a finalist for the Dayton Literary Peace Prize. She has won numerous awards, including the Agatha, Alex, and Macavity awards, and was nominated for the Edgar Award for Best Novel. Originally from the United Kingdom, Winspear now lives in California.

THE NEW LUXURY IN READING

We hope you enjoyed reading
our new, comfortable print size and found it
an experience you would like to repeat.

Well – you're in luck!

HarperLuxe offers the finest in fiction and
nonfiction books in this same larger print size and
paperback format. Light and easy to read, HarperLuxe
paperbacks are for book lovers who want to see
what they are reading without the strain.

For a full listing of titles and
new releases to come, please visit our website:

www.HarperLuxe.com